TOP GUNS

Jeff De Blanc: The Congressional Medal of Honor winner and Marine ace recalls the personalities and aerial battles in the Solomon Islands in 1942, a dangerous ditch landing, a bailout, and his dramatic escape from the Japanese.

Jack Ilfrey: One of the two possible contenders for the title of first P-38 ace of World War II, the Army pilot's remarkable story takes the reader from the dunes and oases of North Africa to an audacious escape across two hundred miles of German-occupied Europe.

"THE BEST COLLECTION OF AERIAL COMBAT STORIES I'VE READ . . . A GREAT BOOK."
—General John W. Vessey, USA (Ret.),
former Chairman of the Joint Chiefs of Staff

"ABSORBING . . . I THOROUGHLY ENJOYED AND HIGHLY RECOMMEND IT."
—Frank Borman, former astronaut
and former President of Eastern Airlines

"FOR EXPERIENCING THE THRILL OF COMBAT . . . *TOP GUNS* IS MUST READING."
—General Robert C. Mathis, USAF (Ret.),
former Vice Chief of Staff, U.S. Air Force

Ray Brooks: Pursuit pilot in World War I's Army Air Service, he recalls hair-raising "seat-of-the-pants" flying and aerial battles with German Fokkers, Pfalzes and Rumplers in the dawn of modern military aviation.

Guy Bordelon: The only Navy ace and the only prop plane ace of the Korean War, he tells what it was like to fly hazardous night-supply interdiction behind Communist lines—and describes the special assignment that resulted in his five victories over Yakovlev and Lavochkin aircraft.

Harold Fischer: This Air Force veteran of both Korea and Vietnam recounts his experiences flying the F-80 and F-86 in an intense, in-depth view of the air war in Korea.

Randy Cunningham: A Navy pilot, he was the first Vietnam ace and one of the only two aces of the war. In his gut-wrenching story he tells of flying against the most sophisticated anti-aircraft in the history of warfare—SAMs, radar-guided cannon and a variety of MiGs—in jets without guns.

TOP GUNS

JOE FOSS and MATTHEW BRENNAN

POCKET STAR BOOKS

New York   London   Toronto   Sydney   Tokyo   Singapore

A Pocket Star Book published by
POCKET BOOKS, a division of Simon & Schuster Inc.
1230 Avenue of the Americas, New York, NY 10020

ISBN 0-671-68318-7

First Pocket Books paperback printing May 1992

10 9 8 7 6 5 4 3 2 1

POCKET STAR BOOKS and colophon are registered
trademarks of Simon & Schuster Inc.

Cover art by Michael Shen

Printed in the U.S.A.

Contents

CONTENTS

THE KOREAN WAR

CONTENTS

Introduction
by Joe Foss

Top Guns is living history, not the kind of history you'll find in a textbook. It was important to gather these stories while our aces were still around to share them. Many of the authors have never before talked about their war experiences. Others may have told stories when they first returned from war, but that was a long time ago, and not enough people wanted to listen. Too often they were introduced as aces, without the opportunity to talk about those events that were important to them. The majority of aces in this collection are unknown to most people, but they are all great men. They led their groups, squadrons, flights, divisions, and sections in battles that changed the world.

The things they did were the kinds of things that have saved this country in times of crisis from its very beginning. Generations come and go, and young people rarely realize what others have been willing to do to keep them free. Here is a chance to understand the contributions of airplanes and air crews in war throughout the span of the twentieth century. These men, especially those who were lost, put their lives on the line, just like people today put money on the counter to buy a loaf of bread or a can of soup. There is never a "safe" mission in war, whether you are in the air, on the ground, or sailing the seas. Wars aren't safe. It doesn't matter what your rank or job might be.

This book is about air aces, but many people who were never aces supplied them, or worked twenty-four hours a day to keep them flying. They made our successes possible. No pilot will ever forget his ground crews or the people who supported him on the home front. This is a long-overdue tribute to all of them. They were patriots, and future generations will produce more patriots. America is a funny place. We always wait until a time of crisis to get moving, but then the whole country moves. They say that great wars and great natural disasters can never happen again, but they always do. They say that something bad will never happen here, never to me, but too often it does. When those things happen, common people have always stepped forward to lend a hand or perform uncommonly brave deeds.

Here are the stories of a few patriots out of millions. Read them and be proud of their sacrifices and love of country, and of our great history.

Introduction
by Matt Brennan

When I accepted the responsibility of working with Joe Foss on this collection, I knew too little about air combat and had no idea how intense and rewarding the next two years would be. In the course of this project, I had the honor of working with Captain Raymond Brooks, a ninety-four-year-old World War I ace who scored his victories four years before my father was born. The great battles of World War II happened before I was born. I had read about the Flying Tigers, the Cactus Air Force, the "Skull and Crossbones" Squadron, and bomber escort fighters as a young boy. America tried to ignore the Korean War, but our pilots there shot down Communist planes in a ratio of over ten to one. Vietnam was my war. Now aviators from each war were telling their stories, often for the first time.

Impressions began to form. What makes one flyer more effective than his fellows? Circumstances had to play a part. A man had to have reliable equipment and be at the right place at the right time. Aerial supremacy might not have been won at Guadalcanal if our marine pilots had been flying some of the earlier fighters. They had the right circumstances—lots of enemy aircraft and their backs to the wall. Luck always plays a major part in war. The same pilot could have been shot down on his first mission, or crashed with a faulty engine, or gone on to become a famous ace. Unique personal attributes had to be important—faster reflexes, better eyesight, a more highly honed survival instinct. Training played its part, and so did motivation. These men passionately believe in what they were fighting for.

The stories came handwritten or typed, on cassette tapes or over the telephone. Their common thread is the matter-of-fact way daring feats are discussed and described. These authors speak from the record. As a group, they learned their strengths and weaknesses early in life and reached the point long ago where they have nothing to prove to anyone, except maybe to themselves. The reader will benefit from their honesty and simple "life-or-death" choices as he shares the cockpit with them on extraordinary missions.

This collection would never have been possible if the aces had not given so generously and freely of their time. They want the world to know, not about them, but about events that have happened, and their small part in them. I am grateful to Jack Romanos, president of Simon & Schuster Mass Market Publishing, for the idea that became this book, and to General Joe Foss for knowing its importance and believing that it could be. My sincerest thanks to Paul McCarthy, senior editor at Pocket Books, for his advice, strong encouragement, and unwavering support. This is truly his book as well as "our" book. Many thanks to Colonel Ward Boyce, executive director of the American Fighter Aces Association, for his kind help. And finally, to my loving wife, Sally Oliver, for her excellent proofreading and many careful and wise suggestions.

WORLD
WAR
I

The First World War was truly the dawn era of modern aerial warfare. America's participation in the conflict was restricted to the western front in 1917 and 1918, although individual American pilots had already flown by that time with Allied units, most notably the Lafayette Escadrille. The first American "pursuit squadrons" were trained and led by experienced Canadian and British pilots, or by American pilots who had served with the French, Canadians, or British, as happened in the case of Ray Brooks's outfit.

Air combat was dangerous and very personal in those days. Pilots operated without parachutes in flimsy biplanes constructed of wood, wire, and fabric. German Fokker D VIIs had a maximum speed of 125 mph and were equipped with twin forward-firing machine guns, and their Pfalz D XIIs had a maximum speed of 120 mph. The American mainstay, the Spad XIII, had a slight speed advantage at 130 mph, but came equipped with less reliable machine guns. Aircraft disintegration or loss of control at almost any altitude usually meant death.

The Allies were conservative about claims of enemy planes destroyed. Many planes shot down behind German lines were never credited to the pilots. However, there were eighty-three American aces in the conflict. Ray Brooks is the only surviving World War I ace. It is our great fortune to have a man with such a clear and valuable memory to contribute to this collection. His historically important account is further enhanced by the mention of other famous aces of the time, including David Putnam (twelve victories) and Jacques Swaab (ten victories).

PURSUIT PILOT

Captain Arthur Raymond Brooks tells a remarkable story of training, "seat-of-the-pants" flying, and aerial battles with Fokkers, Pfalzes, and Rumplers in the earliest days of modern military aviation.

I'm a damn Yankee, having been born in the horse-and-buggy days in Framingham, Massachusetts. I was eight years old when the Wright Brothers flew at Kitty Hawk in 1903, and after that, I was hooked on flying. I built model airplanes out of rattan, tissue paper, and the proper canvas, and carved propellers out of balsa wood. Then I used one of my mother's beads as a thrust bearing and wound-up elastic for power. My models were able to make flights of up to thirty feet. In addition, I built kites, a fishing skiff, a sailboat, and an ice boat on runners. The ice boat would take me across a frozen lake at sixty miles per hour. One of my chief pleasures was to lie atop a hill in the grass and watch for patterns in the great cumulus cloud formations. Below me, the four-wheeled trolley cars traveled along on their rails beside a statue of a revolutionary farmer who was leaving his plow behind and taking up a powder horn to fill his rifle and stop the British at Concord Bridge.

I graduated from high school with honors and had to choose between Sheffield School at Yale and MIT, called Boston Tech in those days. I chose MIT because it was only a twenty-two-mile commute from home on a steam locomotive. In my junior year in college I was certain that America would not stay out of the war in Europe, and I would have to fight for my country. In December 1916 I applied for duty as a private to be able to fly in the Air Service in the Signal Officers Reserve Corps. When I received no word on that, I volunteered for the Engineer Corps in Plattsburg. I had put on a uniform and gone on camping expeditions in rainstorms with a classmate at MIT, but we had gotten fed up with camping out and eating beans out of a can. It wasn't the same as freshman drill in blue uniforms and white gloves inside a building on campus. I preferred the Air Service.

As sometimes happens, both sets of orders arrived at the

same time. I took them down to General Edwards in the Nottingham Building near the public library in Copley Square. He was evidently amused, because he read them and said, "Well, what do you want to do?"

"Oh, I want to fly."

He tore up the papers for the Plattsburg engineer course and I went over to Harvard to take a complete physical. I had spent a lot of time outdoors as a boy and had better than 20/20 vision, so I passed everything and waited for further orders. When I graduated from MIT as an electrochemical engineer in May 1917, I went down to Bridgeport for a second summer of work on submarines at the Lake Torpedo Boat Company. We called submarines "pig boats," and that's what they were: nasty tubs. I never understood how someone could live submerged in them, let alone surface and fire torpedoes. This time I got fed up with the slackers: nine chaps who lived with me in a beach house and were working on submarines to stay out of the war. They laughed at me for wanting to fly and fight for my country, and I had no respect for them. I left Bridgeport early.

I was traveling with a friend in Maine, a state I have always loved, when my brother telegrammed to inform me that I had a special delivery letter at home. It contained my orders for the Air Service. When I joined the army, they made me use my first name, Arthur, and only my middle initial, so for the next five and a half years I was officially known as Arthur R. Brooks. My middle name, Ray, came from the French ancestry on my mother's side of the family. About three hundred years before I was born, there was a St. Raymond, and that's how I got the name I always went by at home. I once asked my mother why she had chosen Arthur as my first name. "It sounded good," she replied with a little smile. If I had been wiser, I would have entered the service as Raymond A. Brooks.

I was soon at Fort Wood in New York City, at the base of the Statue of Liberty. It was there that I wore the OD for the first time. They taught us close-order drill and used us for a few days to hunt rats and handle rough wire for cages without even providing us with gloves. Then one hundred of us, all college youths and aviation volunteers, were sent by train to Niagara Falls, and then by ferry across Lake Ontario, to Long Branch (outside of Toronto) for ground training by Canadian enlisted instructors. Aviation ground school was conducted at the University of Toronto, and we were welcome in private homes in the city. The training was complete, effective, and thorough.

The three available Royal Flying Corps of Canada (RFCC) flying fields were overloaded with Canadian air cadets, so with the RFCC still in command, our group and some of their own Canadian cadets were transported in Pullman cars to Hicks, Texas. We lived in those Pullman cars until some tents were erected for us, then we began flying Curtiss JN-4D "Jennys" with a ninety-horsepower water-cooled OX-5 engine. I loved flying and learned to solo in an hour and twenty-six minutes. Major Campbell took me up one day at dusk when the other fellows were going for their evening meal. I did a good job taking off, but when we came in to land, there was a coal plow and a steam roller on the runway. I didn't see the coal plow in the failing light. The aircraft slid into the plow on the lower right wing skid and went up on its nose, bending in the cowling an inch and a half. Campbell wasn't amused, but he wasn't hurt. To this day I have a knot on my head from the incident. I looked grotesque when I finally arrived for supper wearing a big bandage from the horse doctor. When they saw me, my flying mates gave me the "razoo" and a Bronx cheer.

All was not fun and games. I lost a classmate during flight training. His plane disintegrated in midair as I watched. I gathered flying time and passed every test, but when it was time to receive my first lieutenant's commission, the inducement offered when I volunteered, the adjutant told me they had no records on me. So I had to apply all over again and take another complete physical, even though I now had forty-six hours of solo flying time. My squadron departed for

France, without me and another pilot with the same problem. In the meantime, I continued to build more flight time. One day I landed at a railroad station to get some coffee and a doughnut, something you could do in those days.

The stationmaster said, "Are you Brooks?"

I answered, "Yes."

"They want you at headquarters down at Hicks Field."

I didn't know if I was going to jail or what. When I got there, the adjutant, a hard-boiled egg of a man, threw a piece of paper across the desk to me and said, "Well, here's your commission."

"This is for a second lieutenant," I said.

To this he replied, "That's all you get. Take it or leave it."

I told him, "The RFCC has a naval outfit learning to fly here, not very many of them, but they have offered me two hundred dollars if I can get out of the United States service and meet them at Halifax. The money would allow me to buy a uniform for the Canadian Navy."

The adjutant replied, "Get out of here before I throw you out."

By now the rest of the squadron had arrived in France, and my commanding officer, Major L. C. Angstrom of the RFCC, had telegraphed requesting that I join them when I got my commission. On the basis of these orders I left Hicks as a casual to rejoin them. Arriving in New York after a trip on steam locomotive by way of St. Louis, I was informed by the woman in charge that a boat was sailing for France the next day. I mentioned that my home was only 220 miles north of New York, and I really wanted to see my family and best girl before sailing. The woman was very nice about it and scheduled me on a boat that was sailing in thirteen days. That allowed me a few wonderful days at home, plus a day or two back in New York to enjoy the neighborhoods, the shows, and a few of the best restaurants. New York had everything in those days, and I loved it dearly. Today it's different.

On March 12, 1918, as I was about to sail on a transatlantic steamship for Liverpool, England, a dear friend, Grace Logan, remarked that she would ask a nun, Sister Mary Magdalene of the Assumption, to pray for me. To this day, I believe her prayers saved me on the journey that followed. Prior to leaving, I had spent a couple of days in Greenwich Village, not knowing that the Asian flu was raging up and down the coast, killing thousands of people, nor did I then know that I had caught it. It was not until we were in the middle of the Atlantic Ocean that it hit me and knocked me for a loop. I was attended by two doctors from Pittsburgh, whose efforts pulled me through . . . instead of ending up on a slab of wood with an American flag draped over me and being slid into the Atlantic. March has to be the worst time of year to cross the North Atlantic. I arrived in Liverpool, weak as a cat from the flu and our rough and stormy crossing, but I was alive! This was not to be the last time my guardian angel would intercede for me.

I boarded a train down to London and, on arrival, hailed an old cab-driver with a long white beard. He took me to a hotel in his horse-drawn carriage. I slept for many hours, then refreshed, moved on to the Ritz Carleton, a high-class hotel, to regain some of my strength. The Ritz had a club in the basement, the Kit Kat, where the Prince of Wales occasionally showed up to beat the drums in between trips to France. A few days later I traveled down to Southampton and across the English Channel to France. The trip over the submarine-infested channel was on a dirty, nasty old tub called the *Archimedes*. It was so loaded to the gills with troops and ammunition that you couldn't even sit down. Finally, I paid a crewman two dollars to be able to sleep for thirty minutes in his bunk with cinder-covered sheets in a cabin above the open deck.

Arriving at Le Havre was the beginning of heaven. I traveled to Paris on a real first-class train and immediately took advantage of the restaurants and sights in that beautiful city. I would select seats in restaurants on the second floor of buildings in the vicinity of Notre Dame cathedral so I could gaze on this magnificent edifice as I enjoyed the fine Parisian cuisine. During the course of those meals, with everyone concentrating on the food and drink, as they do in Paris, the quiet would be interrupted by an occasional whistle, followed by a loud explosion, a *boom!* The patrons would look up from their meals without much concern, shrug their shoulders, and comment, "Ha! Another one!" The explosions were incoming shells from the German "Big Bertha" railway gun being fired from far north of Paris. And there was nothing that anybody could do about it, at least not at that time.

I was quartered at the University Union run by an Episcopalian minister by the name of Gibbs. He told me that he would keep in touch with my squadron and tell me when they began further training. One day he told me that my squadron was going to start training at Issoudon, and I left to join them. Issoudon had nine fields that handled training: from taxiing down a strip to aerial maneuvers, artillery spotting and aerial photography. Because we weren't novices who had to learn everything from scratch, we soon got bored. We played a lot of cards, and then we started getting obnoxious to the point where headquarters wanted to get rid of us. We were sent to Paris and divided up. I was assigned to the 139th, designated a pursuit squadron. We were to become "fighter" pilots.

We were first sent to a grass strip about fifteen miles below Toul at a place called Vaucouleurs. We lived in wooden Aldian huts nestled among the trees, waiting for the time when the 1st Pursuit Group would move out of Toul and my squadron could move in. One day during this waiting period, a Spad VII arrived at our strip. I asked Major Angstrom's permission to fly it and he agreed. I flew over the town and around the valley, spinning down among the hills until I was almost out of sight, and I loved every minute of it. Arriving back at the strip, I made three attempts to land. It was important that I make a smooth landing without inflicting any damage to the aircraft so that other members of our squadron would have the chance to fly this Spad the next day. On my third approach I cut the engine (the Spad VII had no brakes) and hoped that I wouldn't veer off the strip. I made it down without incident. On the spot I named the Spad the "flying brick." The Spad was a sturdy machine that could dive under full power and pull out without coming apart, but it had no gliding ability without power and was, therefore, a tricky aircraft to land until you got the feel of it.

At first the American Expeditionary Forces flew French Spad VIIs with one lousy Vickers machine gun and an underpowered 180-horsepower engine. They were soon replaced by Spad XIIIs. These were beautiful birds that were made mostly by the old and the young French people after the cream of their manhood had been conscripted because of the long war and the terrible losses in the Battle of Verdun. Unfortunately, Spad XIIIs were not put together too well, and we had to rebuild most of them. So I personally learned how to tackle the engines alongside the mechanics, because this maintenance was necessary if we were to fly. They arrived with gas tank leaks, broken or unusable cables, high-altitude radiator covers that didn't work, and missing bolts, studs, and nuts.

The Spad XIIIs had 220-horsepower, geared, water-cooled engines, but came with two lousy Vickers machine guns that always seemed to have bad jams. Those gun jams didn't improve until we replaced the Vickers guns with Marlin machine guns toward the end of the war. Unlike the German Fokkers, Spads had no ability to glide down to a landing. You had to pick your touchdown (landing) point from the air, flying in under power until the wheels were some six inches above the turf, then cut the engine, ease back on the stick, and you were down. The pilot steered straight down the strip using the rudder, then he was home. One of my buddies crashed and burned before my eyes when he allowed his Spad XIII to stall out while still fifty feet above the strip.

The United States had allocated 640 million dollars to build planes, but by the end of the war, not a single American combat plane had been built with the exception of Curtiss

JN-4 trainers and copies of the British De Havilland DH-4. A few DH-4s reached France just before the Armistice, but they were not very good. The AEF fought the war in French planes.

While we were building up our forces and were not permitted to cross the lines in our sector of the front, I would travel down to Ourches or Amanty whenever I had the chance, just to see how our American pilots were doing on their bombing and reconnaissance flights. The British had an airfield a few miles from our airdrome at Toul, and I would visit there to watch their night bombers take off for missions over Cologne or the Black Forest, during which the crews would toss out five-gallon cans of fuel and then throw down incendiary devices to ignite them. Not very effective! From my experience, setting fuel afire with incendiaries from altitude was pretty hopeless, but it must have been a good show.

The 139th Pursuit Squadron was stationed at Toul Gengoult Airdrome, a good field with solid buildings that had once been French cavalry barracks. There was one broken-down masonry building we used for protection when the Gothas came over on their night bombing runs from Germany. We would roll out of our bags and run to the building in a part of the airfield that wasn't being used, then watch the bombs exploding and the searchlights from St. Mihiel sweeping the sky. The bombs never killed anyone, but an antiaircraft shell came down through the tile roof of a barracks one night and killed a soldier lying on his bunk. You can't predict anything about war.

The three flights in my squadron (A, B, and C flights) were code-named Red, White, and Blue, and the radiator shutters were painted in those colors for easier identification. The commander of my C flight was David Putnam, a descendent of the famous Putnams who fought at Breed's Hill at the start of the Revolutionary War. Putnam had left America on a cattle boat and gone to France to serve in the Ambulance Corps, the "meat wagons." Then he took the opportunity to fly for France in the Lafayette Flying Corps. He already had eight kills by the time I met him in late May or early June 1918. With all that experience he didn't try to train us by putting us in classrooms with diagrams and lectures. Instead, he asked for volunteers to accompany him on dawn patrols. I wanted to fly with him because he had so much to teach us, but no one else was crazy enough to do it.

We were building up a great strength of battle airplanes at the time, and our orders were to stay behind our own lines. We would take off at dawn and head up to the maximum altitude for our aircraft of 18,500 feet. It would take forty-eight minutes of our hour and forty-five-minute fuel limit to get there. There would invariably be two Fokkers waiting for us when we got to altitude. The German planes were a light gray-green color with small white crosses on their fuselages and red-painted noses. You couldn't tell you were under attack until the bullets started coming at you. We would fight back, returning the fire until low on gas and ammunition, then dive away and head back to the airdrome. I certainly wasn't as effective as Putnam at first, but I learned from him.

One morning we were still climbing when we found ourselves tangling with two red-nosed Fokkers that came at us out of the sun from the rugged Vosges Mountain region to the east. We were caught short because they had the sun behind them and the altitude advantage. We maneuvered with them until we were practically out of fuel, but that was okay, because we were almost directly above our airdrome. When we landed, Putnam's plane and gas tanks were shot full of holes. If his tanks had been full, or if the Germans had been firing incendiary bullets, he would have been incinerated.

On another one of those patrols, I saw a Pfalz, a "Black Beast" as I called them. Putnam immediately attacked from the right side. His gun jammed. I took over and pounded the Black Beast until it disappeared into the clouds. That was my first kill. It was confirmed by the French, who took a picture of the wreckage behind their lines. Putnam complimented me in his taciturn way by saying, "That's pretty good." It was my squadron's first victory.

One day a Rumpler observation and photography plane strayed over our lines. Putnam came up under the tail to properly attack it, while I came in close and shot the rear-seat observer. The plane disintegrated in midair and I flew through some of the debris. I stayed up for a little while to test my guns and the controls of my new Spad XIII. At dinner I sat down in the mess hall at one of our two rows of sawbuck tables.

Major Angstrom saw me beginning my meal and said, "Ray, did you know that Putnam shot down a Rumpler a little while ago?"

"Of course. I shot the observer."

Putnam didn't say a word, but the rest of the crowd was put off because they didn't know whether I was joking or trying to grab some of the glory. I didn't care what they thought. It was a clean-cut victory for Putnam, and I wasn't disputing that.

Putnam was quite an interesting fellow, and his prowess was praised. He was finally killed in a close dogfight after I was transferred to the 22nd Pursuit Squadron. The bullet that killed him went right through the top of his head, so he had almost certainly been in a vertical virage at the time he was hit.

I was assigned to the 22nd Pursuit Squadron as Flight "C" Commander on August 10, 1918. We later joined with the 139th, 49th, and 103rd Pursuit Squadrons to become the 2nd Pursuit Group. The Germans still had Fokkers and bombers coming over. One day I was showing a couple of neophytes, Kendall and Jones, our area—rivers, cities, and so forth. We were heading to the east toward the Vosges Mountains in the St. Mihiel sector when a German Rumpler started throwing explosive bullets at me from about 75 or 100 yards away. I promptly shot him down in flames.

When I landed, someone ran up and said, "There was a plane that went down in flames over by the Vosges a while ago."

"I know. I shot him down."

Kendall and Jones were chagrined because they hadn't seen any of the action. I never heard again about explosive bullets. Maybe they were testing them and I slowed down the development, but they were using them that day.

The St. Mihiel offensive began at dawn on September 12. While it was still dark I was on a high-altitude patrol when the artillery opened up. Guns shot tongues of red flame from the darkness on the ground, and then the front lit up with a red glow from the flaring flashes of explosions. It was the greatest display of pyrotechnics I had ever seen, and it was exciting. We flew continuous patrols for the next two days. We had an early morning patrol on the fourteenth, returned to the airdrome, and organized more patrols.

My commanding officer, Ray C. Bridgeman, was a very fine gentleman who had been an English teacher in Lake Forest, Illinois, and later a member of the famous Lafayette Escadrille. They had been the best of the original flyers in France, and had many victories over the Germans. It was only later that I learned that this was a man who truly hated war. On the third patrol with our untrustworthy machine guns, I was flying as deputy to Commander Bridgeman as he led a flight of ten Spads over our lines. The blue sky was beautifully clear, until I looked high up to my right and saw eight or ten Fokker D-7s. Fokkers were powered with 180-horsepower Mercedes engines and maneuvered beautifully, like cats. They actually reminded me of cats with their tails swishing around when they are ready to fight.

I had no communication with Bridgeman, so I dropped down beside him, wiggled my right wing next to his left wing, and pointed up with my gloved hand. He looked up, saw those red-nosed German devils ready to pounce on us, and immediately dove with the rest of the flight. I didn't know what was happening, but I had volunteered for the Air Service, and that meant being willing to die if necessary. Like a damned fool, I climbed up into those Fokkers. They weren't bothering with me because their flight commander was after

14

our main group. They couldn't shoot at me without hitting each other.

I fought like hell that day and somehow got away with it. I never had such a dogfight again. I could see the features of one Hun and hated to think that one of us had to go. I shot him down. I never wasted a bullet at long range that could be used at a short distance with more effect, so I decided to ram a Fokker. The pilot saw me coming and dodged me. My gas was running low over a big German lake, so I had to break loose from the two or three Fokkers I was fighting and head toward our lines.

One of the German pilots had me dead to rights. He trailed me for miles, firing away, but I kept doing something I was becoming famous for by now—sideslips: left a little, right a little, up a little, down a little. Bullets came winging by me. One bullet hit my "dog suit" (flight suit lined with dog fur) and several whizzed by my head, hit the left side of the windshield, and smashed into the left Vickers gun. Incendiary bullets pierced the wings, and I watched them burning there. Another one cut the control cable for my left rudder. I was a sitting duck as this German pilot poured bullets into my machine. As I crossed our lines, I put on full motor and dived straight down. The German pilot couldn't follow me down and broke off his attack.

My airplane was shot to pieces, but I managed to get back to an advance airstrip just inside the front. There was always an advance landing strip at the front maintained for reconnaissance and observation aircraft. I hit the field hard and crashed my face against the windshield, then climbed out of the cockpit and leaned against the fuselage, blubbering to myself, certain that I was the only survivor of our flight. One of the reconnaissance fellows brought me a flask of brandy. I took a drink and pulled myself together.

They made a call for me back to my headquarters, "Waterfall," on the telephone line. At that particular strip at that particular time there was a regiment of doughboys who were heading for the Verdun fray. For some reason they were allowed to rip the fabric off my beautiful Spad with its "shooting star" emblem and tear it into pieces for souvenirs. Hours later Bridgeman showed up to get me, and we embraced each other with sincerity.

The only fellow missing was Philip Hassinger. Graves registration looked for him for six months. Eventually they discovered a German soldier in the Black Forest who was wearing his belt buckle. Later on a confirmation officer got the necessary credit for two "kills" which made me an ace. I refused the credit unless my buddy, Phil Hassinger, was included with me in the citation. He was.

On the same day, Jacques Swaab was flying toward dusk in rotten weather when he attempted to land at what he thought was our squadron location at Toul Gengoult Airdrome. Instead of landing back at our field, he touched down at a German airdrome. He promptly started shooting before the Germans could react, and destroyed three of their planes on the ground. He took off for our lines and eventually crashed in the Vosges, east of our airdrome, and was rescued.

The commander knew that we both had shaken nerves, so the next morning he ordered Jacques and me to go to Vittel, a beautiful spa, like many of the other watering holes in France, Germany, and Switzerland. We were driven there in a Cadillac. It was a beautiful day in Vittel, and we were in an ideal place for relaxation, so we enjoyed a good night's sleep. The following day we wandered over to the concrete station and found a military train arriving. It held a full complement of grievously injured soldiers. We looked at one another and said, "None of this today. We're trying to get our nerves back." We couldn't relax in a place with so many wounded, so we called back to the airdrome for the Cadillac and returned to the war.

By the end of the war I was credited with six victories and maybe one or two unconfirmed kills. Then I joined General Mason Patrick of the Air Service in Paris. One of my responsibilities for General Patrick at Orly Field near Paris was to close out the remaining planes of the AEF. The first time I was close to "Black Jack" Pershing was when I was stationed there.

Shortly after the war they built a big place near Paris called Pershing Stadium. The idea was to have competitions and other events to take people's minds off the recent hostilities. One day Sam Frierson and I flew Albert Stevens, a famous squadron commander and great photographer, back and forth over the stadium. He took some pictures, brought them back to Orly, and developed them, then dropped them into the stadium by parachute as part of the show.

I wanted to see what was going on, so I got myself a press badge for admission to the stadium. They were having opening ceremonies and I was taking a picture of Pershing from about six feet away when the national anthem began. He saluted smartly. Through the camera lens I could see the nasty look Pershing was giving me as I continued to snap pictures. He wanted me to stop taking pictures and salute.

After the war I accepted a Regular Army captaincy, even though I had a job waiting for me with AT&T Bell Labs. I spent sixteen and a half months commanding the famous First Pursuit Group (94th, 95th, 27th, and 147th Pursuit Squadrons) at Kelly Field, Texas. I had the best plane and the best motor that one could desire. Our SE-5A air frames were made in England and the engines were made in New Brunswick, New Jersey. We used these delightful airplanes to teach aerial combat maneuvering.

I met General Pershing a second time at Kelly Field. I was reviewing my troops one day when he and General Patrick showed up. General Patrick pulled me aside at one point and said, "By the way, Captain Brooks, whatever did become of my Cadillac at Brest?" Somebody had put the word out that I had stolen his staff car, but I had just borrowed it from his exhausted driver to drive up to Paris for the Bastille Day celebrations.

I had an officer burn up on the coast of Texas and went there to investigate. I flew down to a little airport on the gulf in my fine plane. On my way back to San Antonio and my

17

young bride, I had a sputtering engine. The only place to land was in a cotton patch. I came in over a fence and landed the plane at right angles to the furrows. The cotton patch was run by a Mexican with his wife and family. I couldn't speak Spanish and he couldn't speak English, but he gave me some tortillas. I didn't know where I was and wanted to contact my field. Up the trail by the cotton patch came a man on horseback wearing a black suit. He asked me if I knew my way around. No. I was at the south end of the famous King Ranch, which occupied a thousand square miles. The Mexican gave me a plow wrench, and when I removed a spark plug, the oil boiled out. The same happened with the rest of the plugs.

I replaced them, pointed my wheels toward the furrows the plane had already made, climbed in the cockpit, and, like a damned fool, took off. I stalled at the fence, yanked her up, stalled again, yanked her up again and spiraled up to 3,000 feet. I made it back to Laredo and had the plugs cleaned, then flew on to San Antonio.

The first thing I did was call the engineering officer and tell him to yank that engine out and report back to me what the problem was, even if he had to work on it all night. In the morning he told me that the scavenger rings had been put in upside down when the engine was overhauled, and it had been pumping oil over the spark plugs.

I am alive today because of things I learned to do in one case and things I knew nothing about in the other—special flying techniques and my guardian angel. Little sideslips had saved my life in several dogfights in France. I also did it to great advantage on other occasions in America by using an extreme sideslip over high-tension wires to land a Ford Tri-motor on Hadley Field near New Brunswick, New Jersey. Then I would fishtail the aircraft, kicking the rudder left-right, right-left, etc., like a fish swimming through water, to almost kill airspeed and allow me to drop straight down onto that small field. We had no communications in the early days of flying and had to make a lot of dangerous landings in modest airplanes. This last story is an example.

My wife and I moved to Langley Field, Virginia, at the same time as the famous "Bomb Run" by Billy Mitchell. He had demonstrated the potential of aerial bombing attacks by sinking two captured German battleships by dropping bombs beside them, not on top of them. A classmate of mine from MIT, Claudius H. M. Roberts, had designed and built those bombs. It was the era of the "great hurrah!" for military aviation.

Langley Field was a small place in those days and we couldn't find accommodation on the base, so my wife and I ended up sharing a genteel private home in Hampton Roads with Jimmy Doolittle and his wife. After we had settled in, I asked my commanding officer, an ex-cavalryman named Danforth, permission to visit my family in Framingham. He let me use a De Havilland DH-4B, and I requested a good maintenance sergeant to accompany me on the trip. I don't remember the sergeant's name and would rather forget it anyway.

We sailed out in beautiful weather with a fine weather report in hand, but when we were thirty minutes into the trip to Washington the clouds socked in below us. I circled at 6,000 feet and saw no break in the cloud formation. Our compasses were so poor that I couldn't return to Langley, so it was either use up my gasoline by continuing to circle, or try to descend. I dropped gingerly to the top of the cloud mass until the wheels touched the tops of tall trees, then pulled up sharply. Again I circled. Now it was a choice of running out of gas or going back down, and it seemed better to die at least trying to land.

Down, down, down we went through this terrific cloud mass, then we were suddenly below it. We landed in a muddy pasture with cows, and I managed to raise the tail to stop without turning the airplane over. I had stopped the plane just short of a bend on the Potomac River below Mount Vernon. A local man had seen me land and walked down a path from the top of a rise beside the river to ask if he could help. The three of us pulled the bird up the rise, and after a long wait for the cloud cover to lift enough, I took off again. My plan was to land at Framingham at a former muster field of the Massachusetts Volunteer Militia, now a local National Guard airdrome.

It quickly got dark and there were no visible landmarks, just a confusing maze of streetlights below us. Finally I spotted a green field and landed there, somehow avoiding any cross wires. I taxied over to a highway, cut down the engine to low rev, and asked a man in an automobile for directions. He showed me a landmark, a familiar dam. We took off in the direction of my home, but it was the same story—lights here, lights there, no real landmarks. We had to make another forced landing.

My technique in France and America was to look for a field with golden mustard-flower petals, because my experience had shown that these were good places to land. I would point the left wingtip down toward the ground, but cocked up a bit off the horizontal so that the weight of the airplane would reduce airspeed. The nose would start to rise. At the right moment, with airspeed drastically reduced, I would kick the plane around with full force back to the normal flying position and get the nose down. Then I would begin fishtailing to kill any remaining airspeed, being careful to avoid a stall. The wheels would be right off the ground at this point, and the plane would basically drop straight down onto the grass with its last vestiges of speed. We had to do it that way because those crates had no brakes. You needed the feel of the stick throughout these maneuvers to know when you were approaching stall, because stalling in a DH-4B meant death.

I found a place with railroads and buildings on high ground above another river, then spotted a field with those beautiful golden blossoms and made a landing as described above. I stopped just short of an apple orchard on the other side of the small clearing. That was at Concord, twelve miles from home, so a telephone call brought my brother-in-law to pick me up. The next day we backed the plane down to the Sudbury riverbank, and I lifted off on full motor, just clearing the tops of the apple trees. We landed at Framingham and I left the maintenance sergeant with the aircraft.

I returned a couple of days later, and we lifted off for Mitchell Field on Long Island. We weren't twenty miles into the trip when the motor started cutting off. Eventually I found an angle where the engine didn't miss and got to an altitude where I could gently nose down. When we landed at Mitchell Field, they found the spark plugs all fouled up. The sergeant hadn't been near my airplane in two days at Framingham. We flew on to Bowling Field and got another perfect weather report for the last leg of the journey, then ran into the worst thunder and lightning storm you can imagine as we approached the Rappahannock River.

Again I looked until I found a mustard-flower field. The noise of my circling aircraft had drawn a number of automobiles to that same field, and those kind people lined up to outline it with their headlights. I went through all my maneuvers again, made a nice landing, and then all of a sudden my undercarriage disappeared into a brook and the saplings along its edge swept my wings back. The plane skidded to a stop on its belly.

I was greeted by a group of lovely young fellows and their southern ladies, and some of those southern belles told me that they had come out in the storm to see the "dead aviator." I telephoned Langley, and Danforth agreed to pick me up at the other side of a ferry landing on the York River a short distance away. A young man in an open-topped Buick took me to our side of the landing, slithering his pretty automobile down a muddy road through the downpour. I rode across the river with a couple of moonshiners who inquired about the sale of some surplus airplanes at Langley that they might use to transport their product.

I was told that government property had been damaged: not Ray Brooks, but the airplane. I went back up the river in a fishing boat, retrieved the engine and the instrument panel, piled the rest of my plane in a field, and burned it.

So I survived a war and came home. I survived lightning storms, hailstorms, and other dangerous flying conditions, only partly through skill and good luck. Those experiences made me appreciate life and have no fear of death. A guardian angel has been watching over me since 1917, and that has made each day very special for me.[1]

WORLD
WAR
II

While World War I was a European conflict for American pilots, World War II was global in nature. This collection contains memoirs from China-Burma-India (Rector, Scott), North Africa–European Theater of Operations (Ilfrey), the Philippines (Shomo), carrier units in the Pacific (Galvin, Silber, Vejtasa, Vraciu), land-based navy fighters (Blackburn), ETO (Cullerton, Dahlberg, Lowell, Smith, Zemke), Guadalcanal (De Blanc, Haberman, Percy, Swett), and a special story that begins in Java and ends in the Mediterranean Theater of Operations (Morehead).

The pursuit pilot of World War I flew an aircraft armed with one or two machine guns fixed to fire forward through the propellers. His enemy had a similar armament. World War II fighter pilots flew machines capable of speeds of three to four times those of Great War fighters, and carrying up to eight .50-caliber machine guns, or combinations of machine guns and cannons. They faced an array of Bettys, Zeros, Jills, Judys, Tojos, float planes, FW-190s, ME-109s, ME-110s, ME-262s and other aircraft equipped with similar combinations of cannon (up to 37mm) and machine guns. The destructive power of fighters had indeed multiplied.

The variety of American fighter aircraft is impressive. "Swede" Vejtasa shot down Zeros from an SBD dive-bomber and returned to score more victories in F4F Wildcats. James Morehead began the war in P-40 Warhawks and ended it flying P-38 Lightnings. Robert Scott flew a P-40 Tomahawk. Edward Rector began the war with the Flying Tigers, flying a Tomahawk, and returned to fly P-51 Mustangs. Jack Ilfrey and John Lowell flew both Lightnings and Mustangs. Tom Blackburn was a F4U Corsair ace. Roger Haberman, Jeff DeBlanc, and James Percy flew Wildcats. Leslie Smith piloted P-47 Thunderbolts. Bill Cullerton and Ken Dahlberg flew both Thunderbolts and Mustangs. Hub Zemke flew both Thunderbolts and Lightnings. John Galvin and Alex Vraciu were F6F Hellcat pilots. Sam Silber began the war flying Wildcats and went on to pilot Hellcats. James Swett flew both Wildcats and Corsairs. William Shomo flew P-39 Airacobras on photo reconnaissance missions, then went on to pilot an F-6K (P-51D).

The Army Air Corps mission in World War II was worldwide. We have stories from CBI, North Africa, Java–New Guinea, the MTO, the

Philippines, and the ETO. The great air supremacy battles over Europe are covered in some detail. The navy stories are all from the Pacific area and range from the earliest counterstrikes against the Japanese (January 1942), on across the wide expanses of that ocean to the fleet strikes against Japan. The marine stories all begin during the protracted air battles around Guadalcanal, the Marine Corps crucible where Joe Foss won his Medal of Honor. Three of the stories end there. The other one goes on to include carrier operations.

There were approximately 1,475 Army, Navy and Marine Corps aces during the war. In addition, the Eagle Squadron that flew with the British during the Battle of Britain had twenty-one aces. The Flying Tigers had thirty-eight more. There were significant differences between the services in how ace status was awarded. The marines and navy credited only aerial victories. The army credited pilots with aircraft destroyed on the ground as well, and in some cases recognized bomber turret gunners as aces.

These nineteen stories represent aces with at least five aerial victories. They were carefully chosen to provide as wide a view as possible of all air combat operations. Given the number of World War II aces, their whole story may never be adequately told. What we do have is an astonishing variety of experiences: air-to-air maneuvers, ground attack missions, escape and evasion from deadly enemies. We hope that these memoirs will provide the reader with a greater understanding of the war, both in the air and on the ground, and stand as a lasting tribute to all who served.

JAVA TO PLOESTI

Lieutenant James Bruce Morehead's P-40 unit left for the South Pacific immediately following Pearl Harbor and engaged in some of the first actions against the Japanese Zeros over Java, northern Australia, and New Guinea. It was a time when the enemy possessed superior equipment and combat experience. On a later tour, flying P-38s from Italy on escort missions over the Balkans and elsewhere, he saw the tables turned on the Axis, permanently and absolutely.

About the end of December 1941 we left San Francisco aboard a large ocean liner with fifty-five unassembled P-40 fighter planes, fifty-five pilots, fifty-five armorers, and fifty-five crew chiefs. We were at sea twenty-eight days, destined for the Philippines, but the ocean liner was diverted in mid-course to Brisbane, Australia. At Brisbane we were assigned to Amblerly Field and began unloading our P-40s. We pilots worked alongside the crew chiefs and armorers in assembling the planes and then started training in them. The last defense of the Philippines at Bataan was going on by then, and some of the fighter planes from the Philippines retreated to Java, where we made a great effort to support them.

Two flights of aircraft, one with ten planes and one with about fifteen planes, left Amblerly Field for Java and ran into terrible luck. It was the monsoon season. Eleven or twelve of the aircraft in the larger flight crashed in bad weather after they were unable to land at a field in Timor. Most of the pilots were able to bail out. The other flight had similar problems and lost many of its pilots and aircraft. I was on the third flight to Java.

We flew west to the heartland of Australia, then north past Alice Springs and on to Darwin, where we landed at a place called Bachelor Field. A B-17 was assigned to lead us to Java. As we were about to take off, a rainstorm began. The downpour was so intense that there were about six inches of water on the runway. We finally got airborne and followed the B-17 north across the ocean toward Timor. The storm increased and the cloud ceiling dropped down to only a few feet. We were about fifteen feet above the water, flying under the wing of the B-17. I knew that if I lost sight of this bomber, I would be lost at sea. We finally made it through the terrible weather and landed at a base on Timor. We had water buffalo meat for supper and spent the night. The next morning we flew across some beautiful islands to Bali and landed there to refuel. The B-17 left us and flew on to Java.

We gassed up from fuel drums with hand pumps. While we were doing this, a single Japanese plane flew overhead. The flight leader said, "Everybody that's gassed up get in the air! The Japs are coming!"

My plane was not yet fueled. The wave of Japanese fighter planes hit our boys in the air and shot three or four of them down, then a flight of Japanese bombers started bombing the field. I hid behind a coconut tree and thought I was safe, but when the bombs started coming down, the coconuts started falling too. We fled from the field as the bombers flew out in a wide turn to make a second pass. We were running with our Mae Wests on, and unfortunately the Dutch and Balinese soldiers thought we were Japanese and started shooting at us. We finally convinced them that we were friendly. We returned to our aircraft after the second bombing run was finished. Most of our aircraft on the ground had been destroyed, but mine and one other fighter were still flyable. The two of us flew on to Java the next morning, where another raid was in progress at a place called Soerabaja. I crawled under the table inside a hut at the air base while dodging the Japanese bombs for a second time. It was a rude invitation to war.

After a couple of skirmishes at Soerabaja we were assigned to a small grass strip in the center of Java for two or three weeks. On my first combat mission we were attacked by Japanese fighters. I was leading the flight because our more experienced flight leader was stuck on the ground in the mud. The Zeros dived on us, and I turned to meet them head on. I fired at the lead plane as he rushed by a few feet overhead, then dived away to keep them from getting on my tail. We were at too low an altitude to continue fighting Zeros with their superior maneuverability, so we returned to the air base. There I learned that we had lost one of our four planes.

A few missions later I was on a flight when three waves of Japanese bombers attacked the 19th Bomb Group base at

Malang, Java. I was the third man in a flight of three and couldn't catch up with our flight leader as we approached the bombers at about 20,000 feet. A flight of Zeros intercepted the two American pilots ahead of me, made head-on passes and then followed them down, leaving me alone with the bombers. I flew along beside the bombers, made a quartering attack on them, and dived away. I climbed back up to make another attack and wound up in front of the bombers. A Japanese Zero intercepted me, but I didn't believe he could hit me through the wild gyrations I was about to undertake. I did a half roll, pulled up hard, turned back into the bombers, and made a head-on pass at the leader. Then I dived away, losing the Zero on my tail. I was low on ammunition and fuel by then. I swung around after the bombers were gone and landed at Malang for gas and ammunition. As I landed and taxied up to one of the hangers at the base, two men rose from a foxhole and asked if they could help. Yes! They came over to service me. I took off and returned to our base.

When the aircraft carrier, USS *Langley,* arrived at the port of Jakjakarta, another pilot and I took a narrow-gauge native train down there to meet the pilots of the P-40s on board and lead them back to our little grass strip. On arriving at the port, we were met by a couple of American news reporters who told us that they had just learned that the *Langley* and all aboard had been sunk by Japanese bombers. We thereupon reboarded the little narrow-gauge train and returned to our base.

A couple of days later the Japanese started the invasion of Java. We flew missions against them over the beach. One of our boys was shot down and landed on the beach, climbed out of his aircraft, confiscated a bicycle from a native, and rode it back to our base. As the invasion progressed, a number of us were directed to fly to Malang for the escape to Australia. We climbed aboard a B-17 piloted by Colonel Eubanks, commander of the 19th Bomber Group. As we circled over the airfield, Japanese Zeros came down and set a B-24 on fire below us.

We set course for Australia and landed on the northwest coast, then continued down the continent to Perth, around to Adelaide and on to Canberra. I was let off the bomber and assigned to the 49th Fighter Group in southern Australia. We got in a few days of intensive training for the pilots of that group, then flew north again. We had partied at Brisbane the night before. It was getting late in the day and the sun was beaming down into the cockpit of the P-40. I was leading a flight of four when suddenly I found myself diving for the ground. I had fallen asleep. I saw the ground coming up at me, yanked back on the stick, and shot up in a big sweeping pull-up from the dive. The three guys following me screamed out of their dive as well. They pulled up as well. When we got on the ground at Charleyville, the other guys said, "What in the hell were you doing?" I finally got around to telling them that I had fallen asleep. We flew on to our new base at Darwin.

We spent several months at Darwin when the activity was fairly brisk. There were many missions during this time. In November 1942 my squadron commander was leading a flight of four, and I was leading another four-plane flight when we intercepted thirty-one Japanese bombers. They were on the way out of their bombing run, flying low at 16,000 feet, the lowest altitude that I ever had the opportunity to attack them. I asked the squadron leader if he wanted to make the attack or if I was to do it. He had no combat experience and told me to go ahead. I was tickled pink that he let me lead the attack. If he had swung in on a trailing approach, all those bombers would have had the chance to shoot at us. I had the option of flying out in front of the Japanese bombers. I led both flights way out front and made a quartering attack.

As I came in on the lead bomber, I did a slow roll to intimidate them. I don't know if it had any effect, but they had come over our bases before and made a show of flying rolls and loops and so forth. I wanted to do the same for them before I pulled the trigger. I led the lead bomber with my guns by about twenty yards and saw my tracers go right into the airplane. He started smoking heavily. I turned and dived below the bombers, then pulled back hard to gain altitude. To my surprise, I came out right at the tail end of the whole formation, quite close to the rear-end Japanese. I went after him and looked up in time to see that one of my wingmen had swung in on a bomber formation in front of me. His bullets sawed the wing off one of the bombers. The wing came off and the other wing flipped over and struck the airplane that was flying position on him. Both planes went down in a big tangle of wings and propellers. This was only a glimpse, because I was rapidly closing in on the rear Japanese bomber.

I opened fire at the bomber when I saw the rear gunner in the tail of the plane shooting at me with his 20mm cannon. His fire seemed rather slow, and I could see the puff of smoke as each round was fired. I watched my tracers as they stitched across his turret. No more fire. I worked on this airplane until I overtook him, then dived beneath him and went after the next bomber in line. The same thing happened again. The tail gunner shot at me with his 20mm cannon, and I sawed my tracers across his turret. That put him out of action. I fired into the bomber until I overtook him, then dived again. At that point my windshield was covered with oil, probably from my hits on the bomber's engine. Having cut my throttle when firing at the two bombers, my plane stalled out. I dived down to pick up speed and spotted a Japanese fighter as I pulled away.

I turned to attack him, but he cut off my turn. I dived away from him. I pulled up again, saw another Zero, and leveled my sights on him. The bullets went under him. I had failed to elevate enough to hit him. He whished overhead and I dived away from him before he could get on my tail. I couldn't see well through the windshield because of the oil, and I feared that it might be coming from my fighter, so I decided to return to base. I didn't want to become a casualty fifty miles at sea.

On another occasion I was leading a flight of three when we spotted three Japanese fighters below us heading back to their base. I made a diving attack from behind them. My bullets shattered the canopy on one Zero, then I pulled over on another with my guns still firing, pulled up from the steep dive, and gained about 5,000 feet of altitude. I turned back, dived again on a second plane, and followed him through some violent maneuvers until I could get a bead on him. The Zero blew up in my face. I flew through this mess and saw a parachute drifting down. I flew by to wave at the guy, but there was nobody in the chute.

One time I got to see my job from the other end of the telescope. We were in the process of moving from Darwin to New Guinea. This friend of mine flew with the 19th Bomb Group, and he asked me if I would like to go on a bombing mission. Sure I would. He set me up as a waist gunner on a B-17. We didn't encounter any Japanese fighters that day, but it gave me the picture of what it was like for the fellow on the receiving end of our attacks.

There was one sad experience when we were leaving Darwin for New Guinea. The Australians had sent their youth to fight and die for Great Britain against the Germans, and now they asked the British for some help to fight the Japanese. Although the British were in need of every ounce of help they could get, they managed to squeeze out a squadron of Spitfire fighters for Australia. The fighter pilots came in to talk with us about the Japanese and we gave them as much help and advice as we could. I told them that the Spitfire was a very famous aircraft and had done well against the Germans. I was sure that they would not feel very good about running away from the Japanese, but I feared that the Zero was superior in maneuverability. I told them it was better to break off a fight and come back another day on more equal terms. If Zeros got on their tails, they might not be able to shake them off, and until they were sure that they could do so, they should approach wrap-up fights with them with great caution.

I said that twice, very carefully, because of the psychological implication of the Australians taking over the defense of their homeland from Americans. They were very proud fighter pilots. The squadron leader had about fifteen German aircraft to his credit. A few days after we left, the Japanese raided Darwin. The squadron of Spitfires went up to fight them and lost eleven fighter planes and eight pilots killed. It was a sad, sad experience. The Spitfires were soundly defeated. Fortunately the Japanese had decided that they were not going to invade Australia, as they had failed to gain air superiority there. They switched their efforts to New Guinea, although the battles between the Australian pilots and the Japanese were critical at the time they were fought.

The Japanese bombers used to fly over Darwin and keep us awake at night. I made an unauthorized flight one night to try to intercept "Washing-Machine Charlie." My crew chief turned on the headlights of a jeep at the end of the strip to guide me. It was a very dark night with no moon. I got airborne and climbed hard for about fifteen minutes until I arrived at the place where the bombers should have been coming into the searchlights. They were already gone. That very day the radar people had decided that there was no need to sound the alarm until the bombers were practically overhead. There was no reason to get everybody out of bed forty or forty-five minutes before they arrived. Because of this, I got the warning when the Japanese were already over us.

It was very dark and I had no place to land. The strip was blacked out, except for two little twinkling lights from the jeep, and I couldn't tell which way the strip ran. I had to call back to the nearby Australian bomber base and ask them to switch on the runway lights. I landed and parked the aircraft there until the next day. I had hinted to my squadron commander what I wanted to do, but he had never given us permission to make night interceptions. Now I had to explain myself to him and to the Australians. I wanted to be a hero, but that's not the way it turned out at all. I faced considerable blasphemy from my commander for making that flight.

We used to go hunting and fishing in the wilderness outside of Darwin. Sometimes the squadron CO would give us a jeep when we were off alert. One day the jeep got stuck in the mud and the tide came in before we could get it unstuck. We had to walk twenty miles through swamps filled with crocodiles and poisonous snakes. The CO took the jeep away from us. Next we got hold of a little Australian plane called a "Tiger Moth." We would land it in a meadow and hunt water buffalo and wild pigs. One day my friend was flying from the front seat and I decided to crawl out on wing and wave at the guys as we flew over the strip. I grabbed one of the wing braces and tapped him on the shoulder. He damned near jumped out of his seat when he saw me standing beside him on the wing. He started yelling, "Get back in here! Get back in here, you son of a bitch!"

By the time we left Australia for the United States, I had been credited with two kills while attacking Japanese bomber formations over Java, three kills on enemy bomber formations over Darwin, and two kills on attacking Zeros at Darwin.

In the States I learned to fly a P-38 and then helped train new P-38 pilots for a few months. It was a shame we didn't have planes like that when we were first fighting the Zeros. Maybe we could have given a better account of ourselves. There was a historical study after the war. One question asked what was the outstanding weapon of the war. Of course it was the atomic bomb. Another question was used to determine the outstanding conventional weapon of the war. It wasn't the German 88mm gun, or the Spitfire, or the Tiger tank. It was the Japanese Zero fighter.

The first actions with the Zeros over China, or those fought by the British or the Dutch, were Allied disasters. The Zeros were responsible for the initial conquest of the Pacific, because they were able to gain air superiority in every action. Air superiority is so vital to waging modern war. The Japanese fighter pilots had already been fighting for five years in China before Pearl Harbor. God must have been at our right hand when we won some of our battles in the Pacific, because the enemy had the material and training advantages at the time.

In contrast, one of the problems we had in the southwest Pacific was similar to the navy's problems with their torpedoes. When we first started doing violent maneuvers with the enemy, our guns wouldn't fire. I had enemy aircraft lined up several times and the guns wouldn't fire, or maybe only one gun would fire. This was discouraging when your enemy had five or six guns firing at you.

I was sent on a second tour to Italy. There we escorted bombers on mostly long-range missions over Germany, northern Italy, and Ploesti in Romania. The Ploesti oil fields were important to the German war effort, and we bombed them steadily. The evaluation board after the war determined that those strikes against the oil fields were the most telling attacks against the Germans. In addition, we once bombed Monte Casino in Italy in support of our ground attacks there. We supported the landings at Anzio, and later moved to Corsica to support the invasion of southern France.

In the Adriatic Sea our fighters had captured a small island up the Yugoslav coast called the Island of Vis. It was used as an emergency landing strip. I lost my oxygen at high altitude one day over Romania and had to drop to low level to return from the mission. As a result of the long flight and a couple of attacks I had made on ground targets on the way home, I was running low on fuel and had to land at Vis. I was almost sorry that I had to land there after the dramatic scenes I witnessed. Our crippled bombers made emergency landings for a couple of hours with one, two, or three engines shot up, with bullet-riddled fuselages and blood running out of the back ends. It was one of the biggest displays of aircraft crashes I had ever seen. It was heartbreaking to see our Allied brethren shot up, and to see planes leaking fuel, burning, and crashing.

I got back about three hours late from that mission, and everyone figured I had been shot down. They were getting ready to divide up my personal belongings as we often did when a pilot went down. We had quite a reunion at the officers club.

One time I had to shut down one of my two engines over Romania. I was coming home at low level, just skimming the trees and hopping over hills, hoping that no enemy aircraft would spot me. I popped over a hill and saw a line of tanks and trucks ahead of me, broadside. I turned on the gunswitch and gunsight and opened up on those guys. You should have seen how quickly they dived into their turrets and buttoned up. I guess they figured, "Those dirty sons of guns! They're shooting at us when they have only one engine to fly on."

I engaged in a few fighter actions over Romania and Germany and was able to down a couple of Germans on that tour, but my records got messed up. It wasn't until June 5, 1990, that I received credit for one of those victories, after the Air Force Historical Research Center discovered an account of the action in a narrative mission report. On June 6, 1944, during a bomber escort mission to Ploesti, I shot down a poor ME-109 pilot who probably didn't know an enemy was within a thousand miles of him. I was leading a squadron of sixteen fighters and never broke formation. In fact, in the MTO at that time we were restricted from breaking formation to attack enemy aircraft. My aim was true and the Messerschmitt started breaking apart in flames and a shower of Plexiglas shards. He was one of only two enemy fighters, and we were sixteen, so I have never bragged much about the victory. But to learn many, many years later that a victory is only a "claim" is something else again. Now it is part of the official record.

Everything was different in Europe. Our morale in the very first part of the war had been very low. When we were sent to Java, we had a very fine squadron commander named Major Sprague. He could handle a P-40 like a dream. He was shot down over Java and killed. Shortly after we returned to Darwin, our squadron commander, Captain Strauss, was another experienced P-40 pilot. He was shot down and killed over Darwin. After you lose a couple of highly proficient pilots and outstanding leaders, and you are waiting for some guidance and direction, your morale can get pretty low.

They speak of the bravery of the later Japanese kamikaze pilots, but there was little difference between us and them.

The pilots all felt that we were flying suicide missions against enemy pilots with vastly superior equipment and vastly more combat experience. I so admire those early American pilots in the Solomons who never knew when or from where they would be struck. They were like we had been on Java, never knowing when their camp would be overrun by the enemy.

There is also a great difference in attitude between soldiers on the defensive and those on the offensive. Our outlook in the Pacific was one of desperation. Our outlook in Europe was one of great confidence. America was on her feet, going after them and striking back. One of the proudest missions I was ever on happened after all bombers and fighters stood down for several days. Then we got the order to put up a thousand bombers out of Italy. I was leading my group of forty-eight P-38 fighters. Such a beautiful parade of aircraft! As we took off, there were bombers and fighters as far as the eye could see—some en route, some gaining altitude, some taking off. As far as you could see were American fighting men on the way to deliver a blow to the enemy. It was one great feeling.

DIVE-BOMBERS AND GRIM REAPERS

Lieutenant "Swede" Vejtasa was working as a smoke jumper in the forests of Idaho when his notice to report for flight training arrived thirty-one days late by pack mule. He later piloted a dive-bomber on some of the first counterstrikes against the Japanese at New Guinea and in the Solomons, and dogfought Zeros with an SBD in the Battle of the Coral Sea. Vejtasa returned to the South Pacific for some memorable experiences with F4F Wildcat Squadron VF-10, the "Grim Reapers."

In June 1941 my squadron (VS-5), having transferred at sea in Atlantic waters to the USS *Ranger* (CV-4), launched for NAS Norfolk, turned in our biplanes, and drew sleek new Douglas Dauntless SBD-3 dive-bombers. An intensive period of training, bombing practice, war games, and radar familiarization followed. This routine continued until December 7, 1941.

The Japanese attacks on Pearl Harbor came with a shock. All hands reported to the squadron ready room at Norfolk for briefing and instructions. In the hectic days that followed, we loaded our planes on board the *Yorktown* and departed for the West Coast via the Panama Canal. On December 21, 1941, we took off from the carrier and landed at the Army Air Corps base at Albrook Field, spending the night there while the carrier transited the canal. The following day we scouted areas west of Panama before landing back aboard. On December 31 we landed at North Island before heading west to join the USS *Enterprise*.

By the early morning hours of January 31, 1942, the task force was in position and launched aircraft for attacks on enemy targets in the Marshall and Gilbert islands. Our target was Makin Island. I flew wing on the skipper, Lieutenant Commander Bill Burch, as we attacked surface vessels and destroyed a seaplane on the water. The attacks were well planned and executed, and the opposition was light, so we returned to the USS *Yorktown* with no damage. Other units had experienced moderate to heavy AA fire and aerial opposition, and did not fare so well. Several pilots were lost.

The task force turned back toward Hawaii and arrived there on February 6, 1942. VS-5 landed at the Marine Corps field at Ewa for temporary basing ashore. Pearl Harbor, the military bases, and the airfields were a scene of devastation such as I had never seen before, and could not fully imagine from the previous reports received on the December seventh attacks. Sunken ships, burned hangers, and aircraft hulks were visible everywhere. Even though salvage and repair crews had been at work for the two months since the Japanese attacks, there was much left to be done. One of our first tasks at Ewa was to sweep the runways clear of expended bullets and shell casings left behind by aerial strafing. That was an "all-hands" operation.

By mid-February we were at sea again, bound for the South Pacific. The days were occupied by long scouting missions, usually lasting more than four hours. Radio silence was in effect. On March 9, 1942, while we were operating in the Coral Sea, we received orders to attack and destroy enemy shipping in the Lae, New Guinea, anchorage. The next day we flew across the Owen Stanley Mountains en route to the target. There had been some doubt about whether the torpedo bombers could make it with the prescribed load, but all went well.

Bill Burch was leading the flight with me on one wing. He put us in perfect position for attack by taking advantage of the sun, cloud cover, and wind, with a planned recovery and retirement away from the land mass and mountains so that an expeditious join-up could be made. I had a hung bomb after our last dive, so I quickly swerved back and made another dive on a transport before joining up with the rest of the flight. My radioman, Wood, reported a hit on the transport, but at the time I was too busy looking for the squadron and avoiding flack to observe it.

It was in the period after the Lae operation that the *Yorktown* set a record of 105 days at sea without stopping or making port. The ship was fueled, but no supplies were taken on. The menu became very limited until an Australian vessel came alongside and provided us with a deal of mutton. That mutton was not to the liking of all hands.

By early May 1942, the Japanese were moving south, setting up bases on the island chains, especially the Solomon Islands. On the fourth of May, the Air Group conducted all-day attacks against shipping and any enemy aircraft present in the Tulagi area. The operation was well planned and expertly led; however, the results of our dive-bombing were not as good as expected. The windshields and the tubular sights that extended through them fogged up and made it impossible to see. This was due to our chilled aircraft diving rapidly from altitude to the lower layers of warm, humid air. We had not experienced this problem before and it required some corrective action.

Mine was the last plane to dive on the second mission of the day. On starting my pull-out, I saw a Zero fighter on floats attacking from my right rear. Fortunately, Bill Burch had given me many a lesson on countermoves. I turned hard right, into and under the Zero, then hard back, to meet him head on if he scissored, which he now did. As we exchanged bursts of gunfire, I could see him bringing his tracers to bear on my plane. I wished mightily that I had more gunpower on my SBD, but the two .30 calibers firing through my prop were working well. On the second scissor the Zero broke off and dove away, trailing heavy smoke. On each pass my rear-seat gunner, Broussard, had been firing as the Zero made his turn, and he was making that gun chatter. As the Zero sped away, I saw an SBD ahead of me jump on his tail and apply the coup de grâce, sending him down into the ocean in flames. Our attacks had slowed the Japanese thrust and given us a bit more time to regroup and prepare for more action.

Although I was not aware of it yet, the *Yorktown* had received orders for Lieutenant Faulkner and me to be detached and return to California to help form a new fighter squadron—VF-10. Our gear was aboard the oiler *Neosho,* and we were shaking the hands of our squadron mates when the ship's air boss came down and said, "We are not going to detach you fellows just yet. We expect some action shortly and we need all pilots." I was not disappointed because I felt a strong attachment to the squadron and would much rather return with the group. The *Neosho* and its escorting destroyer, the *Simms,* were both sunk a few days later by Japanese carrier planes. There were few, if any, survivors. How strange the hand of fate!

Bomber aircraft of the Army Air Corps reported a Japanese task force with one aircraft carrier north of New Guinea and apparently headed for the Coral Sea. The weather in the Coral Sea was miserable with fog, rain, and strong winds, but we had been operating for months under similar conditions, and this did not pose a great problem. The *Yorktown* was now in the company of the USS *Lexington*, and on May 7, both carrier air groups were launched with orders to attack. Again I was pleased to be flying as wingman to Bill Burch. In my backseat was Commander Shindler, the staff gunnery officer, who would observe and report on the action. I hurriedly checked him out on the radio and the rear-seat gun before takeoff. The carrier was our prime target.

The weather to the north was much improved, and after two hours at altitude we sighted the enemy task force. The carrier was in the center of a number of surface vessels, and all were making great white wakes, indicating they were at maximum speed. I hoped that our fighters were ahead of us, engaging any enemy VF, and apparently they were, because we were not intercepted on the approach. Our skipper put us in an ideal attack position that utilized a fast approach, gaining speed while losing some altitude, then a peel-off at the pushover point, splitting the dive brakes at the last moment and going down with bombsights on the Japanese carrier's deck.

I saw the big bomb detach from the rack on the skipper's plane, take what seemed to be a slight arcing trajectory, and then plunge into the carrier deck amidships. A tremendous blast of smoke and fire shot out from the sides of the vessel. I dropped my bomb, closed flaps while pulling out, and closed rapidly on the skipper. Bill Burch was in a gentle turn that enabled following planes to join up by cutting across his circle. Commander Shindler had his camera out and was snapping pictures as we pulled away and other planes dropped their bombs and torpedoes. I looked back while scanning the area for enemy fighters and saw only a huge black cloud of smoke above the sea where, a few minutes before, there had been an aircraft carrier. We had done the job. Shindler opened on the radio and reported that the carrier had been sunk in seven minutes.

Getting back to the home carrier in bad weather with night coming on was not easy. We hung in close to our leader, who led us to the *Yorktown* like a homing pigeon. Then it was break-up, so much time ahead, a timed turn, so much more time in the straightaway, another timed turn, and hopefully the stern of the carrier would be in sight. The landing signal officer was there, using his night wands to provide better visibility. I landed and taxied forward and the deck crew chocked my aircraft and we got out. Then I saw crewmen rushing around and taking cover, waving madly. One of the strangest events in my experience was about to unfold.

I had no idea what was going on until I saw a plane come in to land, then suddenly take a wave-off with full throttle. As it passed overhead, I saw the Rising Sun on the side of its fuselage! I dashed for the ready room, which was in an island at deck level, and saw another aircraft pass close by on the starboard with a Rising Sun clearly visible on its side. The ship was at general quarters, and I could not get into the ready room, so I took refuge near the island. Guns started going off as some of the lads manning the weapons in the catwalks saw the enemy planes flashing by. As suddenly as it all started, it became quiet. The remainder of our planes came aboard.

When we were squared away and back in the ready room, our skipper explained what was happening. While we were sinking the Japanese carrier, another enemy task force with two carriers, the *Shokaku* and *Zuikaku,* was approaching from the east, searching for the *Yorktown* and *Lexington.* They had sunk the *Neosho* and the *Simms,* but could not locate our carriers through the fog and rain. On the return trip their aviators had come across our carriers, and thinking they were home, started to make their approaches to land.

We were saved by the weather, but I thought of what could have happened if one of the enemy pilots had had the presence of mind to charge his guns and strafe our carrier decks full of planes. We lost two pilots that night, one from each carrier, and oddly, both of them were named Baker.

Our radar had tracked the enemy aircraft and plotted them circling twenty-five miles away. At least one destroyer requested permission to overtake the enemy task force at night in the bad weather and launch its torpedoes. It was a bold and reasonable idea, but it was denied. Through the night the Japanese task force made distance to the north as we took a southerly course. The crews labored all night doing maintenance work, fueling and arming our craft, and spotting the deck with scouts ahead, ready for a predawn launch to seek out the enemy and report his position. Some fighters would accompany the attack group. Others would remain on combat air patrol over our task force. A new concept, of which I was a part, would deploy eight SBDs at low altitude in the direction of the expected approach to intercept and attack enemy torpedo planes. It was not a bad idea, but we had no time to practice and work out the most effective formation, positioning, and attack techniques.

On the morning of May 8, 1942, the weather had considerably improved and we had low, broken cloud layers with a clear blue sky above. Reports of contact with an enemy task force of two carriers and many escorting vessels came early, and the attack units were immediately launched. Our anti-torpedo plane patrol of SBDs took station just above the clouds and in the direction of the expected attack. While orbiting, and without radar warning, we were hit by the first flight of Zeros. Trying to be especially alert, and remembering the many lessons by Bill Burch, I was looking over my shoulder—watching my six—as well as keeping the rear-seat gunner alert. I saw the Zeros coming in fast on our tails, power-diving and driving hard from perfect formation.

I yelled into my mike, "Attack from the rear!" as I turned

hard and underneath the Zeros, then turned back hard to either come out on their tails or meet them head on.

In the ensuing melee I saw a Zero come from underneath the cloud cover. I bore down on him with full power, closed to firing range, and watched the twin .30-caliber tracers hit the airplane. My gunner, Wood, yelled and started firing at a Zero coming up on our quarter, so I swung back hard and reversed course once again, hoping to keep him out of position and gain the advantage for us. At the same time, I saw an SBD, trailing smoke, begin a long dive at a steep angle. It hit the water with only a small splash, like a rock entering the water from a nearly vertical drop. The situation became more intense when I was bracketed by two Zeros with the obvious intent of getting one on my tail, no matter which way I turned. Once again I used the tactic taught me by the skipper—I pulled up into a loop and came out behind one Zero as he passed underneath.

I continued trying to counter the attacks of Zeros coming at me from all directions. As much as possible, I tried to meet them head on or turn to give them only high-deflection shots. I often skidded my plane to give them a more difficult angle of fire. There were many near-collisions as they pressed home their attacks, and many times I felt the impact of the air blast as we passed each other. I had to give way several times when it appeared that the enemy pilots wanted to ram me. Two or more attacking aircraft are most difficult to counter if they coordinate their runs, but this was not happening, and I could pick the greatest threat and counter first one, then the next, with violent maneuvering, using steep diving turns, loops, chandelles, or rollouts on top or out of a turn. The SBD was a marvelous aircraft and very maneuverable, although we could have used a more powerful engine for individual combat.

Firing head on, I could see their tracers coming at me, with the 20mms being fired from a distance before I could come into range. I was wishing that I had the firepower of some of those British aircraft that were being used in the

European theater. It was pretty unbelievable the number of guns they were installing in the wings of their fighters. I saw my bullets hit on several head-on shots. On other passes I was able to bear for a short time on Zeros coming up from underneath and climbing in front of me. I remember thinking that this was not a good maneuver for the attackers. My bullets shot off part of a canopy on one such pass. The plane gave a puff of smoke, and I wondered for a moment if this was a ruse.

On another maneuver I saw an F4F just above the clouds, and with a Zero coming in from my quarter, I thought that we could meet and pick him off. The F4F promptly disappeared into the clouds. I found myself with a single Zero with a most determined pilot who was willing to scissor rapidly and fire head on from a distance. On several of those passes I saw the pilot in his cockpit in his brown flight gear, goggles down, and looking straight ahead. Each time I felt the air blast as we passed each other. On the last scissor he fired his 20mms until the tracers suddenly stopped, making me believe he was out of ammo. I held course until the last moment, firing long bursts. Something flew off his plane. I turned hard as we passed, and he dove away into the clouds, trailing a bit of smoke.

Then as suddenly as it had started, the dogfight was over. Apparently most of the enemy planes broke off the attack on signal or by time. We had lost four of our SBDs with pilots on antisubmarine patrol. We landed aboard the *Yorktown* and received reports from the attack groups. The *Lexington* had taken several hits and could not take her planes aboard, so all aircraft were diverted to the *Yorktown*. The hangar deck was full, the flight deck was packed, and there were still planes in the air. The situation was critical because more planes would prevent the wire barriers from being lifted, and a plane landing long or without a hook would plow into the pack and probably start a fire in which many aircraft would be destroyed. It must have been a quick conference between the commanding officer, the air boss, and Robin Lindsey, the

LSO (landing signal officer). Landing the planes in the water was one alternative and seemed to be the safest solution.

Then Robin Lindsey took a stand, spoke up, and told the CO and the air boss, "Have them land. I can bring them in safely without the barrier."

The CO replied, "Do you know what you are saying?"

"I take full responsibility. Let me bring them in."

What followed was one of the really great feats under tremendous pressure in the annals of carrier aviation. With complete control Lindsey guided each plane in to a perfect landing on either the "one," "two," or "three" wire, well shy of the barriers. A tremendous shout went up from all hands on the deck and on the island as the last plane landed on number one wire. The flight deck was full of aircraft.

Damage Control and the medical staff were working at a frantic pace on the *Lexington* to repair damage, control fires, and care for the wounded. I watched that afternoon from the flight deck of *Yorktown* as those crews fought the fires and finally lost. A most depressing sight, and an indication of the extent of the damage, was when the forward elevator flew high into the air after an explosion inside the ship, then turned over in the air and crashed back into the deck. Shortly after that I witnessed the crew responding to the order to abandon ship. Lifelines were strung from the flight and hangar decks, and men were sliding down them and getting into life rafts floating around the ship. Destroyers were maneuvering slowly about, doing a superb job of recovering personnel from the sea. The *Lexington* was lost.

Thus ended the Battle of the Coral Sea. It goes down in history as the first great fleet battle in which the surface ships did not meet, or come within range of each other's guns.

The *Yorktown* headed south and my logbook for this time closed at Nukualofa, Tongatabu, on May 15, 1942. My next assignment was with VF-10, "The Grim Reapers," then forming at North Island. There we trained hard on our new Wildcats with their six .50-caliber machine guns. Lieutenant Commander Jimmy Flatley, previously unknown to me except by name, was our squadron commander. He turned out to be a true leader, a tactician, a man of superior judgment, a man of vision, and a true friend. Lieutenant Fritz Faulkner and myself were the main junior officers with recent combat experience. We had met the Zero in combat, and our job was to work with the CO to develop tactics that would utilize any advantages our planes might have over the Zero. We settled on the two-plane section, and would work with either two or three sections in a division. Three sections could keep a large enemy formation under continuous attack.

After training at North Island and Maui, we found ourselves aboard the *Enterprise* in October and continued training with the other squadrons of Air Group Ten, a most congenial and close-knit bunch. Action quickly followed our arrival in South Pacific waters. The Japanese forces had been blunted in the Coral Sea, but were still determined in their plan to press on down the chain of islands to Australia and New Zealand. On October 25, while we were on station near the Stewart Islands, word was received that a large enemy task force with two carriers had been sighted well to the north, headed in our direction.

Although the enemy task force was completely beyond our range, the entire air group was launched to locate, attack, and destroy the enemy carriers. I had protested the mission before launch as being impractical because of the distance separating our forces, but had been told that we could do an "out and back." This meant that we would fly to the limit of our combat radius, and if nothing was sighted, drop bombs and torpedoes and return. I had the fighter cover that afternoon, and we took station above the base squadron of bombers. F4Fs at the time were equipped with a fifty-gallon gas tank hung under each wing that could be dropped when action was imminent. Those tanks were made of a type of bean-pod product that would withstand very little stress. They often ripped off in a shallow dive. To add to the problem, it was necessary at altitude to pump fuel from these tanks with a hand pump located to the left and under the instrument panel.

I wore out two pairs of gloves on the flight. Other pilots had similar experiences.

We did not reach the enemy task force, and because we had launched in late afternoon, darkness overtook us as we turned back. The weather was hazy with no visible horizon. Holding station became difficult due to the poor visibility and the tendency of some pilots to succumb to vertigo. I saw one of my VF planes, just to my right, suddenly pull up, roll over, and plunge almost straight down. At the point where my navigation showed the *Enterprise* should have been, there was nothing. I knew that the carrier was leaking oil from a pro-peller seal, so I circled down and fortunately sighted the slick. Taking the most obvious course, we followed the oil slick, and after many miles came upon the ship. The LSO was on the stern and the dust-pan lights had been rigged. We broke up and proceeded to land, all of us very short on fuel.

As I landed and came to a stop, I saw a flurry of activity to my right with flashlight signals and men running past. I looked over my shoulder and saw that another plane had landed at the same time, had hooked the wire and come into a stop in formation. It was my wingman, a really exceptional pilot and very good friend. When we got to the ready room I said, "Coalson, what were you doing?"

He smiled and replied, "If you think you were going to get away from me tonight, you are crazy!" What could I say? We had been in the air over five hours.

We were receiving reports over the sound-powered phones that planes were running out of gas and dropping into the water. The destroyers were busy picking up downed pilots and crewmen. The ship was a beehive of activity throughout the night as all remaining planes were prepared for the next morning's attack. We were now in company with the *Hornet* CV-8, which would launch her air group when we did, at or before dawn.

Action was not long in coming the next morning, October 26, 1942. Radio silence was broken when units of our group reported being attacked by fighters while on course toward the enemy task force. I was on CAP (combat air patrol) station and we were vectored to intercept the squadrons of the enemy attack group that was now being tracked on radar. We pressed forward under full throttle and soon sighted Japanese dive bombers approaching at our level. We turned hard to get into position behind the bombers, which were nearing the push-over point. I cursed, wishing that we had been vectored out sooner to give us a chance of really working them over.

Closing, I saw the Japanese rear-seat gunners swinging their weapons and firing almost continuously. Tracers were going by in great numbers, looking like fireworks. I did not like this type of run, but we had no choice. I remember thinking that the section of bulletproof glass in front of the windshield would stop those 7.7mm bullets. I chose as my target the wing plane on the outside, cut loose with a blast from all six .50-calibers, and felt my plane vibrate a bit from their kick. The dive-bomber exploded. Parts of it flew everywhere. I swung to the next plane, which seemed to be a section leader, as he was pushing over into his dive. In close, I fired once again with all six machine guns at no deflection. The enemy aircraft seemed to stop in the air, out of control. I pulled up to avoid collision as the plane rolled inverted underneath and behind me. We were in an area of intense fire from the surface ships, and I could see the *Enterprise* and a battleship behind her. Both ships and their escorts seemed to be on fire because all guns were in action at the same time. Black puffs of exploding AA filled the air as I turned away.

Word came from our CIC on the *Enterprise* that torpedo planes were approaching from the sector in which we were in action. I broke off with my wingman and we soon spotted them, coming fast in a shallow glide and headed for our carrier. Having altitude, we positioned ourselves on a parallel course and attacked from their quarter. Again I saw the tracers from the rear-seat guns, but most of them were streaming by low and behind us, which was not uncommon if you were in a position to execute a fast S-turn attack. I cut out two guns to save ammunition and fired with the four remaining

.50s at the wing plane on the near side, and then at the section leader on the far side.

Our information on those torpedo planes was that the gas tanks were in the wing roots and were not bulletproof. It was relatively easy to square away for a short time and place the pipper just ahead of the engine which, at a low angle, would put bullets into the forward section of the enemy plane. The incendiary bullets we were using, along with the tracers and steel-jacketed rounds, were deadly. It took only a few hits to set planes on fire. One more pass from the left and I got the first plane, but had to search a few minutes for another one, because the formation had broken up by then.

The next plane was the only one that tried to maneuver, doing S-turns rapidly at low altitude. This presented no problem for the maneuverable F4F, and with my first burst, a fire started at the wing root. The pilot may have been hurt. The plane dug into the water with one of its wings, spun around, and came to rest on the surface of the ocean as the crewmen climbed out of the rear cockpit. My wingman and I had become separated, but I soon located him chasing a torpedo plane that was turning away from the fleet. I could not tell if it was still carrying a torpedo, but immediately attacked it using the two guns I had reserved. With great care I swung in close and gave one burst at the engine. The tracers hit home and a fire started licking its way along the fuselage. This one was already quite low. It hit the water and floated long enough for the two crewmen to climb out onto the tail.

There was still sporadic action. I reported to the CIC and took station near the carrier. At least three other CAP planes were orbiting the area. As I climbed for altitude, a lone plane approached the force at some altitude, in a shallow glide. I could tell from the silhouette that it was Japanese, probably a torpedo plane. I put on full power, climbed up behind the aircraft, and fired a burst. The plane was smoking as I rolled out, so I closed again and fired the last of my ammo. The plane was definitely burning and headed for one of our DDs (destroyers) in the screen that was firing rapidly.

The AA fire was getting close. I broke off and watched the plane continue in its glide, hit the destroyer, and explode. We had been in the air for 3.4 hours and the immediate attack was over, so we landed, refueled, and were launched again as a CAP of eight planes.

The *Hornet* had been hit by the bombers and was dead in the water. I watched it being taken under tow by a cruiser. All seemed to be going well when the CIC reported enemy aircraft approaching the force. I waited for an intercept vector, but nothing came, so I requested one. The reply was "Remain on station." I was sick about the delay. By this time the *Enterprise* was some distance from the *Hornet* and I requested permission to detach one division of four VF to intercept the enemy. Silence, then the reply, "Remain on station." A small number of Japanese bombers approached in level flight and dropped their bombs. The cruiser cut loose from the tow line and left the *Hornet* dead in the water. I saw no hits, but later the crew was directed to abandon ship. The *Hornet* sank that night. The Battle of the Stewart Islands ended as the Japanese task force retired to the north.

The *Enterprise* remained on station in the general area for some time, and on November 13, while I was again on CAP, my division was vectored on a four-engine Kawanishi seaplane that had been shadowing our task group. The seaplane would stay below the horizon away from the ship and pop up occasionally to have a look. The weather was very clear. We went out at best speed and easily overtook it about twenty miles from the ship. We bracketed with one section on each quarter and pressed in for the kill. I got in first and fired one long burst into the center section of the seaplane. The other pilots were like tigers and cut the plane into doll rags. Shortly all that remained was a bit of burning gas on the surface of the sea and a small black cloud floating away on the wind.

During the following months we spent time on the *Enterprise,* at Guadalcanal, and on Espiritu Santo. At the marine fighter strip on Espiritu, I met Pappy Boyington, whom I hadn't seen for years. He was back in the marines after a tour with the Flying Tigers and was awaiting a new assignment. One thing I can say about Pappy—he always met me when I landed, night or day, and took me to his tent for a shower and a bunk with clean sheets. That was special there, on the beach.

During the heavy fighting on Guadalcanal and the air battles up the island chain, I came to know many great pilots such as John Smith, Joe Foss, Marion Carl, Bill Jones, and many others who wrote glorious chapters in the book of aerial warfare while helping so much to turn the tide when the pressure on America was the greatest. I was on patrol one day at about 25,000 feet, in the same area that Joe Foss was orbiting with his division. Word came down that enemy bombers were approaching at 8,000 feet and that they had just passed a well-known point of land. I watched Joe roll over and point that Wildcat straight down. I did the same with my canopy rattling and shaking. Watching for Joe and his division, I saw him pulling rapidly away, and even with throttle open, I fell farther behind. I feared for his safety on the pullout, but he made it and flew right through the bomber formation, firing with all guns. The bombers broke, scattered, and turned back, never reaching their drop point.

I told him after the fracas, "That was a lot of Gs, Joe."

He replied, "If the Wildcat can take it, I can." We looked at his plane a while later and found several rows of rivets along the belly rattling around in holes that had been stretched too far.

In March 1943, the F4U aircraft were being assigned to the squadrons. The marines on Espiritu got some of them. In order to provide some information on shipboard operations with this new plane, one of them, Bureau Number 02232, was assigned to VF-10. I was the pilot. This was an interesting experience because we were able to test the plane against Wildcats in the air. The F4U had a 2,000-horsepower engine and was faster. Its supercharger allowed it to perform better at altitude. I did not like the low tail wheel or the fifty-gallon fuel tanks on each wingtip, but these things were later changed. At first there was a problem with the gun chargers. They had to be loaded hot, a situation that would not have been tolerated aboard ship.

In late May the combat cruise of VF-10, the Grim Reapers, was completed. I was assigned as a fighter training officer at Atlantic City, New Jersey, to provide ground and flight instruction, including gunnery, rocketry, bombing, and individual combat, for pilots of forming squadrons. Many pilots were sent for individual instruction that was always pleasant and very helpful. Besides the Navy officers, there was Corky Meyers of Grumman Aircraft. He got a full course which included qualification aboard a carrier in landing with the F6F. There were two British officers who were top-notch pilots and veterans of the European theater. One of my most interesting experiences was with Colonel Tommy Hitchcock, a P-51 pilot in the Army Air Corps who had spent a lot of time in England. He was undoubtedly one of the greatest polo players of all time and a great athlete in general, besides being a joy to fly with. He quickly absorbed our navy tactics.

With so many returning combat pilots, I was eager for a new combat assignment and expected that it would take me to the Western Pacific. This was not to be. Apparently there was a rather firm schedule for moving the established pipeline of squadrons and air groups to the war zone. I was assigned as a CVL Air Group commander with orders to train for Operation Olympic, the assault on the Japanese home islands. My air group was quickly disestablished after the atomic bombs were dropped and the war came to an end.

HAPPY JACK'S GO-BUGGY

First Lieutenant Jack Ilfrey is one of two possible contenders for the title of first P-38 ace of World War II. Records were poorly maintained in those early days, and the question will probably never be resolved. This remarkable story takes you from the dunes and oases of North Africa to a daring escape across two hundred miles of German-occupied Europe. Ernie Pyle wrote of Jack Ilfrey: "It was hard to conceive of his ever having killed anybody, for he looked younger than his twenty-two years. . . . He was wholly thoughtful and sincere. Yet he mowed them down."

On the morning of November 8, 1942, the news broke over the radio that North Africa had just been invaded. Then we knew where we were going and felt sure that now we would get into plenty of action. Colonel John N. Stone, our group commander, called us all into the briefing room on the night of the eighth and told us that our P-38 squadrons would fly nonstop from England to Oran, some 1,500 miles away. That was a very long flight for a P-38. Charts and maps were brought out, and we spent several days in feverish study, with high-ranking American and British officers giving instructions on every detail. Up until that time, Algiers, Casablanca, and Oran had just been names to us. Now a new world awaited.

We were to fly in groups of eight, with a B-26 bomber from the 319th Bomb Group leading us. The ground crews squeezed every ounce of gasoline they could get into the tanks, including the external fuel tanks, and we were ready. As we prepared to embark early the next morning, the route kept hammering in my brain: fly across the Bay of Biscay, hit the Spanish coast, fly down the Spanish and Portuguese coasts, turn left, and go through the Strait of Gibraltar. Hit the Moroccan coast and fly around it into French Morocco, and then Oran. It was uncertain where the enemy might be on our route, and we were cautioned to be exceptionally alert. We were to fly low level and observe strict radio silence. If we ran into trouble, Gibraltar should be our first emergency stop. I had already been awake four and a half hours by the time we left England at around 6:30 A.M.

My trip was not routine. A belly tank with 150 gallons of fuel fell off my aircraft. We kept on flying and when the B-26 that was leading us dodged a thunderhead, I had the feeling we were getting off course. I was worried after another hour of flying and alarmed after two hours had passed. My gas was running low because we had used a great deal of fuel dodging thunderheads. There was still no coast in sight and we were pretty far out to sea. I decided to leave the group. My gas wouldn't last much longer.

I turned southeastward, climbed to between 8,000 and 10,000 feet, and hoped to hell I would run into the Spanish or Portuguese coast. When the coast came into view, I flew parallel to it for a while, until I realized my gasoline was almost gone and Gibraltar was still too far away. There are no words to describe the feeling you have when you are that high in the air and know your gasoline is going to be exhausted almost any minute. It might be best described as a kind of paralysis, but with part of your mind still functioning and agonizing over what to do next. One minute I wanted to bail out; the next I wanted to crash-land on the coast. Then I came to the mouth of the Tagus River that leads to Lisbon, followed it inland for about thirty miles, and was able to land at a beautiful airdrome just outside the city.

When I completed my landing roll, six mounted men galloped out to meet me. The horsemen looked like something out of a picture book. They wore big, plumed hats, sabers, pistols, and gaily colored trousers. Gesturing wildly, they motioned for me to taxi toward an administration building. Meanwhile, I was hurriedly tearing up maps and papers and throwing them into the wind. I was told to stop the plane on the apron just in front of the building. When I killed the engines, people came from every direction toward me. Some of the crowd flashed the "V for Victory" sign, but most of them just stared at my P-38 and the horsemen who surrounded it. I had the distinction of having the first P-38 to be forced down in Portugal. Their interest was in interning me and making my fighter part of their air force (which was largely composed of impounded aircraft).

As I walked to the administration building I saw the American Douglas DC-3s with the big German swastikas on them. They appeared to be airliners and their pilots were inside the building. After I had been given cake and coffee, the questioning began. One of the officials made the comment that since I was flying a warship and was a fighter pilot, I must have fought the Germans, and all this time, the German pilots were gathered around me, listening intently. You don't have to be psychic to feel hatred from officials who are being superficially polite. The questioning must have gone on for an hour and never once did the German pilots move.

After listening to a speech about Portugal's neutrality and their intention to intern me, I was introduced to a Portuguese pilot. When he directed refueling of my plane with eighty-five octane gasoline, instead of the usual one hundred octane fuel, it was obvious that he was going to fly it to a military airfield. The Portuguese pilot was seated on the wing of my plane, and I was showing him the controls, when another P-38 came in for an emergency landing. The circus started again. I started the engines and the Portuguese pilot attempted to turn off the ignition. The prop blast blew off the pilot's hat and scattered what was left of the crowd. A few seconds later he was blown off the wing. I threw the canopy shut, gave the plane full power, and took off straight across the field. Because of my escape, the other pilot, Jim Harmon, was not treated gently and was interned for about four months. I landed at Gibraltar, received a couple of royal tongue-lashings for violating international law, and was then allowed to proceed to North Africa two days later.

We were first based at Tafaroui, about fifteen miles out of Oran. Most of the rest of the 94th "Hat in the Ring" Squadron had arrived there after a routine flight from England. One of our pilots had crash-landed between Oran and Algiers and had spent several days with the French before joining us; another pilot had flown too close to the coast of Spanish Morocco and had been shot down; Jim Harmon was in a Portuguese jail. We slept on the bare floor of a collapsing building, and when our bedrolls finally arrived from England, we found seventh heaven. Later, we flew several hundred miles to Maison Blanche, an airdrome not far from Algiers. There we inspected the captured German JU-88 bombers and JU-52 transports and concluded that our planes were superior in every way. About a week later my squadron was sent to a place near the front called Youks-les-Bains, near Tebessa, Tunisia. We dug deep two-man foxholes and stretched our pup tents over the top of them. My initiation to combat came the next day.

Eight of us strafed the enemy airdrome at Gabes shortly after daybreak the next morning. We got pretty well separated while dodging the intense ground fire. Newell Roberts and I were flying back across a small space of desert toward the mountains and were about halfway home when he spotted two planes in the distance, heading in the opposite direction.

He said over the radio, "Jack, they don't look familiar. Let's go see what they are."

As we turned toward them, we recognized them as enemy because they gunned their engines, causing black smoke to belch from the exhaust. They were ME-110s—German twin-engine bombers. I said to Roberts, "Let's go after them."

His voice was shaking with excitement when he replied, "Roger. I'll take the one on the right and you take the one on the left."

These were the first German planes we had seen in the air, and it was hard to believe that we were going to shoot them down. We closed in behind them. I must have opened up at 5,000 yards, about five times too far for effective shooting. I pulled in closer, got the bomber in my sight, and let go again. This time the bullets took effect. At about the same time, I saw something red coming out of the back of the bomber and only later realized that the rear gunner had been firing tracers at me!

Meanwhile, Roberts had hit the other enemy plane, and it had crashed and exploded. The plane I shot down had crash-landed. Two members of the three-man crew jumped out, and it was a funny sight to see them running along the flat desert with no place to hide. While I circled around to set the bomber on fire with my cannon shells, Roberts teased the two Germans by diving down low and squirting his machine guns. He wasn't actually trying to hurt them, just scaring the hell out of them. We had made our first real enemy contact and had scored the squadron's first two victories.

The pilots continued to maintain the airplanes, fill the gas tanks, and load the ammunition. When our ground crews finally joined us, arriving in all kinds of English, French, and American aircraft, it was a big reunion.

One morning, four of us were assigned to ground-strafe the pillboxes and gun positions in the Faid Pass, a passage in the mountains on the road to Sfax. We were told to begin strafing at precisely 7:30 A.M. and stop strafing at exactly 7:35 A.M. It came off just as planned. We silenced the German guns and permitted the troops below to begin encircling the enemy positions. We then proceeded down the main road toward Sfax and caught six trucks full of soldiers. In a matter of seconds all six trucks were burning. It was our first chance to shoot at trucks, and I had the feeling that we were shooting at targets, not men. Men were only incidental.

On another day Roberts led a flight of four, including McWherter, Lovell, and me. Our mission was to patrol the coast between Sfax and Gabes and shoot up any trucks, troops, or other targets of opportunity. We soon saw several tanks and trucks under a clump of trees about halfway down the road and left them blazing. As we approached the airdrome at Gabes, Roberts yelled into the radio, "There's four of 'em taking off! I'll take the first one!" He immediately turned and dived on an ME-109.

Bill Lovell yelled that he would take the second one, I took out after the third, and McWherter went for the fourth one. We had the advantages of altitude and speed. It wasn't hard for me to aim and push the button that caused four .50-caliber machine guns and one 20mm cannon to spurt several hundred bullets. My ME-109 had barely left the ground. He had just gotten his wheels up and gone into a bank, and he seemed to stay in the bank. Finally, his wingtip hit the ground and he cartwheeled into a flaming explosion.

Somebody yelled over the radio that six more planes had taken off. I turned sharply and saw dead ahead a Messerschmitt spouting lead. I let loose with my guns and we whizzed by each other. The German had made a direct hit on the high pressure oil line to my right engine, and it didn't take more than a few seconds for the engine to lose oil and freeze up. I feathered my prop to keep it from windmilling and made a determined effort with the other engine to make myself scarce. Two other MEs had seen what was happening and what I was trying to do, and started chasing me.

A P-38 on one engine is no match for an ME-109. I was doing 275 mph right down on the ground, ducking in and out of sand dunes. I started screaming for help. Bill Lovell radioed that he was close behind me. Roberts said he saw me and was trying to get over there. I had to sit there on one engine as each ME-109 made a couple of passes. Just before the first German came in, Bill yelled, "Weave, Jack!" I weaved, but they still hit me. The radio went dead. Lovell got on the tail of one of the Jerries and blasted him. The other one ran away.

During the time the Germans had actually been shooting me, I had kept wishing my damned plane would quit so I could set it down on the desert and get out of it, but the old reliable P-38 wouldn't quit. She kept running until I got back to base. When I was able to lift myself out of the cockpit, I was scared, shaking, and weak. There were 268 bullet holes in the plane, including several large ones from ground fire over the airdrome. A cannon shell had gone through the radio and lodged in the armor plate behind my seat. It had torn the radio to pieces. Another cannon shell had hit my left propeller, the one on the good engine, causing a bad vibration. Another shell had hit the hydraulic fluid reservoir under my seat and left me ankle-deep in fluid. The fighter never flew again.

After several weeks at Youks-les-Bains, sometime around the middle of December, we moved to the airdrome at Biskra to start performing high-level escorts for B-17 bombing missions. The airdrome was a flat field of hard sand on the edge of an oasis. We lived in tents and were glad to be out of the mud of Youks. It was hot and dusty during the day, but the nights were cold. Sometimes the temperature varied from sixty to seventy degrees between day and night. Before the war Biskra had been a winter resort for rich Europeans. When we first arrived there, we dug fancy foxholes and settled in. Later, the Transatlantique Hotel in town was taken over and became a billet for pilots. We slept five to a room in our bedrolls.

Each day we escorted heavy bombers on high-altitude raids over Tunis, Bizerte, Cagliari, and Sardinia. On every mission we were bounced by German fighters that were sitting up very high, waiting for us. Our boys picked up a few hard-earned victories and we lost a few of our own. On one occasion our squadron of sixteen was bounced by a comparable number of Jerries and got split up in a hairy dogfight. Williams, from Marietta, Ohio, was lost. A long time afterward we heard that he was in a German prison camp. We were lucky that the Germans weren't able to put many fighters in the air, because we didn't have too many ourselves.

Another day Rimke was leading our squadron on a mission. While we were escorting bombers near the target, I noticed that a lone B-17 far below us had dropped out of formation and was trying to head for home. Three or four Focke-Wulf 190s were making passes and doing their best to knock him down. I notified Rimke and he told me to take my flight of four down and try to help the distressed B-17. We had an 8,000- to 10,000-foot altitude advantage. I told my flight to each pick a target and I went after mine. I must have caught the Jerry unaware because I made a direct hit on him. He burst into flame.

My wingman, Saul, got another one, and then two Jerries came in on him. I tried to get over to help, but the last time I saw Saul he was shooting at one FW-190 and two more were shooting at him from behind. The four of them disappeared into a cloud bank. He was never heard from again.

Bob Neale yelled that two more were coming in on me, and I evaded the attack as quickly as possible. In the ensuing dogfight Bob and I each shot down a Focke-Wulf and were able to confirm each other's victories. Then we teamed up to get the hell out of there. We saw two P-38s below and dived to join them. They turned out to be McWherter and Murdock, and from the looks of the gathering of Focke-Wulfs above, it looked like we were in for another dogfight. We were well separated from everyone else and low on ammunition, but we knew that we could depend on one another. Eight or ten FWs with altitude on us came in for the attack. We weaved in front of each other to ward off these attacks and eventually were able to outdistance them. It would have been futile to remain and fight opponents with altitude, speed, and numbers in their favor.

We lost three pilots that day, but scored more than three times that number in victories. The bombers and fighters had over twenty confirmed victories and, for several weeks thereafter, we were not bothered by the enemy, just annoyed. The enemy started coming to our base at night in groups of five or six planes. Once a flight of thirty-plus JU-88s really beat up the field. We all rushed to the top of the hotel to watch. Our CO gave us hell for bunching up where one bomb could have killed us all. Bombs scored direct hits on several B-17s and P-38s, and one 500-pounder hit right in the middle of our enlisted men's tent area, knocking down most of the tents and scattering the squadron kitchen. Shrapnel from the bomb blew beans all over the place. The foxholes went really deep into the earth after that raid.

When a fighter pilot failed to return to base, there was no evidence of death. A bomber was different because it brought back its dead and wounded. Ernie Pyle, the famous correspondent, was a quiet little fellow who wandered into our room one night, just to hear about the day's activities. In one of his articles he wrote about us, saying, "Although our fighters in North Africa have accounted for many more German fighter planes than we have lost, still our fighter losses are high. I have been chumming with a roomful of five fighter pilots for the past week. Tonight two of those five are gone."

Ernie later wrote a fine tribute to fighter pilots in which he made mention of me.

Death hit home when Dick McWherter, one of my best friends, was killed. We had been together for almost two years—through flying school, in England, and to the end in North Africa. War leaves scars that are hard to erase.

Christmas 1942 was just a routine day spent escorting bombers. After we returned from our mission, a few of the pilots scouted around and brought in a fifty-gallon keg of muscatel wine, and the enlisted men and pilots proceeded to have a knockout Christmas. I knew about wine hangovers and knew when to stop drinking, but some of the other boys didn't. I've never heard so many Christmas dinners splattering the walls of a hotel.

The next day was different. While leading a flight in the Bizerte-Tunis area, I saw some FW-190s attacking a crippled American bomber. With the altitude advantage, I dove down and picked one out. He turned and went out over Lake Bizerte, but I stayed on his tail, got some good hits, and soon had him smoking and burning. Just as he was about to hit the water, I saw machine-gun bullets kicking up in the water ahead of me and knew that a bandit was on my tail. I banked and turned as hard as I could. As my speed became slower than his, my circumference of turn was smaller. With a great burst of throttles to the engines, I came up under him with my guns blazing. He nose-dived into the lake, giving me a double victory and my fifth kill. I had just become the first ace of the 94th Fighter Squadron in World War II.

We had been scraping the bottom of the barrel to get enough planes in the air, and we had reached the bottom of the barrel when it came to pilots. When some badly needed replacements arrived, ten of us were given a sorely needed rest and flown to the resort town of Agadir, on the Atlantic coast below Casablanca. Agadir compared favorably with the climate of Florida in the wintertime, but certainly not with all the luxuries. We were housed in a nice hotel and had more varied food than we were accustomed to getting. We lay on the beach, went horseback riding, played volleyball, and one day went down a hundred miles to a place called Tiznit, a Foreign Legion garrison. Tiznit looked exactly like the garrisons you see in the movies—surrounded by high walls, lonely, and isolated. The French officers entertained us with elaborate food, and plenty of cognac, anisette, and Calvados. The Arab women put on a special chanting dance for us, with practically just a sash around their stomachs and flutes playing music. The ten days we spent at Agadir were all too short.

The siroccan winds started blowing off the Sahara Desert, bringing with them tons of sand. Preparations were made to leave Biskra, as it became impossible to operate with the sand doing its best to defeat every single movement. We were separated from the bombers and moved to a small fighter strip at Château Dun Du Rhumell near Constantine, the Twelfth Air Force headquarters. Constantine was the strangest city we had yet seen. It was really two cities on very high cliffs and connected by a suspension bridge. It had been built in the days when cities were built on cliffs to prevent seizure by the enemy. We began living in tents again.

Our missions changed a little and we went back to ground-strafing. Rommel's armies were on the Mareth Line, and we spent whole days strafing them on the open roads. Montgomery's Eighth Army was coming from Tripoli and pushing the Germans back up our way, forcing our ground troops to retreat. As a last desperate effort, Rommel tried to surge through the Kasserine Pass and recapture Tebessa, the arsenal for this section of the front. It would have been a disaster if he had succeeded in doing that.

On the day of the Battle of Kasserine Pass, twelve of us were assigned to ground-strafe the pass. Even one year later over Germany I never saw so much flak. It seemed to come from everywhere, not only from below, but from the hills above the pass, *down on us*. Four of our twelve pilots were lost in the pass, two others managed to make our lines and crash-land, and six of us were able to get back to base. All P-38s had suffered battle damage. We had lost Rimke, one of our veterans. Our reaction to that raid was: "If the Germans want this godforsaken place that bad, let them have it!" We later learned that our concentrated air attack on the Kasserine Pass helped turn the tide of battle.

The missions were easier after that. It had finally been determined that a tour would constitute fifty missions or two hundred combat hours, and we began marking the time. Our original squadron had left the States with twenty-seven pilots ten months before. There were eight of us left. The day of my last mission arrived, and it was so routine you might call it casual. I knew nothing could happen to me on that patrol in the straits between Tunisia and Sicily. The Germans were trying to get supplies to Rommel's armies, which were being closed into a gap. We were to spot and report any shipping activities in the straits.

Several miles off Cape Bon we were scooting along at around 600 feet below some low, overhanging clouds when I noticed balloons flying right under the cloud level. At the same instant I realized that they were flying from a convoy of ships. Then I saw a JU-88 below us and to the left. Quinn, my only companion, saw it about the same time I did, and I told him to get a shot at it and I would follow. Then I saw a JU-88 or an ME-110 way off to the right. Just as Quinn was lining up on the first JU-88, I turned and found myself practically staring into six or eight ME-109s. I didn't look twice. Although I was a seasoned P-38 pilot, I knew that we were no match for them.

I yelled to Quinn, "Let's get the hell out of here!"

We tore off, "balls out," ducking around the clouds and streaking for home with the Germans hot on our tails. Fortunately our aircraft were faster, but we still had several hundred miles to go across enemy territory, and we wouldn't have lasted long on full throttle. The gasoline would soon be played out. We sweated along, and I sweated out my forthcoming leave home, until we finally got back to base. Bombers took off and destroyed the enemy convoy before it reached the coast. It was a stiff battle, because the convoy was well protected. But I was going home after seventy-two missions, 228 combat hours, and six victories.

Around March 15, 1944, Jack Landers, Martin Low, and I received orders to report to the headquarters of the Eighth Air Force in England as P-38 squadron commander replacements. We were flown across the Atlantic from New York in sixteen hours, a far cry from the epic first flight of our P-38s across that ocean in 1942. I was assigned to the 79th Fighter Squadron of the 20th Fighter Group. It was odd to be in this unit now, since my old outfit, the 1st Fighter Group, had been in keen competition with the 20th during maneuvers in Louisiana in peacetime 1941. The 20th had really had it rough. They had arrived in England in 1943 and had pioneered long-range bomber escort missions over Germany when the Luftwaffe was still strong in numbers and skilled pilots. But by April 1944 there were many air groups in England and the Eighth and Ninth Air Forces had really been turning the tables. It amazed me to see the large number of P-38s and bombers going to Germany every day. Every square inch of Britain seemed to be crawling with American bombers, fighters, and troops.

About the end of April I flew wing position on R. C. Franklin, my old instructor at Luke Field, as we escorted heavies to Hamm, Germany. This was a new kind of combat for me. In North Africa we had operated in small groups and escorted small numbers of bombers. Now we flew in large groups that stayed close together for protection, and escorted much larger numbers of bombers. Also, I was not used to being strapped down tight in a fighter for long-distance flights of up to eight hours, in temperatures ranging from fifty to sixty degrees below zero. Every detail of the missions was worked down to a science and the forays were carried out with utmost precision.

On my third mission on May 24, we escorted heavy bombers into Berlin, and the very name *Berlin* half frightened me out of my wits. I was leading a flight of four from my squadron of sixteen at 30,000 feet when we were suddenly jumped by a gaggle of thirty to forty ME-109s. We split up momentarily to avoid attack, and I was forced into a head-on pass with an ME-109. I felt a jolt just after firing and looked down to see the ME spinning toward the ground. My own plane was trying to go into a spin, and I could see that the end of my wing looked like shredded wheat. Someone later told me that the ME had come up underneath me and hit my right wing. The collision had ripped open my right wing tank and the engine had temporarily quit, almost throwing me into a spin. I ducked down several thousand feet into some clouds and got the engine running again by switching gas tanks, then purposely stayed in the clouds to avoid detection.

While still in the overcast, I picked up a course that would take me out to the North Sea, because I wanted to get away from the danger in the Berlin area. After flying some minutes on instruments in the overcast at 15,000 feet, heavy concentrated flak began bursting all around me. I couldn't be seen, but radar was picking me up and directing the fire of heavy antiaircraft guns. Taking evasive action, I started diving, hoping to break out of the clouds and see exactly what to do. I popped out of the overcast at 7,000 feet and found myself over what I later determined was Hamburg. The flak was snapping at my tail, and the only thing to do was to dive as fast as possible to get to the Elbe River, which appeared to flow toward the North Sea. My P-38 dug furrows in the water as I followed the Elbe out to sea and headed toward England, four hundred miles away.

I really had to throttle back my engines to conserve what was left of my fuel on the way home. The boys at base had given me up, but I made it. For the next few days I laid off. I had no desire to visit Berlin—Adolf could have it as far as I was concerned. Of course, that reaction soon passed.

When D day arrived, P-38s flew cover over the invasion forces. I flew ten hours the first day, broken into three stretches. The Luftwaffe remained in hiding. During the previous months we had made a determined effort to destroy German fighters on the ground and in the air and now it was paying off. The German Air Force didn't put in much of an appearance over the invasion beaches during the first week, and by that time the Allies were firmly established. D day plus six was my fateful day. It finally happened . . . and to me too.

My squadron had successfully dive-bombed a bridge across the Loire River, at Angers in central France. We had just reassembled at about 8,000 feet when I spied a locomotive with steam up outside a village near Angers. The Germans had become pretty wise to our attacks and usually had a flak car somewhere on the train. Therefore, the attack leader would go after the engine and his wingman took out the flak car. It didn't work that way this time. Just after I opened up on the locomotive, saw the boiler explode, and pulled up, my whole right engine burst into smoke and flame. Somebody yelled over the radio, "Bail out, Jack! You're on fire!"

My cockpit filled with smoke that blinded and choked me. I jettisoned my canopy, the smoke cleared momentarily, and I saw that I was about 600 feet above the ground. I released my safety belt, went out over the left side of the aircraft, and immediately opened my chute. I had just looked up and said, "This damned thing works," when I hit the ground. I threw off the chute, grabbed my first aid and escape kits, and tore off through the woods to get away from there.

I ran through the hedgerows and trees until exhausted, then fell into some tall grass. After a while I gathered my wits and thought, "Well, Jack, it's finally happened to you, and now what do you do?" I got out my rubberized waterproof maps and determined my position to be ten miles west of Angers and five miles north of the Loire River—some two hundred miles *inside* German territory. All I knew was that it was the duty of every American soldier behind enemy lines to evade capture. I took off my helmet, goggles, flying suit, insignia, and boots. That left me dressed in a gray sweater, a shirt with an open neck, a pair of green OD trousers, and GI shoes. I opened the first aid kit and put the contents into my pockets, then regained some strength by eating a Baby Ruth candy bar.

I lay in the grass another hour or so until dusk, at which time I got on a small country road and started walking. In a few minutes two small boys on bicycles approached me from the rear and rode right up. One of them asked in broken English if I was the American "aviateur" who had jumped out of a Lightning a few hours before. Sensing his friendship, I told him that I was. He smiled and told me that he and his brother had just come from the wreckage and the Germans in the neighborhood were looking for me. They took me to their home in Andigne after dark. It consisted of a restaurant with living quarters in the rear and upstairs. There were five children, two boys and three girls, and the father was a farmer. They had an Italian cousin from Florence, Maria, living with them. The only one who spoke English was Jean, the younger brother. We talked far into the night, and I learned that my plane had exploded in the air just after I had bailed out.

I stayed with them for a while. My first paralyzing fear of the Germans was partly overcome by watching them through the window when they passed on the road outside the café. Once I was sweeping up the floor when some young German soldiers came in for a drink of cool wine. I immediately started sweeping toward the back, and right into the kitchen, and they didn't seem to notice my casual but nonetheless hurried retreat. Eventually the family gave me some French clothing and one of their bicycles. I gave them all the money in my escape kit, which included American dollars, English pounds, Belgian and French francs, German marks, Dutch guilders, and Spanish pesetas. It was the least I could do in payment for the bicycle and the wonderful treatment I had received from those kind, simple folks.

One of the daughters, Emily, wrote a little note which she thought might aid me. It read:

To Whom It May Concern:
    This boy, Jacques Robert, from Angers, is trying to

get to Bayeux (which is in American hands) to see his parents. He has been injured in a bombing raid and is deaf and cannot speak.

Please let him pass.

Dr. P. Armand

I left after a good breakfast one morning dressed in Papa's black beret, Robert's pants, Maria's green shirt, and a pair of Jean's old slippers. I had only French identity papers and ownership of a bicycle. With much kissing and embracing, I departed at daybreak with bon voyages echoing in my ears. It was good to be out of doors again.

Five kilometers from the village I reached a main road and headed north. A short distance to the south were three parked German trucks, and I was relieved that I didn't have to go that way. A few kilometers farther on, I came upon a lone, parked German truck. A soldier jumped out and started yelling at me, but I had the presence of mind to realize that he was looking for the other trucks. When he asked if I had seen them, I answered with a *"Oui, monsieur"* and he allowed me to proceed. I had seen my first German at close range. He had spoken to me and I hadn't died yet.

I passed a lot of German men and equipment that day and continued on until I suddenly noticed that the main road led through an airdrome. I was right upon a sentry post and a soldier stepped out to stop me. It would look too suspicious if I turned around now, so I put on the deaf act and showed him my identity card. He shook his head and said, *"Nein,"* then stepped back into his booth and punched a buzzer. I knew for sure the game was up. A German officer appeared from a building beside the road and the guard explained the situation to him. I handed the officer my note from the doctor. He read it and passed it back to me, then waved me on. I almost fainted with relief as I got back on my bicycle and quickly shoved off.

I rode straight through the airdrome and saw a few German planes and what was left of the installations. Most of the buildings and hangars had been destroyed, and I took pride in the fact that I had dive-bombed this airdrome several times and had contributed to some of the wreckage on the ground. I saw two wrecked P-38s and wondered what had happened to the pilots. There were also a couple of our external belly tanks lying around. As I continued into the town of Laval, I saw my first big damage from American bombers. The railroad station and yard were demolished, but so were surrounding blocks of houses. That night I slept in a barn.

The next morning I discovered that my bicycle had a flat tire, but it wasn't long before a priest on a bicycle happened by and offered his assistance. He took me to his parish, where I was given a hearty meal. One of the priests didn't like me very well. He made some remark about how American aviators had bombed him out of his church and killed many of his friends in Laval. I felt invigorated after the meal and was offered the chance to stay at the parish as long as I liked, but I was eager to continue my journey. I left about noon after another meal. My saddlebag was full of more food.

I rode for a long time before reaching a blockade where a German sentry asked me for my ID card. He looked me and my knapsack over very thoroughly and then allowed me through. Late in the afternoon I was stripped to my birthday suit and bathing at a secluded spot on a pretty river when I met my next friends. Two French boys had at first assumed I was a tramp, but when they discovered my identity, they were eager to help me. I stayed with them for three days, then got itchy feet again and moved on. Now I began to cross the hilly, rolling country of Normandy, and oh! how I cursed those hills! If I pushed a bicycle up a hill once, I did it a thousand times, each time falling on it and coasting swiftly to the bottom, only to start all over again.

In midmorning I played tag with a convoy of six trucks full of Nazi youths, none of whom appeared to be more than seventeen years old. Once, after passing each other three or four times, the soldiers motioned for me to hang on if I wanted to, and as tired as I was, that's what I did. The Germans all continued laughing and talking. We had covered a few more miles when six P-38s appeared. Did those Germans stop and get out of their camouflaged trucks in a hurry! I pedaled for all I was worth and got to the top of the next hill in time to see the Lightnings set all six trucks on fire. Now I was without a lift.

Toward late afternoon I approached the town of Flers, which appeared to be a very beautiful place, sitting up high on a hill. Everything was pretty and green, and there were large, open valleys all around. Then I heard the sound of B-17s in the distance. I sat down on a high hill to rest and watch the show as the bombers, escorted by P-38s and P-51s, came right to the town and bombed the railroad yards. After the planes left, the whole center of town was a maze of dust, fire, and smoke rising several thousand feet into the sky. I was soon passing the devastated railroad yards. Many of the bombs had fallen long or short and crashed into the surrounding buildings. The streets were full of rubble. Almost all the Frenchmen I had seen asked me why Americans flew in such concentrated numbers and so high, while the British flew in scattered groups with each bomber doing its own aiming. They had forgotten that the British were night bombers, while the Americans bombed in daylight and had to fly at high altitudes in large groups for mutual protection.

More kind French people helped me after I left Flers. It was then that it dawned on me that I had traveled over two hundred miles and hadn't spent a cent. I'd like to see that happen in the United States. It took me three or four hours the next day to get through Conde, a town the size of Galveston that had been reduced to one big mass of rubble. Instead of streets there were lanes several feet deep in toppled buildings. A river ran through the town with bodies floating in it and no intact bridges, and I wondered how I was going to get across. I finally inched over on a piece of bridge understructure. I gradually worked out toward a less heavily damaged residential section of the town. The guns were very loud and noisy now, and I knew that the front was close by.

There were more Germans and lots of equipment. Communications men were busy stringing wires, and I saw large 88s in camouflaged positions in the surrounding fields.

After riding for several hours, passing more and more soldiers and equipment and watching the Germans fire their big guns, I turned off the main road to Caen and pulled into the little village of Fontenay. Dead cows and horses were lying around, and I could hear the whiz and explosions of shells from Allied long-range guns. I didn't know if I was in front of American or British troops. Again I confided that I was an American aviator and again people risked their lives to help me.

The next morning I pushed on, leaving the village on a narrow road that was filled with branches and leaves knocked off the hedgerows and trees by shellfire. It must have been a sort of no-man's-land. Shells from both Allied and German guns were whizzing over my head by the time I was a mile or so out of the village. I met two German soldiers who were carrying one of their wounded comrades. They wanted my bicycle to put the wounded soldier on and I let them have it at once. A mile farther along were quite a few Germans on the roads and in the fields, all dressed in camouflage suits. They didn't seem to notice me. Next I came to a point where the trees stopped and the road ran off through a clearing.

As I was about to step into the clearing, I heard voices off to my left and saw some Germans entrenched in the tall grass. They yelled for me to get down. I dropped to the ground, and one of them crawled out and motioned for me to follow him back into the grass. We crawled a hundred yards or more to a group of soldiers lying around holes in the ground. They spoke to me in German and I didn't understand. They asked me if I spoke English, and I put on one of my "don't-understand-a-word-you're-saying" faces. We lay there for a long time, until one of the soldiers near me was hit in the leg and stomach with shrapnel. The soldiers motioned for me to take him to an aid station in a wheelbarrow. I dragged him through the grass, put him in the wheelbarrow, and started wheeling.

It was easy at first, but soon proved to be real labor. The boy couldn't have been over seventeen and was in a great deal of pain, and I felt sorry for him and wanted to ease his pain. But after wheeling him for more than an hour, every bone in my body ached and I began wishing he would hurry up and die, so I wouldn't have to push him anymore. He didn't. The wheeling got pretty rugged, and I had to stop and rest frequently, but we made it to an aid station. As I was leaving, one of the medics yelled "Hey!" and I froze in my tracks. He handed me two cigarettes and a chocolate bar.

There was nothing to do but return to the village and spend another night. My French hosts suggested that I head toward the town of Tilly, six miles to the west. The countryside was more open there and I would be able to see quite some distance ahead. I followed their directions the next morning, passing several large German gun emplacements along the road. Some Spitfires came over low, probably looking for targets to strafe, and I saw the Germans shoot one of them down. At the intersection of the road where I was to turn were several knocked-out British tanks and trucks. This appeared to be the work of both antitank guns and mines. I turned north and started down a small open road, watching carefully for mines. It must have looked funny to see a poor, dumb French farmer out on the road, jumping over places and sidestepping others to avoid being blown to pieces.

About a half mile farther I approached an intersection of hedgerows and heard several limey voices. "Wot the bloody hell . . . a French civilian doing out there?" I saw the good old British helmets. One of them yelled at me in French.

I yelled back, "Sorry, bud, I don't speak French."

He looked surprised, took a tighter hold of his gun, and said, "Don't pull that stuff around here." It took a while, but my identity was finally established. I had made it.

Ahead lay many more interrogations and a lot of adventures. I was in London for another debriefing when a V-1 buzz bomb hit nearby. There was a loud putter like a motorcycle, then the putter coughed and died. People stopped talking and stood rooted in their tracks. There came a kind of *boom!* and then an ear-splitting roar. Two blocks away a building was lit by fire and crumpled into the street. It seemed like tons of glass were crashing down everywhere around me.

I got back to base as the changeover from P-38s to P-51s was going on. The Mustang was a better all-around airplane for our long-range escort work. Morale and victories went up while our losses went down. We got new "G" suits that allowed us to withstand a dive in a P-51 pulling nine or ten "Gs." We had the excellent new British gyroscopic gunsight that was so good that we called it the "No-Miss-'Em." Missions became fairly routine, and only once in a while did we meet any German opposition. Now we lost people to flak on ground-strafing missions, or to the weather. London was being hit by V-2s by then, and we would watch them flying by miles above us. We were seeing a few German jets. Occasionally some of our boys would box in a jet and nail him when he came down. We were no match for jets, but they didn't have any range and couldn't dive any faster than us. When they came down, we could nail them.

One of our missions was a shuttle run to Russia after we escorted around seventy B-17s to a target near Chemnitz, Germany. We landed at our base at Piryatin, near Kiev, and saw little else but the base. Our only excursion was a truck ride through Kiev, accompanied by a driver with orders not to stop or let us get off. Damaged German and Russian equipment gutted the road leading into the city and Kiev itself was pockmarked with grim reminders of fierce house-to-house fighting. On the way back to Piryatin, the driver let us go swimming in a small lake.

On the way back to England, we stopped in Italy. I took the opportunity to ride over to Bari and see my friend, Alden Sherry, who was working in air force headquarters. He had been one of the aces in the 94th "Hat in the Ring" Squadron in World War I. The 94th had been my squadron in North

Africa, and I wanted to compare wars. He told me that we'd had it tougher than they did in 1918. They even had a sort of comradeship with the Germans. They talked with captured German pilots and went over air battles together. They had gone so far as to wave to one another when they ran out of ammunition.

I took an unauthorized tour of Paris on my way back to England. The normally thrifty Parisians were generous and treated us to everything. They couldn't do enough for the Americans, their great liberators. The mademoiselles were vivacious and seemed to have a capacity for dazzling smiles. The lovely girls on bicycles waved at us. They had pretty legs and they didn't care who knew it. Gay Paree was an enchanting city, and the French seemed to have a special gift for living and making you feel welcome.

All the way back to England I kept thinking that this flight would be my last one—the last time I'd roam the skies, 30,000 feet up, a part of two worlds. Maybe I'd helped make a little bit of history with the tradition of a squadron that had gone through the hell and triumph of two wars, a tradition that would carry into the future. The future. I was wondering what it would be like.[2]

AMBUSH AT KWEILIN

Colonel Robert Lee Scott was considered too old to be a fighter pilot, but that was before he begged a lone fighter from General Chennault and took on the Japanese over Burma. When the AVG (American Volunteer Group—Flying Tigers) was disbanded, Scott was chosen to head its successor—the 23rd Fighter Group. Tokyo Rose threatened the group's destruction on the day it was to come into being. This story tells how that threat was turned into a great American victory.

My most unforgettable day of World War II began in a cave in the Kuangsi province of China near the city of Kweilin. If you look at a map of China today, it will be spelled Guilin, because Mao changed some of the spelling of the cities. But I assure you that it is the same place on the River Li which flows southward, down toward Canton. It will always always be Kweilin to me, regardless of what Chairman Mao said.

The evening of a day in late June 1942 had been one of the most exciting days of my life. I had been chosen to lead the 23rd Fighter Group that would replace the Flying Tigers. I had learned about it in the morning, and slowly I had come to the realization that I was the luckiest thirty-four-year-old fighter pilot in the whole wide world. My spirits had soared from the depths of despair, where they had been back in the training command when they told me that I was much too old to be a fighter pilot, to jubilation as I sat there in the dining room of the little house that Generalissimo Chiang Kai-shek had given General Chennault. We had just finished dinner, and even that soon I was beginning to consider the character of the man who had selected me for what I considered to be the best job in the entire war.

The day was memorable too, because my soup had been so charged with hot peppers that I'm certain I would never have withstood the fire had it not been for the excitement of the day. There was a rumor that had come to me a long time before, that those hot things had been sent to the "Old Man" from all over: from Louisiana, from Mexico, South America, anywhere they felt their peppers might be sharp enough for him. There was a veritable collection of them in bottles in front of his plate. Thank goodness I had watched how carefully Doc Gentry dashed only a bit on his soup from one of the bottles. I knew that he had lived there with General Chennault for a long time, so he knew these things. Of course I followed him to the letter, yet careful as I was, the first taste of the soup had blasted my sinuses wide open. I was to live there with Chennault, Doc Gentry, Wang Cook, Wong Chauffeur, and the rest of his household for a long time, and it comes to me now after all these years that the Old Man ate those high-octane peppers as though they were candy.

The big event must have started on July 2, but whatever date it was, it became a turning point in my life. For the first few days I was there, I felt almost like a guest in General Chennault's house. I had been in combat before with the single ship he had loaned me, and I had to make decisions. Now there were no decisions to make, except maybe the one about being careful with the peppers. But my life changed abruptly. We had just finished another meal and were listening to the shortwave radio. The program came out of Shanghai, I thought, and it was occupied by the Japanese then, but it could have originated in Japan, because it was Tokyo Rose. As usual, she was blasting us Americans with lamentations of doom. We had to listen to her no matter what, because this was the only broadcast we could pick up out there in China.

"Greetings, you American bandits! Now hear this! Listen, you hired assassins known as the Flying Tigers." Her voice was dripping with venom. She hated them all. "Pay heed, especially you green American kids who'll be taking their places, for these Flying Tigers have today terminated their bloody contract with Chiang Kai-shek. They know they have been beaten by the Imperial Japanese Air Force. They are sick and tired of it all and will go home now with their pockets full of gold, ill-gotten gains from the Chinese people. Facing the invincible Japanese Air Force from now on will be a group of green Yankee pilots, trying to take the place of those other, hired assassins. What is more, they will be led into combat by a Hollywood playboy by the name of Robert Scott."

I looked at General Chennault. "Hollywood playboy" delivered as a kind of epithet didn't bother me, but it was sobering to realize that the Japanese knew this much about me. I had been a technical advisor in Hollywood on a couple of pictures, but how could the Japanese be aware of such an inconsequential assignment?

But Tokyo Rose had more with which to taunt us. "Yes, these paid killers are running out on the Chinese now that the Japanese Air Force has thrown its might across Burma and far into China. They have found out that they are mere pawns of the real aggressors. Chennault is left with only the dregs of the AVG and a few rosy-cheeked schoolboys to be commanded by this playboy. The Japanese hereby give warning. They will utterly destroy this new 23rd Fighter Group on their first day of activation—the Fourth of July—their Independence Day."

General Chennault was sitting there, casually looking at me with a ghost of a smile on his face. "Well, you heard her, son. What do you recommend?" Here was the first opinion asked for. Here I had to make a decision.

All the time the shortwave radio was a bedlam of static in my brain. I felt a shiver, not the braggadocio of what might really happen with those green kids on my wing, instead of the experienced AVG, but in finding out that an enemy nation, speaking from far-away Tokyo, considered me to be a pawn ready to be sacrificed. The prickly sensation I had in my face could have been a flush all over. My hands were perspiring. I had to say something though. "I think they'll be mighty surprised, sir."

I looked at General Chennault. He was playing a card game called Coon Can with Doc Gentry, just waiting to hear me out, although he appeared to be unconcerned. Over in the corner, his dachshund, Joe, was vigorously digging at the plaster wall in in his never-ending battle to exterminate rats, and barking furiously. At least the general called them rats, but they were the strangest-looking ones I had ever seen. The first one I saw was when the general called me over one day and pointed to what Joe was trying to dig out of a hole. I was surprised to see a long-nosed rodent that could have been a rat, but this one wasn't squeaking like mice do. It was barking, actually barking back at Joe.

But still I had to say something, and I did. "I think that they will be very surprised, sir, that we won't be sitting here and waiting for them to come out and get us on the Fourth. I suggest you let me take off early that morning and attack them instead. Anything's better than waiting."

The general sat there, flipping cards at the pile on the table and said, "You got the right idea, son. A good one too. I like it because you've learned something already—not to think defensively. Never think defensively! Always play it offensively! It's the best defense anyway. You're absolutely right, everyplace except in your date." He was looking at me now, almost pinning me up against the wall with his black eyes. "Just your date's wrong. That's all, Scotty. Don't wait for the Fourth. Get them the day before. Hit them tomorrow on the third. Go set up the planes."

I almost committed a serious mistake. I caught myself just in time, before saying we couldn't do that because we wouldn't be an official part of the Army Air Force until our inauguration day, the Fourth of July. I remembered just in time though. What the devil did official activation mean to guerrillas like us? Tokyo Rose had called us paid killers, bandits, and playboys. Well, we would beat them to it by a whole day. This would be a real trap. I thought all the way back to those amateurish traps I had tried to set with my lone P-40. I hadn't been ready then. Was I ready now?

General Chennault was setting up this trap and he must know. And he set it up in secret too. The Old Man had learned the hard way that you didn't trust anything to encoding and decoding, that most of the time there were leaks, no matter what precautions you took. He didn't go to the trouble of giving me a written order. He just sat there at the Coon Can game and told me to load up every flyable P-40 I could find. He said that a few of the experienced AVG, the Flying Tigers, had agreed to stay over just for him, and they would go with me. We'd infiltrate the field at Kweilin, five hundred miles eastward, and not go barreling in there in formation and thereby warn the enemy that we were up to something unusual.

I called in the maximum force from all three squadrons, and they amounted to twenty-nine planes. So we gathered our skeleton group of old ships and new kids, and a scattering of those other veterans—six, to be exact. Then on July 2, that same day, we left the field at Kunming a couple of ships at a time and flew leisurely along to the east. We landed by single ships and by twos and threes, without even circling the town of Kweilin. No need to advertise the fact that we were there. Spies would get the word through soon enough. From there we could strike Hong Kong, Canton, or Hankow. But this time we were not going to strike any of those places. We were going to sit tight and supposedly wait to be struck.

We hid our ships under camouflage nets, scattered at random in the boondocks, and in the shadows of the strange-looking mountains bordering the Kweilin field. In the slots beside the runway where we would have normally parked our fighters, the Chinese had placed dummy P-40s to bait the trap. These pseudo-airplanes were really very crude, made of light wood in the general shape of a Tomahawk P-40, covered with canvas and then painted to resemble the actual fighter—grinning shark's teeth, wooden props, and the insignia of the Chinese Air Force. So often they would fool a close observer. I had noticed them on other fields, and until I landed and was taxiing close to them, I thought they might be actual fighters. They were so convincing that sometimes, in the half light of dawn, or in the excitement of a *jing-bao* (air raid), normally sharp-eyed pilots, fooled by a planned gag of the Chinese mechanics, would jump onto the wing of a dummy, thinking it was their ship.

That night, to bait the trap further, General Chennault sent some of the old hands into town with instructions to visit certain establishments and "accidentally" pass out fake information that he wanted to reach the Japanese. As they drank wine and acted as though they had drunk more than they had, the pilots talked louder and louder for the benefit of the informers. They called rather boisterously that they were newly arrived, and that Chennault had sent them to the nearby field to practice. The squadron would be at Kweilin for a day or so, and then would fly back to Chunking to defend the capital. We hoped the acting had been good. Even if the enemy came in too early, they would probably get only the dummies. We sat on alert that night in the operations cave at Kweilin and played cards.

July 3, 1942. The hours dragged by and I kept watching the action of the Chinese warning net, for the plotting board was situated right there in the cool, damp cave. The net had been showing action ever since early morning, all around the main bases from which we could expect the enemy: Kai Tak at Kowloon, White Cloud near Canton, and farther north, all around Hankow and Nanking. At exactly two P.M. the atmosphere of the cave suddenly became charged as though with electricity. The little Japanese flags on pedestals were shoved out across the plotting board. Starting at the danger points, they formed a straight line that pointed directly at us there in the cave. They showed the formations to be crossing the outer circle. Twenty-four were airborne from Kai Tak, a similar number from White Cloud. My hopes rose, but so did my nervousness, and the tension in the cave increased.

Again I wondered if I was ready. Were any of us ready? Somehow I wished I hadn't heard that radio announcement from Tokyo Rose. I wished that we had waited for July 4. It was a whole day away. At 2:45 the waiting was over. General Chennault signaled for me to scramble with my command. There we went, an imaginary outfit taking off for combat the day before we were to be born. Maybe we would never be officially activated, going out to meet forty-eight airplanes of the enemy with our piddling twenty-nine fighters. The last words I heard the Old Man say were that the enemy was a hundred miles away, and we were not to come down from our altitude until he told me so. That no matter what happened, we were to maintain strict radio silence until he told me when to attack.

I ran toward my ship past the Chinese operations people as they played with little flags on the plotting board, where tiny "red meatballs" stared threateningly at me in the dim yellow glow of a twenty-five-cycle bulb. We saddled up then, took off as fast as we could in a cloud of red dust, and climbed to 21,000 feet, an altitude simple to remember, since it was as high as the P-40s would go. Some of them had a tough job getting even that high.

My orders kept running through my mind so vividly that it was as if they were being repeated to me over the headset in my flying helmet. "Orbit west of the field. Radio silence. Nothing, but nothing, to make you break that silence. High in the sun. Stay there circling and watching to the southeast, low down. Attack only when the word comes. No matter what the enemy does, you watch and wait."

I circled and strained my eyes, drying my sweating palms on the leg of my flying suit. I could hear the crackle of static and the drone of my engine, and suddenly there was a new sound of strange, high Japanese voices calling to one another on our frequency. They surely weren't observing radio silence. They were probably out on a holiday flight and telling each other what they were going to do to the unsuspecting Americans. Their overconfidence worried me one moment and chilled me the next. Then they were there, just flashes at first, flashes of windshields in the sunlight, and we were between them and the sun. I could make out black dots—twenty-odd here, another twenty-odd there. It looked like a hundred, but there couldn't be more than the forty-eight they had predicted.

My throat had been dry with excitement, and now my tongue seemed to stick to my teeth. Good Lord! I wondered how it would be when we went down among all those. We had to go. There was no getting out of it now. I had argued myself into a mess like this once too often. I looked around in the other direction to rest my neck. We kept circling, circling, circling. My neck soon ached on that side too, and my eyes burned. I could see dots all over the sky in every direction. I tried to count the air armada, and then I tried to keep my eyes focused somewhere else so I couldn't count them, but my eyes kept being drawn back. I had to look. I counted my own formation, hoping that somehow it would grow in number. I remembered Tokyo Rose's words and I had to agree with her. This just might be our first and last flight together, even though we had changed the date.

At 3:10 P.M. the enemy formation was over the town of Kweilin. I could count them with ease now, and when they turned and the sun was at a certain angle, I could see the big red meatballs on the wings and the fuselages. They dove for the ships they saw waiting for them on the field, the Chinese dummies. I wanted to go down and get it over with. Over my shoulder I looked at my formation and wondered why Chennault didn't give the word. It didn't matter now when we went. "Oh, General, call me down! I'm ready! We're ready! As ready as we'll ever be," I kept thinking.

The sky above the field was filled with circling, diving, strafing enemy fighters. A few of them stayed high to form top cover for the strafers. When the fake P-40s were blazing, and I would think it was apparent to the Japanese that they had caught the green Yankees on the ground with their pants down, even the top cover couldn't resist. They, too, came down to strafe and try to drive small frag bombs into the mouth of the operations cave. They must have been overjoyed that none of the ships on the ground had even started an engine, that not one of the Americans had tried to take off. Back and forth the Japanese Zeros went. I could see the phosphorescent lines of their tracers arching across the Kweilin airdrome from mountaintop to jagged mountaintop. The fires of the dummy planes looked realistic, for the Chinese had placed a Jerry can of gasoline inside each fake P-40. Now wrapped in flames, they looked so real that I was sorry to see them burn.

But why didn't the Old Man pass the word? Maybe his

radio was out. Perhaps one of those bombs they had lobbed at the cave had gone inside. My hands moved to the top of the throttle to press the throat mike button a dozen times, but it never quite got pressed. Circle, circle! We kept circling and watching and waiting. The air was filled with smoke, and the enemy's arrogant ships were all over the sky. They looped and rolled and chandelled off the runway above the burning dummies. High in the sun waited the P-40s, our real P-40s. Every now and then I'd note that my altimeter was unwinding. By some reflex I had let the pressure of my hand push the nose of my ship down. The formation would follow me, but I'd remember in time and win it back and return to orbiting. Finally the decoys were nothing but ashes, and the pall of smoke had thinned out and risen so high that I could smell the fires.

Then the word we had been waiting for so eagerly came. "Take 'em! Take 'em, Tigers! Take 'em! They're ripe and waiting! Take 'em, Scotty!"

Down we went. No verbal orders, just a flip of my rudder and a dipping of my wings to the direction. Behind me, the various flight leaders relayed my signal. In a flash we were closing in on them. All the Zeros had been pulled into a tight formation by their leader. They were practically waiting over the city of Kweilin. They loomed in my gunsights a thousand yards away, and I fought the temptation to open fire. We'd waited a long time, and the first pass had to be good. I had forgotten how outnumbered we were; I'm very happy now that I did. But it was such a relief to get the word after endless suspense and go down from that incessant circling that perhaps we would have been relieved to attack twice that number.

The formation was so perfect and so close that we couldn't miss. Even the new kids remembered not to shoot at the whole formation, but to concentrate on one ship, one lone ship at a time with short bursts, then skid to another. Hang on, aim, then fire, always short bursts. They didn't see us until it was too late. Twenty or more were already going down, and those we didn't burn in the first pass broke and ran in all directions. After the first dive, when we climbed back into the sun for altitude, we broke, too, and took out after the stragglers. I followed one with my wingman all the way to Canton, two hundred miles southward, and shot him down when the pilot lowered his landing gear preparatory to landing at White Cloud airdrome. By that time we'd shot down thirty-four planes in the victory, but more than that, we had become blooded combat men.

When I dragged in on the final approach I noticed that my tanks were almost dry. My voice sounded strange and foreign in the side tone of my radio as I called for landing instructions. I sounded like another person, and maybe I was. If I could have heard Tokyo Rose that night, it would have done me good, but she didn't come through there in the mountains of Kweilin. Later on we received a report from British intelligence, hiding in the outskirts of Kowloon, saying that she had raised hell that night.

She emphasized that we had continued in the cowardly tradition already established by the mercenary killers of Chennault, and had shot down one innocent student pilot as he was about to land at the airdrome at Canton. She bragged about the forty P-40s the Japanese had caught and destroyed on the Kweilin field, but no mention was made of the thirty-four ships we knew they had definitely lost. The Chinese of Kweilin and the surrounding rice paddies had gone out and brought in the evidence of those thirty-four planes to Chennault as proud testimonials. Tokyo Rose asserted that by raiding the Japanese training base at White Cloud the day before our fighter group was officially activated, we had violated some covenant of the Geneva convention. We were starting out in the same dastardly fashion with which the AVG had left off.

Coming in to land, I was more than careful that day, watching closely for bomb craters in the runway, but the Chinese had been out there almost before the strafing had stopped, to repair those pockmarks as well as to remove all the debris. I parked my ship in the boondocks again, far away from the hot ashes, and by the time I had walked up to the cave, I had time to breathe deeply and compose myself just a little.

General Chennault, as usual, appeared younger than he had when I had left him before the battle. He always relaxed when something that he had planned went off well. I found him Indian-wrestling with one of the Tigers, a sport in which, to my knowledge, he had never been defeated. When he saw me come into the mouth of the cave, he stopped his exercise to congratulate me. I couldn't help being happy, nor could I hide the joy that I felt.

"See how easy it is, Scotty? Any questions?"

"Yes, sir," I said. "I do have a question. Please tell me why we waited so long. Why did we keep circling all that time?" Since I didn't mean to question his judgment, I hurried to say that I thought his radio might be dead, that maybe one of the bombs had hit it, or maybe my radio was out.

He leaned down to rub Joe's ears and took a cigarette out of the pocket of his leather jacket. "Now, Scotty," he finally said, "put yourself in the place of that Jap commander. What would you have been thinking about if you had been sitting where he was instead of up there where you were? What would you have been thinking when you first arrived and saw all those fat targets down there?"

Well, that was easy. He wasn't going to catch me with that one. "I would be thinking about how many I was going to burn up on the ground. I'd have been calculating those two lines of P-40s, one on each side of the runway. Catch them before they started their engines. That's what I'd have done."

Chennault just kept rubbing Joe's ears, kneeling down there close to the little dog on the floor of the cave. Then he stood up and looked me right in the eye, practically laughing out loud. "That's just what the Jap colonel was thinking. After that, you saw him dive and zoom and use up most of his ammunition, and most of his gasoline, and let his disciplined formation get sort of out of hand. All the time you were hiding up there, he was becoming more and more uncertain about those dummies down below. They burned too fast. Twenty minutes, thirty, and all the time he's getting more and more overconfident, but he's worrying too. In fact, he's just about to conclude that things are not the way they seem to be when I called you down. He looks up at the danger quadrant, up in the high sun, but it's too late. He looked there when he began to be worried about something else. Know what that was, Scotty?"

Sure I did, finally. That cunning old fox. I found myself feeling a little guilty too, but I was happy just the same. "His fuel, General! I see it all now. I'd have been worrying if I had enough to take me back to Kai Tak or White Cloud or wherever I had to go."

He grinned all over and winked at me then. He had seen it all the time. So many times he had seen it, and this afternoon he had been down there on his lookout point, thinking it all out while I orbited up there and wondered what in the world everybody was waiting for. "That's why you shot down over half his planes, son, and didn't lose a single one yourself. Remember it!" And from that moment I never forgot.

So the 23rd Fighter Group was born in combat a whole day before Washington said it was to be activated. With the added confidence of the stalwarts of the AVG that stayed with us, few as they were, all those green American kids didn't stay green very long. We took on the aura of the real Flying Tigers, and the Chinese continued to call us Tigers. Leading a bunch like that, I came to be pretty proud of myself. I had to move fast to stay ahead of a group that figured they outnumbered the enemy, even when the ratio was twenty-nine to forty-eight.

That first day I shot down two and was credited with damaging two more. Within a month I was an ace with five enemy planes definitely destroyed in aerial combat. Five little Japanese meatballs on the side of my ship testified to this mythical honor. I was as cocky as any of the original Flying Tigers had ever been. I found myself dressing as they did and talking as they had talked. Maybe to some of the brass that came out to India from as far away as Washington I was insufferable too. Maybe I was. But in three months, when September came, I had ten planes and was a double ace, so the newspapers said. The Chinese cheered me, and when I drove my operations jeep through the streets of Kunming, the little kids stood on the curb and called, "Ding-hao!" ("You are number one!") It made me happy and I always felt a shiver run up my spine as I tried to sit a little straighter in the jeep.

Why, there was nothing to this. I had run my spirits up so high that by the time the year was over, I'd have a hundred victories. My confidence was brimming. Then one day I caught on. I came to realize a single truth that I should have known the first afternoon back there among the jagged, inverted, conelike mountains of Kweilin. I owed everything to Chennault. Sure I shot down the enemy planes. That is, I flew the ship and pressed the trigger, but I flew it when he said to fly and put it up in the part of the sky where he said to put it. He passed on to me a wealth of knowledge, strained and restrained from seven years of combat and thirty years in China, and from a quarter century's work and research on fighter planes. I merely carried out the operations for him. I was his hatchet man. I was his executioner. Most of all, though, I was just his long right arm, extending high into the skies of China. But for his knowledge, I would have been just another pilot.[3]

WE'RE HERE TO STAY

Lieutenant Roger Haberman was a division leader in Joe Foss's eight-aircraft flight. His story is unique because it covers so many different facets of the early days on Guadalcanal—Pistol Pete, Washing-Machine Charlie, Japanese naval shelling, ground attacks, and aerial combat. Roger also tells about the day he shot down a Zero and forced three others to ditch after they attacked a PBY returning from a very unusual mission.

Marine Fighter Squadron VMF-121 trained in San Diego with very limited time in Grumman F4F Wildcats. There was a shortage of rubber and there weren't enough tires for our aircraft, hence very little flight time. I got twenty-five hours of flight time in the Grumman Wildcat before we went overseas. My wingman, Oscar Bates, had only nine hours. We had hardly any preparation for the operations that were planned for us. VMF-121 sailed for the South Pacific on September 1, 1942, and landed in Numea, New Caledonia. While we were there, Joe Foss, me, and six others went out to the airfield at Tantuta and test-hopped our aircraft before putting them aboard a carrier. On October 9, 1942, we boarded the carrier USS *Copahee* and sailed to within 175 miles of Guadalcanal. We launched from there and flew to a dirt strip on Guadalcanal called Fighter One.

Taking off from Fighter One was an experience. The eight pilots in a flight taxied out and lined up. The first plane off would leave a great cloud of dust. Each succeeding pilot would count to ten—"one thousand one, one thousand two, etc."—and take off into the dust. You were flying when you came out of the dirt and dust. After it rained you would have to push the plane through six to eight inches of mud, slop, and water to get airborne.

The planes were the best available at the time. They had blowers (superchargers) that were not supposed to be engaged below 10,000 feet. The blowers were wired open so that we could get the maximum power out of an aircraft on takeoff. That meant that an engine would last twenty-five to fifty hours before it blew up and had to be replaced. An engineering officer told me that the pressure on the cylinder walls was equivalent to sixty inches of mercury—a standing sixty-inch column of mercury at sea level. The F4F didn't have electric fuel pumps. When you got up to 10,000 feet, you maintained fuel pressure with a pistol-grip hand pump. Eight to ten seconds after you stopped pumping, the damned engine would quit. We would secure the throttle setting, then to maintain fuel pressure in the engine in order to get to altitude, we would fly with our left hand and pump with our right.

The first planes didn't have any shoulder straps, so if you had to make a water landing, you were guaranteed ten to fifteen stitches on your forehead where it would hit the gunsight. Water is very hard when you land on it. Looking back now, it seems to be a miracle that any of us got out of there alive. We were so short of gasoline that we had to salvage it out of wrecked aircraft. We would have air raids and the cooks would go up into the hills for two hours. When it was time to eat, we never knew if there would be any food ready, but we really didn't care. I lost twenty-five pounds in five weeks. The mosquitoes were as big as the middle fingernail on a man's hand and all over you day and night. If you went to bed at night and any part of you touched the mosquito netting, there would be a big red welt in the morning where they had stung you through the netting. Everybody except me caught malaria. I was stung to hell by the mosquitoes, but must have had a natural immunity, because I never contracted the disease.

The daily "menu" was twenty-five to thirty-five Japanese Zeros, about ten minutes ahead of twenty-seven horizontal bombers—fourteen in a front formation and thirteen in a second echelon. There would be only eight of us against fifty-two to sixty-two Japanese aircraft. We would climb as fast as we could up to our maximum altitude of 23,000 or 24,000 feet and watch the Zeros at 31,000 or 32,000 feet doing wingovers and other aerobatics. They could look down our throats and do whatever they damned well pleased. This was one of their tactics. By flying in so many different directions, they had a 360-degree view. On the other hand, we flew in a close-knit formation to protect one another. The Zeros had superior maneuverability. In two and a half turns against a Wildcat they could have you boresighted. But our planes were heavier than theirs, so if you got into trouble, you could dive away earthward from them.

After aerial combat at 24,000 feet or so, we would make two or three 360-degree turns while diving straight for the ground, and then land at Fighter One. The Japanese planes we had blown up would have been blasted free from their wings, and burning debris, wings, and pieces of fuselage rained down around us like falling leaves, even after we had landed. There was a correspondent with us, Harry Keyes of the London *Daily Times*. He had once had a newspaper up in Malaya, but the Japanese had run him out. Harry told us that he had been in London during the Battle of Britain, but the aerial combat at Guadalcanal was far more intense.

We didn't get much sleep because of "Washing-Machine Charlie," a Japanese aircraft that flew over nightly at 22,000 feet, just above the maximum altitude of our antiaircraft guns. This was strictly a nuisance flight to cause us to lose sleep. The engine had a peculiar drone compared to ours, and he flew back and forth all night long. We weren't allowed to smoke in the open—no lights on the ground at all after dark. The reason was that the Japanese troops on the ground were close to the field, and the night bomber had to drop his bombs pretty accurately to avoid hitting his own people. We never knew when he would drop one of his big 500-pound bombs. It might come at nine o'clock at night, or at four in the morning.

When we later returned to Guadalcanal, the ground marines had pushed the lines back and we erected three GP tents on a little hill. We were pulled out on the twenty-sixth day. The next day, Washing-Machine Charlie dropped a bomb that killed three of the navy pilots who had occupied the tents we had slept in the night before.

When we were on the island the first time (late 1942), up in the hills, about a quarter-mile away, there was a Japanese field gun that we called "Pistol Pete." The Japanese gun crew would fire on the field anytime they wanted to— ten o'clock in the morning, three o'clock in the afternoon—

whenever they felt like it. You'd hear a *whoomp-shoosh-bang!* You didn't know what the hell to do or where to go.

Frank Knox, then Secretary of the Navy, came out one day to look around the island. He came in about ten in the morning and was walking up and down the flight line, shaking hands and talking with the mechanics. He had scheduled himself to leave about ten o'clock the next morning, but that was before he was subjected to a couple of those shots from Pistol Pete and the usual night bombing by Washing-Machine Charlie. About two o'clock the next morning somebody shook me awake for a mission. Joe Foss and his flight took off about three A.M. in weather so dark that we couldn't even see the instrument panels, and escorted General Geiger's PBY (with Frank Knox aboard) out about one hundred miles. Knox had decided not to wait until morning.

We were so close to the front lines that we could hear the rifles and machine guns firing all night long. A friend of mine from Devil's Lake, North Dakota, Lieutenant Philip Wayne Kelly, came to me one day and said, "Come on, Roger. Let's go up to the front lines."

I told him, "I don't have any business up there. What the hell's the matter with you?"

He said, "Come on. I want you to go up with me because the National Guard outfit from Devil's Lake, North Dakota, my hometown, is on the front lines and I know every one of them."

I said, "Fine. I'll go along."

We drove his jeep about one half mile up a jungle trail to the front lines. These were the circumstances when we got there. Ten days earlier, a National Guard patrol was returning to our front lines after dark, but what they thought was their patrol returning was actually a column of about four hundred Japanese. The Japanese jumped into the American foxholes and there was hand-to-hand combat. The National Guard started firing their mortars out from our lines and then walked the shells in as close as possible. The guard killed hundreds of the Japanese.

When we arrived, the bodies had been lying for ten days in the hot tropical sun, just a few degrees off the equator. The mortars had blown most of the clothing off those guys, and they had swollen up two or three times normal size. There were so many maggots around that it looked like snow had drifted up into their armpits and across their faces. Big black flies were swarming everywhere. The stench made your eyes burn.

I said to one of those guys from North Dakota, "Good Lord! How can you be so close to this stench and go down one hundred feet from here to your mess hall and eat?"

He said, "I haven't had anything of consequence to eat in ten days. I can't eat."

They couldn't pick up the bodies and bury them because there were Japanese snipers in the hundred-foot-high trees around the grassy clearing where the bodies lay. The snipers were finally cleared out, and engineers blew holes twenty feet in diameter and sixteen feet deep. Japanese prisoners were made to throw the bodies into the holes and they were buried with bulldozers. It was the damnedest scene you ever saw.

On October 13 the Japanese came down with a battleship with thirteen-inch guns, two cruisers, and four destroyers for a naval engagement. There weren't any American vessels around for a naval engagement, so they decided to pelt us all night long. They cruised back and forth in column for about three hours, first firing the port-side guns, then turning and firing the starboard guns. Henderson Field was parallel to the shoreline, and naval gunfire destroyed practically all of our aircraft that night. It's a helpless feeling to be shelled, because you can't run from it. I went out to the latrine about 9:30, reached around in the dark for some toilet paper, and burned my hand on a big piece of hot steel from an exploded shell.

We were a good target. The beachhead was three quarters of a mile deep and a mile long with Japanese on three sides and the ocean to our backs. Major Gordon Bell was the commanding officer of the dive-bomber squadron on the main strip. A shell hit the foxhole he was in and killed him, his executive officer, his doctor, his flight officer, and another officer. They shelled us all night long, with an observation plane overhead directing fire. They used star shells and searchlights to light up the beach. The star shells put out five times more light than daylight, and the effect was just eerie. The exploding shells made the damned ground shake. Sixteen or seventeen of our planes were set afire. When that magnesium and aluminum starts to burn, it's like burning a Fourth of July sparkler. The ammunition dump was hit and it burned for twenty-four hours. Our fuel dump was hit and continued to burn for two and a half days.

On the morning of October 15, 1942, we were recovering from the third straight night of aerial bombing, and shelling from Japanese warships offshore. All of the torpedo planes had been put out of action on Henderson Field. We were on constant alert, but weren't taking off to pursue flights of fewer than fifteen Japanese planes, because of the fuel shortage. The Japanese were so desperate that they had run some cargo ships ashore about seven miles west of the field and had gotten their personnel and materiel off any way they could. Major Jack Cram took General Geiger's PBY patrol boat, lashed two torpedoes on the thing, made a run on the ships up there, and sank one of the Japanese cargo vessels. Using a patrol boat to launch torpedoes had never been done before or since.

Foss, with our flight, was climbing out of the field to give the six or eight dive-bombers some protection from the Japanese air patrol over the cargo ships. We were climbing up in a tight spiral, heading inland while still in the cone of potential protection from our antiaircraft guns from the field. I looked down and saw Jack Cram, flying the general's PBY, reach the edge of the field with four Zeros just shooting the hell out of him. They later counted 160 holes in his aircraft, in addition to other damage. I was about 1,500 or 2,000 feet above them, so I peeled off and gave what I call a "spraying shot." Our guns were bore-sighted at 250 yards, so this wasn't considered effective, precision shooting. As I pushed over toward them, one guy peeled off to the left and up to 500 feet. I pursued with a speed differential in my favor of 75 to 100 mph until I opened fire from about a hundred yards behind him. He caught afire and pieces began flying off his aircraft. I flew into the fire and had to turn out to avoid crashing into him. Then I dropped my wheels and landed. This was my first kill.

In mid-1989 I was in contact with John B. Lundstrum, Assistant Curator of History at the Milwaukee Public Museum. He has written a book about the Battle of Guadalcanal and is now researching a book on the Battle of Guadalcanal from the Japanese perspective. He told me that the Japanese records are much more detailed and accurate than our own. He had reviewed the Japanese records of my run and discovered that I had shot down one Zero in flames and forced the other three pilots to ditch their planes because of battle damage from my strafing run. The Japanese records included the pilots' names. I was the only pilot who made a run on those four planes that were shooting up the general's transportation.

On November 11 I was wounded while attacking a bomber. We had a rule that you broke off the attack and went after other enemy planes when you knew the one you shot was going down. But that son of a bitch had shot me through the right leg and the right arm and it made me double mad. I wanted to tear off his right aileron and crash him, even though he was already doomed. You never forget the burning intensity of moments like that.

After I got out of the hospital I joined what was left of the squadron in Numea, New Caledonia, and shortly after that the Foss flight was sent to Australia for two weeks of rest leave. When we got back to New Caledonia, Joe Foss had a talk with General Roy S. Geiger, the general in charge of marine aviation on Guadalcanal. General Geiger asked him, "How do you feel, Joe?"

He replied, "Hell, I feel fine."

Joe Foss, me, and the other six guys in our flight went back up to Guadalcanal on January 1, 1943, for twenty-six days. The rest of the squadron was sent to British Samoa, where they remained until they returned to the States about eighteen months later. They were denied their rest leave in Australia, and it's a damned shame, because that was what Major "Duke" Davis had in mind when he sent our flight down first. He wanted to be sure that no one was cheated out of that leave. The Foss flight left Guadalcanal a second time and spent thirty days in New Zealand. We then boarded a liberty ship and sailed for twenty-eight days before arriving back in the United States.

When I came back from overseas the first time, my sister took a look at me and said, "Well, I think the Marine Corps has made you a little bit crazy." That was the way she summed up the changes she saw in me as an individual.

My retort was, "Well, that's possible, my dear, but in order to be an effective fighter pilot in the Marine Corps, you have to be a little bit crazy."

After a thirty-day leave I was assigned to a training squadron in El Toro, California. I was later sent to Mohave, California, to an observation squadron, VMO-251. They were so short of fighter squadrons that we were converted into a fighter unit. After more training I returned to the Pacific in February 1944 for operations all over the Philippines, from Manila to Zamboanga. I flew cover over the Subic Bay invasion. When you are flying at about 10,000 feet and there are about eighty vessels, both capital and support ships sailing in convoy formation below you, the effect is like a beautiful water ballet. The ships would travel on a certain course for about ten minutes and then turn at the same time with their wakes trailing behind them. It was a magnificent sight.

During my total time in the Marine Corps (four and a half years), I flew over two hundred combat missions and was given credit for seven and a half kills. How do you get credit for half a kill? Two people start firing simultaneously and the enemy plane goes down. One time, three of us opened up at the same time at a Japanese plane and shot it down. They didn't give credit for a third, so we tossed coins to see which two guys got half a kill.

While on Guadalcanal we flew in flights of eight planes, divided into two divisions, each having two sections. Each division had a leader with three men flying wing on him. I was the second division leader in Joe Foss's flight. Our squadron (VMF-121) went into Guadalcanal with forty pilots. Fourteen were killed in combat, four of us were shot up, and two pilots broke down under the pressure and had to be evacuated. Everyone had malaria except me. We were pretty damn well ravished by the time we got out of there after six weeks of combat. VMF-121 shot down 132 Japanese planes during those six weeks. Joe Foss and his flight of eight accounted for seventy-two of them. Of those seventy-two enemy aircraft, Joe Foss shot down twenty-six and became America's top-ranking ace of the war to that time.

I feel in my heart that there were probably any number of young American men who could have done the same things we did. But the fact remains, we were the ones who did them. Words can't explain the camaraderie we felt on Guadalcanal. We never knew if we would be driven into the sea the next day, or even live to see the next day. Air Transport Support was flying bombs and gasoline to the island in DC-3s, and those planes couldn't carry much of that kind of cargo. One time, our support people tried to send a barge loaded with gasoline to us across the strait from the neighboring island of Tulagi. The Japanese sank the barge. Enemy warships shelled us at will. Daily air raids, Pistol Pete, and Washing-Machine Charlie made our survival touch-and-go all of the time. But we figured, "What the hell. We came to Guadalcanal to stay." And stay we did!

FLYING THUNDERBOLTS

Lieutenant Colonel Leslie Smith flew P-47s with the famous 56th Fighter Group. His story covers a wide range of topics, including bomber escort missions and the many types of strafing missions for which Thunderbolts are so well known. Leslie also tells about several special missions conducted by his fighter group.

I was assigned to the 61st Fighter Squadron of the 56th Fighter Group. On January 3, 1943, we boarded the *Queen Elizabeth* and headed across the Atlantic for Scotland. Land was sighted five days later. We disembarked in Scotland and boarded a cold, clammy troop train for a long overnight ride to our temporary base near Peterborough, England. We received new P-47C aircraft and began slow-timing the planes and making orientation flights from our little airfield at Kingscliffe.

My first flight in England took place on February 10, almost three months after I had last been in the airplane. I decided to give a nearby bomber base a one-ship flyby and let the bomber crews know that the fighter pilots had arrived to protect them. I got clearance from the tower for a low pass and initiated the approach from about 5,000 feet. When I crossed the base fence, the ship was at full throttle and near maximum speed, about ten feet off the ground.

Halfway down the long runway, I lifted the nose slightly and started a slow roll. Initially the roll was smooth and the plane was gaining altitude, but once I was on my back, the runway looked too close to my head. I pushed on the stick, but it didn't respond quickly enough. I pushed harder, creating a high-speed stall that immediately converted the slow roll into a snap roll. As the airplane spun quickly through 180 degrees, my right wingtip clipped the weeds at the side of the runway. I kicked the right rudder hard and slammed forward on the stick, regaining control. I returned to Kingscliffe without looking back. I have often wondered how much damage was inflicted on the bomber crews' morale by my display of ineptitude that day.

The group's first combat mission took place on April 13, 1943. Since it was our first mission, the 56th Group put up only one twelve-ship squadron, then joined with the 4th

Group (formerly the RAF Eagle Squadron) and 78th Group (also flying its first mission). We organized our twelve ships in the traditional RAF javelin formation, where each of three flights fly line astern. Our group commander led the first flight with three other planes in trail and stacked down behind him. The second and third flight leaders flew on either side of the group commander at his altitude, but slightly behind. The planes following them were also stacked down in trail. Looking down from above gave this formation a spearhead appearance.

The flights were separated from each other by about a hundred yards, and the planes within each flight were separated by fifty to seventy-five yards. This tight formation provided almost no field of vision to the rear and very limited maneuverability. Fighter pilots always prefer to attack other airborne planes from behind, since the shooting angle (deflection) is much easier and the relative closing speed between the two planes is much lower. For that reason the trailing planes in any formation are the ones most likely to be fired on during an enemy attack. It was therefore decided by our senior officers that the last planes in the 2nd and 3rd Flights should not be piloted by captains and above, but by lieutenants, whose loss would not be of as much concern to the war effort. Lieutenant Mahurin of the 63rd Squadron and Lieutenant Leslie C. Smith were honored to be the 56th Group's first "Tail-End Charlies." It says something for the youth of America that those junior pilots not chosen were very disappointed.

Major Loran G. McCollom, CO of the 61st Fighter Group, led the second flight on the left side of Lieutenant Colonel Hubert Zemke (see "Mayhem—P-38 Style," page 189), the group commander. Captain Eby, the squadron operations officer, was flying in the number-two slot; Captain Don Renwick was number three, and I was number four.

Members of the 61st Squadron's flight started across the English Channel in the prescribed in-trail formation. However, as we proceeded across the water toward the enemy coast, each of us moved forward and closer to the plane flying ahead of him. By the time we crossed into enemy-occupied France, we were not in trail, but in a vertical formation with no one really in the tail-end position. Fortunately none of the yellow-nosed German fighters from Abbeville rose to challenge us, and there was no need to defend ourselves from this awkward formation.

We returned to base and immediately began working on a combat formation that would give us more maneuverability and equal visibility for everyone in the flight. After considerable discussion, chalkboard diagrams, and in-flight practice, we developed a widely spread, almost line-abreast formation for each flight. Each flight within a squadron would be deployed in a widely spread fingertip formation. This provided all flights with all-around visibility, more maneuverability, and better fuel management for the wingmen (once they learned to make crossovers in the turns). This new formation was widely adopted in the ETO and was later used extensively in Korea.

Flying out of England was rarely routine. Some of the hazards we faced were the weather, the cold North Sea, and the altitudes at which we operated. The weather was usually bad; often it was downright rotten. We frequently took off with a ceiling of only a few hundred feet or less, then had to climb thousands of feet through the dense clouds before breaking out on top and reassembling. The flight leaders would climb out on instruments at uniform power settings, headings, and rates of climb. The lead squadron would take the designated heading, and the second squadron would take a course five degrees to its right. The third squadron would then climb out five degrees to the left of the lead squadron.

Often the clouds were quite dark. The wingmen would have to fly in close visual formation, separated from the leader by only a few feet, and sometimes further hampered by canopy icing. The strain on them was enormous. If they lost sight of the leader, wingmen would instantly have to go to instruments. This sudden switch was often accompanied by a period of disorientation and the danger of a spinout or a midair collision. I can remember early missions where I switched to instruments and experienced vertigo so badly that it felt as though the plane were skidding sideways with one wing much higher than the other. I was delighted when I became a flight leader and had to worry only about instrument flying.

The weather could also severely complicate our return to England with very low ceilings and only an occasional compass vector from one of the RAF tracking stations. When the ceiling was down to near zero, we would sometimes let down to fifty feet or less over the North Sea and pray that our altimeters were still correctly calibrated. We would look for the fog dispersal airfield along the coast, or any recognizable landmarks for orientation.

Another problem was the high altitudes required for bomber escort missions. Oxygen starvation occurred fairly often. This was because the oxygen system—the tanks, tubes, and valves—could develop leaks. The most common problem was ill-fitting or leaky oxygen masks. We tested them before every mission and continued testing them frequently during flight, in addition to checking to see if our fingernails were turning blue, a sure sign of oxygen deficiency.

On the last day of 1943 I was leading our twelve-ship squadron on a bomber escort mission to the Brest peninsula. We had just leveled off at about 30,000 feet and were approaching the French coast when my wingman's plane nosed up and began climbing above the formation. The pilot was Bill Marangello from New York, I believe, a new pilot who was a bit older and more reliable than our typical replacement. I suspected a radio or oxygen problem. I called and got no response. Then his plane did a slow wingover away from us and fell into a near-vertical dive, convincing evidence of oxygen starvation. I followed him down, yelling at the top of my voice, imploring him to wake up. As far as I know, he never did. His plane crashed into the North Sea at close to the speed of sound.

After the first combat mission, several fighter sweeps

inside the Belgian and Dutch coasts resulted in little enemy reaction, but allowed us to familiarize ourselves with the area and practice the new combat formation. The 61st Fighter Squadron's C Flight was led by an able captain who closely followed our orders to stay close to the bombers we were escorting. We couldn't engage enemy fighters at great distances from the bomber train, and this put us in a defensive mode. Other flight leaders interpreted the orders more loosely and had more aerial engagements. Eventually the Eighth Air Force came to agree with us that enemy fighters should be attacked wherever they were found. Under this new aggressive policy we could move away from the bombers in search and pursuit of the Germans.

On July 3, 1943, I was appointed C flight leader. A few missions later I got my first good shot at a German plane. We had flown over Holland to take over escort duty for B-17s on the way home from a deep-penetration raid. As we approached the bombers we could see enemy fighters attacking. We dropped external tanks and went to full power. Our arrival "en masse" discouraged most of the Germans, and we wasted a lot of fuel trying to catch up with them. My wingman, Dick Mudge from Edwardsville, Illinois, reported "bingo fuel" (just enough to get home). We reduced power and started for home.

We spotted four German fighters following us as we neared the Dutch coast, but couldn't turn back to engage them because of our fuel state. Shortly thereafter we approached the last of the B-17s flying in ragged formation. One lone bomber was trailing at least a thousand yards behind the others with its wheels down and a Focke-Wulf 190 flying close formation on its left wing. While we were still out of range, the 190 slid behind the B-17 and fired into the bomber. There was no return fire. The Focke-Wulf then moved back up into tight formation to look over its prey. We closed with the FW and I fired, scoring hits on his fuselage and right wing. It pulled up sharply, spewing dark smoke, executed a split-S, and headed for home. We didn't have enough fuel to give chase.

Now we were attacked from above by the four German fighters that had been trailing us. Dick was several hundred yards to my left in our line abreast combat formation. As the Focke-Wulfs approached, Dick called, "Break left!" and we easily turned inside the attackers. The enemy fighters climbed above us for position. We continued heading for home to gain a few more miles. When the next attack came we again broke inside while firing short bursts to show that we still had ammunition, then completed our turn toward home. They made one more halfhearted attack, then broke away and disappeared back toward Holland. After reaching my hard stand back at base, Joe Gibson (my crew chief) calculated that I had enough fuel left for three or four additional minutes of flying.

Many combat missions followed. For various reasons of weather, aircraft malfunction, being in the wrong place at the wrong time, or just poor gunnery, I was able to only damage more enemy aircraft. That changed on February 22, 1944. I was leading Red Flight in the group's lead squadron while we provided bomber escort into Germany. Nearing the front of the bomber train, we saw two groups of enemy aircraft making head-on passes through the bomber formation. When they turned back to make another pass, my flight swung out to the right, and back to the left, to attack about eight FW-190s approximately 5,000 feet below us. We dove on them from high and out of the sun (a favored attack position) and they took no evasive action. I opened fire on my target from about two hundred yards. It always seems closer than that, and I initially guessed that the distance was fifty yards. There were hits on the fuselage, several big flashes, and then heavy smoke. I fired again, got more good strikes, and pieces of the plane began flying back toward me. As I pulled up and off to the left, the plane slowly turned into a shallow right downward spiral.

Next I saw two enemy fighters that were trying to get

into firing position behind two of my squadron's P-47s. We were closing slowly and still out of range, but I was going to fire anyway to discourage the attack. The pilot closest to me must have seen us, because he suddenly split-Sed and headed for the deck. I followed him in a near-vertical, full-power dive and could tell from the stiffness in the controls that we were approaching the speed of sound. The German pilot started to level out at about 7,000 feet, but I was still out of range. We followed the Focke-Wulf on down through a thin cloud at about 3,000 feet. He must have thought that he had lost us, because I was able to get very close behind him before opening fire. My guns hit his fuselage and tail section. Debris came spinning off his plane, and the left wing dropped in an awkward manner, as if he were out of control. As we passed over him, I noticed that our altitude was about a thousand feet. I continued to climb and watch as the enemy fighter descended in a wing-low, shallow spiral. We later discovered numerous dents and scratches on my propeller from the pieces that had been knocked off the enemy plane. My claim for two FW-190s destroyed was confirmed by gun-camera film and reports from my wingman, Willy Aggers, who had stayed right with me through those difficult maneuvers.

Two weeks later I was leading the group of aircraft patrolling to the right of the bomber stream when our other group reported a large flight of enemy fighters approaching from the northeast. We dropped our external tanks and went to full power to climb and cross over the bombers without being shot down by our Big Friends. There was a huge swarm of enemy fighters about ten to fifteen miles away, flying in what seemed to be a totally unorganized formation. They reminded me of a flock of starlings swarming toward the bomber track. Our lead group intercepted the enemy fighters first, keeping them away from the Big Friends. A few minutes later we arrived over the top of a giant Lufbery, in which our lead group, and a group of P-51s, were engaged in a giant air battle with over a hundred Focke-Wulfs and ME-109s. All of them were turning to the left so hard that no one seemed to be able to get enough lead for an effective shot.

Looking for a target in the mass of planes below, I saw a red-nosed P-47 (our squadron's colors) near the top of the whirlpool. He was trying to get his gunsight on a 109 ahead of him while avoiding being hit by the 109 to his rear. As my wingman and I dived to give assistance, I recognized the plane as that flown by Evan McMinn. I called and told him that we were coming. His response was: "Get that bastard off my ass!"

Evan did not abandon position behind his target. I tried to get into position behind his pursuer, but after more than another 360-degree turn could still not get enough lead. "Mac" could see my problem and called to tell me to get ready—he was going to execute a snap turn to the right on the count of three (a very dangerous maneuver to attempt with an enemy directly behind you). When he counted two, I eased off my left turn and was in a perfect position by the time the 109 altered his turn to follow McMinn to the right. I hit him in the wings and fuselage. A sheet of smoke erupted from the Messerschmitt. The German pilot rolled his plane over on its back and bailed out.

My wingman called a right break as a 109 tried to get into position behind him. As we turned, McMinn turned into formation with us. Now the 109 pilot changed his mind about what had become three-to-one odds. He dived away with his greater speed into the top of a nearby cumulus cloud. We turned back east to find another target, but all we could see were towering cumulus clouds and the long stratus clouds made by the bombers' contrails as they continued toward their target. The fight had lasted only a few minutes, and now there wasn't another plane in sight. It's amazing what could have happened to two hundred airplanes engaged in a desperate dogfight below us. Exhausted and low on fuel, the three of us turned back toward England, satisfied that we had kept the Germans away from the Big Friends, at least for our part of the mission.

On March 27 we were assigned a short bomber escort mission to the French city of Nancy. Little opposition was expected, so each flight was assigned a separate airfield to attack on the way back. After leaving the bombers, we flew at 10,000 to 12,000 feet over Gael Airfield in Normandy. It appeared to be empty, except for one plane parked in front of a hangar. That looked suspicious. I instructed the other pilots in the flight to maintain altitude while I made a solo low-level pass. Pretending that we had not seen the aircraft and intended no attack, we flew perhaps ten miles farther on toward England, then I split-Sed to the deck and returned to the field going full throttle at treetop level.

I crossed the open airfield too low to put the gunsight on the target, so pulling up just enough to pop the stick forward momentarily, I brought my guns to bear on the strange-looking plane. I hit it, but it wouldn't burn. The antiaircraft guns were firing by then. As I pulled up to avoid hitting the hangar, a stream of white-hot tracer bullets flowed over my left wing like water from a fire hose. I jammed the stick forward, dropped behind the hangar, and got away. It had been a trap and I was lucky to escape. I very nearly joined Bud Mahurin, Gerry Johnson, Eve Everett, and John Fields, all of whom went down that day doing exactly what I had done.

On April 9 I was leading B group on a bomber escort mission into northern Germany near Denmark when we engaged a group of about twenty 109s that were dogfighting with a smaller group of P-47s. I picked a target. After I made a full 360-degree turn behind him, he rolled off into a steep spiral toward the ground. My wingman and I followed at full throttle. I got off a short burst from my eight .50-caliber guns at three hundred yards and saw a few hits on his wing. I was closing too fast to stay behind, so I pulled up, rolling back and down to regain firing position. My second burst hit him in so many places that the flashes and smoke momentarily obscured his plane. As I passed over him, I looked down into the cockpit and saw a young man fighting for control of the plane. As I turned back for a third pass, the canopy flew off and the pilot bailed out. The 109 rolled to the right in a lazy spiral toward the ground.

I was at an altitude of less than 1,000 feet, and decided to record the crash on my gun camera. Although I could have switched to camera only, that didn't occur to me in all the excitement. I put the gunsight on the empty plane and fired. The film clearly shows the plane and its shadow racing together toward the ground with dozens of flashes of light on the ground from exploding bullets. Rapidly the plane and its shadow converge into a pillar of flame, dust, and smoke. It was a long, depressing flight home over the North Sea as I considered the possibility that I had unintentionally hit the pilot in his parachute while confirming my victory with the gun camera. Happily the developed film proved that my bullets had not hit near the downed pilot.

On April 15 the 56th group sent two groups to attack airfields and targets of opportunity in Denmark. My group attacked Flensburg airdrome, where many twin-engine and single-engine planes were parked. My flight of four had approached from the southeast so that no turns would be necessary as we cleared the field. I scored many hits on a HE-111 bomber, but didn't see it burn. Approaching the hangar, I fired and set aflame another HE-111 and saw multiple hits inside the building. We had seen no ground fire on our first pass, so after flying north twelve to fifteen miles, I decided to circle around and make a second pass. My flight again fired at parked Heinkel bombers and ME-109s, leaving the hangar and four or five planes burning vigorously.

Captain Dick Mudge, my roommate and best friend, was flying with the other group that day. He was hit while strafing Heidbeck airfield, bailed out successfully, and spent the rest of the war in Stalag Luft 3. He returned to our base in England just before V-E day and entertained us with stories of life in a POW camp. I particularly remember his telling us about the shortage of food before their long trek back from East Germany ahead of the advancing Russians. There was sometimes ample food when the Red Cross packages arrived, and everyone tried to save some of it for later, but it would eventually run out. As would be expected, the Kriegies, as the POWs called themselves, became obsessed with food. When Dick Mudge returned to our unit, he couldn't bear to see food wasted. At breakfast the day after he returned, he ate all of his food, including the powdered eggs he had once shunned, then proceeded to eat the leftovers from everyone else's plate. Mudge had grown up in the lap of luxury as the son of a wealthy lawyer, so eating the leftovers from other men's dishes was surprising behavior.

Mudge told us a story about one fellow who was particularly good at hoarding his food. He had saved a piece of meat and a piece of cheese long after everyone else had consumed the contents of their packages. He kept the meat and cheese on top of a rafter above his bed, and would lie there, looking up and thinking how good the food would taste when he finally ate it. It was cold in those barracks and the meat and cheese were filled with preservatives, so they didn't rot. After some days of this, he awoke one morning to find that the pet cat had eaten his food cache. The pilot went into a state of deep depression and refused to talk to anyone, in part because the others had laughed at his misfortune. Instead, he spent his time brooding and watching the cat. Several nights later the other pilots found him cooking a piece of meat over the barrack's pot-bellied stove. It was the cat.

On May 19 I was leading our sixteen-ship squadron on an escort mission deep inside German territory. As we approached our rendezvous point, we saw many enemy fighters attacking the Big Friends. As we looked for targets, we spotted a group of about fifteen FW-190s above and to the rear of a combat wing of B-24s. The Focke-Wulfs were above us and out of range, but we dropped external tanks and went into a full-power climb toward them. They apparently had not seen us, or were concentrating on the bombers, because we had no difficulty getting above them. As we approached, they started a left turn and split into three separate flights.

I closed on a plane that had dropped behind the closest

flight. I got hits on the first burst and the pilot took violent evasive action. He made a beginner's mistake of reversing his turn, and when he leveled out briefly, I fired again and scored many hits across the fuselage. Smoke poured out of his plane. My third burst knocked pieces off his plane. The 190 slowly rolled over onto its back and fell off into a vertical dive, trailing smoke.

There were still three FWs ahead of me, so I attacked the next plane in trail. A short burst at 300 yards produced no visible hits. A second burst at 250 yards showed no hits. The third burst at 200 yards hit his wings and fuselage. He rolled over into a steep dive and turned under me. We followed, but had difficulty getting back into range. He dove into a small cloud and we followed. When we came out of the cloud, we were still out of range, but in good position to press our attack. Suddenly the enemy fighter pulled up, streaming vapor trails from each wing, and rolled over on its back. The pilot bailed out. The FW plunged earthward and blew up on impact. The element leader had destroyed another FW. Seeing no other targets, we headed home.

On May 20, 1944 I flew my hundredth combat mission, an uneventful bomber escort into Germany, thus fulfilling my "contract" with Colonel Zemke. I returned to California for a thirty-day leave the day before the Allied invasion of Normandy. My next combat mission took place on September 26. We were pretty much in control of the skies over Europe by then, and seldom thereafter did we encounter the big air-to-air battles we had known before.

Colonel Hub Zemke was our group commander when we went overseas and had remained so until the fall of 1944. Dave Schilling, who had been the exuberant, gung-ho commander of the 62nd Fighter Squadron, then became the group commander. Dave had a wonderful imagination and complete self-confidence, and was always volunteering us for special missions that were believed to be too difficult or impossible for the bombers.

Once we took a flight of thirty-six P-47s on a medium-level, tight-formation bombing mission to a war factory near Koblenz in Germany. We had radar stations in France and Belgium by that time, and Dave and the radar experts thought that they could direct us to a perfect bomb drop by radar triangulation. All we had to do was fly a tight formation on a straight course, at a fixed speed and a fixed altitude, for about five minutes. That's all a good antiaircraft battery needs. The flak burst so perfectly that it hit in the exact center of our formation. Because we were flying in a diamond formation, there were no planes there, but we got a few holes in our aircraft. We dumped the bombs and headed for home. Another time we tried low-altitude skip-bombing into the mouth of an old mine shaft in the mountains of western Germany, where the enemy was making aircraft parts. That didn't work either, but Dave didn't give up.

He volunteered us to knock out three synthetic oil plants deep in German territory. He planned a daring simultaneous low-level attack with three flights of four ships each. My target was a plant at Leuna, and the Eighth Air Force built a three-foot model of the facility for the flight to study. It had four very large concrete chimneys on one side that were three to four hundred feet high. The only way to skip-bomb the generator, our primary target, was to fly between those stacks. Three times we were scheduled for this attack, and three times the strike was canceled due to bad weather over one or more of the plants. The last time we tried, we had gotten as far as Germany before being recalled. After V-E day it was discovered that the Germans had stretched heavy steel cables between the chimneys at my target. We probably wouldn't have been able to see them in time to turn away four planes flying at full throttle, line abreast at treetop level. To climb over the stacks would have been extremely unhealthy. Intelligence reported 165 antiaircraft guns around the plant. The bad weather that kept us away from those targets on three different occasions was the best bad weather I have ever encountered.

Another of Dave's ideas to shorten the war happened

during the airborne drops in Holland, after we learned that Field Marshall Montgomery was again unable to achieve a breakthrough to relieve his troops. We heard that our airborne troops and paratroopers were desperately low on food, so Dave volunteered to fly a low-level fighter sweep over Holland and drop K rations to them in our external fuel tanks. He scrounged all over England for enough food, while our ground crews cut doors in our big 150-gallon metal tanks. Thirty-six of us set out from England to deliver food to the encircled troops in Holland. We found them, and apparently dropped the tanks in the right location, because word came down the next day that the troops weren't really that hungry. A streamlined wing tank traveling at high speed and filled with five hundred pounds of canned food is just about as dangerous as a heavy artillery shell.

On another bomber escort mission over Germany we found no aerial opposition. After the P-51s relieved us on station, we split up into flights of four and dropped down to hunt for targets of opportunity. I picked out an airfield that turned out to be very heavily defended. As our flight raced across the open field, the sky turned into a Fourth of July fireworks display, but we miraculously escaped to the shelter of some trees on the far side of the field. Several miles past the field we tried to regain our altitude. But each time we were reengaged by antiaircraft fire. I told the flight to stay at treetop level, head west, and we would try to reform over the North Sea. I came upon an embankment heading west with a wide canal on the other side. That embankment made me feel more secure.

Suddenly I realized that I was going to fly a few feet in front of a German gunner in a concrete emplacement on top of the embankment. He had twin machine guns in his little fort, and when he realized that we were going to have our own personal war, he swung them around to engage me. I couldn't turn to engage him without gaining more altitude, and if I did that, he would have a much easier target. Knowing my eight .50-caliber machine guns would sound like an entire army to him, I pressed the trigger and held it down. The German opened fire at me, but just as he did so, he dropped down out of sight in his fortress. As I went by, ten to fifteen feet in front of and below him, my guns were still firing down the canal, not endangering him at all. His two guns were firing straight up at the clouds and not endangering me.

I shot down my last German aircraft on December 26, 1944. While we occasionally found a German fighter plane in the air after that, our targets consisted mainly of enemy planes on the ground, trains, trucks, canal barges, and specially built flak towers (antiaircraft gun emplacements). While these targets may sound quite tame by comparison with aerial combat, they often turned out to be very dangerous.

The airfields had very heavy concentrations of guns, which were ever-increasing as the Germans abandoned fields farther to the west. Truck convoys had their own moving defenses, as did some of the barges. Trains usually had some AA defenses and, toward the end of the war, these were concealed inside ordinary-looking boxcars. As we approached to attack the locomotive, the sides of the fake boxcars would drop to reveal a nest of deadly 88mm antiaircraft guns. While attacking a train, there was also the possibility of hitting an ammunition car and creating a fireball that could reach hundreds of feet into the air above your aircraft.

On March 31, 1945, I completed my second combat tour with an uneventful bomber escort into Germany. The last mission was routine, except for the two ME-262 jet fighters that made a head-on pass through the bombers. We had been told by our ground radar control that they were in the area, but they came on fast, and we had no chance to intercept. After their first attack they made a wide turn miles behind the bomber train and started another brazen attack from the rear, in plain view of our 48 Thunderbolts. Normally, giving away a 5,000-foot advantage (we were that much higher) to an enemy that outnumbers you twenty-four to one would be fatal. As they came back under us for their second attack on the Big Friends, I gave the order to attack. All forty-eight

P-47s dived after them. Even in a near-vertical dive at full power, and with our altitude advantage, we didn't even come close. Their speed in level flight was absolutely amazing to us. How lucky we were that the Germans had only a few ME-262s, and very little fuel for them.

My official combat record included 138 missions. I changed my mind about a military career soon after returning to the United States and returned to banking, but still with a yearning to fly fast aircraft, so I joined the California Air National Guard. I remained a banker and a weekend warrior from 1948 to 1962, flying F-51s, F-86s, and, briefly, the F-102. On June 30, 1962, I retired from the Air Guard as a brigadier general.

FIGHTING EIGHTEEN

Lieutenant Commander Sam Silber's first squadron (VG-27) participated in the invasion of North Africa, then sailed for the South Pacific
in time for aerial combat over the Russells. Silber later assumed
command of VF-18, one of the first F6F Hellcat squadrons. His experience reads like a battle guide to the Pacific war—Rabaul, Tarawa,
Kavieng, Kwajalein, Truk, the Marianas.

My first years in the fleet as an air cadet were very special ones. In addition to becoming adept pilots, we learned how to exercise leadership. This came through our association with the many fine officers with whom we were in constant contact: people such as Jim Flatley, George Anderson, Tom Moorer, Tom Blackburn, Joe Clifton, and one of the finest of them all, Johnny Hyland.

My tour of duty at NAS Opa Locka (Miami) as an instructor in fighter operational training probably contributed more to my abilify as a fighter pilot, instructor, and leader than any previous experience. These abilities were incredibly helpful in organizing, training, disciplining, developing, and coordinating the complex tasks of getting my first wartime squadron, VGF-27, aboard the USS *Suwannee* (a converted oiler) ready for combat operations. The commanding officer was a bit too old for his job and the executive officer a bit too young and inexperienced for his, so it fell upon me as the operations officer to put the squadron together.

Our first mission was the invasion of North Africa in the early part of November 1942. The less said about this "so-called invasion" the better. Never have I participated in a more fouled-up (I hesitate to use the more expressive "F" word) operation. No one seemed to know what was going on—whose side the French were on, what our targets were, or who was supposed to do what to whom. It was a general mess. Nevertheless, we escaped without too much damage to ourselves or the enemy, whoever they were!

The *Suwannee* sailed directly from North Africa to the South Pacific. We were first land-based on Efate, a small island with a very small fighter strip, just south of Espiritu Santo. Later we were sent to a land-based assignment on Guadalcanal (Cactus) for a few very exciting weeks.

It was on April 1, 1943, that our Wildcat squadron had

its first real combat mission. At about 0930 hours, a raid of Japanese planes was intercepted over the Russell Islands (where my brother Bernard was stationed with the Medical Corps) by a group of twenty Wildcats led by VGF-27's Cecil Harris. Harris destroyed his first Zero in that action and later became one of the navy's top aces. Later, at about noon, an assorted group of navy, army, and marine planes intercepted another wave of Japanese planes. Lieutenant Ken Walsh of the USMC, later one of the Corps's leading aces, shot down three Japanese fighters.

My section was directed to 24,000 feet, so we had a great altitude advantage over the incoming fighters, who were 2,000 feet below us. I singled out a straggler flying third in a very loose formation, and with a couple of quick turns got on his tail. He pulled sharply to the right. I found that I could follow him even though I nearly blacked out and my sturdy Wildcat nearly spun out. I started shooting from much too far away, and in spite of the admonition that every good fighter pilot knows about shooting in short bursts, kept my hand tightly wrapped around the trigger until "my" Zero disintegrated. The feeling I had at that moment was an ecstatic combination of an incredible orgasm and immeasurable fear. My guns were completely burned out and absolutely limp, and so was I.

These actions lasted about three hours, and there were about forty Zeros involved. We shot down eighteen of them and lost six of our fighters. It was the first combat experience for almost every American fighter pilot involved, and although many tactical errors were made, as a whole we proved ourselves more than equal to the task. Tokyo reported that their Zeros encountered forty Grummans on the first wave and shot down twenty-four of them. On the second wave the Japanese reported shooting down ten P-38s, twelve F4Fs, and ten F4Us. They were claiming credit for shooting down fifty-six American aircraft while losing only seven of their own. Tokyo Rose reported: "U.S. mass production turned into *mass destruction!*"

I left VGF-27 in late spring 1943 and was given command

of one of the first thirty-six-plane Hellcat squadrons. We were going on the offensive! Nothing I have ever done can measure up to the fierce pride I have in that squadron—Fighting Squadron 18. We were commissioned in late July 1943, and on November 11, 1943, we participated in our first action as part of Air Group 17—an attack on Rabaul. In spite of the fact that my squadron had the shortest training period of any squadron in naval aviation, we acquitted ourselves like seasoned and experienced combat veterans.

We were flying bomber escort, with specific groups of fighters assigned to specific groups of dive-bombers or torpedo planes. I was flying with a group of fighters escorting dive-bombers. As we approached Rabaul, we saw a lot of Japanese fighters, waiting above and all around us. We kept good formation over the dive-bombers and made no attempt to go after the Japanese. The dive-bombers went down after their targets and started their dive through scattered clouds and some rain squalls, and we managed to stay with them. We were making no attempt to strafe ahead of them, so we went into a shallower dive than they did, picking them up as they came out. We did strafe a couple of merchantmen on the way out. The pilots assigned to escort torpedo bombers strafed ahead of them and silenced most of the AA, so the VT could concentrate on their runs. Hits were made on two cruisers, but none of the damned torpedoes exploded.

The four-plane division behind me was engaged by about twenty-four Zekes. By using the offensive and defensive weaving we had practiced in San Diego and Kaneohe, three of them managed to get back okay. The Japanese fighters were lining up and making regular runs on these boys, wobbling their wings, coming right in and making their runs, pulling simultaneous runs—every damned thing. But the three of them managed to stay in there by weaving violently. Weaving never presented a good target to an enemy fighter.

After we landed, the admiral decided to send another strike in the afternoon. We took off at about 1300 hours, and when sixteen of us had gotten off and were up to 4,000 to

5,000 feet, we suddenly saw a couple of Japanese dive-bombers diving on our ships. We had heard vague reports over the radio about bogies, but had no other information. This was probably because one fighter director was trying to control three entire carrier groups of fighters and it was just too much of a job for one man. We shot down most of the dive-bombers that day, either just before they released their bombs, or just afterward. We couldn't get far enough out to do any intercepting, but two other squadrons did and pretty well disorganized the attack group. I shot down two Vals in that fight. My squadron shot down thirty Japanese planes and lost one pilot.

That was a pretty good job for our first "group tactics." The commanding officer of the USS *Bunker Hill,* my carrier, wrote a glowing citation for our squadron after the battle. I am almost as fond of that as I am of the letter of reprimand issued on September 3, 1943. It cites a navy shore patrol report and bans me and my squadron pilots from reentering Mexico (Tijuana). The reprimand came after a particularly raucous night that helped us to become the cohesive squadron that we were in later combat actions.

After a short stay at Espiritu, we went up to Tarawa. We prepared for that in the ready room as much as we could. The group commander pinpointed the target for each division of dive-bombers, torpedo planes, and fighters. We thought that we had pretty well destroyed the place after three days of fighting. There didn't appear to be anything worthwhile on the ground to strafe or bomb. We were amazed when we heard the reports of all the casualties.

During our time around Tarawa, we shot down a number of Bettys. One night just about dusk, eight of us were vectored out, intercepted about sixteen of them approximately seventeen miles from the force, and dived down to attack them. We managed to divert the main attack, and although a couple of them got within the screen, I think most of them were eventually shot down. When making runs on Bettys low over the water, there weren't many choices. About the only thing we were able to do was to make a beam run, allowing ourselves to be sucked astern. You had to forget about the 20mm cannon in the tail. Although a few of our planes were hit by them, only one pilot in the squadron was hit seriously enough to effect a water landing. So we ignored the stinger in the tail.

After Tarawa we stopped at Nauru on our way back to Espiritu Santo and watched the battleships lay a few million pounds of shells on the island. We first went in just before dawn and attempted to strafe planes on the field. We knew they were Japanese aircraft on the field, but couldn't see them until we got down low, and then we couldn't strafe effectively. The torpedo planes came right down behind us, and they pockmarked the runway so that the planes on the field couldn't take off. Just at dawn we were able to see well enough to set afire practically all the planes on the field. We decided after that, it would be much better for the bombers to go in without the fighters, dropping their bombs and incendiaries ahead of us. They could do fairly effective glide-bombing at night, while we couldn't do very effective strafing. That's how we did subsequent similar missions.

On New Year's Day, 1944, while escorting our SB-2C bombers on a second mission over Kavieng, I was able (with the help of my very capable wingman) to shoot down three Japanese Zeros. On our first mission on Christmas Day, the AA had been light and there had been no aerial opposition. This time there were thirty to forty Zeros waiting 5,000 to 10,000 feet above us. They made no attempt to intercept before we got to our targets—two cruisers and two destroyers, ten miles west of the harbor. My wingman, Bob Beedle, and I started our dives with the intention of strafing a destroyer, but decided not to go on when we were down to 4,000 feet and realized that eight Zeros were following us down in the dive. They were on the starboard, in a column at about 6,000 to 7,000 feet. When we were down to 3,000 feet, they initiated an attack on my section leader, and we were able to counter by weaving and making one complete circle.

It was a series of wild, unpredictable maneuvers, both on the part of the hapless Japanese pilots and me. Bob and I were weaving toward each other. It was simple and they were stupid about the whole thing. The Japanese pilots made no attempt to put up any opposition. They just turned away from us and presented nice targets. We were able to shoot down four Zeros between us.

On our next mission over Kavieng a few days later, Bob Beedle and I were attacked by about eight Zeros as we were escorting bombers low over the water. It was during the vulnerable part of our weave maneuver, when we were crossing each other, that Bob was shot down. A few seconds later I heard a tremendous explosion. I had been hit in the left wing flap, and it was completely gone. What I thought was hydraulic fluid all over the cockpit later turned out to be my blood. I avoided further attacks by weaving over the retreating bombers. Finally I managed to land on the carrier without flaps after three attempts!

After that we took part in the Marshalls invasion. We launched our flight of twenty fighters an hour or so before dawn, about 130 miles away from Kwajalein. We were divided into two groups, one high at 20,000 feet and a lower group at 10,000 feet. We got there just before dawn and watched the torpedo planes drop their incendiaries and hundred-pound fragmentation bombs. We stayed at our altitudes until we were sure there wasn't any aerial activity in our vicinity, then strafed the seaplane base and the field. There were one or two planes on the field and quite a number of seaplanes at the seaplane base. All our strafing runs were steep, at high speed, picking a definite target as soon as possible and staying with it. We were satisfied with one burning plane on one pass, and never attempted more than one unless we were sure that the first target had been destroyed. We were also able to strafe quite a number of small ships in the harbor on the way out.

We went into Kwajalein a few more times that day and raised general hell. Then we steamed all night and arrived at

Eniwetok early enough to launch a group of torpedo planes in the same manner as at Kwajalein. We arrived as they were dropping their bombs, and when it was light enough, we assured ourselves that there was no aerial opposition. The planes at 10,000 feet started strafing, while the others stayed fairly high. We caught fifteen Bettys on the ground, two of which were ready to taxi out. We stayed around Eniwetok for about four days, wreaking destruction. We didn't think there was much there when we left, but apparently there were still enough people around to offer slight opposition to the marines when they went ashore.

Later we steamed undisturbed to within a hundred miles of Truk. We launched an hour before dawn and hadn't been gone more than twenty minutes when we found ourselves on the outskirts of the lagoon. As we were assigned high cover, we skirted the lagoon and climbed up to 20,000 or 25,000 feet. Most of the Japanese planes were caught on the ground, and of those who got airborne, approximately seventy-five percent were shot down between zero and 2,000 feet. The defense of Truk was completely disorganized, and few of the enemy aircraft made any real, concentrated attacks. As a result, we were able to maintain air superiority after the first hour and a half. In the afternoon we shot down three Vals that must have come from the field. They were loaded to the gills with bombs, and probably intended to strike at one of the carriers. I don't know what they were thinking, because they had no chance in the world of doing that. Our torpedoes worked at Truk. We stayed there for two days, strafing ships in the harbor and strafing ahead of the torpedo planes and dive-bombers.

After Truk we steamed toward Majuro and then back to Tinian and Saipan for the Washington's Birthday strike. Unfortunately we were picked up the afternoon before we were scheduled to attack, and were harassed that entire night by many twin-engined torpedo planes—Kates, Mavises—everything they had available, including a twin-engined fighter. Everyone expected quite a heavy attack at dawn, but there was no attack at all, just a couple of bombers flying around and one twin-engined fighter that made an attack on the *Yorktown*. It dropped a bomb that didn't hit anything, and managed to get away.

At daybreak my flight of twelve Hellcats was ordered to attack the Tinian airstrips. We climbed through a thick overcast and were blown southward by a strong wind. When my "dead reckoning" indicated that we were near our objective, we descended through the clouds, and at about 6,000 feet, discovered a big airstrip. A couple of fighters were just getting ready to land. They apparently hadn't seen us, and we waited until both of them had their wheels and flaps down before we strafed them. They had just about hit the ground when we polished them off. We made a few more runs on the field and polished off three or four Bettys, some fighters, trucks, and equipment. After our third run we found two Bettys a half mile away, coming in to land, and shot them down before they had wheels and flaps down. We were low on ammunition by then, so we headed back to the *Bunker Hill*. It was not until we were headed back that I realized we had hit Guam and not Tinian!

We were able to get into Tinian again on the last flight that afternoon. There were seventy planes parked on the field—bombers, twin-engined fighters, and various other types. We strafed most of them with the help of a couple of other squadrons. Practically every plane destroyed that day was sitting on the ground. It was hard to figure out why, because they'd had all night and practically all day to do something. We decided that since Tinian was a training station, those boys weren't ready for their "final check."

That about ended our tour. We went back to Pearl Harbor and then returned to the United States.[4]

TURKEY SHOOT

Lieutenant Alexander Vraciu completed three tours of duty in the Pacific. Each time he would request more action. He held the title of top navy ace in the theater for four months, and survived two crash-landings, two bailouts, and five weeks with the Filipino guerrillas.

My first combat assignment was flying F6F Hellcats for five months as wingman to Medal-of-Honor–winner Lieutenant Commander Edward H. "Butch" O'Hare, commanding officer of Fighting Squadron 3 (later changed to 6). It was while flying section lead in Skipper O'Hare's division that I shot down my first enemy aircraft, a Japanese Zero fighter, at Wake Island in October 1943. I got a reconnaissance Betty bomber at Tarawa, and on January 29, 1944, qualified as an ace after downing three more Bettys over Kwajalein. The third bomber was downed after a long pursuit at low level. Only one of my machine guns was firing part-time as the bomber jinked and turned into me as I made passes.

Then came the first strike on Truk atoll on February 16, 1944. That two-day operation began at dawn and was a new and enjoyable experience for the carrier fighter pilots—a fighter sweep by seventy-two Hellcats with no bombers to protect. Three divisions (twelve planes) of VF-6 took off from the Intrepid at 0640 hours to rendezvous with the remainder of the task force fighters. Our primary mission was the destruction of enemy aircraft over the airfields on Moen, Eten, and Param islands. Our strike force approached Truk from the southwest at an altitude of 1,000 feet until we were approximately forty-five miles out, then climbed for our assigned intermediate altitude. We arrived over the atoll at 13,000 feet, just before sunrise, and circled over Moen Island. Enemy planes could be seen on the airfield, including two Bettys that were just taking off. Antiaircraft fire had already commenced, and had found the level of our flight, but the bursts were off to both sides.

The flight leader spiraled down, preparatory to initiating a strafing attack on the Moen airfield. My section was at the tail end of the flight. I remembered Butch O'Hare's wise advice to always look back over my shoulder before commencing a dive, and rubbernecked once again before pushing over. Our first ten fighters were already well into their runs when I spotted a group of enemy fighters 2,000 to 3,000 feet above us and on the port side. They were starting a high-side run on us. The Zeke enemy leader's guns were already firing. I quickly tallyhoed, and turned my section into the attack, getting off bursts at the leader and causing him to break off his attack and head downward. Enemy planes were all around us by then.

Maintaining our speed, we pulled up into a steep chandelle and aileron-rolled down on a Zeke trying to stay on our tail. The Zeke pulled up into a climbing turn and spun out at the top. We started to jump him, but I had to let him dive on down because the other Zekes seemed to be preparing to strike us from above. By scissoring with another Hellcat, we soon worked all the Zekes down to our level or below. From there on the picture completely changed, and we were able to press home the attack. The Japanese pilots weren't reluctant to attack us, but once they were countered, they would dive steeply for the deck or a cloud.

The Hellcat could outmaneuver the Zero at speeds of 250 knots or better, so we began to follow them down. I followed three planes in this manner, two Zeros and one Rufe, setting them all afire. All crashed into the Truk lagoon. As I climbed back to altitude after the last attack, I saw another Zero that was skirting a not-too-thick cloud. I began a pass at him, but he promptly headed for a thicker cloud. We played cat-and-mouse for several minutes, then I climbed into the sun and let him think that I had retired. When I came down on him the last time from five o'clock, he never knew what hit him. His wing tank and cockpit exploded.

An afternoon hop produced no additional air-to-air combat. We had returned to our usual role by escorting a bomber and torpedo strike against enemy shipping that was attempting to escape to the north. At one point our flight strafed a listing enemy cruiser that was dead in the water. That evening the USS *Intrepid* was torpedoed by a Japanese Kate and forced to withdraw from the action. This was Fighting Squadron 6's second carrier torpedoing, and the unit was returned stateside.

I felt that there was still a job to be done and requested continuing combat duty. The navy obliged by assigning me to Fighting Squadron 16 (the "Airdales") aboard the USS *Lexington*. There I participated in the second carrier strike on Truk, on April 29, 1944. The mysticism that had surrounded the atoll in the past was missing this time. We were returning from an escort mission with a morning bomber strike when our flight was attacked by a small group of enemy fighters. We quickly pounced on them and destroyed them at low altitude (where they performed best). It was a no-contest affair after we had them boxed in, and I was fortunate enough to down two Zeroes from the six o'clock position.

The afternoon hop was a little more exciting, and ended with my spending the night on one of our task force destroyers. Out on another mission, I'd been setting up at 9,000 feet for a strafing run on one of the island airfields when my Hellcat was hit by medium AA fire. Part of the flak passed through my cockpit just in front of my face, showering the cockpit with Plexiglas. The hydraulic system was riddled and the landing gear dropped down partway. I aborted the strafing run and was escorted back to the task force by my wingman. Since I was unable to lower the landing gear, I had the choice of parachuting over the fleet or ditching in water alongside one of our DDs (destroyers). I chose the latter option, and after spending the night aboard the destroyer, I was highlined back to the "Lex" the next day. Amazingly, although some Plexiglas had embedded itself in one of my eyes, I never felt it until the middle of the night, following which the ship's doctor deadened the eyeball and scraped out the offending glass.

On June 14 I led a team of Hellcats with five-hundred-pound bombs in an attack on enemy shipping in Tanapag Harbor, Saipan. We made a low-level bombing attack in the face of intense AA fire, and I sank the largest Japanese ship in the harbor, a 6,500-ton merchantman, with a direct hit on the stern at the waterline. I got another kill on June 12, north of Saipan. This time it was another Betty snooper. Those big, fat-bellied, versatile bombers had been my prime preoccupation ever since I was told that one of them had shot down Butch O'Hare in a strange nighttime encounter. We were at 3,000 feet, on a strike against enemy positions on the islands north of Saipan, when I spotted the Betty at 18,000 feet. Despite its altitude advantage, by keeping in its blind spot I was able to overhaul the bomber and shoot it down in flames.

The American task force protecting the Saipan operation was expecting an attack by over four hundred Japanese carrier planes on the morning of June 19, 1944. Bogies were picked up on radar approaching in several large groups, and our carrier fighter aircraft were scrambled to supplement the combat air patrol (CAP) already aloft. I was part of a group of twelve fighters launched from the Lex. The VF-16 skipper, Paul Buie, was leading our three divisions of four planes each. I led the second division of Hellcats. As we were climbing for altitude at full military power, I heard the fighter director officer (FDO) saying, "Vector 250! Climb to 25,000 feet, pronto!"

Overhead, converging contrails of fighters from other carriers were heading in the same direction. The skipper was riding behind a new engine, and after a while he began to steadily pull ahead until he was out of sight. We had seen his wingman drop out. The full-power climb was just too much for his engine, and the propeller had frozen, forcing him to ditch in the water. Luckily he was picked up twelve hours later by a destroyer. My own engine was throwing an increasing film of oil over the windshield, forcing me to ease back slightly on the throttle.

My division stayed with me and two other planes joined us. When I found out that my tired engine would not go into high power, our maximum altitude became 20,000 feet. This limitation was reported to the FDO. All the way up, my wingman, Brockmeyer, while observing radio silence, kept insistently pointing toward my wing. Thinking that he had spotted the enemy, I attempted to turn over the lead to him, but he would only shake his head. Not being able to comprehend what he wanted, I finally shook him off to concentrate on the mission. Later I found out that my wings weren't fully locked. The red safety barrel locks were showing, and that had caused Brock's frantic pointing.

It was all over before our group reached this particular wave of attacking enemy planes. I was ordered to return with my group and orbit over the task force at 20,000 feet. We had barely returned when the FDO directed us to Vector 265 degrees. There was something in his voice that indicated that we had a good one on the string. The bogies were seventy-five miles away when reported, and we headed out, hoping to meet them halfway. I saw two other groups of Hellcats converging from the starboard side—four in one group, three in the other.

About twenty-five miles out I tallyhoed three bogies and closed toward them. In the back of my mind I remembered the seriousness in the fighter director's voice and figured there had to be more than three enemy planes. Spot-gazing intently, I suddenly picked out a large, rambling mass of at least fifty planes 2,000 feet below us on the port side. My adrenaline flow hit high C. They were about thirty-five miles from our ships and heading in fast. I remember quickly thinking that this could develop into a once-in-a-lifetime fighter pilot's dream. Then, a little bit puzzled and suspicious, I looked around for the fighter cover that normally would be overhead. But there did not seem to be any top cover. By this time we were in a perfect position for a high-side run. Giving a slight rock of my wings, I began a run on the nearest in-board straggler, a Judy dive-bomber.

I was peripherally conscious of another Hellcat that seemed to have designs on the same Japanese. He was too close for comfort, almost blindsided, so I aborted my run. There were enough cookies on this plate for everyone. I streaked underneath the Japanese formation and got a good look at the planes for the first time. They were Judys, Jills, and Zeroes. I radioed an amplified report, pulled up and over, and picked out another Judy on the edge of the formation. It was doing some mild maneuvering, and the rear gunner was squirting away as I came down from the stern. I worked in close, and gave him a burst. He caught fire and headed down to the sea, trailing a long plume of smoke.

I pulled up again and found two more Judys flying in loose wing. I came in from the rear and sent one down, burning. Dipping the Hellcat's wing, I slid over on the one slightly ahead and got it on the same pass. It caught fire and I could see the rear gunner still peppering away at me as he disappeared in an increasing downward arc. For a split second I felt sorry for the little bastard.

That made three down, and we were getting closer to the fleet. The enemy planes had been pretty well chopped up, but a substantial number still remained. It didn't look like we would score a grand slam, and I reported this information back to base. The sky was full of smoke and pieces of planes, and we were trying to ride herd on the remaining attacking planes to keep them from scattering. Another meatball broke formation up ahead, and I slid over onto his tail, again working in close because of my oil-smeared windshield. I gave him a short burst, and that was enough. It went right into the sweet spot at the root of his wing tanks. The pilot or the control cables must have been hit also, because the burning plane twisted crazily out of control.

In spite of our efforts, the Jills were descending to begin their torpedo runs, and the remaining Judys were at the point of peeling off to go down with their bombs. I headed for a group of three Judys in a long column. By the time I had reached the tail-ender, we were almost over the outer destroyer screen but still fairly high. The first Judy was about to begin his dive, and as he started to nose over, I noticed a black puff in the sky beside him. Our five-inchers were opening up. Foolishly I overtook the nearest Judy. It seemed that I scarcely touched the gun trigger when his engine started coming to pieces. The plane started smoking, then torching alternately off and on, as it disappeared below.

The next one was about one-fifth of the way down in his dive, apparently trying for one of the destroyers, when I caught up with him. Another short burst produced astonishing results. He blew up with a tremendous explosion, right in front of my face. I must have hit his bomb. I had seen planes blow up before, but never like that. I yanked up sharply to avoid the scattered pieces and flying hot stuff, then radioed, "Splash number six. There's one more ahead and he's diving on a BB. But I don't think he'll make it."

Hardly had the words left my mouth when the Judy caught the direct hit that forever removed it from the war. He had run into a solid curtain of steel from the battle wagon. I looked around at that point and could see only Hellcats in the sky around me. Behind us was a thirty-five-mile-long pattern of flaming oil slicks on the water. This battle became known as the "Marianas turkey shoot." Because of my oil-stained windshield and the need to work in close, I later found out that I had used only 360 rounds of ammunition to shoot down six enemy aircraft in less than eight minutes.

The following day I shot down a Zero, my last enemy kill, and damaged another. We were flying escort for bomber and torpedo planes on a record, over three-hundred-mile-long-range strike against the Japanese fleet in the First Battle of the Philippine Sea. We returned from the strike and landed aboard the carrier in total darkness. That final victory made me the navy's top ace for a four-month period. I was awarded the Navy Cross for my actions from June 12 through June 20, 1944.

Fighting Squadron 16 returned to the United States. I talked my way back into combat several months later, after learning that I was being lined up for a war bond tour. My luck ran out early this time. On December 14, 1944, I was shot down by antiaircraft fire on my second mission while strafing near Clark Field in the Philippines. I parachuted to safety and spent the next five weeks with the USAFFE guerrillas. They gave me the honorary rank of brevet major. For the final week of this episode I found myself in command of 180 men, dodging the Japanese to meet General MacArthur's advancing troops. I marched into an American camp, sporting a Luger and carrying a Japanese sword.

Because I was forced to return home due to regulations, I was unable to make the first Tokyo raid. After surviving service on six carriers (two of which were torpedoed), two ditchings, and two parachute jumps, and becoming known as "Grumman's best customer," my war was over. I had shot down nineteen enemy aircraft and destroyed twenty-one more on the ground. I spent the last months of the war as a test pilot at the Naval Air Test Center, Patuxent River, Maryland, helping evaluate the tactical performance of U.S. and enemy aircraft.

BIG JOHN

Colonel John Lowell told the army that he believed they would like to have him as a fighter pilot. Subsequent events proved how true that statement was. In a wartime career as a test pilot, squadron commander and group commander, he managed, among many other things, to develop an effective P-39 recovery technique and a successful P-38 "clover-leaf" attack tactic, sink Japanese minisubs, duel one of Germany's top aces, and shoot down an ME-262.

When the 360th Fighter Group transitioned from P-39s to P-38s, we began standing alert for immediate takeoff in defense of the San Francisco area. One afternoon my flight of four was scrambled and vectored to the Golden Gate area, then out to sea. The cloud base was low, just a little below the tops of the two tall pillars of the Golden Gate Bridge. I led the flight under the Bay Bridge, then under the Golden Gate Bridge, and then out to sea, where we were directed to four Japanese two-man subs. We surprised them and sank three of the subs with the 37mm cannon in the noses of our early P-38s (the later models used against the Germans had six .50-caliber machine guns in the nose).

After this first exciting contact with the enemy, I got the flight together, turned on wingtip lights, and signaled for "tight formation" (as usual when we did tight-formation aerobatics). We headed back to the Golden Gate Bridge from twenty miles out to sea, under a cloud base at 2,000 feet that sloped down to the top pillars of the bridge. Since my flight had done lots of tight-formation aerobatics with me, and because we had just sunk three Japanese minisubs, I decided to fly under the Golden Gate Bridge. This was authorized on a scramble mission. I suddenly decided to pull up in a four-ship tight-formation loop on instruments around the bridge. I remember thinking at the top of the loop: "If I do too tight a loop, we'll hit the bridge. If I do too loose a loop, we'll be in the water." So I kept the typical smooth "feel," and we came out of the loop perfectly. We continued on to fly under the Bay Bridge, then landed at Mills Field (now San Francisco International Airport).

About two hours later I received a call at squadron headquarters from General Kepner's headquarters in Oakland, telling me to report to the general. When I arrived there, he ate me out viciously, not even mentioning my flight's victories.

Seventeen "head-to-tail" car accidents had occurred on the Golden Gate Bridge, and four people were hospitalized. He told me: "If one of them dies, I'll bust you to a private, transfer you to the infantry, and see to it that you are on the front lines in a few days. Now get out of here!" I had been promoted to captain eleven months after graduating from flying school, mainly because of the large amount of time I had amassed in fighter aircraft at Wright Field. Ironically General Kepner preceded me to Europe, where he promoted me to major, lieutenant colonel, and colonel by the end of the war.

When the 364th Fighter Group was activated in 1943, the group commander, Colonel Fred Grambo, selected me to be the commander of the 384th Fighter Squadron. In late '43 the fighter group was trained in P-38s in the Ontario-Oxnard-Van Nuys area. Then we were assigned to the Eighth Air Force in England. We traveled via train to New York, sailed across the Atlantic on the *Queen Mary,* and arrived at Honington RAF Base in East Anglia. Our first missions were flown by our group commander, deputy CO, and each squadron commander and operations officer, all with the nearby 20th Fighter Group.

I can never forget my first combat mission with the 20th Fighter Group. After crossing the North Sea and flying over Holland, Freddie Grambo was hit by high-altitude flak. One engine caught fire and he went straight down to a crash. Within about thirty minutes we approached a rendezvous with a long string of B-17 bombers. A B-17 went down in flames and about eight men floated down on parachutes. An ME-109 closed in on a parachutist and blasted him to pieces, and I watched the chute floating in the air without any weight aboard. Two other Messerschmitts were shooting parachutists. I was above them by then, because I had followed Grambo down for several thousand feet after he was hit, telling him to bail out, but he must have been unconscious. That separated me from the squadron I was flying with. By radio and known direction I was trying to rejoin them when the Germans started shooting bomber crewmen.

This affected my attitude *instantly, violently,* and *permanently!* I went about half nuts, and could think only about destroying those bastards and butchers. Quickly I got on the tail of an ME-109 that was lining up on another parachute. I waited until I got in close and gave him a long burst from six .50 cals. He blew up like a little bomb. I spotted another 109, chased it down to the deck, got into a tight Lufbery, and began the clover-leaf attack that I had used successfully so many times in mock combat against friendly adversaries from the army air corps, navy and marines. I destroyed him rather quickly. I got into the area of the other P-38s, but could not identify any 20th Fighter Group aircraft. When the other P-38s left the area for home, I followed them.

On my second mission our squadron got into a tough, aggressive group of ME-109s. It seemed that the Germans were constantly attacking our entire P-38 group from above and "out of the sun." Only by being carefully defensive, and then quickly becoming aggressive, did we begin to even the odds with the attackers from above. I worked with my wingman for mutual defense, but when a split-second opportunity showed that I could attack the enemy, the odds became closer to even, based on relative speed, position, aircraft capability, and, particularly, pilot capability. I was fortunate enough to surprise and shoot down one ME-109 below me. The pilot had been concentrating on a P-38 that was not yet in a defensive maneuver. Later I decided that my fuel was low enough for me to set course for England. Suddenly I was attacked from above and behind.

I saw the ME-109 coming from high above at seven o'clock. I broke left at the crucial time and maneuvered to tail him as he screamed to the deck. I kept him in sight, but the P-38 couldn't outdive a Messerschmitt (or anything else) because of compressability. As he leveled out on the deck and saw me following, he turned around to fight. I fired head on and got several strikes. As I passed above and on his right, he turned ninety degrees, slowed down, and bailed out. Smoke trailed behind his plane as it plunged to the ground. I left the German pilot alone as he floated down. I couldn't bring myself to shoot a man in a parachute.

On my third mission I experienced a high-altitude attack on my P-38 by an FW-190. My evasive tactics were fortunately effective, and I finally tangled with him at 16,000 feet. This plane (and/or pilot) was no match for me and my fighter. It was a surprisingly easy victory. The rest of the mission was devoid of enemy sightings.

Flying our early missions out of Honington had its highs and lows—its victories and losses. As I look back, it is obvious that the Germans had mastery of the skies over Germany, Holland, and France in early 1944. The 364th entered combat with seventy-five combat pilots. Thirteen were left after thirteen weeks, and all thirteen finished their first tours. Twelve of them volunteered for a second tour and they all made it. As replacement pilots arrived, I always insisted that each of them fly against me in mock combat so that I could evaluate his combat skills. I sent seven pilots home due to their inability to achieve a reasonable degree of excellence in the P-38.

Freddie Grambo's replacement, the original deputy group CO, was a total failure. I asked General Anderson, the 67th Fighter Wing commander, to relieve him of any combat missions because of his lack of leadership ability. Anderson immediately sent him back to the States. Brad McManus, 383rd Squadron commander, and I led most of the missions before a new group commander, Colonel Roy Osborn, was appointed.

On one such mission to southern France, I led the group on a fighter-bomber strike. Following a successful delivery of our bombs on the target, I spotted two ME-109s and had a running speed chase with one of them. My element leader shot down the other German fighter. My ME-109 led me over central Paris before I caught him. He set up a tight Lufbery around the Eiffel Tower; the pilot was too low to bail out even if he tried it against those six .50 cals in the P-38's nose.

Fortunately I got good strikes on him by using my clover-leaf tactics. He lost power and was smoking badly as he aimed the 109 down a street near the Eiffel Tower. The crash wiped out many cars. The plane burst into flames. I got good film on that one.

Many times the gun-camera film was undistinguishable because the camera was located in the P-38's nose, and the six .50-caliber guns vibrated it so badly that it was often impossible to verify a victory, and it became a "probable." The miracle of this Eiffel Tower victory came twenty years later when I met Vincent LaRolle of Paris. He had witnessed the fight and the crash in the street in front of the building from which he was watching. He and I became business associates in 1963 in a Paris company which we created in the field of industrialized housing.

Shortly thereafter, General Anderson sent me to lead the 479th Fighter Group on its first eight P-38 combat missions. This was the last P-38 group to become operational in the ETO before all such groups were converted to P-51s. The P-51 had longer range, "identity" advantage, and the ability to high-speed dive better than any Allied or enemy aircraft (until the ME-262 arrived in '45). The 479th did well, but soon lost their group CO. As a result, the remarkable P-47 ace from the 56th Group, Colonel Hub Zemke (see "Mayhem—P-38 Style," page 189), was given command.

Hub and I struck up a recurring acquaintance after missions, and when we had no missions scheduled on a particular day. Soon after we met he told me of a creative plan of aggressively "sweeping" enemy territory, looking for enemy planes below 10,000 feet. He called it the "Zemke fan." I worked with him on the details, and the 479th and 364th both used it very successfully. The plan was to spread a squadron out line-abreast with quite a distance between planes, sufficient that upon attack from above and rear each P-38 could turn into each other to cover each other's tail. Primarily the Zemke fan gave us a massive horizontal spread to search for enemy planes. Whenever they were spotted, the identity call of the spotting P-38 defined exactly where they were, and the flight, section, or entire squadron was close at hand to engage them. Victories in both groups accelerated as a result of this tactic.

Unfortunately, shortly after both our groups changed to P-51s, Hub was involved in a high-altitude instrument condition. His flight "spun out" with full external tanks. He bailed out and was a POW for the last few months of the war.

I remember a rough P-38 mission in very bad weather conditions, deep into Germany east of Berlin. Our mission was to strafe German airfields. The bombers did not fly that day, and we were at 30,000 feet when we identified Berlin from the intense ack-ack. We let down on instruments and broke out at the planned spot, computed from when we knew that we were over the German capital. I had the second section of my squadron (two flights) stay up to cover our attack on an airfield northeast of the city. We made a coordinated strafing pass from east to west on at least fifty parked fighters. Our attack did not surprise the Germans.

My wingman, a college light heavyweight boxing champion, was hit in the supercharger on his right engine. It disintegrated and cut off the cockpit at waist level, killing the pilot instantly. I happened to look back over my shoulder as the upper half of the cockpit and the pilot's body came off. His plane rolled to the right, climbed a little, and crashed into a steeple. The other two pilots in my flight were also shot down. My own plane was badly damaged from groundfire, primarily in the tail and the right engine. I feathered the right prop and stayed at treetop level all the way back across the continent and the North Sea, landing "wheels down" at Honington.

Eight of us had shot up over twenty parked German fighters, but we lost three planes and three men. I had ordered the rest of the group to abort any attack due to the intensity of the German antiaircraft defense. The mission was not a total loss, because our pilots strafed three German trains west of Berlin. An inspection of my plane after landing showed that the right rear fuselage at the horizontal stabilizer had been blown apart by a 20mm shell, but the control cables had remained intact and kept the stabilizer from tearing off because of my very slow return speed. Fortunately no enemy aircraft spotted me as I sneaked back across the Channel.

Our group received several P-38Ls just before the P-51s arrived. This latest "Lightning" had dive flaps under the wings, improved power, and a gun camera located away from the nose. On a day that we were "stood down" (no missions), General Eisenhower arranged for one of the top English aces, Wing Commander Donaldson, to come to Honington and show us slides of English Spitfires that had been equipped with external tanks like U.S. fighters. Those tanks allowed Spitfires to penetrate deep into Germany. Most of the U.S. pilots didn't know about the Spit's long range, and some Spitfires had been fired upon before American pilots realized that their insignia was the Royal Air Force circle and not a German swastika. ME-109s, P-51s, and Spitfires were not easily distinguishable from one another until close enough to "make combat."

All 364th Fighter Group pilots attended Donaldson's slide picture presentation in our briefing room. When he was finished, he described the new Spitfire XV he had flown to our base. It had a five-bladed prop, a bigger engine, and improved firepower. Then he said, "If one of you bloody bastards has enough guts, I'll fly mock combat above your field and show you how easily this Spit XV can whip your best pilot's ass."

The entire group started clapping and hollered, "Big John! Big John!"

That was me, so I asked him, "What is your fuel load?"

He replied, "Half petrol."

"What is your combat load?"

He said, "No ammo."

We agreed to cross over the field at 5,000 feet, then anything goes. I took off in a new P-38L after my crew chief had removed the ammo and put back the minimum counterbalance, dropped the external tanks, and sucked out half the internal fuel. I climbed very high, so that as I dived down to cross over the field at 5,000 feet, I would be close to 600 mph. When Donaldson and I crossed, I zoomed straight up while watching him try to get on my tail. When he did a wingover from loss of speed, I was several thousand feet above him, so I quickly got on his tail. Naturally he turned into a full-power right Lufbery as I closed in. I frustrated that with my clover-leaf, and if we'd had "hot guns," he would have been shot down. He came over the field with me on his tail and cut throttle, dropped flaps, and split-Sed from about 1,000 feet. I followed him with the new flaps, banked only about forty-five degrees, but still dropped below the treetops.

The men of the 364th were watching this fight and saw me go out of sight below the treetops. Several of them told me later that they thought that I would crash. But they were wrong! All I had to do was move over behind his Spit XV again. He was apparently surprised. He had stated at our briefing that he would land after our fight to explain the superior capabilities of his Spit XV, but he ignored that promise and flew back to his base. I was most pleased with the reception I got upon landing. There are several pilots at our 364th Fighter Group reunions that witnessed that fight. One of them lives near my home in the Denver area.

One of our last P-38 missions was a flight to protect bombers on a mission near Berlin. My squadron was flying top cover. We were attacked from above, out of the sun, by sixteen long-nosed FW-190s. I was alerted by a flight leader in our squadron. I saw a flight of four Focke-Wulfs coming in from too high to effectively fire on my flight, so I quickly slowed the flight as we opened up laterally for a defensive break and a head-on attack that the Germans never wanted when they were fighting P-38s. The lead German flight passed very close over me with throttles back, trying to slow down.

I looked up at a German plane. The pilot was looking down at me as he eased ahead and close above me into sure death, unless he could take violent evasive action. He split-

Sed and I followed him. He nearly got out of sight because the P-38 high-speed compressability problem kept me from staying with him in a vertical dive. I stayed out of trouble by doing a vertical barrel-roll to pull several G forces and keep my speed under control. Finally he turned to find me, and I cut across to close with him. Then the fight started.

He was a fantastic, wild, talented pilot who pulled all the tricks I had ever seen. But finally I got into a tight Lufbery with him and used my clover-leaf surprise to get a few strikes. None of them harmed his power unit. The long-nosed FW-190 had methyl injection that was usable for ten-second spurts. Then a pilot had to quit using it for a while, because the twenty-six percent added boost to the engine would burn it up if used too long. This pilot used his methyl injection very advantageously to keep me from shooting him down. When his methyl was gone, he dived to the deck and dropped into a tar pit that was about five hundred feet deep and wide enough to fly a fighter in a tight turn. I got a few more strikes on him. A portion of his vertical stabilizer and one wingtip flew off. Unfortunately I was getting low on gas and had to break combat and head for the North Sea and England. After two more circles in the pit I pulled up and flew away to the west. I looked back over my shoulder to see the FW-190 going the opposite way, waggling his wings as if to say, "I'll see you tomorrow and we'll go at it again."

A few years ago the American Fighter Aces had their annual reunion at Maxwell AFB near Montgomery, Alabama. The base commander invited five of the top living German aces. The first day, I arrived in a large hall where over one hundred Maxwell and AFA officers were gathered. Ace Gabreski, the highest-scoring living USAF ace, who is a friend and a man that I admire to the hilt, was talking with the German aces, along with several other U.S. aces. One subject was the German attitude and tactics relating to the P-38. Gabby saw me come in the opposite side of the room, waved, and hollered for me to come over. He introduced me as the highest-scoring P-38 ace in Europe.

When I shook hands with German General Adolf Galland (over three hundred victories), I said, "Adolf, did you ever shoot down a P-38?"

He said, "Yah. I shoot down eight."

Then I asked him if any of his pilots told him about a fight in a long-nosed FW-190 in late '44, against a P-38 that wound up in a huge pit with water and two crashed P-38s in the bottom. I described what had happened and the strikes I got on the long-nosed 190, then told him that when I ran low on gas and had to leave, the German pilot waggled his wings as he flew away in the opposite direction. I was using my hands and looking down as I talked and wasn't watching General Galland. When I looked up, he was pale white.

He said, "You son of a bitch! You dom neer keel me dat day!"

Holy mackeral! All the pilots that heard our conversation bellowed their surprise, including me. Adolf wouldn't let me out of his sight for the rest of the day, asking me how I got the P-38 to do what I explained was my clover-leaf in a tight Lufbery "fight-to-death" tactic. He wanted to know how I trained our pilots and had many other questions about tactics.

Colonel Osborn (Ozzie) led us on many missions after he took over the 364th Fighter Group. My 384th Squadron operations officer was Major Roy E. Spradlin. I considered Sprad's excellence as a fighter pilot the equal of mine. He did such a masterful job of leadership in our many months of combat that he always led my squadron when I was leading the group. He came closer to beating me in individual mock combat than any other pilot I ever fought. A super pilot in the 383rd was Major George Ceuleers. Neither he nor Spradlin ever whipped me, but both came close on occasion.

On one mission Colonel Osborn had three FW-190s close to shooting him down, but Sprad shot them off Ozzie's tail and destroyed all three. This allowed Osborn to get back close to the field in his badly shot-up plane and successfully bail out. Unfortunately Sprad couldn't handle the heavy odds against him. His plane was shot down. He bailed out and spent the rest of the war as a POW. I located him after V-E day and got him assigned to Williams Field, Arizona, and got him checked out in P-80s. He soon finished his military tour and returned with his beautiful wife, Mabel, to Everett, Washington.

Later, Colonel Gene Roberts came from the 67th Wing and took command of the 364th Fighter Group until V-E day. He did an excellent job as commander of our group, which had by then been unofficially designated "Every man a tiger— no pussycats in this outfit."

Major George Ceuleers shot down four enemy fighters on one mission. He and Ernie Bankey were rough competitors with me in our efforts to wind up with the top number of victories in the 364th by war's end. Colonel Ceuleers stayed in the air force and completed a twenty-year tour.

One of my missions in a P-51 took us southeast of Berlin to cover B-17 bombers. The long-nosed Focke-Wulfs were very active that day. My flight tangled with several of them that didn't have the altitude, speed, or surprise advantage. I wound up on the tail of a "190" that tried to dive away from me at 21,000 feet. I was able to stay close enough in a vertical power-dive to continue to get occasional strikes on him. He did a large barrel-roll while going straight down. Our speed had reached the maximum I was willing to risk, and he was still going straight down. Finally I decided that it was the last moment I could recover at my altitude and speed. So I cut my throttle and pulled out just above a high-speed stall. I barely did pull out of my dive and leveled out at about fifty feet, right in the middle of the German Penemunde air base.

I looked over my left shoulder and saw the FW-190 go straight into the ground. I must have killed the pilot, because he had made no attempt to pull out of the dive. I had lost sight of my wingman when I was about halfway down in that vertical dive. He made it back to Honington safely and later told me that I and the FW-190 had just "disappeared going straight down." As I streaked across in front of the German hangars, I saw several ME-163 rocket fighters and blasted three of them.

Several months before V-E day, the 364th was ordered to fly a deep-penetration low-level attack mission far east of Berlin. The total time from takeoff to landing was a little over seven hours. I was group leader that day. As we were in a spread formation going north, my far eastern plane called, "Bogies at three o'clock." It was a formation of sixteen Russian Yak-9 fighters flying the same "four finger per flight, four flights per group" formation as my squadron was. The other two 364th Fighter Group squadrons were farther west and not within sight of the Russians. I alerted my squadron to closely watch the Russians as they flew parallel and slightly above us. Gradually the Russians eased over behind my far easterly flight and cruised for about three minutes in that position. Suddenly the lead Russian fighter opened fire on the number-four man in the most easterly flight. We immediately broke into the Russian formation and they dispersed. I shot down one Yak and my squadron mates shot down two more.

When I reassembled the squadron, I learned that the number-four pilot had been hit badly in the right foot. I talked him into using his belt as a tourniquet, and stayed with him all the way back over the North Sea, until we landed safely at Honington. The poor guy was hospitalized, lost a portion of his foot, and was crippled thereafter. No other contact was made by the 364th with the Russians at any time. I reported the incident to the 67th Wing commander for his knowledge, but there was no other written report. The wing commander told me that he sent the information to the commanding general of Army Air Corps, ETO, and was advised that our action was "totally correct and without blame, and should be kept confidential at all times."

In the spring of 1945, while on a P-51 mission to cover bombers, I witnessed an ME-262 jet fighter perform the most devastating attack on our B-17 bombers that I had ever seen. A single ME-262 would climb high above the bombers (and our fighter escort) to wait until the bombers turned at their designated "initial point" (IP). The IP was the signal to all bombardiers to arm their bombs. Then the pilot had time to line up on the final bombing run and drop the bombs. When the bombers turned at the IP, the ME-262 would dive in a head-on attack with 20mm-cannon fire spread out to hit and detonate just one armed bomb. This would blow up several B-17s in the close formation. On that particular day the German jet made a pass that apparently blew up several B-17s before they dropped their bombs. One ME-262 killed ten men per plane on six or eight bombers in just one passby. Then it pulled up high and fast and set course for home.

I swore to myself that I would track and destroy that 262 if it was the last thing I ever did. If only I could keep him in sight. I pulled away from the squadron as they continued flying cover for the bombers, then kept the enemy jet in sight as I pushed full throttle with the nose down a little bit, knowing that the 262 had only forty-two minutes endurance from start-up to dead stick (out of fuel) landing. He became a tiny black speck against the sky, and I almost lost sight of him. Then the speck got bigger, and I knew that he had slowed down and begun to lose altitude.

I cut across to gain speed, heading for what appeared to be his ground destination. By cutting across at about a twenty-five-percent dive, I began to see his plane clearly. I finally caught up with him when he had already started to turn on the base leg of his landing approach at his airfield. His wheels were down, so I closed in and fired viciously from close behind him, getting many strikes and watching pieces of his plane come off, including the canopy. But there was no fire, smoke, or explosion. On final approach the 262 hit the edge of the runway hard and bounced off the ground (because his speed was still enough). The plane rolled over and crashed upside down on the runway.

Here I was at about 150 mph over a heavily defended German base. The antiaircraft defense had been holding its fire to avoid hitting their own plane along with me, but now all hell broke loose. The crossfire shot off my canopy and shot up all my instruments. There were numerous hits on the armor plate behind me, and the top four inches of my joy stick were chopped off. Fortunately I was holding it farther down. Only the help of "God—my copilot" kept me from being hit bodily, or being incinerated from the hits in my self-sealing gas tanks, or having the engine quit from the hits it received. Not one bullet hit the oil cooler radiator just below the cockpit. A hit there would have stopped the engine.

I stayed just above the ground, zigzagging violently, often below the treetops. My engine kept running; I stayed away from congested areas and navigated by the sun to "go west." Miraculously I found the Zuider Zee and followed the coast-line just out to sea at about two hundred feet, until I could cross over the narrow straits to England. I crash-landed at Manston on the English coast, unscratched and very thankful to be alive. I was flown to Honington and immediately went to the officers club to get cleaned up for supper.

Next day my great crew chief, Master Sergeant Joe Jennings, came into my headquarters office and said, "Colonel, come with me in the jeep to see the holes in Penny III." (My P-51 was named after my wife, Penny.) "I have painted red on each hole."

We flew down to Manston in one of our base C-47s. There were 147 holes or bullet damage scars in the armor plate, seventeen in the propeller, nine in the gas tanks with no explosion (apparently because the self-sealing material prevented "hot bullets" from causing one), and twenty-nine scars on the side of the engine that had somehow caused no electrical damage. There were no holes in the oil cooler radiator, although it had been badly damaged.

Ironically no gun camera record or other pilot witness gave me a "victory"—only a "probable." But one thing I will always remember is that an ME-262 pilot killed many Americans in one head-on attack and lost his life to one P-51 tail-on attack inside the shelter of his own base.

Adolf Galland told me that over eighteen hundred ME-262s were assembled and waiting for jet engines at the end of the war. The engines were waiting for the ball bearings that our bombers had destroyed at Schweinfurt, thank God! Adolf said that over one hundred German pilots had been checked out in 262s by V-E day. Witnessing a head-on jet fighter attack that was so successful against our bombers at the crucial time when the bombs were armed caused me to realize how close the ME-262s may have come to changing the outcome of the European conflict.

I finished the war with 157 combat missions. On V-E day plus one I flew to the Zuider Zee area to get to Geithoorn, where Colonel Fred Grambo had crashed on our first World War II combat mission. I met the burgomaster's wife on arrival, and she told me the following story:

Grambo crashed in a large canal at Geithoorn near the Zuider Zee. The German commander in the area ordered two of his guards to use two Dutch divers to pull the body from the wrecked P-38. While still underwater, one diver found a packet of papers in the zipper pocket on the lower leg of Grambo's flight suit. The diver hid the packet under his pants. They buried Colonel Grambo in the Geithoorn churchyard. Immediately the natives began putting flowers on his grave each night. The German commander put a twenty-four-hour guard at the gravesite. Soon the body was dug up and moved a half mile out of town. Flowers began to show up every night at the new gravesite. The twenty-four-hour guard was again maintained.

The Dutch diver had dried the packet (a detailed typewritten list) and given it to the Geithoorn burgomaster, who hid the papers on his office wall (under identical wallpaper) that same night. The diver made love to his young sweetheart and told her about "the list." She in turn was later wooed by the German CO and told him about it. The German commander quickly called all inhabitants to a town meeting under guard and threatened to kill an eighteen-year-old native girl if "the list" wasn't turned over to him within twenty-four hours. The burgomaster left town and joined the Underground in case the diver should expose him. The deadline arrived, but no "list" was produced. Instead of shooting the girl, the German commander and his butcher boys cut off her right hand. She survived with the help of a local doctor, and the Underground later got a prosthesis from London. The burgomaster's wife introduced me to that beautiful young girl with her right hand cut off at the wrist.

We were still talking about noon when the burgomaster walked into town with two other men of Geithoorn. All three of them had joined the Underground, had been caught by the Germans and imprisoned, and had escaped to return home that very day. There was a mad scramble by the townsfolk to greet them. Soon the burgomaster's wife brought him to see me at their home. He tore off the wallpaper in his home office and handed me "the list"—names, serial numbers, grades, home addresses, phone numbers, names of wives and children of all 364th Fighter Group pilots. What a tool it would have been for the Germans to use to threaten our fighter pilots who became POWs! I took "the list" back to Honington, wrote a full report, and sent it to Wing headquarters. Then I wrote a long letter to Fred's wife, Dorie Grambo.

Shortly after the war ended I was sent to the Pentagon for assignment as the first military test pilot on the new P-80 jet fighter. I spent most of the first fifty hours flying the P-80 out of the Lockheed factory at Burbank. Later I was assigned to Williams Field, Arizona, to command the USAF Jet Fighter Transition School. During those days at the end of 1945, Major Dick Bong was sent to me for transition training. He acquired about twenty hours of flight time in the new fighter at the factory. One day I was in front of the operations shack at the Lockheed factory in Burbank with Johnson, the P-80 creative engineer, when we saw Bong take off in a P-80. Just after he was airborne, heading south toward Burbank, we saw a massive burst of flame come out of his tail cone, and then no flame at all. A flame-out! He guided his P-80 down a street in Burbank, released his canopy, jumped out, went straight through the roof of a house, and was killed instantly. The jet wiped out several cars but did not kill anyone else.

The obvious cause of the crash was his habit of pulling back on the throttle just after takeoff. We always did this in the P-38, and he had become the all-time top U.S. ace while flying that fighter in the Far East theater. He had realized that this habit was not correct for a jet engine and, apparently, had jammed the throttle forward, thrusting the flame out of the tail. He was too low for an "air start." I did the same thing once while practicing landing approach and go-around at 15,000 feet, but I had enough altitude for an air start. The lack of aneroid engine acceleration fuel control killed that wonderful, "best of all" fighter pilot. An aneroid control that allowed only safe acceleration of fuel to the engine solved this problem for all future jets.

The P-80 that blew Miles Burcham to bits at Walker Air Force Base (then Murock Dry Lake), and the three P-80s brought to England before the war ended all had the problem of fuel igniting ahead of engine combustion. The three P-80s in England had been destroyed by this problem. It happened this way. Several of the top aces in ETO volunteered to fly the P-80 against the Germans. I wound up number five on the list, until the engine on the first P-80 flown in England caught fire, and the pilot bailed out and was seriously injured. Then I was number three on the list. The second P-80 caught fire at low altitude. Another pilot bailed out and was seriously injured. Then I was volunteer number two. The third jet caught fire on takeoff. The pilot cut the engine, folded the gear, slid off the end of the runway, and was badly burned. Now I was number one. V-E day came shortly thereafter. This may have had some impact on my being chosen as the first military test pilot to fly the P-80.

Some of my scariest moments at Williams Field came while I was checking out senior USAF officers in the P-80, mainly because, on the landing approach with throttle back, the jet maintained a glide ratio far greater than a fighter plane with a propeller.

One day while commanding the Transition School, I was at 26,000 feet above Kingman, Arizona. I noticed a sudden loss of power, looked over my right shoulder to the skin around the jet engine behind me, and saw a jet hole about eight inches in diameter, blowing flame out at ninety degrees to the motion of the plane. The hole was growing fast! I cut off the engine, jettisoned the canopy, and was ready to bail out when I looked at the hole again. It had stopped burning and growing, so I radioed the tower at Williams Field and said I was coming in "dead stick." Have the fire equipment ready. Having plenty of altitude, I circled the field once and came in to a normal landing.

I stopped at the end of the runway and climbed out on the wing at about the same time that a fire truck arrived and sprayed foam massively over me and the plane. I slid off the wing, fell to the runway, and sprained my ankle. Ironically that was the only injury I had in the war. Three months later I had coccidiomicosis (Valley Fever), which became tuberculosis from breathing the foam. It kept me coughing for ten days, then I was sent to the TB ward in Fitzsimmons Hospital in Denver. There I was told that I could never fly again.

While I was there I received my appointment as a permanent USAF lieutenant colonel (I had been promoted to colonel at age twenty-six), but turned down this long-term dream because I would not be able to fly again. However, I continued to try to get back on flight status. About one year after I left Fitzsimmons, I hand-carried my AF64 physical through USAF headquarters with a waiver, and was again authorized to fly. Since I had left active duty and was discharged as a reservist from Fitzsimmons, I joined the Colorado Air National Guard and became CO of the 140th Fighter Group. They were equipped with P-51s. During my tenure, the 140th got P-80s, F-84s, and F-86s.

When the Korean War broke out, the 140th Fighter Group was called to active duty and assigned to Clovis AFB, New Mexico. Shortly thereafter, when General Joe Cannon, commander of the USAF Fighter Bomber Division, visited Clovis to inspect the group, I urged him to challenge the fighter groups of the entire United States Air Force to a gunnery competition. I told him that my 140th was a hot outfit that could "whip their asses." He bellowed with laughter, but thought that the timing was excellent for such an exercise. Six months later at Elgin Field, Florida, over twenty USAF fighter groups and two ANG groups competed. There were six trophies at stake: top group, top squadron, top group CO, top squadron CO, top individual, and top ground gunnery—napalm.

After two weeks of elimination competition, the four surviving groups competed for another week. The final, formal announcement day arrived with every officer in full uniform, in addition to the air force band, the USAF commanding general, and several other air force generals. The master of ceremonies was General Joe Cannon. He awarded the first five trophies to the 140th Fighter Group. At the last award presentation to my group (I was required to join each winner), General Cannon said, "By God, you really meant what you said that your outfit would whip everybody's ass!" This was recorded on sound camera. I was told that it is in the air force archives. This gunnery meet was the origination of the ensuing "top guns" competition that is now so well known.

Shortly thereafter, our unit was sent piecemeal into combat. I was given orders to go to Nellis AFB in Las Vegas to await assignment as CO of the 56th Fighter Group in Korea. I waited four and a half months while flying F-86s on two to four gunnery missions a day, five days a week. But my final orders never came. I became convinced that my being an ANG colonel with several years "age in grade" probably kept me out of that combat opportunity. Not long after that I left the ANG and entered the business world in construction, banking, and investment banking.

As I look back now at the continual and recurring performance of our P-38 and P-51 fighters, I am keenly aware of the constant and untiring excellence our maintenance and armament crews provided to us pilots. Without their timely and effective mechanical achievements, our 364th Fighter

Group would have been a total loss in World War II. I remember so many times when my wonderful crew chief and his crew worked throughout the night so that my fighter plane would be ready for another mission the next morning. We can talk about pilots all we want, but without those unsung heroes at the base, doing their jobs with whatever sacrifice was required of them, we pilots would have been of no value to the war effort.

A LIFE FOR A SACK OF RICE

First Lieutenant Jeff De Blanc came from Louisiana and felt that the Spanish and French names of the South Pacific islands were familiar and a good omen. The world was young and he wouldn't die there. This is a sensitive story filled with insight and bravery. He tells of the personalities and the aerial battles in the Solomons chain, a dangerous ditch-landing, and a bailout where he was rescued by natives, with more adventures to follow. For his accomplishments and dramatic escape from the Japanese, Jeff was to receive the Congressional Medal of Honor.

After an accelerated course of flight training with less than 250 hours of actual flight time, I joined Fighter Squadron VMF-112 stateside in late October 1942, and left the States for Guadalcanal when the unit received overseas orders. The veteran pilots on "Canal" had been in combat for a month, and replacement pilots were arriving after rudimentary training in gunnery and instrument flying. We were facing enemy aces such as Saburo Sakai, Hiroyoshi Nishizawa, and Junichi Sasai.

On my first flight I accompanied Lieutenant Bill Marontate, a pilot from Joe Foss's division in Major Duke Davis's squadron. Bill pointed out the various landmarks while I checked the oxygen mask and blowers on the little fighter. We were fired upon by Japanese troops as we landed, a factor that was considered a fringe benefit by fighter pilots of the Cactus Air Force, as we were called. We were always under fire on takeoffs and landings.

It took this enemy gunfire to make me realize just how close we were to the front lines. We held only the airstrips and were protected on the perimeter by marine ground troops. We could not leave the tents at night for any reason, because Japanese would infiltrate during nighttime hours. Marine guards, located in fixed firing positions with rifles ready, would shoot anything that moved. Toilet facilities were indeed a problem, but could be handled under these conditions.

By sunset on that first day I had become familiar with the flying area and the Solomon slot map. I could hardly believe my eyes, and felt as if I were home in the Atchafalya basin. The names of most of these islands in the Solomon chain were French and Spanish. Both languages were common in Louisiana, and I could speak each fairly fluently. This was a good omen for me, and I felt that the world was young and I would never die here. I could survive in the jungles of this island chain if I were forced down. That this was a home away from home gave me an added edge of confidence in the air combat battles that followed.

We were awake before dawn and had a breakfast of hardtack and C rations with "coffee" to wash it down. Since only a few fighters were in commission, the flights were rotated among many pilots from different squadrons. I missed the dawn patrol of two fighters, but got in the eleven o'clock daily action over Henderson Field. It was my first combat action and my first view of death in the skies. I had been assigned as number-four man in Lieutenant Marontate's fighter division, and as such flew wing on Staff Sergeant Joe Palko. Joe was a smooth-flying pilot and an experienced one, yet I would witness his death that very day.

Fighter Command managed to get ten F4F-3 Wildcats airborne before a flight of fifteen Japanese twin-engined Betty bombers reached the airfield. This was an almost daily affair and, unknown to me at this time, coastwatchers up the chain of islands would radio these flights to us. This would give us the altitude advantage on the Japanese planes. It is axiomatic with fighter pilots that the man with the altitude advantage generally wins all the marbles. We were climbing through 10,000 feet and heading up to 25,000 feet when we spotted the enemy bombers at about 15,000 feet, starting in on a bombing run on Henderson Field. We didn't have the altitude advantage and had to get that position before beginning a firing overhead run on the bombers. I could not see the advantage of this maneuver that we had been taught in flight school and were now using in combat. These were World War I tactics that would leave us at a disadvantage against enemy fighters, but second lieutenants simply follow orders. My duty was to fly wing on Joe Palko and follow through the firing run on the bombers while protecting Joe's tail against enemy fighters. In the first overhead pass we dropped two bombers on fire but failed to scatter the others that were already locked in their bombing run.

I believe today that a head-on run would have dropped

more bombers, scattering them from the bombing run and giving us the position to cut off their escape, if some of them managed to complete the run. We went by the book, the Japanese dropped the bombs after our first pass, and were on their way home before we could get a second pass. Our division of four planes went after the two crippled bombers. One was immediately blown up in the air by our first two fighters. The other one, still on fire, was heading for the Japanese-held island of Tulagi. I could not see the wisdom of attacking a crippled bomber that could do no harm with its bomb load, but followed Joe Palko and the others down toward it. I scanned the skies for enemy fighters, but saw none and radioed this information to the others.

Joe started a high-side run on the flaming bomber and I followed, only to see another fighter making the same type of run from the other side. Before I could pick up the mike to yell a warning, I watched in horror as both Grumman fighters began firing at the crippled bomber at the same time as its rear gunner opened up with his 20mm cannons, concentrating on Joe's fighter. To this day I don't know if Joe was hit by gunfire, or if it was the slight collision of the two fighters as they flew past the tail of the bomber. That may have knocked out Joe momentarily. I saw a flash of fire and one of the pilots bailing out. It was Lieutenant Pederson from the other fighter. I followed Joe down, and it looked like he had control of his fighter, but at the last minute he crashed on the beach of Tulagi. I marked the spot on my knee-pad map, and the spot where Lieutenant Pederson landed in the water. Then I went after the Japanese bomber, but it was too late. The pilot landed the burning aircraft in a lagoon among friendly Japanese forces.

Back at Henderson Field I was told to report to Captain Joe Foss. I briefed him on what had happened, and he immediately took off in a J2F float plane to search for Palko and Pederson. I was ready for coffee and a rest and prayed that Joe Palko was all right, but he did not survive. Pederson was picked up and returned to the field. I will never forget that first, vivid action. I had fired on a bomber and put a few holes in it, but failed to bring it down. I will always remember this first action as we flew alongside the Japanese bomber stream, climbing for position to make a firing run. I could see the Japanese rear gunners swing their guns around toward us as we climbed out of range. Forever etched in my subconscious mind is the flaming Japanese bomber and the death of Joe Palko.

I lay awake on my cot with the sounds of ten thousand mosquitos trying to penetrate the mosquito netting, hoping somehow to rationalize the three-plane formation flying we were taught in cadet training. These were World War I tactics that didn't apply here. We were told to scissor-maneuver with our enemy in a dogfight, but here in combat we were instructed not to dogfight the highly maneuverable Zero fighters. I began to think in terms of aggressive fighter tactics, but with an outlet for survival. I realized that I would have to develop my own tactics in order to survive in the Solomons. Later I was in a position to understand my part from combat experiences. It appeared that about eighty percent of the fighter pilots on each side stuck with the ways they were taught in flight school. Come hell or high water, many pilots trained to follow a certain pattern will fly that way in combat—the same throttle settings, the same smooth climbing turn, the same breakaway regardless of any dogfighting they may do. This training pattern is easy to note, and easy to lead with gunfire.

My second air battle was on November 12, 1942. This time I flew with members of my own squadron. Major Fontana, our skipper, was scheduled to lead a flight of eight fighters for the eleven o'clock daily action. I was one of the eight and would fly wing on Lieutenant James L. Secrest. I was low man on the totem pole in terms of flight hours, hence my position as wingman for a while. This soon changed, and I would be leading flights as the war progressed.

Captain Joe Foss had eight fighters at Angels 25 (25,000 feet) flying early patrol when "condition red" sounded and we scrambled. Our first four fighters off the deck created a cloud of dust that enabled the Japanese mortar expert, Pistol Pete, to get a fix on the runway. My group of four took off through a barrage of bursting mortar shells. I didn't pick up any arrows from this fire as I cleared the coconut trees at the end of the runway and climbed for altitude, banking sharply over our fleet off the shore of Guadalcanal. As we passed through 5,000 feet, Major Fontana's voice crackled in my earphones, directing our attention to the AA fire from the fleet below.

Looking down at the fleet, I saw fifteen or more twin-engined Betty torpedo bombers coming around the 'Canal and starting a high-speed run on the fleet at about fifty feet. They were in the most perfectly strung-out run I have ever seen, and this time we had the advantage. It was a fighter pilot's dream. The altitude was ours and we would not have to compensate for speed and position, just dive on the sitting ducks below us. Under no circumstance would I ever be a bomber pilot in combat! Our fleet was at a disadvantage. They could not maneuver to avoid the bombers, and had difficulty in lowering the deck guns from the "up" position to the "down" position at the water line for firing purposes. Regardless, they were sending up a huge barrage of antiaircraft fire that we had to fly through.

Joe Foss and his flight had spotted the Japanese bombers and were on the way down from 25,000 feet to engage them. My flight dived through the AA fire, and two of our fighters were hit and crashed into the ocean. Then we hit the enemy bombers at high speed. The action was too fast and fierce for fear to catch up with me. I flew through the barrage from the fleet and locked onto the tail of a Betty and opened fire, killing the rear gunner and watching my tracers strike the engines. The plane burst into flames immediately, and I almost flew into the bomber due to target fixation. I was awed by the winding down of its two engines' propellers as seen through my own propeller turning at greater revolutions. The stroboscopic effect was hypnotic. Flying through the heat generated by the flaming bomber, I quickly recovered and locked onto the tail of another bomber, adjacent to me at about fifty feet off the water. I sent this one crashing in flames with a short burst of the six .50-caliber machine guns.

I had cleared the fleet by this time, knowing that there were other bombers coming out of their runs and clearing the fleet as well. A wingover placed my fighter back in the action fifty feet over the waters. Sure enough, there was a last bomber clearing the run and starting for home base. With a little motion of the rudder and stick I lined up the Wildcat for a head-on run, coming down on him from a little above his flight path. It didn't take long to bring the bomber fully within the rings of the projected gunsight on my windshield. I locked on fast and quickly let go a short, deadly burst of machine-gun fire. The burst caught the left engine and smoked it as my tracers also hit and shattered the pilot greenhouse area.

As I flashed by the bomber and looked down into the cockpit, I clearly saw a third man, kneeling behind and between the two pilots, reach over and pull the pilot in the left seat (who was slumped over the controls) off the controls so that the copilot could take over. This was a flash view at high speed, but as any pilot will agree, motion in the cockpit or on the ground is readily seen, regardless of velocity. Motion in a cockpit and velocity are mutually exclusive. The motion of this third man was the factor that caught my eye. The pilots looked like mannequins at the controls. I could not confirm this aircraft as destroyed, so it went on the records as a probable kill. I wonder if they made it back to the airfield. I know many pilots after the war said that fighter pilots shoot down planes and not men. I could never accept this. Although I knew that I had killed men in the planes I shot down, it was either kill or be killed, and I felt no remorse for them. We were at war!

For the balance of November, flights were routine as the air action slowed. It was then that we lieutenants became aware of RHIP (rank has its privileges). We were scheduled for the dawn and dusk patrols where little or no action would be forthcoming, while the captains and majors had the noon flights—the action period. During the early part of December, word came down from Fighter Command about how Japanese float planes were shooting down some of our dive-bombers' during their rendezvous after pullout. It was suggested that we change tactics when escorting them. After every four dive-bombers would make their bombing run, one fighter would dive down with them and be there for the rendezvous. It was a good idea.

Lieutenant Jim Percy (see "Survival," page 203), a truly top fighter pilot, had a big dogfight over Munda one day. His division of planes was sent on a fighter sweep to represent our squadron, VMF-112, and ran into a heavy overcast. Suddenly a lone Zero appeared and made a run on all four Wildcats. Jim laughed at such a stupid move by a Japanese pilot, and figured that the Japanese was not long for this world, as his division took on the fighter. To make a long story short, this Japanese pilot must have been one of their top aces. He made fools out of all four pilots.

Lieutenant Percy had the Zero in his gunsights and started firing when both planes disappeared in clouds as they dived straight down. Soon the lone Zero came climbing out of the clouds like a homesick angel, heading straight up. On his tail and firing blindly came Percy. The tracers came through the cloud cover before Lieutenant Percy emerged. The Zero sped away. Percy's plane stalled and spun out at the top of his loop. We did not know that he had blacked out in the dive and was holding down on the trigger while semiconscious. After he recovered from his spin, Jim's wingman pulled up, noticed he was covered with blood, and assumed that the Japanese pilot had wounded him. Such was not the case. Lieutenant Percy had pulled too many G forces and blacked out while climbing after the Zero with such force that he struck his face on the gunsight. We did not have shoulder straps on those first tour planes. Regardless, he made it back to safety. We all had a good laugh about the top Japanese ace.

At high noon on December 18, I flew one of the fighters escorting a group of dive-bombers scheduled to bomb the Japanese airfield at Munda on New Georgia Island. It was a beautiful day for an escort mission. Weaving over the slow-flying dive-bombers, I became distracted and splashed around in my mind the awesome firepower of this little fighter. What destructive power for one man to handle! Why, only yesterday I was a college kid, roaming the campus and looking at all the beautiful girls. Now I was in this environment. What a change! The sound of conversation over the airways broke my daydreaming, and I focused on the situation developing rapidly before me. We were at the target area and the dive-bombers were doing their thing.

After the first twelve had completed their run on Munda Field, I dived with the last four. Still in my dive, I spotted a float plane on the tail of one of our bombers. The Japanese plane was below and behind the tail and unseen by the rear gunner of the dive-bomber. Both planes were heading directly into my line of flight, and my gunsight. To save the lives of the pilot and his gunner, I would have to fire above his cockpit into the Japanese plane on his tail. I usually fired with four guns during combat and saved two guns to come home on as added insurance, but this time I switched on all six .50s. It would be a close, quick action. If I missed, the enemy pilot would shoot down our dive-bomber. But I couldn't miss since his plane filled my gunsight and I had the proper lead on the gunsight rings. I surprised the Japanese pilot when I opened up. In his rush to make a sure kill, he had failed to see me coming until it was too late. I could see his frantic motion to maneuver out of my line of fire when he did spot me. I had put enough rounds in his plane before he could break clear of his position on our dive-bomber's tail. The float plane went down.

In my anxiety to protect our bomber, I failed to realize that all the expended brass from the fired rounds were falling free of my aircraft below the wings. The Law of Free-Falling Bodies would take over! With the same velocity as my fighter, the shell casings rained down on Lieutenant Poole's plane. The result was awful. It almost knocked them out of the sky, but luck was with them. They were not injured, but sore as hell. The plane would have to be repaired or scrapped. I completed a wingover and blew the damaged float plane out of the skies with a short burst from six guns.

It was then that Lieutenant Tom Hughes of VMF-112 joined up on my wing for the return trip to Guadalcanal. He had witnessed the whole action. As we cleared the area, Tom's voice came over the radio. He had spotted another Japanese float plane returning from antisub patrol, heading right for us, but a thousand feet below. The pilot saw us, and his rear gunner began to swing his machine gun in our direction. I pulled into a wingover and hopped down onto the tail of the float plane. I didn't bother to dive below his plane and come up under him for a firing position to avoid the rear gunner. I felt that firing six .50s instead of the usual four would get him before that peashooter could reach me. I was wrong. The rear gunner put about five arrows into my fighter before I chopped him down. I was closing too fast to stay on his tail and shoot the plane down, and had to pull up quickly to avoid crashing into him.

At that moment Tom Hughes boresighted the float plane and opened fire. His firing was very accurate, striking the gas tank and the depth charges of the Japanese aircraft. I felt rather than saw the explosion, and witnessed small pieces of plane fly through the clouds all around me as my fighter lurched upward with tremendous force, as if seized by a giant hand and flung aloft. By the time I straightened the fighter, Tom was on my wing looking for damage to my aircraft. Finding none, he proceeded to move his hands in Hollywood film pantomime, taking my picture and laughing. I did the same thing to him since this was his first kill. We proceeded all the way back to Guadalcanal doing these motions. Fortunately there were no Zero fighters around.

Upon landing I was greeted by Lieutenant Poole. He was a little bit unhappy about the brass falling all over his plane, but was glad we all made it back okay. He said his gunner was going to nail the Japanese, but from my position I doubted that he had the angle to fire without doing damage to his tail. Regardless, he thanked me for my help. Lieutenant Poole was killed later during the war in an operational accident.

Predawn of January 29, 1943, was one for instrument flying. The moon was down and it was as black as the inside of a 1926 ink bottle. I was assigned a mission to fly this hop with three other pilots in a predawn takeoff and vector east of Guadalcanal to 10,000 feet, then orbit until daylight. Word had filtered down from Fighter Command that a Japanese force of Betty bombers would strike at dawn from the east. My plane was a klunker with a right wing tank attached and dirty from mud splashes. After just clearing the trees on take-off, I sweated out the long climb on instruments. Movement from the bay below caught my eye as destroyers began to turn at high speed in the water. This created huge phosphorescent waves as the propellers churned the ocean. It was a beautiful sight and lit up the entire bay. It gave me a feeling of security as I relaxed, flying on instruments. I was oriented with the earth below. It was then that I noticed a film of oil rapidly spreading all over my canopy, and the oil pressure needle on the engine unit gauge dropping. Soon the oil pressure was zero and the engine began to seize. I was too busy to radio my troubles to base, or to the other fighters, as I dropped below into the blackest of nights.

I had just cleared 6,000 feet and was on the way down. My only sensible option was to bail out. Only a fool would ride down a fighter with a dead engine at night over water. I could no longer see the bay because the ships ceased to churn the waters below. I had trimmed the fighter to a speed of 130 knots and stepped out on the wing three different times as I held on to the canopy. Each time I lost my nerve and stepped back into the cockpit. I had had a flashback of one of our pilots bailing out during a dogfight and watching him go down pulling at his jacket in frantic gestures when his chute failed to open. Usually our chutes were repacked every thirty days, but here in the humid climate the chutes were opened and repacked every fifteen days. My thoughts were wild. Did I have a chute that needed repacking? The one I wore was not my regular chute, so I elected to ride the fighter down on instruments. At night with no moon, it was suicide to try it.

Luckily for me, the air raid alarm sounded and came over the radio to us. This started a chain reaction with the ships in the harbor below as they began to swerve and churn up the ocean with high-speed evasive movements. This provided me a "landing field" complete with lights furnished by the sea-animal life acting like thousand-watt bulbs. The USS *Jenkins* steered a straight course for about two hundred feet before turning. Here was my runway. I dropped the seat as low as I could get it and went on the gauges. As I approached one hundred feet of altitude, I went on contact vision and dropped the little fighter wheels up in a most beautiful water landing. Seconds before I hit I remembered the wing tank I should have jettisoned, but this probably prevented my wings from dipping into the water for a possible cartwheel landing. The fighter simply skidded on the waters, nosed up past the ninety-degree-vertical plane, and bounced back below the vertical. This gave me time to get out of the aircraft before it sank. The tail disappeared below the surface as I popped my Mae West life jacket.

The men aboard the *Jenkins* spotted me and yelled to pick me up on the run. This I refused to do. Any fighter pilot in his right mind will *never* board a destroyer during an air raid. I would take my chances in the water. I personally saw Japanese dive-bombers sink one of our destroyers in seconds. Later they fished me out of the water and laughed at my fears about boarding a destroyer during an air raid. Visual (light) communications were established with Guadalcanal, and three hours later I was back with the squadron. Little did I know that I would bail out of my fighter two days later without the slightest hesitation.

The air war heated up around the Solomons and Fighter Command began to send strikes at maximum range against the Japanese. This finally put us on the offensive. All during the dark days of 1942 we had been fighting a defensive action over Henderson Field. Now the action was moving up the chain of islands. The range of the Wildcat fighter was about two hundred miles without external fuel tanks, provided the engine was functioning properly. External tanks were experimental and not too reliable in the hookup stage. However, emergencies in war have priority over safety, and the Wildcat was the only fighter we had to oppose the Japanese. The Corsair fighter would have had the range with its internal fuel tanks and efficient external tanks, but it was still a month away from the Solomon Islands campaign.

The coastwatchers on Vella Lavella sent word to Fighter Command that a Japanese fleet was seen entering the Kolombangara area between New Georgia and Vella Lavella, escorting cargo ships, and requested immediate dive-bombing action for a "sitting-duck" attack. This sighting led our leaders to believe that another attempt to regain control of Guadalcanal was in the making, but the reverse was actually true. The Japanese planned to evacuate their troops from the 'Canal. The big fight was on January 31, 1943, as a handful of fighters (six Wildcats) escorting twelve SBD-3 dive-bombers were ordered to strike a fleet located 250 miles away from Guadalcanal. It would be one of my wildest dogfights, and would earn me the Medal of Honor.

Eight pilots from VMF-112 were on standby alert for the afternoon action. We had been playing acey-deucey when word came down from above that an escort action was handed to Fighter Command. We scrambled for the flight line and, with parachutes strapped on, headed for the assigned Wildcat fighters. The briefing had been short and concise. The time was 1500 hours, the distance was 250 miles out, and there would be instrument conditions for the return trip since the moon was down and the weather was closing rapidly up the slot. Belly tanks were quickly strapped on the eight Grumman fighters, and we were ready to go. Now the fighter action would be reversed. We would be fighting away from our field and over enemy waters with the added burden of a belly tank. Before engaging in combat, a fighter pilot had to jettison his belly tank for two reasons: the added weight hindered maneuvers, and if the external tank were hit by bullets, it would explode because it was not self-sealing.

I was assigned a fighter that had a blond "bombshell" painted on the cowling with the title "Impatient Virgin" lettered underneath. The plane captain handed the yellow sheet to me for my signature of acceptance and I signed. We made small talk as he helped me strap in, and said that he hoped I would get my first kill this day. I mentioned that I already had a few planes to my credit and this aircraft was not the one I usually flew. There was a misconception after the war that all fighter pilots were issued a personal fighter. Such was not the case. Planes were put into commission on the flight line and then assigned at random. Each plane did have a flight captain who was responsible for seeing that the aircraft was in commission. I wish that I had taken the time to remember this one's name, but I didn't and I regretted losing his plane in the coming action.

The afternoon flight was not one of the more lucrative ones and was usually shunned, if you could get out of it. But we were on call and had no choice. It was after 1500 hours by the time we were airborne, because the slower bombers had to take off first. All eight of our fighters took off, and soon the pilots switched to belly tanks in order to use all the petrol from those tanks first, then release them to have a "clean" fighter and lots of fuel remaining for the coming fight. Twenty minutes into the flight, one of the pilots called in with a rough engine and aborted the mission. Two minutes later another fighter pilot called over the radio, stating that his fuel pressure gauge was acting up. I wanted to tell him to smash the gauge and not worry about it, since we needed all the guns we could get on the escort mission, but I decided not to say anything. He aborted and returned to base. That left six fighters to do the job. I resented this a little since almost every fighter we flew into combat had something wrong with it. If we were stateside and in training, I venture to say that out of twenty planes we flew in combat, only two would meet flight standards. Some pilots were aggressive. Others were not.

Of the six fighter pilots remaining, all were members of VMF-112 (as were the two who had left), except Staff Sergeant Jim Feliton (a member of VMF-121). The VMF-112 pilots were Lieutenant Tom Hughes, Lieutenant Joe Lynch, Lieutenant Jack Maas, Lieutenant James Secrest, and me. It was decided that Maas and Hughes would fly high-cloud cover, and the rest of us would wing it right over the bombers for the dive on the Japanese fleet. It was never clear to me how this decision was reached, but the die was cast. After this decision we leaned the gas mixture as much as possible to conserve fuel. I had settled down to cruising speed, drawing fuel from the belly tank and scanning the area for enemy planes. We were now deep in enemy territory.

It was during this scanning action across the cockpit instrument panel and out the canopy that I noticed the gas-gauge needle starting to fluctuate. Fighter pilots are able to scan over the main instruments in the cockpit by simply looking across the panel briefly and watching for vibrating gauge needles. Movement of any gauge needle meant trouble. I quickly threw the emergency fuel pump switch and started working the wobble hand pump to build fuel pressure back to normal. The gas selector switch was on external tank, the needle continued to drop in spite of my efforts, and I quickly switched my selector valve to main internal gasoline tank. The pressure needle jumped back to normal and the engine picked up the added revolutions. I could not have used up the fifty gallons so soon, or had I? Either the tank had run dry from a gas-guzzling aircraft or suction was lost through the external connecting feed lines, the latter being a common occurrence in the experimental phases of auxiliary tank connections.

Quickly I got out the plotting board and did some fast figuring with the circular slide rule located in the lower quadrant. I could make it if I leaned out the fuel mixture some more. We were past the point of no return, and I could see the island of Kolombangara sliding below my wing 14,000 feet below. The Japanese airfield looked empty. Where were the Zero fighters? We crossed the island and I checked my fuel gauge again. It was dropping rapidly despite my efforts to lean out the engine. I now knew that I had drawn a gas guzzler or had a main leak somewhere. I leaned out the fuel mixture until the engine began to drop RPMs. That was the signal to quit the procedure. It was going to be a close one getting back. I notified the others of my situation.

By this time we were over the target and the fleet below. All hell broke loose as the dive-bombers went into action and the AA fire started reaching for us. Secrest and Lynch went into a strafing action against a cargo ship below, and Feliton and I were in position to protect the dive-bombers against float-plane action. I picked up a call for assistance as the dive-bombers came under attack while regrouping at 1,000 feet for the trip home. It had been a lousy run for them. All twelve had succeeded in getting near misses—no hits. I broke off my engagement and saw the usual old "Munda airfield" setup. That is, float planes racing in to clobber the dive-bombers after they started to join up. I was well experienced in this type of action and had the altitude advantage.

Two of the Japanese float planes were closing in for the kill, one following the other in a tail-chase pattern. With luck I could nail them both. I called for Staff Sergeant Feliton to follow me down and cover my tail in case I missed and overshot. In this way he could nail the float if I missed, and I would go after the next one. I had the feeling of perfect control as I pulled the little Grumman fighter flat on the trailing float plane for a no-deflection shot using only four guns. The rear gunner opened up on me, and I dropped quickly below his flight path to the six o'clock position and opened up with my guns when his plane filled my sights. It flamed immediately and dropped off in a slow graveyard spiral, burning furiously. The float plane exploded as I flew over and settled on the tail of the second one, the leader. Evidently there was no communication between this rear gunner and the pilot, since no evasive action was taken.

I settled onto his tail (below sight of the gunner) at six o'clock to him and twelve o'clock to me. When the aircraft filled my gunsight, and with the cross hair dead center on the cockpit, I opened fire and watched the plane flame immediately. The float plane started a slow climbing turn to the right from an easterly direction to a westerly one. Upon reaching the westerly heading, the plane exploded in a flash that matched the setting sun. For a moment I was mesmerized by the sun and this flash. It all seemed unreal. What appeared to be a slow-motion bit of action was only a matter of seconds. All other float planes cleared the area. I pulled up in a climbing right bank to verify Feliton's position and clear my tail. As I raced for altitude with Feliton on my wing, somebody over the radio yelled, "Zeros!!"

About ten Zeros were heading straight for us and holding a fixed altitude. They failed to see Feliton and me, since we were about 500 feet below them in a climbing-attack approach. I pulled up into a smooth gunnery run on the leader, and it was like shooting at a fixed-target sleeve that I had fired upon during advanced cadet training. I placed the gunsight in line with the leader's flight path and a few mil-rings above the nose of his oncoming aircraft, and squeezed the trigger when he was in range. There was no way to miss. The leader never knew what hit his plane or where the fire was coming from. With a jerking motion of such violence that it almost tore the wing off the Zero, he rolled out of my sights in a tumbling flip to the left. I either killed him instantly and his last reflexes resulted in this motion, or he was the fastest evader I had ever seen. I never saw him again and could not claim him. His wingman started upward in a slow left spiral climb, looking around and trying to figure out what was happening as I locked onto his tail. The Zero pilot started a slow roll upward and I followed the roll with him. As he came out of the roll, I fired. He never knew what hit him because his plane exploded violently.

This started one of the wildest dogfights I had ever been in. To this day I cannot tell how many Zeros came down on us. Targets were everywhere. Staff Sergeant Feliton and I flew a defensive scissor weave covering each other's tail. On one turn he pulled too wide and in the first few seconds, which seemed like a lifetime, I watched his fighter take a hit in the engine cooler as he banked across the nose of my fighter, leaving the fight with a huge trail of black smoke. The Zero broke off firing at him and cleared out when he saw my fighter. Staff Sergeant Feliton would be safe from further fighter action. Crippled aircraft were usually left alone in dogfights until all the action was over. Then they are shot down. By this time Feliton would have bailed safely out.

For ten seconds the air was clear of fighters. My fighter had taken a few arrows during the dogfight, and I remembered seeing a Zero plunging in flames from above. It was a kill by Lieutenant Maas, who was up on high cover. The dive-bombers had all assembled for the return trip and were preparing to take a heading back home. I noticed two Zeros closing in from behind me as I started a climb toward a position which would take me above the dive-bombers that already were fast disappearing in the distance. A glance at my fuel gauge shocked me. I had used up quite a bit of fuel during the dogfight. I could easily join the dive-bombers and fly wing on them as added protection for the return trip. The rear gunners and I could handle the Zeros if I could reach them in time.

The fighter escort mission was completed with safe retirement of the dive-bombers from the immediate combat area. If I stopped to engage Zeros, my chances of returning safely would be in question because I would probably run out of gas. With total darkness for the return trip, I kept thinking about the night water landing, something I did not want to consider again so soon. I decided to challenge the Zeros and take my chances, and at the same time draw them away from the dive-bombers, if they tried to catch them. This was hardly likely since fuel and speed were factors for them as well, and I was in the immediate combat area—a definite target for the Zero fighters. I knew that I could not outrun them and would have to accept combat. If I ran out of gas returning home after the fight, I would bail out this time. No more water landings on the gauges for me.

The coming action would be in full view of the rear gunners in the dive bombers returning to Guadalcanal and, unknown to me at this time, in full view of Missionary Sylvester on the island of Vella Lavella. He mentioned it to me later when I was brought to his mission. I switched on the last set of guns, the ones I usually kept for the return flight home, as added insurance. I have always maintained that if you can't hit them with four guns, you certainly won't hit them with six of them. But I was in an "all-or-nothing" position.

Those Japanese pilots were aggressive. Both fighters came at me as I turned head on into them. Again I was in the better firing position. A climbing head-on run is better than a diving head-on run. The Zero pilot had a trim problem diving on me as he picked up speed, while I was slowing down as I climbed toward him. I had six .50s against his two 7.7mm machine guns. I assumed my bullets would reach him before he could hit me. Besides, he couldn't use his slow, low-muzzle velocity cannons until he had me boresighted. My fighter became more stable as I slowed in the climb, and the Japanese pilot started shooting out of range. The tracers looked like Roman candles and a pair of railroad tracks coming at me. We closed in less than a heartbeat and I fired. The Zero caught fire immediately, but kept coming straight at me. He was going to ram! The firing slowed my fighter about fifteen knots or more (Newton's Third Law) and my controls became sluggish. I really became frightened. Could I maneuver out of the way? I held the trigger down and the Zero blew up in a flash of fire. Pieces flew everywhere and some struck my fighter. I struggled to regain control from an almost stalled position after flying through the debris.

I banked sharply to get on the tail of the other Zero as he flashed by, but he had already pulled up high above me and completed his turn. He came in on me in a high-side run. Lieutenant Colonel Bauers always claimed that if ever a Zero gets on your tail, don't worry because he will open fire with the twin 7.7mm machine guns to line you up, then cease firing and open up with his twin 20mm slow-firing cannons. You will have plenty of time to skid out of the way. Even if they hit you, the armored plate behind you will take the shock. This man had convinced us long ago that the Zero was *not* invincible, but could be dealt with head on, or on your tail. He said, "Dogfight them, for they are paper kites."

The Zero pilot coming down on me was too eager for the kill and did not judge my speed correctly. With his altitude advantage and his closing rate of speed too great and increasing during the diving run, he stood a good chance of overshooting me, a factor he realized too late. I chopped the throttle, skidded, and dropped my flaps. The Wildcat was down to a few knots above stalling speed. The Zero pilot, closing too fast, sailed by and overshot me, at the same time fishtailing his aircraft to stay on my tail. This he failed to do. I can still see his face as we locked eyes in that instant. He "froze" on the controls and flew straight ahead of me without making any attempt to get away. I shot him down with one short burst. It is odd how this action is still so clear in my mind today. I have often wondered if this Zero pilot knew that others were on my tail and, by flying straight, they would shoot me down after I got him.

I had made the almost fatal error of not clearing my tail before I shot this Japanese pilot down. Unknown to me, there were others behind me, already in firing position and making a run on me. With a quick glance I looked at the watch strapped on the inside of my wrist and noticed the time approaching 1800 hours. Night was rising fast from the earth below. Night and lightning rise from the earth to the sky. In the next instant I felt the watch fly off my wrist. The instrument panel erupted in flames caused by a 20mm shell that came over my left shoulder. The gasoline from the ruptured primer on the instrument panel had a good fire going in the cockpit, aided by the floor auxiliary fuel tank. In the next second I caught another burst in the engine. It flamed and lost power. In my frantic effort to get out of the line of fire I caught a glimpse of the Zero banking for another run on me. In the meantime the damaged canopy worked loose from its railings and, with a loud bang, was lost in the slipstream. With the aircraft falling apart, I unbuckled my safety belt and jumped for the trailing edge of the left wing. Feeling a jerk on my neck, I realized that I had forgotten to disconnect my throat mike cord.

How peaceful it felt to be free of the noise and watching the waters far below as I tumbled through the air. What a sensational feeling! I felt free as a bird and got a beautiful view of the earth from "space." I had the feeling that I could land without getting hurt. I often wonder how others who have parachuted felt on the first jump. I don't remember pulling the rip cord (D-ring), but the next minute the canopy of silk was above me and I was on my way down. This Japanese pilot had seen me shoot down his buddies, and some Japanese pilots shot at Americans in parachutes, so I was eager to get down. Upon parachuting out of the stricken fighter, I had reacted too quickly. Instead of free-falling at least 1,000 feet, clear of the dogfight arena, I found myself in the same sky with the Zeros. I decided to play dead in the chute. I let myself go limp, with head sagging, as the Japanese pilot circled me twice. He even pulled his canopy back on the second pass and gave me the once-over. I guess he was an exception, because he sped off back to Kahili Field on Bougainville Island.

The sun was setting as I floated down, and the waters below looked calm and glassy. I would not have to fight choppy waves, but would have trouble judging when to release my chute before hitting the water. We were trained to let our feet touch water before jumping out of the parachute harness in order to prevent the chute canopy from settling over your head and drowning you before you could clear the area. I concentrated on the glassy ocean and had to wait an eternity, since I had left the fighter at about 2,000 feet. Finally I knew that I was close and said to myself, "What a piece of cake." I unstrapped my chute harness and sat comfortably in the seat pack, ready for my feet to touch the water. As usual, these instructions were for choppy waters, not glassy ones.

Depth perception over glassy water requires a great amount of concentration. If the waves below are choppy, the pilot will see 3-D immediately and will most probably judge the proper parachute height. A glassy ocean will not be readily judged in terms of height above the water. Compounding this factor in combat, a downed, wounded pilot would have more of a problem judging distance. This flashed through my mind as I was coming down, and I knew that with little wind the chute would collapse on top of me as I hit the water. Therefore, I would release about ten feet above the water and avoid this danger. I thought that I had excellent eyesight, but I misjudged the distance, an understandable error after the fight I had just been in. What I had thought was ten feet turned out to be over forty feet.

It seemed like an eternity before I hit the water while my chute collapsed and I fell clear of the shroud lines. My plunge into the ocean was a deep one. I was so far under that I had to pop my Mae West life jacket to help me reach the surface. I could see the reflection of the sunlight on the surface of the ocean, but it seemed like ages before I broke clear and gasped for air. Only half of my Mae West was inflated; the other half had been cut by shrapnel. The adrenaline was flowing and I didn't realize that I had been wounded in the arms, leg, and side. My .45 automatic, canteen, and extra shells had been ripped off my waist when I bailed out. Had I worn my shoulder holster, this would not have happened. The back pack of my parachute harness still attached to my body contained survival equipment.

I had landed in the Vella Gulf between Kolombangara and Vella Lavella, and beat Jack Kennedy to the island by seven months. I started to swim toward the island of Kolombangara, hoping to get ashore and possibly steal a Zero from the Japanese airfield that I had spotted as we flew over earlier. This may sound far-fetched, but I knew of no other way and figured this was my only option, unless I elected to hide in the jungles for the duration of the Solomon action. I thought that I could survive in the jungles with no problem.

All aviators flying over water carried chlorine pills in their shirt pockets. These we were told to break in the water every fifteen minutes to ward off sharks. Sharks are vicious in the South Pacific, especially the great white ones. My wounds were not too bad, but bleeding filled the water and I feared sharks. I broke some chlorine pills every few minutes and let the smell permeate my flight clothing. I found out after the war that they have no effect on sharks. The bombing may have scared off the sharks in this area, but that is only a guess.

The darkness gave me a sense of security from the Japanese, and I hastened to swim. Swift currents kept sweeping me out to sea, and it took about six hours to reach shore in my weakened condition. Even in the darkness, the shoreline appeared menacing and the mangroves treacherous. I was so tired by then that I simply pulled off the Mae West, hid it under the coral rocks, proceeded inland about fifteen feet, and went to sleep on a pile of branches. I awakened to raindrops pelting my aching body and noticed that my sleeping quarters were overhanging an entrenched gully. I had a breakfast of fresh water and a piece of concentrated chocolate from my survival kit, dressed my wounds from an emergency first aid kit fit for a medical operating room, and headed east toward the far end of the island, toward a huge volcanic crater.

I remembered seeing the volcanic crater as we flew over the island. It was split into two halves and covered with jungle growth, but rose 5,000 feet above the jungle floor. I was well oriented and felt that I could locate the Japanese base with no trouble while living off the land. Once I got within a few miles of the field, I heard aircraft engines and the usual airfield activities. I had absolutely no knowledge of any coastwatcher activities in this area. Munda Airfield, the Gizo Island Japanese float plane sea base, and Villa Field surrounded my position. I knew that I was deep in enemy territory.

While I was moving toward the end of the island, a series of unlikely errors were acting in my favor. Sergeant Feliton was shot down before me. Our other four fighter pilots had returned to Guadalcanal where Lieutenant Joe Lynch was debriefed in a session attended by General Mulcahy. Joe told the general that he had seen "a chute open up at a very low altitude above the trees of Kolombangara and collapse immediately among the trees." He marked the exact spot on his aerial strip map and showed it to the general. The general instructed the intelligence officer to pass that information on to the coastwatchers. He had seen Feliton's chute over the island. Lieutenant Maas reported that he had seen a chute open over the waters during the dogfight. That was actually my parachute.

I am enough of a mathematician to know that the Law of Probabilities is not to be reckoned with. What would be my chances of fighting in the skies with Zeros over a great field of cloud actions, and covering considerable distances, being shot down over a spot in the ocean that enabled me to swim to shore, head through the jungle and arrive at the exact place where Feliton's plane had crashed and his chute had snagged in the treetops? Remote, you will say. Absolutely not. Two days later I was camping below the tree where Feliton had landed.

When I realized that the jungle was too thick for me to make headway, I took to the trees. My wounds bothered me and I dressed them often, dropping the old dressings on the jungle floor below. I slept in the trees, in a "bed" between two huge limbs on the second night. I didn't know what to expect on the jungle floor, because animal tracks were all around. The next morning I spotted a clearing and dropped to the ground. I followed a trail through the jungle, holding my big survival kit shark knife in full readiness until I reached a clearing of coconut trees with a native grass hut in the center.

The birds were singing as I listened carefully for signs of Japanese or other human life. I knew the sounds of the swamps of Louisiana well, and it's no different anywhere else. If the birds are singing, all is well.

The hut was neat and had a straw sleeping mat on the floor. Pretty soon I had a pile of coconuts and firewood, plus a fresh supply of water that I had obtained by brute force from huge leaves that acted like rain barrels. There were fishhooks and matches in my survival kit, and I would be careful not to leave any articles of civilization hanging around in case the Japanese crossed that way. A brackish stream ran through the compound and headed toward the sea, and I found native footprints on the banks. I wondered if they were friendly natives or headhunters.

After a repast of coconut milk and fruit, I decided to explore across the stream in the direction of Vella Field. Clearing the other side of the stream, I noticed the tops of the jungle trees were chopped off in a neat path and realized that a plane had crashed. I hurried to the scene, and twenty minutes later came across the remains of a Grumman fighter with the sound of flies all over the place. I searched in a radius of a few hundred yards but could find no body. During the search I found the remnants of a chute—shroud lines and harness but no silk canopy. The canopy had been removed by someone. I got paranoid about the Japanese, until I noticed native footprints all over the jungle floor. I salvaged what I could from the wreckage and returned to my hut.

I followed the stream to the ocean that afternoon and discovered a beautiful inlet with a beach across it. I was waist-deep in the water when I saw a huge shark fin cut the surface fifty yards away. I got back to shore just in time, losing one of my boondocker shoes in the process. The shark circled the spot where I had been for a few minutes, then went under. I returned to the hut shaking and prepared for a good night's rest.

I awoke to the usual jungle noises and decided to make this a day of fishing. But by the time I had the lines prepared

and was setting them in the stream, the rain was coming down in buckets. I returned to the hut. I didn't really know how to open a coconut and had been using the brute force method with my shark knife. When I tried that again, I broke the blade's end off in a coconut and discarded it with the blade tip still embedded. Later I slept.

I awoke to a clear morning and listened for the usual jungle bird songs. The jungle was still. I grabbed my broken shark knife and looked out the hut door to see a short native standing at the edge of the clearing, looking at me. He had reddish hair in an Afro style, with a big bone through his nose and a bolo knife in his hand. I felt rather than saw the other natives behind me. There were six of them. I dropped my knife and they closed in to throw at my feet all of my discarded bandages, the tip of the shark knife and the coconut itself, all the while grinning at me. They had been tracking me from the very first day. They touched my skin with one finger and marveled at the whiteness that appeared around redness, then one of them showed me how to open a coconut with a sharpened stick. I could see that I was out of my element in jungle ways, and I never forgot that lesson.

We had to communicate by signs. They moved me down a trail to the ocean until we came to a twelve-man outrigger canoe, then I was placed in the middle while they paddled near the shoreline for hours. We left the canoe in another inlet and followed a trail that led into a native village deep inside the forest. There were no women or children around, and I was placed in a cage with two native guards outside. As night fell, jungle drums started which raised the hair on the nape of my neck. These drums were huge, twenty-foot hollow logs with a full-length narrow slit at the top. One native beat a tattoo code with two sticks and the women and children emerged from the jungle. They disappeared again at dawn. I was later told that they were hiding because they had been abused by the Japanese.

Later a group of seven new arrivals entered the village. They threw down a sack of rice and I was released from my cage to their custody. We quickly left the village without a word being spoken, but I knew that I had been bought for a sack of rice. This changed my whole outlook on life, and I realized how values of different cultures varied. The U.S. Navy would spend millions of dollars and use an entire fleet to rescue downed pilots, but this one had been purchased for a sack of rice. Very few people today know the extent of their wealth. I know *exactly* how much I am worth—one sack of rice!

We took a break after about an hour, and the leader spoke to me in pidgin English. He talked about the coast-watchers, but not in those terms. We entered another village and the chief wanted my belt buckle with the marine emblem. When he took it, I grabbed his nine-foot spear in trade. It is a beauty with a beautiful basket weave, plus flying fox (tropical fruit bat) teeth and wing bones in position on one end. It hangs in my den today. We were told by the chief that a party of five Japanese were aboard a beached barge on a coral reef about fifty yards offshore. It was decided to get rid of them and make off with the goods aboard, since the Japanese had no idea that a native village was in the vicinity. The chief already had a cap from one of the guards that his natives had obtained while the Japanese slept. He gave me the cap. Since I was a guest of the group, it was native protocol to attend all functions; so I went along on the raiding party.

We reached the jungle clearing near the beached Japanese barge about two hours later, and waited until dark to make our move. I don't know how the natives did it, but by the time I arrived there were no Japanese aboard. I searched the radio cabin and found a bundle of papers that I brought back to Guadalcanal after my rescue. The natives took lots of clothing, guns, etc., and I searched a foot locker for clothing to replace my rags. I got a complete officer's summer khaki uniform, two pistols in holsters, a beautiful hara-kiri knife in a gold and silver case, and a bottle of sake. I was feeling no pain when we left the ship. A picture of me in that uniform hangs today in my den.

I was eager to leave the island of Kolombangara, and a twelve-man outrigger was brought from out of nowhere. A fresh crew of powerful young men from a nearby village did the paddling. We couldn't make the trip in one night because of the distance, so the journey would be in two steps. Between us was the island of Gizo with its huge float-plane base from which regular patrols were flown and native canoes were often strafed. The natives navigated in total darkness in a rainstorm with no landmarks or stars to guide us. I tried to help with a paddle, but only broke the natives' rhythm, so I settled down to bailing out the extra water while getting a good soaking from the downpour. We arrived at Gizo Island before dawn.

The young natives left me with a guide and headed back to Kolombangara that evening. We followed a path that took us close beside a Japanese outpost. I knew the penalties for being out of uniform in time of war, and although I could see the Japanese eating around a campfire in a squatting position, we were not challenged. I could have sworn that one of the soldiers waved, but I didn't wave back. It was pitch black by the time we got to the other side of Gizo Island, and I could hear the roar of float-plane engines. Maybe I could steal one and get back to base, but I would probably be shot down by one of the squadron mates.

A fresh outrigger crew covered me with coconut palm leaves and would not let me up. This was a new ball game to me, and I had the feeling that this part of the trip would be more dangerous. I was right. We failed to reach Vella Lavella in darkness, and dawn found us an hour from our destination. Float planes buzzed us at daybreak, and the natives would stand up and wave every time one would pass fifty feet overhead. When the leaves were finally removed, I sat up in the canoe at a wharf adjacent to a huge red farm warehouse. I couldn't believe my eyes and ears when a white man and five native men appeared. Missionary Sylvester called me by name with no errors in pronunciation. How could a perfect stranger in the middle of a war zone call me by name and rank? It was only later that I was able to comprehend the vast network of coastwatchers throughout the Solomon chain.

I attended a beautiful Church of England service with the missionary after he told me that it would be an insult to the natives if I were not present, even though I am Catholic. I was amazed how beautifully they sang the hymns, and almost fell out of my seat when one native stood up and recited the twenty-third Psalm, "The Lord is my shepherd, etc." I had surrendered my weapons to Missionary Sylvester, but had felt the hara-kiri knife was rightfully mine and had kept it. I was wrong. He informed me very politely that I had a hidden dagger and the natives expected me to turn it in. There were smiles all around when I did so. The next afternoon Sylvester and I sat on his porch while our dive-bombers struck Munda Airfield. We sipped tea at three as I watched the dive-bombers join up for the return trip to Guadalcanal. The air was clear of fighters and float planes. I left for a coastwatcher outpost "somewhere in the mountains" within an hour, after being informed that a Japanese patrol was on the way to the mission.

I accompanied a party of eight natives as jungle drums relayed our progress along the way. We found Feliton in a village called Parmata. He was in bad shape and suffering from cracked ribs he had received during the descent into the trees. We didn't talk much because of his pain, but he was glad to be alive. They fed us fish cooked in coconut oil. We were visited by one of the coastwatchers the next morning, namely, Lieutenant Henry Josslyn, a mining engineer from England who had been commissioned in place after the outbreak of the war. This satisfied the terms of the Geneva Convention. I would later meet the other coastwatcher, a tall Australian officer named Lieutenant Keenan. They made a good combination and were very effective. Since I was physically fit, Lieutenant Josslyn asked me to join them at the outpost and I quickly accepted.

We climbed for hours through the jungle before reaching the outpost. It was well planned for quick escape. The shelters holding the radio and other equipment were platforms over a deep ravine. They were secured by a stout rope tied to a common point overhead and beautifully braced into a dragline configuration. All they had to do to strike camp and escape after the radio was removed was to sever the ropes with a single swish of a bolo knife. Everything would vanish into the deep ravine. The antenna wire for forty meters could be removed in short order.

They used voice transmissions to pass the word to Guadalcanal. If one were to look at the "slot" of islands in the Solomon chain, he could readily see that Japanese planes leaving Rabaul and Bougainville (Kahili Field) had to pass within sight of Vella Lavella, or they would run out of fuel on the return trip. There was no other way. A group of planes would be counted on the way out and counted again on the way back for the record. I saw the whole picture then. I had thought our radar was picking up these planes for advanced warning, but it was the coastwatchers all the time.

The next day I got a full indoctrination on radio fix. The Japanese were restocking an outpost on the beach that we could see at the base of our lookout. There were six Zeros flying cover for a Kawanishi flying boat. Three orbited at about 3,000 feet and three more were at 6,000 feet. Their orbits were clockwise for the first group and counterclockwise for the second. I could see myself in a Wildcat fighter, diving from 20,000 feet at high speed through the formation of planes and burning the four-engined flying boat, a target I had been searching for a long time. They soon finished, and a destroyer pulled into the bay with a four-engined flying boat over the island. We knew that planes would be coming down and that they were in a position to get a fix on our station when we opened up. Sure enough, a flight appeared. We counted them and transmitted twenty-five before shutting down the transmission. It was not enough time for a fix, but I watched Japanese soldiers running out of the outpost below with fixed bayonets, looking like the Keystone Kops. They didn't know where to go and soon settled down. The Japanese destroyer quickly left the area.

It was time for Feliton and me to leave the island. The rescue mission was set up for the afternoon of February 12, three days before my twenty-second birthday. I was eager to get away from the hazardous life the coastwatchers led, so I joined Feliton on the beach to wait for the arrival of an escorted P-boat. Under the very noses of the Japanese outpost and within sight of three enemy airfields I saw for the first time our new gull-winged fighters, along with army P-38s, flying escort for the P-boat. We were already in a canoe, having bid farewell to our benefactors, when the flying boat landed. I was ushered in with Feliton, spear and all. Dr. W. W. Evans, known to us as "Big D," was along for the ride. He handed me a bottle of brandy for medicinal purposes. He had heard that I was seriously wounded and had braved this flight to help. On the flight back one of the P-38 pilots had an engine run wild near Munda Airfield and had to bail out over the ocean. We landed to pick up the pilot. Upon landing back at the 'Canal, I was brought to General Mulcahy's quarters for a debriefing and a medical checkup by Dr. White (De Blanc in English).

My leave was over and the F4U-1 Corsair birdcage had at long last reached the front lines. Our squadron was pulled out early and sent to the rear to get checked out in this new fighter. I had the "distinction" of being rescued on the first mission that any Corsair pilots flew in the war zone, a rescue mission to pick up Lieutenant Jeff De Blanc and Staff Sergeant Feliton. Ken Walsh was one of those Corsair pilots. He was soon awarded the Medal of Honor for fighter action.

I spent another tour of combat duty in the Pacific war. It included the Okinawa Campaign, Kamikaze action, a UFO sighting, and the humor associated with the winding down of the war in 1945.

MAYHEM—P-38 STYLE

Colonel Hub Zemke was already a famous P-47 ace and group commander before he took over the 479th Fighter Group. This is the story told in the distinctive Zemke style of the preparation, attack and follow-up to the raid on the German airfield at Nancy/Essey, where forty-three enemy planes were destroyed and twenty-eight more possibly damaged.

Midair collisions and losses to the weather had plagued the 479th Fighter Group. Fourteen pilots and aircraft went down in the month of June 1944 alone. Inexperience and too much in the way of desperation tactics contributed to some of their losses. No enemy aircraft were destroyed, but innumerable railroad busting sorties to France and the Low Countries attested to their determination. As the group became proficient in strafing and bombing, they sought out the French and German railroad system wherever they were sent. Locomotives, oil cars, freight cars, bridges, and dams came under the gunsights of the Lightnings. By August they had conducted 115 missions against the Nazis. A number of Jerry aircraft had been dispatched, but here again, fourteen first-line pilots had "flown west." Replacements filled the ranks, but the morale of the troops did not espouse confidence.

On August 10, the 479th Group Leader, Lieutenant Colonel K. L. Riddle, took a number of direct flak hits in the left wing while strafing a marshaling yard northeast of Paris. Riddle was not seen to parachute, but he did go on to escape and evade. He lived with the French Underground for a while, and was then liberated when the Allied front lines overran his position.

After turning over command of the 56th Fighter Group at 1400 hours on August 11 to my executive officer, Lieutenant Colonel Dave Schilling, I arrived at Wattisham with all my worldly possessions, a packed steamer trunk and a B-4 bag, in time to address an assembly of 479th pilots at 1600 hours. They were told to informally sit on the parade ground grass while I listed a few pet policies on military demeanor and what was expected of them—discipline, devotion, and dedication, down to the lowest ranks. They would be tested from time to time to determine if the "good words" had penetrated. It had been my experience long ago that indoctrination and training were a matter of repeating lessons—lessons often learned the hard way. Some things would be repeated many times. There was a "Zemke way." Let's see if it would work again. They were told that it was a pleasure for me to become their commander, but I had no secret formula for combat success. As I looked around at the serious faces confronting me, I told them that I was certain that we could muster a combat unit that would make the Germans cringe.

Having acquired only a few hours in a "droop snout" P-38, it became impingent upon me to fly a few more hours in a combat Lightning. For certain, a pilot should have wrung out his fighter aircraft a few times to learn its characteristics, not least of all the emergency steps and procedures that should be taken in the event of any malfunction. The P-38 was controlled by a wheel mounted on a central column rather than by a stick. This was something new. It was different, but not unmanageable, to regulate and synchronize two engines at double throttle. I logged about ten hours of orientation flying before venturing into combat. Those flights were tacked on the tail of one of the squadrons performing some local training.

The next few mornings saw me saddled up a P-38, trying to memorize instrument positions, in addition to the pips and squeaks of the little beast. It took some doing, but the tasks were not insurmountable. My afternoons were spent on the flight line and in the engineering shops, the pilot ready room and the airmen barracks.

Evenings were livened with "skull sessions" with the flying executive and the squadron COs. These took place in my quarters, and attendance was required. Tactics and more tactics dominated the conversations. Those rap sessions were continued to reemphasize my evaluations of the group's capabilities, and where I wanted emphasis placed or changed. In particular, considerable time was devoted to explaining tactics in various situations, both air-to-air and air-to-ground. Those same sessions had been never-ending in the 56th. In the case of the 479th, certain immediate upgrading and changes in tactics were indicated.

From those discussions it was determined that the pilots had better-than-average accumulated flying time in their chosen fighting machines when compared with other outfits in theater. Pilot for pilot, they were far more experienced than the Luftwaffe. All they needed was more time and experience in the "assault and support" phases of aerial combat. That philosophy applied to the lowly two-pilot element, where the leader conducts the attack and is wholly supported by his wingman. The rule prevailed up to squadrons in the assault, being supported by one or more other squadrons. Likewise, tactics were reevaluated and modified as they applied to "free strafing," especially against heavily defended ground targets. A little more thought and planning was needed, rather than the opportunistic strafing of any and all targets that presented themselves. Losses had been too high.

The morning of August 18, 1944, broke clear and bright over East Anglia. Mission number 136 had come over the teletype in the wee hours. I was called to look over the "frag orders." The 479th would escort two combat wings of B-24s on a "round robin" mission to neutralize the German-held Nancy/Essey airdrome in eastern France. The airdrome was not too deep into enemy territory anymore and looked like a natural for an inauguration mission. For a long time we in the 56th Fighter Group had taken pictures of the airfield and monitored its activities, hoping someday to pull a coup when it was loaded with aircraft. Its features were well known. Personally I welcomed the chance to give the Luftwaffe station commander a rousing demonstration of how a coordinated bomber-fighter assault could turn his day into a splitting nightmare.

The group operations officer on duty in the briefing room was directed to scrub the name of Lieutenant Colonel Woods as mission leader and substitute Zemke. The pilots were told at the briefing that we possibly had a good mission. The target, an active airfield of long standing, offered a lot of strafing potential if the B-24s laid their bombs properly. The bombers carried two-and-a-half-pound "daisy cutter" canisters and 500-pound general purpose bombs—a load with the proper ingredients to put every German flak battery into safety shelters for a good spell. With two B-24 combat wings, the airdrome personnel would get a thundering blast of bombs from the first wing. A second load of bombs would come crashing down to stir up the dust and spread more confusion. Then the strafing would begin.

I liked those attacks by heavy bombers on airfields. By quelling the flak, they made the job of fighter strafing so much more in our favor, and much more intimate. With the ground shock, fires, explosions, and confusion, fighters could nip around the fire and dust for twenty or thirty minutes and administer more havoc on any surviving aircraft.

The participating pilots were told that I would break off the escort of the lead squadron (code-named "Lakeside") fifteen miles before the target to proceed ahead and reconnoiter the airfield. If the airfield was loaded, and the bombers did a bang-up job of laying their eggs, and not least of all reduced the flak, Lakeside Squadron would set up a circular strafing pattern in a string of flights. One after the other. One of the two remaining escort squadrons would establish top cover to prevent any enemy fighters from bouncing us. They could also spot and attack any uncovered flak batteries that had the courage to fire. Once Lakeside Squadron had expended most of its ammunition, they would exchange positions with the top cover and permit them to drop down for some strafing on their own.

The third squadron had to continue escorting the B-24s (as indicated by the field order) to ensure a safe return to "home plate" by the Big Friends. No designation of the task could be given at this briefing. We might all return home if the bombing results were poor, or if the field held no aircraft. All pilots were warned to keep the radio chatter down. They were told that I wanted to see the reaction of the 479th to a little excitement, then wished them "good luck!"

Taking aloft forty-nine P-38s in a leisurely climb out across the English South Coast, the group made rendezvous with the 2nd Air Division bombers on penetration of the French coast at Bayeux. I called for the "four finger" combat formation. The 436th Fighter Squadron took up escort on the left flank of the bombers, while the 435th Squadron slid over the top to patrol the right flank. To guarantee that all enemy head-on attacks were nullified before they started, I took the sixteen P-38s of the 434th Squadron ahead of the bomber tract to continue to weave across the forward route of the penetration.

The route to the target first carried us due south to a point beyond Paris. Here an abrupt ninety-degree turn to the east took us past Paris and straight for Nancy, in eastern France. The weather was beautifully clear with visibility measured in double figures. No enemy opposition rose to challenge our progress.

At the appropriate time I took the last section of Lakeside Squadron (eight P-38s) from in front of the bombers and made a dash for Nancy/Essey. The second section of the squadron maintained its escort coverage of the B-24s. We arrived over Nancy at over 12,000 feet and began orbiting in a wide circle around the target area while observing the layout down below. The airdrome with its runways, hangars, and dispersal areas showed evidence of previous attacks and damage repairs. There were a good number of twin-engine light bombers parked at random around the field and its dispersal area. A hasty calculation of visible aircraft indicated that there were more than seventy JU-88s and HE-111s. Because there were so few visible single-engine aircraft, it was concluded that this was a night fighter or light bomber base rather than a fighter defense airfield. For certain it was loaded, vulnerable, and ready for plucking. All that was needed was for the bombers to pattern the airfield with an array of bombs that would silence the ground defenses. The 479th could take care of the rest.

I relayed back to the escorting P-38s that the situation

was ideal for strafing. The squadrons were told to break off escort while the bombers unloaded, and form in a wide circle south of the bombing area and free of the city of Nancy. The 436th Squadron would take up escort immediately after the bombing and escort the two combat wings back to England. They would have to reduce coverage to put a section (eight aircraft) on each flank. I would judge the damage—smoke, fires, winds, etc.—as soon as the bombing was finished, then determine a strafing pattern.

Switching the VHF radio channel to fighter-bomber frequency, I talked with the bomber commander, telling him about the ideal situation and wishing him luck. Nancy extended to the very edge of the airfield. I recommended that he make a run south-southeast to north-northwest to keep from scattering any hung-up bombs into its residential areas, as if he didn't have that figured out well before his bombers were airborne. Shortly thereafter, the first combat wing of about fifty B-24s appeared to the southeast, plowing along in a deliberate and laborious manner, on a direct course for the airfield. The four-engine heavies looked up to their task.

Loads of 500-pound bombs left the bomb bays and curved toward the target with ever-increasing velocities. A few wasted bursts of flak appeared near the bombers but stopped abruptly as a string of several hundred bombs covered the northern half of the airfield. Dust and smoke rose 2,000 feet into the sky. The first B-24s slowly cleared the airfield and swung to the northwest on a homeward-bound route. The bombing phase of their task was completed.

Next came the second combat wing of heavies, loaded with two-and-a-half-pound antipersonnel bombs clustered in canisters. Being perhaps two or three miles directly astern of the lead combat wing, it took them only a few minutes on "bomb run" to dump their full load in a string through the south center of the airfield. Smoke and fires belched from the destruction. There was no enemy opposition whatsoever. The chief bombardier must have considered this to be another training run on a practice range.

All of this action was viewed from a safe sideline seat at 10,000 feet south of the strike area. We couldn't have asked for a better bomb-dispersal pattern. Concussion from the explosions rocked us a bit, but our lives remained otherwise serene. The crash and explosions of the bombs must have been ear-shattering and earthshaking at ground level. No doubt the flak gunners and other military personnel had pulled their helmets farther down over their heads and remained cringing in their shelters. It was enough to rattle the staunchest of nerves.

When the 436th Fighter Squadron was told to take up escort again, a bit of radio reaction arose. Major D. Biscagart pleaded that he wanted to stay and participate in the strafing. He was bluntly cut off with, "Dammit, Bisket! You've been told once already that you and your squadron would escort the B-24s back to England. You have your instructions." He probably ground his teeth in his oxygen mask, but the 436th took up their assigned duty.

For what it's worth, there's only one commander in an air battle. For better or worse, his directions are absolute and final. In other words, there's no room for discussion—lesson number one to the "troops." It's not incidental to say "*no* bombers were lost on this mission." They had been covered on the entire route over occupied territory.

I directed the first section of Lakeside P-38s to follow me on a wide circling sweep while individual pilots took their places for strafing, each man covering the aircraft ahead of him. If flak opens up, divert to take it out first. Then came the order of the day, *"Follow me!"* Thus began the assault.

The 435th remained above us at two levels, 6,000 feet and 10,000 feet, patrolling in a wide circle, scanning the sky for any enemy aircraft and checking the ground for reactivating flak positions. Their vigilance allowed us to devote all of our attention and energy to the task at hand. Their turn at exploiting the situation would come.

My first run on a two-engine aircraft that was partly surrounded by trees saw me put a good five-second burst into the kite. Just as I was about to close in for another burst, I noticed another P-38 out of the corner of my eye, firing at the same target and fast converging on a collision course. A midair was averted, averted by only a narrow margin, by a fast roll of the ailerons to the left and by pulling back on my elevators. I don't know where the other P-38 came from, or where it went. I announced over the radio, "Whoever the SOB was who just tried to cut me out, you'd better watch out or I'll shoot you down! I'm serious. Report to me after the mission is over."

No one ever reported, and though I suspected a certain pilot, the culprit was never identified. An accepted practice of long standing among all fighter units was that you didn't cut in front or try to outgun a leader, whether he was a squadron commander or a two-ship element leader. This was not tradition or a precedent, but a common-sense tactic that had to be followed in the heat of battle.

To maintain a semblance of continued attack order, I took my wingman up to 6,000 feet and untangled the array of swooping P-38s. They were having a field day, every man to his own choosing. The strafing planes were put back into circular strings and maintained that way for the remainder of the mission. There was too much discussion and radio chatter. I was forever against extraneous radio chatter and hoopla.

Captain Claire Duffie found a dispersal area well south of the airfield and requested permission to take a section and work it over. "Permission granted." Soon a new plume of smoke shot skyward as Duffie and his boys shot up the area. By now the cloud of smoke and dust over the main air base had become so intense that the strafing pattern had to be altered several times to keep away from burning debris. It was impossible to fly directly over or across the airfield because of the intense burning black cloud.

Once everyone had an opportunity to make two or three strafing runs and expend some ammunition, the operation was called to a halt. In my book, each man could now justify his claim of having become a fighter pilot. All had blown the tape that covered their gun barrels. Evidence from later gun-camera reviews showed several P-38s in the picture frames, with other attackers also firing at ground targets, all of this with one or two P-38s hammering targets in utter disregard of the apparent hazards. The strafing pattern and distances between aircraft were anything but proper. Some of the pilots overran each other, or fired at ground targets ahead of the P-38s they were supposed to be supporting. It was a case of overeagerness and inexperience. For certain, not an example of combat refinement.

Although a few more enemy aircraft might have remained, flying was becoming more hazardous. The stunned flak gunners were regaining their composure and mustering the courage to man their guns. A coup is a coup. Why overdo it? The 479th was no longer operating to its best advantage, so we returned to base.

Lieutenant P. W. Manning of the 434th Squadron turned up MIA when the group finally reported back at home base. Later in the war it was reported that he had crashed in Nancy. Although the flash combat report gave the apparent cause of his death as flak, it was known that very little flak had been seen during the raid.

As motley and amateurish as the strafing phase of the mission had been, the returning fighter circus knew that they had administered a thrashing to the German station commander and his crews. By now he should have been shaking his head in complete despair and crying into his beer stein. Inwardly I knew from the billowing fires and columns of black smoke left behind at Nancy/Essey that the 479th had vindicated itself in one fell swoop for the losses and frustrations of its previous two months of combat.

Returning to Wattisham, I climbed down from the cockpit to behold P-38s buzzing and performing victory rolls as never before. Everyone airborne had gone berserk. Immediately I drove to the control tower and climbed the catwalk into the control room. Facing two ashen-faced air traffic controllers, I directed them to start copying aircraft numbers of

P-38s trying to blast down the wind sock. After they copied down eight or ten numbers on a pad, I took the microphone, calmly announced who I was, and told those clowns to stop the tomfoolery. "Anyone taking a low pass, making a victory roll or a loop, is fined fifty dollars a violation. Put your kites on the ground immediately. All pilots, and I mean you, report to the group briefing room immediately after landing."

Waiting in a straight-backed chair in the briefing room and smoking a much-needed cigarette, I watched a somber group of hotshots file individually into the room and silently take their seats. They didn't show the youthful exuberance they'd displayed on the mission. All three squadrons were eventually in attendance.

The debriefing was opened by expressing my concern about the unprofessional conduct exhibited at times during the mission. Assembly, escort, and general-formation flying was as good as any organization, but when the tempo of action was stepped up, this exuberance made things fall apart. It was beyond me from where this laissez-faire attitude toward military conduct had come. If I was expected to command and lead them, I would lead. My policy and decisions must be obeyed and performed. A list of the aircraft that had violated my policy on airdrome buzzing was read. Frankly I detested such insolence when it applied to air discipline. It had been pointed out a few days before how much I detested buzzing, victory rolls, and aerobatics close to the ground.

It was explained that I had written too many letters to grieving young brides or aging parents about overconfident, deceased flyboys. I'd certainly welcome them to do the same things in the face of the enemy on the other side of the English Channel. Those whose aircraft numbers had just been called out were expected to visit the station finance officer and pay fifty dollars American for flying violations under Article 104 of the Uniform Manual of Courts-Martial. Those who felt that my policy denied some sense of their flying rights could request trial by military courts-martial. I would be available the next day to sign the appropriate papers for such trials.

The speech was greeted with blank stares and blinking eyes. For once they believed the new commander spoke in all seriousness.

It was not my intention to dishearten them completely on the mission in general. A valiant attempt had been made to completely disarm the Nancy/Essey aircraft. Certainly the results were gratifying. What concerned me was the amateurish display of strafing technique. Every pilot had seemed to want to be a self-proclaimed exterminator—firing from all angles, all distances, and all directions. Had we not had ideal conditions by virtue of the bombers and a complete absence of AA fire, the tide of battle might have been very different. The request from Major Biscagart wasn't mentioned. That was handled later in a personal conversation.

Extraneous radio chatter had to stop. That cluttered the channel and endangered everybody. Veteran organizations had a plan of action and didn't jam up the single fighter radio channel with "nothing" conversations. If I gave an order, there would not be time for explanations or discussions. Just do it. Cutting off people from the pattern or taking the offensive away from a leader was taboo. Each pilot had a specific job to do on the team and was expected to do it rather than give displays of rugged individuality and cutting each other off to get to a target.

The mission appeared to be a resounding success, but we needed a lot of improvement before the 479th was a smoothly functioning fighting machine. I felt a degree of satisfaction to have pulled such a coup on my first mission with the 479th. Perhaps they had overreacted from enthusiasm and the desire to excel, but the fact remained that combat was a terribly dangerous business. My stern lecture was designed to save lives on future missions.

There must have been some low-level grumbling when the pilots returned to their respective squadrons for intelligence debriefing, but now they knew where the "old man" stood. While we were waiting for the flash reports of actions and claims from each squadron, Lieutenant Colonel Sid

Woods (the flying exec), Major Evans Pillsbury (the group intelligence officer), and I tried to reconstruct the fast action on a mission that almost went out of control. We finally concluded that combat excitement and the evidence of mounting success, after so many dismal losses, had caused the troops to throw caution to the wind.

By seven o'clock that evening a consolidated group claim of more than one hundred aircraft destroyed had come from conflicting claims. Considerable discussion continued among the pilots over the exact number and types of aircraft destroyed. With this in mind, a short teletype was sent to Fighter Command, stating that no flash report could be rendered that evening. The successful bombing by the 2nd Air Division, plus the strafing by two Fighter Squadrons of the 479th had caused such destruction—fires, smoke, and general havoc—at Nancy/Essey that it would take some time for a proper evaluation and justification of claims.

My request for an immediate aerial post-strike photo could assist in assessing the actual results. Two days later a large set of overhead photo shots of the airfield laid on my desk. It took an evaluation board to review and act upon each pilot's claims, and they had to be verified. An attempt was made to obtain affirmation by fellow pilots. We had to wait two more weeks for the actual combat film to be developed. That film cleared up many of the questions about actual damage. It was concluded that the B-24 strike pilots had destroyed seventeen parked aircraft. Then the overlapping claims of the fighter pilots were evaluated. In some cases, as many as three pilots had claimed the same aircraft destroyed. The combat film helped to clarify who did what damage in those cases. Aircraft that were hit but did not burn or break down were relegated to the category of "possibly damaged."

Realizing that a true awarding of claims was impossible, we made a breakdown of credits (shared ground victories) in some cases. Some pilots may have lost and others may have gained, but all were given a share. After two weeks of juggling and reevaluation, it was concluded that on Mission 136, August 18, 1944, the 479th Fighter Group had destroyed forty-three enemy planes and possibly damaged twenty-eight more. Fifteen of the sixteen 434th Squadron pilots held claims. The sixteenth pilot, Lieutenant P. W. Manning, may have had a claim, but had crashed into the town of Nancy on the mission. Thirteen of the sixteen 435th Squadron pilots were awarded credits for ground victories. In my case, the shooting up of the twin-engine aircraft was thrown into the pot to share the wealth among the lieutenants. Two others had claimed the same aircraft. Neither of them came forward to say that he had come close to shooting me down that day.

Since that resounding kickoff with the 479th Fighter Group on my first mission, I've often wondered how exacting were the claims of ground victories by many other fighter groups. Supposedly, the top score on the ground by one group was 125 destroyed late in the war. More power to them. It will never be known how many were actually destroyed, but if the true figures were known, there wouldn't be anything to argue about in the future.

SURVIVAL

Lieutenant Jim Percy arrived at Guadalcanal in early November 1942, just in time for eight days of intense aerial combat that was deciding the fate of the marine beachhead. The next months were more of the same. He was shot down in June 1943 and should never have survived the events that followed—plunging 2,000 feet to the water with a chute streaming out behind him, being stalked by sharks, floating throughout the day on the current, being inspected by a deadly coral snake, and finally pulling himself halfway onto the beach of a tiny island with only the use of his upper body. It's an incredible story.

Following graduation from flight school in the spring of 1942, I was sent to NAS North Island to attend the navy advanced carrier training program. During the months of July and August I was able to accumulate approximately 120 hours in the F4F Grumman Wildcat and was trained in all phases of fighter tactics. Upon completion of that training, I and five other ACTG graduates were ordered to MCAS Kearny Mesa, just outside of San Diego, and assigned to the newly formed marine fighter squadron, VMF-112. The squadron consisted of Major P. J. Fontana (the skipper), Captain Bob Frazer (the executive officer), and twenty-four relatively brand-new second lieutenants. By the time we sailed for overseas about five weeks later, the squadron's average flight time in the F4F was twenty-two hours. My ACTG training had been a real boon. I had more flight time in type than anyone else except the skipper and the executive officer. Some of the pilots barely had enough time in the F4Fs to get safely airborne.

We left for overseas in early October 1942, heading for some place called "Cactus." The trip over was great. We traveled on a converted passenger liner that really hadn't been converted yet and still had its civilian crew. We ate like kings—menus, waiters, and small tables complete with white tablecloths and silverware. War didn't look too bad. We were let in on the big secret after we had been at sea for a few days. Cactus was the code name for Guadalcanal. No kidding? Where is that?

We landed in New Caledonia in late October and spent approximately a week there, then went on to Espiritu Santo, where we established our squadron rear and maintenance base at a newly completed fighter strip. On November 8 pilots and ground crews were flown by transport to Guadalcanal. As far as I was concerned, this was it. Right out the side windows, people were shooting at each other. Could I really handle it?

Only time would tell. When the transport taxied to a stop, all we could see from the door were wrecked aircraft. It just happened that our plane had pulled up facing the salvage yard or "bone pile." It was a disconcerting first look at the island. We were trucked to our bivouac area and assigned to tents in a coconut grove, then we were sent to the flight line. Some of us were sent on local orientation flights, while the rest of us were given intelligence briefings. Mainly, though, we listened wide-eyed to the tales of aerial combat being spun by the old-timers.

We were told that an all-out Japanese effort to retake Guadalcanal would begin at any time. Thus began eight of the most fantastic days of my life. I will relate only a few of the events that directly affected me. On November 11 I was standing scramble alert when word came down that a high-altitude bombing raid was inbound. Eight of us immediately scrambled and started climbing to intercept the raid. At 14,000 feet I shifted from low blower, the first stage of the two-stage turbocharger, to high blower. The engine began to run rough and then it quit. I shifted back to low blower and the engine restarted and smoothed out. I couldn't keep up with the others without high blower, and prudence dictated that I return to base, but I had spotted twenty-seven medium bombers flying in a V of Vs. I was fiercely determined to get into combat.

The bombers were about five miles away, flying at 24,000 feet, when I first spotted them. I continued to climb very slowly on low blower, but it was obvious that I wasn't going to reach their altitude in time to intercept. As the bombers passed about 3,000 feet over me, I noticed that their bomb-bay doors were open. As I grasped what that meant, their bombs started falling toward me. All I could do was duck my head and pray. Bombs passed all around me, but my plane was not hit.

I was considerably shaken up and opted to return to base. At that point I spotted three Japanese Zeros, high and to the right. One peeled off and commenced an attack. I turned toward him. He broke off. I turned back on my course. Another one peeled off. I turned toward him and he broke off the attack. I returned to my course. This went on for what seemed to be hours but probably wasn't more than a few minutes. The worst thing was that I wasn't making much progress toward home. Then, to my eternal joy, I saw another Wildcat returning to base. What a wonderful sight! I rapidly joined up on him and we both headed home. The three Zeros left the area. I was a very chastened and subdued fighter pilot by the time I got home. I hadn't fired a round and had broken almost every rule of fighter combat, but somehow managed to survive.

During the night of November 12–13, a major naval battle took place off Guadalcanal between Florida and Savo islands. That place was later called Iron Bottom Bay, because so many ships were sunk there. Even though we were in our foxholes, the battle was awe-inspiring. Every salvo lit the horizon from end to end. The noise was shattering. Our imaginations were working overtime. At about two A.M. a Japanese battleship began shelling both the bomber strip and the fighter strip. The huge shells passed over our heads sounding like roaring freight trains, exploded on the fighter strip, and set aircraft on fire. This went on for three and a half hours. There were only four fighters left flyable for dawn patrol.

Shortly after dawn the battleship was discovered almost dead in the water a short distance from Savo Island. Four destroyers were escorting it. More fighters were being returned to flight status, so my four-plane division was ordered to escort dive-bombers and torpedo-bombers attacking the battleship. If there was no opposition, we were to make strafing runs to suppress AA fire and divert it from the bombers. We found no aerial opposition and peeled off into our strafing runs. Tom Hughes (my wingman) and I concentrated on the battleship. John Stack and E. V. Wagner concentrated on the destroyers. Getting into position for a dive, I remembered the hairy stories we had heard about the amount of antiaircraft fire that destroyers, and particularly larger ships, could lay down. On passing through 10,000 feet and not having seen any AA fire that I could identify, I stopped worrying about it.

I started firing at approximately 4,000 feet, and was surprised at the number of ricochets flying around. Some of them looked as big as baseballs floating through the sky. So be it. I continued my run, pulled out over the mast of the battleship, and climbed for altitude for another run. I dived, again watching ricochets fill the sky around me. I ignored them and concentrated on my attack. By then I was almost out of ammunition, so I joined up with the rest of my flight and returned to base. It wasn't until I was making light of the supposedly heavy antiaircraft fire back at base that it was pointed out that my ricochets were really enemy fire aimed at me. I felt extremely foolish and naive. From then on I kept my mouth shut unless I was sure about what I was saying.

Aircraft from Guadalcanal and naval carriers continued attacks on the battleship throughout the day. It was hit by nine aerial torpedoes and fourteen 1,000-pound bombs, but it was still afloat at dusk. The battleship sank that night. Three of the four escorting destroyers had been sunk during the daylight strikes.

That night we were told that a Japanese invasion force was on the way to reinforce the garrison on Guadalcanal and provide enough punch to retake the island. An on-call air strike was scheduled to take off as soon as scout aircraft could pinpoint the enemy location. Our squadron was assigned fighter cover for the dive-bombers and torpedo-bombers on the first strike. Only eight fighters were available—Bob Frazer's division of four aircraft and my division. The scouts located the enemy force approximately 120 miles northeast of Guadalcanal. It consisted of twelve troop transports and four cargo ships, escorted by thirty-eight destroyers and light cruisers. Our attacking force was made up of eight Wildcats, twelve SBD dive-bombers, and six torpedo planes. This sounds like a puny force now, but at the time we thought that we were a pretty potent group.

As we approached the target area at about 15,000 feet,

eight Zeros turned toward us. Their intent was to at least scatter us so that they could disrupt the dive-bomber attack. I alerted Bob Frazer, and both our divisions turned to meet the attack. I picked my target and maneuvered to make a head-on run, knowing that my six .50-caliber machine guns could outgun the two 7.7mm machine guns and two slow-firing 20mm cannons on the Zero. I opened up at maximum range and was gratified to see immediate results. Small pieces started flying off the Zero and black smoke spewed from the engine compartment. Due to the high speed of closure, I was able to fire only one more burst, then had to rapidly climb to avoid a midair collision. As the Zero passed under me, I could see the pilot slumped over in the cockpit as a fierce fire burned in the engine compartment.

I turned to check on our two divisions and saw six other Zeros going down, some burning, and some out of control. I spotted another Zero diving for the ocean, closely pursued by two F4Fs. The lead Wildcat fired a long burst and the aircraft virtually disintegrated. I found out later that Bob Frazer had been doing the firing. Eight for eight—not a bad morning's work. The most important thing to me was that it was my first aerial victory.

Our bombers were able to make their attacks free from aerial opposition. Three troop transports received direct hits. Others got near-misses. In many cases, a near-miss could be more lethal than a direct hit. Marine and navy aircraft continued their attacks throughout the day. All twelve transports were sunk. The four cargo vessels were damaged so severely that their captains ran them ashore on the northeast coast of Guadalcanal. If the 45,000 troops on that convoy had reached Guadalcanal, there would have been no way for our ground forces to prevent them from overrunning the island.

On February 1, 1943, word was flashed to the ready tent that two U.S. destroyers on patrol near Savo Island, just off the northeast end of Guadalcanal, were in danger of aerial attack. Ten F4Fs were scrambled, with Bob Frazer leading and the rest of us following in no particular order. It took only a few minutes to reach the area. The first thing we saw were six Aichi-99 dive-bombers commencing their attack on the destroyers. As we turned to engage them, I saw a large number of Zeros (thirty-five to forty) off to the side. Frazer and two other Wildcats were already attacking the dive-bombers, so I called the six others and told them to form a line on me, pick a target, make one pass, make a 180-degree turn, and head generally back toward base. By doing this, I hoped to buy some time for the fighters that had gone after the dive-bombers, and create confusion among the Zero pilots.

I missed my target, or at least didn't do enough damage to bring him down, but some of the others were more fortunate. The air was still saturated with enemy fighters. I instructed all aircraft to join and commence the "Thach weave." This was a defensive formation devised by Commander Jimmy Thach for use when you were outnumbered or outgunned. We qualified on both counts. The maneuver normally utilizes two or four aircraft that line out on a course and weave back and forth in a series of running figure-eights. When done properly, you can protect each other's tails. I began weaving with Captain Michael R. Yunck. To his chagrin and my delight, most of the Zeros in our little piece of the sky picked on him instead of me. I exploded three Zeros off his tail in a few minutes.

We were relatively clear of the fight and just catching our breath when I looked to the side and saw an F4F in a screaming dive for the ocean and home base. It was followed by two Zeros that were pressing in for a final attack. I peeled off after them but was rapidly losing ground, so I aimed as far in front of them as possible and fired a short burst. Both Japanese pilots obviously saw my tracers. One immediately broke right. The other one pulled up in an extremely steep climb. I picked him to continue my own attack because I could cut across to intercept his climb path. I was rather far away, but he appeared to be slowing in his climb.

One Japanese fighter tactic was to complete a zoom, then

do an Immelmann turn and dive down when the opposing pilot was most vulnerable—flying at low air speed that would restrict his ability to maneuver to avoid attack. It almost worked. He completed his turn and dived, but I still had enough airspeed to stand on my tail and bring my guns to bear. I had time for one desperation burst and caught the brass ring. He burst into flames and went out of control. The wreckage passed so close that my cockpit filled with smoke, and my wingman was sure that we had had a midair collision. This impression was further heightened in his mind by the fact that my aircraft was obviously not in control. In getting into position to fire on the Zero, I ran out of airspeed. As soon as I fired my guns, I went into a spin.

I recovered from the spin and joined the other aircraft to assess our situation. There were no other enemy aircraft in the area. We returned to base, and after debriefing learned that our ten F4Fs had accounted for six dive-bombers and thirteen Zeros confirmed, with no losses on our side. Four of the Zeros were credited to me.

Around late February or early March 1943, our squadron was relieved of combat duties, ordered back to Espiritu Santo, and transitioned from the F4F Wildcat to the brand-new F4U Corsair. Learning to fly Corsairs was a thrilling experience. We returned to Guadalcanal with our new aircraft for a third combat tour in early May.

All was routine until early on the morning of June 7, 1943. We received word that the Japanese were launching a maximum-effort air strike against the island. This meant an attack with well in excess of one hundred aircraft. VMF-112 was on scramble alert and launched sixteen Corsairs on order. We arrived on station at 30,000 feet, at our assigned orbit point just to the north of the Russell Islands, and prepared to engage the Japanese. Just as we got there, one of the pilots alerted us to Zeros, high, starting an attack. I looked up and saw twelve to fifteen Zeros peeling off and diving from a position 3,000 to 4,000 feet above us. We spread out our formation to make maneuver room, and the dogfight was on.

I found myself on the tail of a Zero with both of us wrapped up in tight right turns. I couldn't turn sharply enough to get enough lead to hit his aircraft. He couldn't turn sharply enough to get a lead on my aircraft or safely break away. Stalemate. As I tried to arrive at a solution, I looked below us and spotted a Corsair a few thousand feet below us with three Zeros converging on him. Without thinking, I rolled over into a full-power vertical dive and opened fire on the Zeros. As far as I know, I didn't hit anything, but the sight of my tracers caused them to break off their attack.

By this time I had built up a tremendous amount of airspeed, and when I tried to pull the nose through, it refused to respond. The only thing I could think of doing was to cut the throttle completely, slow down, and keep trying to get the aircraft to respond to my controls. The nose finally did come through, much faster than I would have liked. This resulted in excessive G forces, and I blacked out completely. I came to, flying straight and level at 16,000 feet with the sky completely to myself. Being a more prudent pilot by now, I set course for home.

As I approached the Russell Islands, I spotted three aircraft flying in a V formation, followed by two others in column. All five aircraft were on a reverse course about 3,000 feet below me. They had to be enemy aircraft heading back to their home base, and they apparently hadn't seen me. I positioned myself to make a high-speed diving attack from the rear. I closed on the last of the two aircraft in column and fired a burst. He exploded and went out of control. I shifted aim to the second one and fired another burst. Heavy smoke poured from the engine area and he dropped rapidly toward the ocean. I was now overrunning the three-plane V, so I pulled up sharply with the intention of continuing on home. I regained altitude and saw the three planes again. They must not have seen anything because they were still heading blithely back toward Bougainville. One more quick pass seemed indicated.

As I rolled into the attack, all hell broke loose. My right wingtip disappeared, the right aileron virtually disintegrated, a row of bullet holes marched down the right wing to the center fuselage, and explosions racked the cockpit and accessory section. It felt like I was sitting on top of a hydraulic jackhammer. A stream of hot oil and hydraulic fluid shot out of the fresh-air vent located between the rudder pedals. I had been very thoroughly shot up by an aircraft that I had not even seen. I jammed on full throttle, rolled over into a vertical dive, closed the fresh-air vent, built up speed, rolled sharply to the right, and violently pulled out, straight and level. The Zero could not follow that kind of maneuver. It was not aerodynamically stressed to withstand those forces.

That rid me of the Zero, but I still had a problem. My first reaction was to make an emergency landing on an almost completed airstrip on one of the Russell Islands. I slowed the aircraft down to check it out and discovered that the right wing dropped at speeds under 220 knots and I couldn't control the aircraft. I knew the engine wouldn't last the sixty to seventy miles back to Guadalcanal, so I decided to bail out as close as possible to that strip in the Russells. The normal bailout procedure in a Corsair was to roll inverted and fall out, thus decreasing your chances of hitting the rudder or the elevators. I didn't have enough control of the aircraft to do this. I slowed down to approximately 240 knots, reduced altitude to about 2,000 feet as I passed over the strip, opened the hood, released the safety belt, put my foot on the control stick, and shoved forward as far as I could. This catapulted me out of the cockpit. I missed the rudder by approximately one thick coat of paint.

After clearing the aircraft I pulled the rip cord and confidently awaited the shock of my chute opening. Nothing happened. I looked up and saw that the chute had come out of the pack and was streaming out above me. I pulled on the risers, but that did no good. I had no sensation of falling. It felt as though I were floating through space. I looked down and regained my depth perception in time to see that I was getting close to the water. I straightened up, grabbed my crotch, and hit the ocean. I regained consciousness underwater, how far underwater I do not know. When I realized where I was, I pulled the toggles on my Mae West and floated to the surface. It was a strange feeling. I didn't know whether I was alive or dead. I took a deep breath and felt pain, so I concluded that I must still be alive.

Many people have asked me what I thought about when I realized my chute wasn't going to open. They wanted to know if my life passed before me, if I was conscious throughout, and so forth. It has been calculated that falling at 126 mph, it would take ten seconds to fall 2,000 feet. That's not much time to think about a lot of things, particularly when you cut that time in half. That's about how long it took me to realize that the chute wasn't going to get any air in it. I was conscious throughout. My life did not pass before me. I did think that this was going to be a bum deal for my squadron mates, because they would spend days looking for me with no hope of success. I knew how frustrating it was to find nothing on searches and never know what had really happened. I felt sorry that I was going to be the cause of this. There were no other thoughts, except those connected with trying to make the chute work properly.

My first thought on surfacing was to inflate the life raft that was attached to our parachute harnesses and formed the seat we sat on. The 20mm cannon shells had torn holes in the life raft and parachute, rendering both of them useless. I jettisoned both. I wasn't concerned, because I had gone down approximately in the middle of the Russell Islands, a gathering of two hundred small atolls. No matter which way I went, I could make landfall in an hour or two. Normal breathing didn't hurt, but breathing deeply did. I could move my arms, but when I moved my legs I could feel bone grating in my hip area. My ankles didn't respond well. I also noticed that there was a small leak in the inner compartment of my life jacket. I inflated it with my breath and continued doing so whenever it was required. I decided that a minimum movement of my arms would keep me afloat, so I would do just that and let the current take me to a landfall.

I had gone down around eleven-thirty in the morning and felt sure that I would make shore before dark. All went well until I had been floating in the water for a while and noticed movement in the water around me. I was being circled by sharks, but given my mental state by that time, it didn't bother me too much. We were issued glass vials of potassium chlorate which, when released in seawater, liberated free chlorine, a substance that sharks apparently did not like. I carried nine vials. I would break one each time the sharks began to close in, and they would disappear for a while. I discovered that the reason they kept coming back was the 20mm shells that exploded in the cockpit had peppered my chest, stomach, and legs with shrapnel, causing many open, oozing cuts. The sharks lost interest when the blood stopped flowing from my wounds.

I kept myself afloat and let the current carry me along. By late afternoon I had been carried to a reef just offshore from a small island. I figured if I could get across the reef, I could make shore. But I didn't have the strength to climb onto the reef. I decided to wait for the tide to rise, if it was going to rise, and body-surf onto the reef. After an hour or so, just before dusk, I made the attempt. All was fine, except a wave caught my left leg and flipped it up and over. I had no control over it. I passed out from the pain. I awoke the next morning, still lying on top of the reef, but apparently none the worse for wear.

I managed to roll off the reef into the lagoon side, where the water was calm and only two or three feet deep, and began to make my way the few hundred feet to shore. At one point while I was sitting on the bottom and resting, I noticed movement out of the corner of my eye. A coral snake was swimming my way. I stayed as I was, not moving, as it swam by not more than two feet in front of my face. It continued on by, stopped, turned around, and came back, stopped, and looked me over again, and then finally swam away.

Shortly after this I made shore and was disappointed to discover that I couldn't pull myself out of the water. I was on the beach sand only from the waist up. Nothing was working right from the waist down. It was then that I realized how violently thirsty I was. I grabbed a fallen coconut but couldn't open it. My survival knife was missing. I tried beating the coconut with pieces of coral and sticks and so forth, but to no avail. Frustration supreme! I happened to glance out toward the reef and saw a canoe with three natives in it. What a joyous sight they were.

I screamed, hollered, and waved, and finally attracted their attention. They immediately came over and checked me out. One of them went off in the canoe while the other two stayed with me. I signaled that I was thirsty, and one of them scrambled up a coconut tree and cut green coconuts off with his machete. After all that I had been through, I almost became a casualty to falling coconuts. The native returned and cut the end off a coconut, and I enjoyed a drink of the most delicious liquid ever devised.

The canoe returned not long after that. It was leading a Higgins boat containing two U.S. doctors who had taken some time off to go fishing. They had been just off the opposite side of my island. They made a stretcher out of oars and spare raincoats and put me aboard the Higgins boat for transport to a medical facility located at the new fighter strip, a distance of only three miles from where I went down. I felt no pain at all until the doctors showed up, but it began as soon as they tried to put me on the improvised stretcher. The pain was excruciating by the time they had me in the Higgins boat.

A medical examination showed that I had two broken ankles and a crushed and separated pelvis. All of my back muscles had been torn and pulled loose from their attachments. There were also multiple shrapnel wounds. Thus started another story. I spent one year in various hospitals, a journey that started in the Russell Islands, continued on to facilities in the New Hebrides, New Zealand, Pearl Harbor, and Oakland, and finally ended at Yosemite Convalescent Hospital.

BLACKBURN'S IRREGULARS

Lieutenant Commander Tom Blackburn was the commander of F4U Corsair Squadron VF-17, also known as the "Skull and Crossbones" Squadron. They tested many innovations, including a highly successful roving high-cover tactic. Fighting 17 shot down 154 Japanese aircraft, more than the number claimed by Pappy Boyington's "Black Sheep" Corsair Squadron.

At 0630 on November 1, 1943, we were circling at 25,000 feet, ten miles to the west of Empress Augusta Bay of Bougainville. As the light increased, we could clearly see the 10,000-foot peak of Mount Balbi to the northeast, and due east of us, the volcanic cone of Mount Bagana, spewing forth a steady cloud of black smoke from its peak of 8,500 feet. Bagana's plume streamed off to the south-southeast, indicating a wind of about twenty knots at that altitude. These two mountains were part of the great backbone ranges of Bougainville: the Emperor in the northern part and the Crown Prince to the south. The dark green of the heavy jungle cover of these ranges went right down to the shoreline, where the water was a bright apple-green, shading off to a deep blue as the water deepened.

It was a spectacularly beautiful view of the island's ninety-three-mile length, from adjacent Buka Island at the northeast tip to the southeast with its two major, though vacant, airstrips. Close by were 35,000 Japanese who were separated from the invasion area by fifty-five miles of barely passable terrain. Transit was by trails through the dense rain forest and across the many rivers flowing off the mountains. There were no roads at this time connecting Kahili and Kara airfields with Torokina.

At Empress Augusta Bay itself, code-named "Cherry Blossom," we could see the twelve transports of the landing force with landing craft, like beetles, swarming around them and heading in a great procession into the beach at Cape Torokina. Outboard of the transports were ten destroyers, steadily engaged in throwing shells into the beachhead half a mile from the shoreline and well clear of the landing parties. Four cruisers created a diversion by shelling Buka.

I had been unable to get a response from the fighter director whose call sign was "Dane Base," but heard him talking with a flight of New Zealanders (whose accent came through clearly) and three other fighter flights at lower altitudes, also in the immediate vicinity of Empress Augusta Bay. I was flying with seven companions. Doug Gutenkunst was on my wing. The heavily black-bearded Jim Streig was flying number three, and Tom Killefer was number four. Leading the second division was "Juggy" Bell, with Earl May flying number two. The second section of the second division was led by Ray Beacham with wingman Don Malone. We were in a loose, wide-open formation with approximately fifty yards separating each section within a division, and a couple of hundred yards between the two divisions.

Dane Base excitedly reported: "Bogies inbound four-zero miles north of Cherry Blossom, angels one-five, course one-eight-zero, speed one-four-zero!"

I sighted them shortly thereafter. It was a flight of eighteen Val dive-bombers at approximately 15,000 feet, covered by twelve Zekes (Zeros) 3,000 feet above them. The Zekes were in three flights of four planes each in a loose V. The dive-bombers were in two tight V of Vs.

I keyed my mike. "Tallyho! Tallyho! This is Big Hog Gem One. Eighteen Vals, twelve Zekes, north-northeast four-zero miles. Proceeding to attack, over."

Dane Base did not reply, so I called Juggy Bell. "Juggy, this is Big Hog, Big Hog! Did you get my tallyho? Did you get my tallyho, over?" No response. My transmitter was dead.

I rocked my wings and fired a short burst from all six guns to alert my flight, then swung to a course of zero four five to intercept the incoming Japanese flights. I was concerned that there was another flight of Japanese fighters up sun from the two flights that I had in sight, and that the pattern we were seeing was a booby trap. When we came in to attack, the fighters up sun would have an advantageous altitude and tactical position from which to cream us. I pointed down at about 350 knots, a high approach speed for gunnery purposes. My plan was to hit the Japanese fighter cover from the rear, then chandelle up to the left, into the sun, to counter a probable attack by the ambush group.

As I closed with my seven companions following in good shape, the Japanese fighter leader rocked his wings violently and pulled up sharply to the right to head back into us to counter our attack. All three enemy divisions swung into us in unison. We were presented with very difficult shots with a turning, head-on, constantly changing deflection, and a relative speed of approximately 500 knots. I opened fire at the fairly long range of about 300 yards, and my tracers appeared to be going into the Japanese fighter leader. But I saw no evidence of any damage as we approached a 100-yard range and I pulled up to pass over him. It's hard to believe, but none of the other seven in my flight had seen the enemy planes until I opened fire.

We chandelled into the sun, and finding no additional group of enemy fighters waiting, turned back to renew the attack. Meanwhile, the Japanese dive-bombers had broken up. Some of them were scooting for home; some of them had pushed over into dives to attack the transports. We mixed it up with the twelve Zekes. I flamed a Zeke from very close range, so close that when he blew up, I got hydraulic fluid or lube oil on my windshield. It was a wild scramble for what seemed like a long time but was probably only two or three minutes. Killefer, Streig, and Beacham each shot down a plane, and Doug Gutenkunst inflicted damage on still another Zero.

After the brouhaha had subsided, I found myself very much alone, and was happy to see Don Malone's Corsair shortly thereafter. We joined up and resumed our patrol at 25,000 feet. We saw nothing further of any of the Japanese aircraft, nor of the remaining six planes of my flight. After our appointed time on station was completed, Malone and I swung out seaward and started letting down to a lower altitude, where we could get rid of our oxygen masks and relax. As we did so, we sighted a lone P-40 headed south off our starboard bow, with a single Zero about two miles behind it.

We slanted down to overtake the Zero, but it was evident that we would not reach a firing position before he got close enough to the P-40 to shoot it down. So I pulled up my nose and fired a fairly long burst, hoping that the tracers falling into the sea ahead of him would spook him, and that he would break off his attack. Amazingly and blessedly, that's just what happened.

He pulled around in a tight turn to the left, which we followed, and made no attempt at evasive action, although he had to know we were there. It was a very short time before we overtook him. Malone swung out a couple of hundred yards to the side to counter any evasive action by the Japanese pilot, but he held course and speed at approximately 2,000 feet. I closed to 150 yards and flamed him with a very short burst. Malone and I then joined up in close formation and returned to our base at Ondongo ("place of death") on New Georgia.

When I got back to the ready room Quonset hut for debrief by Duke Henning, our superb air combat intelligence officer, I learned that the other six planes in my flight had all landed safely. Ray Beacham had a 20mm hole in the port wing of his plane, which required changing the outboard panel. None of the other planes suffered any damage. Our total kills were five with no losses, which was very gratifying, although tactically the action left a lot to be desired. This was not too astonishing, since it was the first time we had even seen Japanese airplanes, much less gotten into a scrap with them.

That afternoon Roger Hedrick, leading eight Corsairs on combat air patrol over Empress Augusta Bay at 20,000 feet, jumped a flight of nine Zeros and seven Vals. Roger shot down a Zero, and his flight damaged two others. Again there was no damage to any of our planes.

The next bit of action occurred on November 8. We were scheduled to make a predawn launch of twelve F4Us to rendezvous with twelve B-25s that were to attack shipping in Matchin Bay at the north end of Bougainville. The morning was rainy and pitch black when we took off at five o'clock. I circled the field a couple of times with my lights on, hoping to get the flight properly rendezvoused, picked up four "hogs," and headed to our rendezvous point, some twenty miles to the northwest. The five of us circled there until it was full daylight and the weather had ameliorated to the point where visibility was good, but no more Corsairs, and no B-25s showed up. There was no response to attempts to raise them on the radio. Accordingly we headed north to carry out the mission, flying at 1,000 feet where it was comfortable. At that altitude we went at fast cruise, not high enough to be picked up by Japanese radar on Bougainville.

The B-25 strike was to be a low-level attack on shipping in Matchin Bay, just south of Buka, to be followed by a pass over Buka-Buna to beat them up with machine guns. We reached Matchin Bay going flat out at twenty feet above the water and saw no shipping whatsoever, so continued on to the airfields some ten miles to the north. "Dirty Eddie" March and Whit Wharton were flying in a V with me, and Tom Killefer was flying on Jim Streig's wing as a second flight. I elected to take the Buka airdrome to our left. Jim and T.K. swung away to the right to attack Buna. As we three came in on Buka, a light transport, a Ruth, was on final approach to landing dead ahead of us. Dirty Eddie and I fired simultaneously and flamed him almost instantly. We then proceeded to shoot up the 150-man formation which was lined up to receive whatever dignitary had been in the Ruth. Whit Wharton shot up a Zeke that was parked near the control tower. Streig and Killefer hit antiaircraft positions around Buna. There was no return fire until we had pulled clear to the southeast, very pleased with ourselves.

Shortly after landing back at Ondongo I was summoned by telephone to fly over to Munda to talk with the chief of fighter command, Colonel Oscar Brice, and give him the run-down on the morning's activities. Oscar was more than pleased to hear my account of our successful venture. Another navy fighter squadron commander was there, a rather stuffy type. As I finished my tale, he said, "Well, fools rush in!" Upon hearing this, Colonel Brice and his ACI officer just looked at him. Brice got considerable mileage out of the morning's action by needling the bomber command people: their B-25s couldn't get through the weather, but *his* fighters could, and would carry out their mission for them.

As I taxied out to the runway to return to Ondongo, I held clear for a B-25 on final with one prop feathered. It lost altitude rapidly short of the end of the runway, impacted with a high sink rate, sheared off the landing gear on the rough ground, skidded onto the runway, and burst into flames. I taxied over as quickly as I could to the burning aircraft, hoping to blow the flames away, so any survivors would have a chance to escape. The meat wagon and the crash truck came screeching up, but halted a discreet 300 yards away from the scene of the wreck. I soon realized why they were holding clear, and releasing my brakes, pulled off a couple of hundred yards just before the bomber blew up with an enormous explosion. I'm happy that the meat wagon and the crash truck had been there to alert me. Otherwise I would have been part of the disaster.

On the afternoon of November 9 I was summoned to Munda again, this time for a conference with the commander of the air force, Solomons, Major General Nathan Twining, U.S. Army Air Forces. Colonel Brice and the various ACI officers, plus the other fighter squadron commanders in the area, were in attendance. General Twining turned the meeting over to Colonel Brice, who explained that there was to be a carrier strike against Rabaul on November 11, for which Fighter Command was to provide as much protection as possible. The carriers *Saratoga* and *Princeton* were to attack from the east at daybreak, followed at approximately nine o'clock by a strike from the south mounted from the carriers *Bunker Hill, Essex,* and *Independence*. The southern task force had been diverted from the Gilberts operation for this attack.

It was desired to get maximum strength on this attack from the south, and to use all the fighters from that task group to cover the bombers going in. In order to do this, ComAirSols was to provide fighter protection from the beach. The first question before the house was whether or not Fighting 17 could go out to this task group, provide cover during the initial launch, land aboard *Essex* and *Bunker Hill* for refueling and possible rearming, then be airborne when the strike aircraft returned from Rabaul to provide cover and defense for the expected Japanese counterattack. This was a much more positive method than relays of flights and required far fewer fighters. We were being considered for this assignment because we were carrier qualified. However, we had not had any carrier experience since the latter part of September. Most of our pilots were brand-new, green ensigns who had never even seen a carrier before mid-1943 and had only a few carrier landings and takeoffs under their belts.

ComAirSols said, "Blackburn, C_onel Brice tells me that VF-17 is his first team. Can your pilots find that task group before dawn, then land aboard one or more times during the day? Protection of those ships is vital. We can't afford a foul-up."

"General, these men qualified for carrier landings aboard a jeep carrier in Chesapeake Bay with minimal winds, and have found that operating off a full-sized carrier like *Bunker Hill* or *Essex* is a piece of cake. I have no concern whatsoever that we will do the job. We can and will accomplish the mission with no sweat."

General Twining beamed at my affirmation. He said, "Okay, if your people are that good, we'll set it up so that you fly out to the carriers on the morning of the eleventh."

Duke Henning and I returned to Ondongo from Munda, and I directed that the tail hooks be reinstalled on our Corsairs. I had previously had them removed as a minor weight-saving measure, and also to eliminate the possibility of hooks dangling inadvertently and making aircraft with that problem a likely target for Japanese fighters. All hands were very mystified by the obvious carrier operations that reinstallation of the hooks and checking out their dash pots (antihook bounce) portended. Duke and I could not brief people until after all flights were completed on November 10. This lest someone was shot down and taken prisoner, spilled his guts, and spoiled the surprise attack security.

Twenty-four F4Us took off at about three A.M. on the morning of the eleventh, and twenty-three of us proceeded on course. While cruising at 10,000 feet in the pitch darkness, we reached the point where the task force should be. I could get nothing from *Bunker Hill*'s navigation aid ("hay rake") on my set, but Chuck Pillsbury picked up the hay rake from *Essex*. He called, "Big Hog! Big Hog! This is Chuck. I have Judah's hay rake. We are approximately overhead, over."

"Chuck, this is Big Hog. Roger. Out." No further radio transmission was needed. We were sure that the ships had been tracking us on their radars and had heard Chuck and me. We went into a racetrack holding pattern overhead.

The radio came alive after daybreak, "Big Hog! Big Hog! This is Judah, Judah, over."

"This is Big Hog. Go ahead, Judah. Over."

"Big Hog, this is Judah. Bogie zero-zero-zero, distance three-five, angels fifteen. Buster." (Loose translation—a single aircraft due north, thirty-five miles out, altitude 15,000 feet. Proceed at best speed.)

We climbed fast, northbound, to 20,000 feet, and spotted a lone Tony headed south. He saw us shortly after we saw him, and slanted down desperately to get cover in a cumulus cloud. Unfortunately for him, the cloud was too far away. I flamed him just in time. There were a bunch of eager fighter pilots following me down. Had I missed, they would have gotten him.

"Judah, this is Big Hog. Splash one Tony. Returning to station. Over."

"This is Judah. Roger. Out."

The strike force for the Rabaul attack was taking off as we resumed circling the ships. They were on their way by eight o'clock. We dropped to 1,000 feet in response to a searchlight signal from *Essex:* the letters PC (prep Charlie)—

standby to land aboard. We dropped our hooks and went into the landing pattern above the ships. As they swung into the wind, we executed the standard carrier breakup. When they hit the wind line, Roger Hedrick was 200 yards astern of *Essex* in a final approach for landing, and I was in the same position astern of *Bunker Hill*. The red flag on the ramp meaning "foul deck, no landings" was replaced with a white flag signifying "clear for landings," just in time for the landing signal officer to give the "cut" signal. "Cut" says, "cut your throttle and land aboard." Our twenty-three planes came aboard in smart fashion with close intervals, no waveoffs and no problems. I was gratified beyond measure, and so were many others.

After I landed aboard *Bunker Hill* and my plane was secured, I went up to the bridge to report to Captain Ballentine and receive his congratulations, and to collect ten dollars from his air officer, Kit Carson. I had made a bet with Kit at Pearl Harbor that Fighting 17 would get into action before *Bunker Hill* did. Carson had seen the three Japanese flags painted on the side of my airplane, so he had the ten dollars ready when I got up there. We went below for hot showers and then a sumptuous meal in the ward room. The meal was quite a change from our usual fare at the "Hotel Mud Plaza" on New Georgia. We sat at a table with tablecloths and napkins and were served palatable orange juice, bacon, and scrambled eggs by the stewards, in lieu of the army air force's breakfasts on Ondongo. There we ate battery acid flavored with grapefruit juice, Spam, and powdered eggs.

After breakfast we proceeded to the fighter ready room, where the teletype screen had printed out, "Welcome Fighting 17." It then began to print intelligence information on the progress of the strike. The strike forces had no difficulty getting into Rabaul and making an effective blow at about nine o'clock. The strikes that morning, combined with the effects of those from the *Saratoga* and *Princeton* on November 5, were devastating. After this the Japanese no longer based any major shipping at Rabaul. The only enemy ships around were destroyers making high-speed night runs, in and out before daylight, plus submarines and auxiliaries. This marked the beginning of the end of Japanese operations in the Solomons.

We launched about ten o'clock and were in position by the time the strike aircraft returned to the ship. We climbed to 25,000 feet for our combat air patrol station and orbited in a pattern five miles long by two miles wide, throttled back as much as possible to conserve fuel. Shortly before one o'clock, when the cumulus clouds to the north and west had built up to enormous size and heights up to 40,000 feet, the fighter director on *Essex* excitedly made the following transmission: "This is Judah! This is Judah! Many bogies, various altitudes. Distance three-zero miles, course one-eight-zero. This is Judah, out!"

This was far from precise fighter direction, but the fighter director had been unable to pick up the blips of enemy aircraft due to interference from the heavy cumulus cloud formations. The Japanese had cleverly used them as a screen from both visual and radar sighting, until they were nearly on top of the task force that was operating in a large, clear area. Shortly after the transmission we sighted the Japanese approaching in two groups on either side of a huge thunderhead. To the east of it were about thirty-five Val dive-bombers covered by some forty Zeros. To the west were about thirty-five Kate and Judy torpedo planes covered by a like number of Zeros. It was to be the heaviest counterattack launched against a U.S. task force in World War II.

I had turned over to Pillsbury the lead of my flight from *Bunker Hill* because I had experienced radio transmitter failure once again. He led us into an attack against the dive-bombers. Hedrick had come up on our left and, seeing us attack the dive-bombers, elected to attack the torpedo planes. Pillsbury came in very fast on the top cover of the dive-bombers. I was somewhat off to his left with my wingman, Gutenkunst, and Jim Streig.

I attacked the leader of the Japanese fighter formation, but unfortunately he saw me as soon as I began setting up for him. He did a split-S to evade the attack, and I made the mistake of following him. We went screaming down in a vertical dive with him a good thousand yards in front of me. I was closing very slowly at a speed that was almost terminal velocity for the Corsair. He twisted and turned, belying the stories we had heard about the Zero having poor aileron control at very high speeds. I was the one with aileron problems, because at that speed they tended to overbalance. It took very careful monitoring and gentle controls to prevent excessive movement and uncontrollably high rate of roll that could have had disastrous consequences.

As we passed through 10,000 feet, I fired a long-range burst at the quarry. It had no apparent effect, except that he made a violent pullout from his dive, pulling six or seven Gs with great vapor plumes coming off his wingtips, and escaped into a cumulus cloud. I was following and endeavored to knock him down but couldn't hit him. As soon as he was in the cloud, I realized that I had bitched things up, was out of the fight for the time being, and was completely fogged in. The rapid change in altitude and the very damp atmosphere had caused condensation on the inside of my bulletproof windshield and sliding hatch. It was easy enough to wipe off the sliding hatch, but I couldn't reach the other surfaces, so I was blind forward. I pulled into a cloud to let things warm up and give the glass a chance to clear.

I stooged around in the cloud at around 5,000 feet for several minutes until the glass cleared, and then stuck my nose out to see what was going on. The first thing I saw was a flight of six Tony fighters at about my four o'clock position about 3,000 feet above me. The flight leader of the Tonys saw me almost as soon as I saw him and rolled into a dive in my direction. I honked around for the safety of the cloud, expecting at any minute to hear the thug! thug! of 7.7mm and 20mm bullets hitting my airplane. Apparently he was not able to get into position before I disappeared from view. I went back to a general circling inside the cloud, where I calmed down after having the living bejesus scared out of me.

When I was calmer I eased out again. No sooner had I

come out of the cloud than I saw two Corsairs at my nine o'clock position, close aboard. To my horror, the leading edge of the wing of the flight leader erupted in gun flashes. Simultaneously I heard the trip-hammer blows of .50-caliber bullets hitting my airplane. There was only one short burst fired, but three of the bullets hit just behind my cockpit and three went through the accessory section just forward of the fuel tank. The two Corsairs turned out to be Roger Hedrick and his wingman, Mills Schanuel. They pulled up alongside me with worried contrition written all over their faces as they checked my airplane for damage. They could see none and so indicated with hand signals. The three of us mutually decided through hand signals that we were getting low on fuel, so we headed for home. We had had enough for one afternoon.

In that day's action, Fighting 17 got eighteen and a half kills, including several torpedo planes in the final stages of their run-in on the carriers. None of the ships suffered any bomb or torpedo damage. We lost no planes, but some of them were shot up pretty badly, including Johnny Kleinman, who took a friendly 20mm on his bulletproof windshield just before he splashed a Kate close aboard *Essex*. It sprayed his face with shards of glass and cut him badly. He was able to get home, but he sure was a mess. Ike Kepford distinguished himself by knocking down one torpedo plane and three Val dive-bombers. He had to land aboard *Bunker Hill* to refuel in order to get home. Windy Hill also flamed a torpedo carrier as it attacked. He was unable to reach Ondongo because of fuel shortage and had to ditch at sea near the Treasury Islands that we had occupied two weeks before. He was picked up by a PT boat after twenty or thirty minutes in the water.

This was a classic case of the projection of carrier air power. The Fifth Air Force had been attacking Rabaul for eight months and the Japanese were still using it both as a naval base and as a potent air base. The Japanese never again tried to use it as a naval base.

On December 2 we were relieved by Fighting 33 and

returned via Guadalcanal to Espiritu Santo. Our box score for the first combat tour was forty-eight and a half enemy aircraft destroyed in the air and two on the ground, four cargo ships and fourteen barges destroyed. We had lost three pilots. Keith and Pillsbury were lost to enemy antiaircraft fire, and Brad Baker was lost to enemy aircraft in a fight on November 17. We lost additional planes that had ditched to enemy AA fire, but there were no other injuries of any consequence.

We returned to action on January 26, 1944, after seven weeks of rest and regrouping in Sydney, Australia, and Espiritu Santo. We had devoted part of that time to the training of replacement pilots to bring us back up to strength. On January 24 we went back into the combat area, taking off from Espiritu at nine o'clock, landing at Guadalcanal to refuel, and then flying on to Piva Yoke on Bougainville. We gained a lot of character with our marine ground crew upon landing, because each aircraft had four of the big ammunition cans full of beer. We had gone to 25,000 feet for the last part of the flight to cool them. When each plane captain opened an ammo can, he was able to get two ice-cold beers, one for himself and one for the pilot. That was the brainstorm of Lieutenant Hal Jackson.

On the twenty-sixth we launched twenty-four Corsairs as part of a strike of SBDs and TBFs on Lakunai Airfield at Rabaul. The Japanese flirted around the edges of the big formation on run-in, but didn't make any attack. Once the dive-bombers and torpedo planes had broken formation to make runs which we covered with strafing attacks, the Japanese fighters mixed it up with us. The aerial battle continued until the bombers completed rendezvous some fifteen miles south of the target. In the course of this action I shot down one Zero who made a head-on run as we were pulling out from the target. Doug Gutenkunst destroyed two Zekes and Tom Killefer got one, as did Cordray, Hedrick, Miller, and Gile. Total kills: eight. Landreth and Dunn shared one probable.

Bob Hogan's plane had been hit by a fairly large caliber

AA shell as we dove in to the target. It blew off his right wing. He parachuted, but we didn't see anything further as we were in the midst of a big scramble. He was never heard from again. Jim Farley was shot down while he was flying wing on Tom Killefer. We saw him going down, although we didn't see the impact with the ground. Windy Hill took three 20mm hits in the wings of his airplane which did a lot of damage. He cracked up on landing back at Bougainville and suffered a lacerated scalp. He was out of action for about a week. We suffered minor damage to other airplanes but lost two pilots.

The following day I led twenty-two Corsairs covering B-25s on an attack at Lakunai. The Zeros were very aggressive, mixing it up with us all the way into the target and all the way out. We were very fortunate and scored fifteen kills with only one loss. Lieutenant Juggy Bell disappeared early on in the melee and was listed as missing in action and presumed dead. Nothing further was ever heard of him. "Teeth" Burris got shot up and suffered a major oil leak so that his engine froze up and he had to ditch fifty miles out of Rabaul. He was picked up by a Dumbo after being in his raft for about half an hour. Once again we didn't lose any bombers to enemy aircraft. At no time during our combat tours did we lose any bombers to enemy aircraft, nor were any ships for which we were providing cover hit by enemy bombs or torpedoes.

We launched another flight of twelve Corsairs at one o'clock in the afternoon to escort B-24s bombing Lakunai Airfield. This flight was led by Lieutenant "Butch" Davenport. I had a division of four as his number-three division. The enemy antiaircraft fire was meager and inadequate as the B-24s went in at 20,000 feet, and there was no interception whatsoever. Apparently the morning's attack on the same airfield had produced significant damage.

We launched twenty-four Corsairs the next morning to cover another SBD/TBF strike on Tobera Airfield at Rabaul. We were intercepted by fifty to seventy Japanese fighters about ten miles southeast of the field. Gutenkunst, Cordray,

March, and Killefer each destroyed two enemy aircraft. Hedrick, Miller, Meek, and Jackson destroyed one each, and Bobby Mims shared destruction of a Zeke with a marine pilot. Three of our F4Us were seriously damaged by gunfire from enemy aircraft. One of them cracked up on landing. The pilot was uninjured.

On January 29 we again went into action in a big way, this time with sixteen Corsairs covering the dive-bombers on a strike at Tobera. We weren't as successful as we had been; however, Burris and Kepford each shot down four Zeros, and Gile and May each got one Zero. This was our first employment of roving high cover. Two aircraft free-wheeled ahead and well above the main formation to intercept the Japanese fighters as they were forming up, and before they could attack the main group. It was an innovation that we had dreamed up and executed with the approval of Fighter Command. The tactic itself was not new to warfare, but this variation was a first in that area. We repeated it happily and very successfully several times thereafter.

On January 30 in the morning, I led sixteen F4Us providing cover for B-25s attacking a supply dump in the Rabaul area. Twenty to thirty Zeros intercepted the attack, and Roger Hedrick and "Fatso" Ellsworth each got a kill. Miller, Smith, Bowers, Malcolm, and Keller each got probables. One Corsair was seriously damaged by gunfire from an enemy fighter, but was repairable.

This, we thought, was the end of our commitment for the day. After lunch Doug Gutenkunst and I traveled five miles down to the beach in a jeep. There was no surf at Bougainville and the sand was pitch black. Although it was soft and pleasant, it was unattractive-looking. The beach shelved out gradually, and Doug and I enjoyed leisurely swimming, then lay around for a little while, discussing the world's affairs. We were very much at our ease when all of a sudden we heard a number of aircraft engines tuning up, a complete change in the usual noise level. We hastily donned our clothes, and watched fighters, torpedo planes, and dive-bombers taking off from Piva Yoke and Piva Uncle as we climbed into the jeep.

By the time we got to the field, the strike was on its way, and we were informed that it was an emergency strike in response to a report of a Japanese carrier standing in to Rabaul. Bomber Command had gotten together as many available aircraft as possible. The fighter squadrons contributed what they could on a scramble basis. Thirteen of our aircraft were being led by Lieutenant Oscar Chenoweth. Gutenkunst and I manned aircraft as rapidly as we could and took off in pursuit of the main body.

We came in over Rabaul well above the main action taking place at altitudes of between 10,000 and 15,000 feet. From our vantage at 25,000 feet we had a good view of what was going on. There was no carrier, so the TBFs were turning around to take their torpedoes home. The dive-bombers were dropping their bombs on small shipping in the harbor. Japanese fighter opposition was fairly strong as Gutenkunst and I came in on top of the Zeros attacking the main formation. I got two kills and Doug got two probables. I had seen a pilot bail out from one of the Zeros I had flamed, and I watched the chute open. I flew back to inspect the chute and saw that the risers had burned through and it was now empty. The pilot had made a free fall from about 25,000 feet.

It began to get dark on the way home, and by the time we got to Bougainville, it was fully dark. Many of the fighters had been badly shot up in this action, and by the time we got there, our field was closed because of wrecks on the runway which included our men "Beads" Popp and Ike Kepford. The other field, normally used just for the dive-bombers and torpedo planes, was a maelstrom of fighters and bomber aircraft, all trying to land in the dark. The radio chatter was unbelievably bad. There was no radio discipline at all, and the tower was completely unable to control the activity. I saw a slot in the landing pattern that appeared to be big enough for the two of us and we slipped into that, Gutenkunst taking a thirty-second interval behind me.

I landed without incident. As I was completing my roll-out, I looked in my rearview mirror to see if it was clear to turn off. To my horror, I saw a huge orange ball of flame at the down-wind end of the runway and instantly knew that Gutenkunst was part of that fireball. As he had been making a normal turning approach, a wounded marine, Major Johnson, was making a straight-in at high speed with a badly damaged airplane with no lights and no radio. He had been escorted back to Bougainville by his squadron mates and was seconds away from getting down safely when he and Doug collided just short of the end of the runway. Both of them were killed in the resultant crash and fire.

I was completely wiped out by this loss. Doug Gutenkunst and I were very close. He was somewhat like a son to me, or a younger brother. We had been through a great deal together during the course of training, shakedown, our first combat tour, and the trip to Sydney. It was a freak accident and nobody's fault, but it was truly hard for me to take. It was bad enough to have people shot down and killed, but this was just happenstance, and it devastated me.

During the last six days in January we accounted for sixty and a half enemy aircraft shot down. But the cost was steep. Six of our pilots had been killed and we had lost thirteen aircraft. Most of the lost aircraft were crackups on landing as a result of gunfire damage. Fortunately the first and second of February saw the whole area completely shut down to any aircraft activity by torrential rains and very low cloud ceilings with zero visibility. We got back into hot and heavy action on February 3. It continued until February 13, then tapered off for a few days.

Toward the latter part of the aerial battles over Rabaul, I was leading a roving high-cover group of four planes when we tangled with thirty or thirty-five Japanese planes. My wingman was a new lieutenant who had flown a couple of missions with us and was doing pretty well. Bobby Mims was leading the second section, and he and I worked as a team, attacking those Japanese from opposite sides in succession. Each of us got four flamers out of it.

My last one was after Bobby ran out of oxygen and had to head for home. The new lieutenant and I were stooging around, looking for trouble, when we spotted a lone Japanese plane whose pilot had apparently secured for the day, leaned back with his feet up on the dashboard, and lit a cigarette. He was flying along with an open canopy at about 125 knots, completely oblivious to what was going on. I slowed way down and fired from very close range, about 100 yards behind him. Metallic chunks bounced off the lieutenant's wings. When we got home I was very pleased with the whole operation. We had shot down ten Japanese planes with no damage to any of our own.

I turned to the lieutenant and said, "Well, wasn't that a great hop?"

He replied, "Skipper, I would like to be detached from Fighting 17 today. You guys are all crazy."

"Okay. Go pack your bags, Jack."

After February 19, when we got an intense response from the Japanese to a strike of SBDs and TBFs, there was no enemy air activity over Rabaul. The carrier strikes on the Truk Islands, plus the attrition that ComAirSols had wrought on enemy air forces, combined to convince the Japanese that they were pouring money down a rat hole and that it would be only sensible to pull back to Truk and the Marianas and defend a more restricted perimeter.

We in Fighting 17 felt that we had significantly contributed to the victory. We didn't suffer under the illusion that we were the only factor in the Japanese defeat, but took pride in the fact that we did our share and were on the cutting edge of one of the most effective air forces of World War II. Fighting 17's accomplishments can be highlighted by our proving out the Vought Corsair as a viable carrier fighter aircraft, by our combat record of 154½ enemy aircraft shot down to a loss of thirteen of our own pilots, by the development of cruise control techniques for the F4U (which extended its range and usable time on station), to the development of the "spoiler" device that significantly improved low-speed safety, and by pioneering the bomb-carrying capability of the aircraft.

Fighting 17 was sometimes referred to as "Blackburn's Irregulars." Our tactical innovations in the Solomons were not earthshaking, but they did prove effective. In addition to being powerful morale builders for us, they destroyed enemy morale. We have learned from later writings that our roving high-cover, free-wheeling attacks in advance of the strikes was very much feared by the Japanese fighter pilots who characterized it as "attacks on us by wolves."

TRADING THREE FOR FIFTEEN

Captain Ken Dahlberg's Ninth Air Force unit was unusual because it transitioned from P-51s to P-47s instead of the other way around. Dahlberg didn't mind the change. On two missions in P-51s he shot down seven German fighters. On his first mission in a P-47 he shot down four more. In the course of a short tour in the ETO, Dahlberg was shot down three times, evading the Germans on two occasions and escaping from them twice more.

To my way of thinking, there were two significant events in 1917. Communism was born in Russia and I was born in St. Paul, Minnesota. I mention this coincidence because it would have a profound impact on my life. I moved to Wisconsin and grew up on a farm. Meanwhile, Russia was busy, by hook and by crook, powering the USSR. By the time I was drafted in 1941, Stalin had chosen Hitler as his partner in progress. They enjoyed great kinship, each having slaughtered millions of his own people.

I was commissioned from the army air corps flight school at Luke Field, Arizona, in 1942, and was a flight instructor for about one and a half years. By the time I arrived in combat (ETO, 1944), Russia had switched to the "Allies" as a partner. By the time the war was over, I had been shot down three times, had escaped twice, and had experienced the loss of liberty in a POW camp. But I managed to shoot down fifteen German planes in the meantime. And Russia, after annexing half of Europe and several hundred million people against their will, declared a new war against us—cold war—with all its misery and economic ramifications. So, being born under the Red Star changed the horoscope of my life!

My most hyperactive year was from June 1944 to June 1945. Arriving in England just in time for the invasion, I had a quick transition to live targets. My first mission as a new pilot in the 353rd Fighter Squadron (354th Fighter Group, Ninth Air Force) was flying top cover over the invasion, combined with emptying my guns—strafing anything that moved in front of the Allied troops fighting for a secure beachhead. The reality of war became more complete on D + 10 (June 16) when I landed our first P-51 at airstrip A2 at Criqueville, France. "This is an airport?" I wondered. It was just a cow pasture between hedgerows (reinforced with some heavy wire mesh), and a lot of tents for eating, sleeping, and operations.

The reality of war meant being fired on during takeoff and landing. It seemed questionable to me to risk planes and pilots so close to the front, but the rationale was more missions per plane per day, in addition to the advantage of avoiding the "London fog" weather of England. France turned out to be just as bad.

Our mission was to patrol the skies above, and in front of the Third Army, keeping the Luftwaffe at bay, and dive-bombing before each patrol and strafing afterward. We also flew escort for B-17, B-26, and B-25 bombers. We sweated out the news of slow progress by our ground forces during June and July. The British could not get through Caen on the north, and the Americans were stuck at St. Lô in the south. A 3,000-plane bombing mission, accompanied by great ground heroics, finally gave us space to enlarge and enhance air operations.

My first aerial kill was in July over Chartres, when I saw a lone ME-109 in a shallow turn. I was a wingman, but some-how my flight leader had missed seeing him, so I turned into the German with very little effort. A thirty-degree deflection burst and instant smoke and flame! All my stateside experi-ence as a gunnery instructor had paid off. But was aerial combat really this easy? I found out later that it was not. This guy must have been newer to combat than I, or I had just caught him off guard.

Now it was August. Our airstrip was near the village of Rosaire-en-Hay, dubbed by us, of course, as "Rosie in the hay." It was a very wet month—mud, mud, and more mud. The worst problem was mud on the wheels. At altitude they would freeze while locked up, and getting them down was sometimes a big problem. The solutions were handcranks, low altitude "thaw time," or wheels-up landings.

During a late afternoon mission on August 16, our eight-ship squadron was patrolling just a few miles southeast of Paris when we ran into a huge formation of eighty ME-109s near Dreaux, France. They were aggressive. We turned into each other for the attack, and since we were so badly outnumbered, we automatically went into the "every man for himself" mode. The adrenaline was flowing! Broken cloud conditions made for a real challenge in the use of fighter tactics. Either side could use a cloud defensively. If a pilot was in a deteriorating position, he would be able to break into a cloud and lose the pursuing plane. When the target plane uses a cloud as a sanctuary at the last second, the pursuit plane may find itself momentarily in the dark, with a bunch of surprises waiting as it zips back into visible conditions.

The battle was filled with many high-degree deflection shots with pairs of planes locked in combat. I managed to get three victories and one probable. The last plane exploded right in front of me, and I'm not sure whether it was debris damage or the 109 on my tail that caused the smoke in cockpit. My instant reaction was to get out. Luckily I was at the edge of a cloud. I ducked in there and bailed.

I made a precise landing in the presence of an attractive Frenchwoman who had witnessed much of the aerial battle. She asked me in perfect English if I was an American pilot. When I said yes she told me to go that way to the water and hide. German soldiers were all over the place. Quickly getting out of my chute, I ran to a pond and submerged myself in the water, among cattail bullrushes.

At dusk a civilian of small stature with a very French accent came looking for me. He was saying softly, "American pilot, where are you?"

I decided he looked friendly, so I exposed my position. His name was Dennis Baudoin. He owned the property and was a member of the Free French Underground. After dark he brought me a trench coat for warmth and some bread and wine, then instructed me to stay in hiding overnight, until he could arrange my escape. The next day, through a series of maneuvers, I was brought to the main château, "Le Gue D'Aulene." Several days later, dressed in civilian garb and riding a bicycle alongside my French host, we passed through the departing Germans and reached the advancing Americans. The journey was scary, but without incident. By the time I found my way back to the squadron, my buddies had already divided my clothes and personal possessions among themselves—a ritual of respect for a fallen buddy.

Being a fighter pilot in the ETO during that stage in the war was not always the indescribable exhilaration of air-to-air combat. To be so well trained, to be so ready, and then patrol for days on end without seeing an enemy plane would have been boring had it not been for the dive-bombing and strafing that began and ended each mission. Except when we were given a specific target, such as an airdrome, our strafing was mostly against targets of opportunity. We found our own targets—anything that moved. A favorite was a nice, long train. When eight .50 caliber machine guns, each expending 3,000 rounds a minute, converge at 200 yards, things happen! A train engine bursting into a big steam cloud, and the camouflaged petrol cars exploding into smoke and flames made a great sight, better than your own Fourth of July fireworks. Trucks, cars, and buses would not only explode, but could be rolled right in the ditch.

The worst job was strafing airdromes. They were protected by batteries of 20mm and 40mm guns that literally rained lead from the ground. So numerous were the guns that they did not aim at our planes, instead creating a "lead box" we had to fly through. To my mind, it was an inefficient way to knock out enemy aircraft. One day in July we lost two squadron commanders attacking the same airdrome.

Our squadron commander, Jack Bradley, and his deputy, Glenn Eagleston, had just left for the States for R&R after completing their first tours. Don Beerbower of Hill City, Minnesota, became the squadron commander. Wally Emmer of St. Louis was his deputy. Our morning mission was to strafe a heavily defended airdrome. Don led the mission; I led a flight of four. The flak was murderous. On the second pass I saw Don get hit and go straight in on the strafing run. "Damn," I thought, "not Don!" But it was, and it had happened so quickly. By training and experience, not much emotion was usually evident among us, but on this occasion we had lost two planes and two pilots, one of them a super leader. Our emotions ran high.

Wally automatically became the squadron leader and asked for volunteers to go back and hit the same base in retaliation. Most everyone volunteered. I again led a flight of four. We flew the deck until we were near the airdrome, swooped up, and approached the target in single file at full diving speed, nearing 500 miles per hour. They were ready for us. Ugly flak, and so much of it!

We shot up the planes and the hangars. I was just coming down run with all guns blazing when I saw Wally's plane smoking as he came off the target. There isn't much time to aim at that speed and in that time frame. There is fire, smoke, and explosions, and the uncertainty of not knowing whether the plane's vibrations are from exceeding red-lined speed limit or having been hit. I would much rather have fought the Germans one on one in the sky.

Although we had agreed to only one surprise pass at the target, we had paid the price. Again two planes; two pilots. We had lost radio transmission with Wally, but pulled up to 12,000 feet (as briefed) and headed for home. It wasn't a good day for our squadron. Months later I learned that Wally was in rather bad shape in a German prison hospital.

The fall season was wet, muddy, and interrupted by another move. As Patton moved east, we followed. Our 354th Fighter Group was making history in the sky with its leading record. We were a hot group. The abrupt news that we were switching to P-47 Thunderbolts was devastating to the pilots and crews. But I didn't mind so much, having flown the '47 in OTU just prior to going into combat. I lucked out four more Focke-Wulf 190s, following a strafing mission on September 12, 1944—a fitting tribute to a great bird. I got three more German fighters before our last mission in P-51s in December.

On my first combat mission in that big bird (P-47) on December 16, I got four more ME-109s and damaged a fifth one. We were on an armed recce in the area of the German breakthrough which began the Battle of the Bulge when we spotted two gaggles of ME-109s, jettisoned our bombs, and attacked. It was eight against eighty at high altitude, where Thunderbolts could maneuver with the best. Four of us had destroyed ten German fighters, but we lost two of our own.

The Battle of the Bulge was Hitler's last stand in the Ardennes Forest. The Third Army had come to help the First Army that was bogged down by the Wermacht. The weather had grounded the air support. When the weather lifted, General Quesada's 9th TAC (Tactical Air Command) directed us to dive-bomb German tanks, but there was too much new snow and the Germans had captured many of our tank color panels. There was no such thing as a battle line. The cloud cover was low. The question was how to bomb and strafe the right tanks.

On a dive-bombing run I decided that we were lined up on some of our own tanks. I radioed to "Hold bombs! Tanks friendly!" then the groundfire knocked out my engine and electrical systems. Not being able to disarm the bombs, I veered to an open field and dropped them. With that action, guns of both sides thought I was bombing them, and small antiaircraft fire from both sides let me have it, knocking off the canopy as I came in for a dead stick crash landing in a lightly wooded area. I was grateful to the American tank commander who risked coming into hostile territory to rescue me. After a briefing and an overnight stay at General Quesada's headquarters, it was back to the squadron and back to work.

On February 28, 1945, I was leading our squadron of eight Thunderbolts home from a successful dive-bombing/strafing mission. We had climbed to 10,000 feet and I had just received a radio check from the flight leaders behind me—"Roger Red Two," "Three" and "Four," and "Roger Blue One," "Two," "Three," and "Four"—advising them that we were crossing friendly lines. My report was interrupted by puffs of ugly 88mm flak. The next thing I knew, I was less than 500 feet from the ground in a just-opened chute. It seemed incredible that I could be blown free, not only from the plane, but the seat-belt harness as well, free-fall unconscious through 9,500 feet, then regain consciousness in split-second time to pull the rip cord (by rote, I have no memory of it). The landing was very hard, but I was safe.

Safe, did I say? Army air had done a lot of bombing and strafing in the area. Waiting for me on the ground were about a dozen angry civilians armed with pitchforks and clubs. They looked like farmers and they were mad. I emptied my .45 and its extra clip at them as I retreated into the woods to a place that looked like a bivouac area, but without soldiers. I lifted the canvas cover on a jeeplike tow trailer and hid underneath it until dusk. I could feel and hear the trailer being hooked up to a vehicle and starting to move—an eerie feeling.

Knowing that I was close to the U.S. lines, I wanted to keep perspective on my location. It may have been the instinct to survive, with every move a guess, but escape was the only thing on my mind. Don't get caught! Sounds told me that we had moved into another bivouac area. I wondered how soon they would be lifting the tarp to use my hiding place. Peeping out from time to time, I could see it getting darker. Artillery fire increased. Finally, as the voices died down and the darkness came, I decided to make a break into the woods. It was overcast, leaving me with no sense of direction except for the sound of artillery. The cold night drained my strength. My head hurt and I was bleeding from a wound in my forehead. A piece of metal was stuck there.

"Think! Where am I? How much German activity between me and the American Army? How will I get there, and will I last long enough to try?"

Although I couldn't see my compass very well, I moved through the forest in a northwest direction until I arrived at a river. According to my memory of the area, it must be the Prum River in the general area of Bitburg. With the help of a branch for flotation, I managed to cross the cold, cruel water, losing my compass in the process. That was a bad break. After moving cautiously and painfully throughout the night, I wound up back on the river at dawn. I had traveled in a complete circle. Now a critical decision had to be made. I could hide out during the day and attempt the American lines that night (but would my strength last that long after so much blood loss and a still-bleeding wound?), or I could try the seemingly impossible and unlikely effort of getting through during daylight. The head wound and dizziness persuaded me to keep moving. I might not last until evening.

Walking along the edge of the road and trying to look like a refugee, I advanced perhaps a couple of miles amid heavy military traffic that was interrupted by farmers with their horses and old trucks. There was also some foot traffic heading mostly in the opposite direction. I knew it was over when a German military policeman challenged me. After identifying myself, I was taken to an army tent and given first aid to stop my bleeding. I was grateful. I was given some black bread, then taken by truck to a small stockade next to an airport and locked in a room. From the window I could see an ME-109 and listened to a lot of takeoff activity.

The next day I was marched by a single English-speaking guard to a POW collection station near Nuremberg. The guard was young and congenial. He wanted to talk about American jazz music (I knew too little!) and baseball. As we hiked through most of the day, my mind remained on escape. While I appeared to be involved in his conversation, I was noting his actions and habits. Then we stopped for a rest and he put his rifle down for the first time. I pounced on him and we struggled until I struck him on the head with his rifle butt, leaving him unconscious.

I retreated to the woods and soon came to a small town. Parked there was a French Citroën car with German Red Cross markings. It was unoccupied. Luckily I had expropriated a similar car in France and knew how to operate it. Luck again—the key was in the ignition. I just got in and drove off, heading west. I went past a lot of traffic with my heart thumping, hoping that there would be no checkpoints or barriers to the American side. But there were! The Citroën's flashing lights did nothing to move a huge log that barred the road. I knew that I was going to be challenged again, but this time I would be an escapee and not just an ordinary shot-down airman. As I desperately tried to run the blockade, the end of the log went through my windshield, tipping over the car and wrecking it badly. Now we would call it "totaled." Then all hell broke loose. I was identified as an escaping airman as they were pulling me out of the wreckage.

This time under heavy guard, I was taken to an army building and eventually faced the German intelligence officer who grunted those awful words, "For you the war is over." Those words disgusted me because I was only about two minutes from friendly territory. Perhaps I should have been happy just to be alive, but the finality of knowing the most thrilling show on earth was over, that of being a fighter pilot in the thick of it, devastated me. I didn't have time to think about my aching head, or the ordeal of the last forty-eight hours. Exhaustion masked all other emotions.

After a short stay in confinement in Nuremberg, about a thousand captured airmen were marched in the cold of winter, in substitute shoes (my good boots had been confiscated), toward Stalag 17A in Moosburg, a suburb of Munich. About a day or two into the march, a German-speaking Norwegian captain and I decided to try to escape. Since there weren't enough guards to prevent escapes, we had been strongly advised not to try it—we would surely be caught and suffer dire retribution. Nevertheless, the two of us left the formation at an opportune time and ducked into the woods. The main roads seemed to cut through the forest. The problem was, we never knew how deep the forest was. Maybe it wasn't a forest at all, but just clumps of trees alongside the road.

Here my memory is blurred. I believe it was caused by sheer exhaustion, because my new friend was helping me carry even my light pack. Anyway, we were eventually discovered hiding among the trees . . . by a unit of the SS. We expected the worst and were surprised when they treated us decently.

Perhaps they knew more than we did about how near the end was—for them. We were escorted back to a little town, loaded on a vehicle, and driven to Stalag 17A in Moosburg. The escape attempt had its good side: at least we got to ride the final distance to camp!

Being a prisoner for a few months was relatively easy compared to those who had been in for years. It wasn't fun, but it was tolerable and I learned a lot in that short time. I learned how to get along better with other people under duress. I learned to appreciate very small things like a shower once a week, or once a month. And a piece of bad dark bread (partly sawdust) three times a day, and a wormy cabbage soup once a week.

I also learned about inflation and free enterprise. Every so often we would receive Red Cross parcels from Switzerland. In addition to some concentrated high-calorie food, they contained seven little boxes of five cigarettes each. I was twenty-eight years old and a nonsmoker, having never taken up the habit, but I quickly learned to trade a cigarette for a turnip with one of the prison guards. Wonderful! My cigarettes were money. Soon the local turnip supply began shrinking and the price went up—two cigarettes per turnip until there were no more turnips. The law of supply and demand had worked. But inflation! So I started to smoke, because we had learned by then never to waste anything. Our camp was liberated at the end of May by Patton's Third Army.

So, in a rather short combat tour of one year, I had lost three fighter aircraft (one P-51 and two P-47s) and some good parachutes. I had also managed a kill ratio of fifteen to one against ME-109s and FW-190s. Whoever started that war sure caused a lot of commotion in my life, but I did outlast that pesky Red Star. Praise the Lord!

A DIVE-BOMBER RAID AND KAMIKAZES

First Lieutenant Jim Swett arrived on Guadalcanal in February of 1943 and thought he had missed most of the action, but that was before he shot down eight Japanese dive-bombers on a single mission and won the Congressional Medal of Honor. He later flew missions across the Pacific, until the day the war ended for his Corsair squadron when kamikazes attacked the USS *Bunker Hill.* His many adventures are a portrait of what it was like to fly 103 combat missions in the Pacific War.

Marine Fighting Squadron VMF-221 arrived at Espiritu Santo in early February, received brand-new F4F Wildcats, and flew on to Guadalcanal to replace another Marine Corps fighter squadron. Our CO at the time was Captain Robert Burns. He was a marvelous person who recently died (late 1980s).

Not much was happening at Guadalcanal in those days, except for night bombing raids on the airfield by "Washing-Machine Charlie." By arriving when we did, we barely made the sobriquet of "Cactus Air Force." We didn't see the terrible combat experienced by Joe Foss, John Smith, Bob Galer, Marion Carl, Jeff De Blanc (see "A Life for a Sack of Rice" page 158), Ken Walsh, and the super pilots of their squadrons. Things changed on April 1, 1943, when our squadron got tangled up in a big Japanese raid. I was circling Henderson Field at the time and didn't get into the fight at all.

On April 7 I was on a 4:30 A.M. flight to the Russells. We circled over the islands and exchanged pleasantries with a fighter control fellow, call sign "Knucklehead," who advised us that there was a Japanese raid preparing to come down and greet us. By the time we had landed back at Guadalcanal, nothing much had come of the raid, but our coastwatcher, Martin Clemons, informed us that the raid was then passing over Bougainville. We left on another combat air patrol, circled over Cape Esperance to the west of Henderson Field, and finally came back and landed. At about eleven o'clock, we learned that the Japanese were coming down in earnest. They had about 150 dive-bombers and escorting Zeros. We were told to take off, circle over Tulagi, and try to intercept the dive-bombers that were coming after our destroyers and tankers, and a couple of Canadian Corvettes.

As we started our climb, we heard Smiley Burnett of

VMF-214 over by Cape Esperance holler, "Jesus Christ! There's millions of 'em!"

I was leading a flight of four aircraft. We were climbing like mad in our Wildcats, which don't climb well at all, and finally got up to roughly 15,000 or 20,000 feet of altitude. We could see the Val dive-bombers peeling off and going into their runs at Tulagi. Ten or twelve of them were going into a dive on the ships below, so we sidled in behind them. Because we were already in a dive, we were going a heck of a lot faster than they were. I exploded three of them with small bursts of ammunition on my way down. Those six .50-caliber machine guns were extremely destructive. It took only a few rounds from each gun to really put the screws to them. Every one of the Vals caught fire and blew up. On pullout from the dive I was hit in the left wing by our own antiaircraft. It made a nice little hole in the outboard end of my wing and disabled one of my guns. The AA fire also damaged my wing flaps.

As I was trying to get out of that mess, I flew over to the other side of Florida Island and looked for the rest of my flight. They had been jumped by the Zeros. Only Jack Pittman, my wingman, had been able to get away. Red Walsh and Wally Hallmeyer had been shot down. Jack made it back to Guadalcanal with a plane shot full of holes.

On the other side of Florida Island were a number of dive-bombers that were trying to rendezvous. They were spread out all over the sky. I sidled in behind each one of them, fired a few rounds, set them on fire, and put them into the ocean. The fifth Val that I attacked, number eight for the day, was a different story. I got too close to him, and the rear gunner stuck his .30-caliber machine gun right in my face, and blasted my windshield and my oil cooler seconds before I killed him and set the aircraft on fire. I claimed that Val as a probable kill. Later on, Navy Lieutenant Pete Lewis took an excursion over to the other side of Florida and found number eight down on the beach on one of the little outlying islands. The rear gunner was dead. The natives had killed the pilot. They were able to retrieve a decoding key from the wreckage, and it helped the intelligence people immeasurably. I have the engine plate from the aircraft in my trophy room today, but I never got credit for shooting down that plane.

After the rear gunner nailed my oil cooler, I turned around and headed for Florida Island and managed to get over the bay at Tulagi before the engine froze up. That old propeller was sticking up right in front of me like the middle finger of the right hand. I made a water landing without flaps, because the antiaircraft damage made it impossible to lower them. The aircraft bounced once and then dove into the water. Very quickly I was under fifteen or twenty feet of water and it was getting dark and cold. I unlatched my safety belt, but the parachute straps hung up on a boat release hook, which was a two-hook handle. After what was only a few seconds of struggling but seemed much longer, I managed to pull myself free. The rubber lifeboat and I rose to the surface. Only half of the lifeboat was inflated, but it and my Mae West gave me something to hang on to.

A few minutes later I attracted the attention of a Coast Guard picket boat by firing tracer bullets from my .45 automatic. They came over, pointed their rifles down at me, and said, "Are you an American?"

"You're goddamned right I am!"

One of the coast guardsmen said, "He's just another marine. Let's pick him up."

The picket boat took me to Gavutu, a small island near Tulagi, to wait for the colonel to come across and pick me up. When the colonel got there, he took me to his quarters on Tulagi. I had a bashed-up face and cut-up chin, cheeks, and nose from the hits in my windshield and the crash. The doctor gave me a shot of morphine and the colonel gave me a shot of Scotch. The whiskey promptly came back up. I couldn't even hold water down. The colonel let me use his bunk. I was trying to get some sleep when Red Walsh arrived. He had some scratches and bumps on him, and the doc had also given him a shot of morphine. We spent the whole darned night throwing up by the numbers.

The next morning a PBY took us to the Koli Point Naval Hospital, where we stayed for a few days. The doctor who took care of me was Olin M. Holmes, from my hometown of San Mateo, California. He later became my wife's obstetrician and would bring my son, James, Jr., into the world. After that stint in the hospital, I returned to duty to learn that I had been recommended for the Medal of Honor by Admiral Mitscher, ComAir, Solomon Islands. He would later be my boss and the commander of Task Force 58 while I served aboard his flagship, the USS *Bunker Hill.*

I was back on flying status about May 1. Shortly after that we were relieved and spent ten days down in Sydney, Australia. It was a welcome vacation. After a drunken brawl in Sydney, we returned to Guadalcanal loaded down with fresh fruit and chickens and other things for our enlisted personnel. We learned that we would be checked out in F4U Corsairs. That checkout was something where the Corsair was just flying me and the others all over the sky. Later, at the end of June, we moved to the Russell Islands.

We spent our time on combat air patrols, escorting dive-bombers to Munda, Vella Lavella, and Kolombangara, and flying cover for Arleigh Burke's destroyer attack group ("Thirty-one knot Burke's little beavers") and Admiral Merrill's cruisers. We covered the June 30, 1943, landing at Rendova, and supported both battles of Kula Gulf by escorting retiring cruisers and destroyers. At Rendova I shot down two Betty bombers, and a Navy Wildcat and I downed a Zeke. That raised my total kills to nine and a half. The enemy flight had consisted of twenty-four Mitsubishi Bettys and thirty to thirty-five Zero fighters. None of the enemy planes survived.

On July 11, four of us had taken off on a combat air patrol over Munda on New Georgia Island when we learned that another enemy raid was coming down. My section leader ran into engine problems and couldn't keep up with us at all. I sent him and "Tail-End Charlie" back home. Manny Segal and I orbited the area. The Japanese strike came in very close to us. They started to turn just before they got to New Georgia, and we decided to make one pass and get the hell out of there. I set a Betty bomber on fire as I went by. Manny got either a Zeke or a Betty. We dove into the clouds and flew around in them, trying to find each other. All of a sudden I saw this Corsair, Manny's plane, smoking like the devil. It had a Zero on its tail. I peeled in behind the Zero and let him have it with all six barrels at one time. The bullets sawed the wing off the Zero and down he went. I lost track of the Corsair.

I came down out of the clouds and saw a Betty bomber flying low over the water, possibly trying to make a sneak attack on our troops. I thought that it had one Zero escort, but there was another one that I had not seen. I waited until the Zero got out of position, dove in, and splashed the Betty bomber. Suddenly my instrument panel went to hell in a handbasket. The engine and everything else was shot up. The second Zero had spotted me diving on the Betty and had come in on my tail. I was 100 feet off the water with a dead engine, so I went into the water about five miles offshore at the entrance to the reef at New Georgia.

It took a very long time to paddle five miles to the shoreline in a rubber boat. I arrived around midnight. Every time a coconut would drop from a tree, I would be peeing in my pants, jumping in my rubber boat, and paddling back out to sea. Finally I calmed down and started looked for the friendly village at Segi. Captain Donald Kennedy, an Australian Army coastwatcher, was also down near Segi. I was still paddling two days later. At a point fairly close to Segi I suddenly heard a noise behind me. It was a dugout canoe with two natives. One of them had an ax and was ready to split me wide open, if I turned out to be a Japanese.

He asked me, "Are you American?"

"Yes! Yes! Yes! For heaven's sake!" It turned out that I was worth fourteen dollars of calico and canned bully beef.

They put me in the dugout and took me to the little village

of Segi, fed me some boiled sweet potatoes, and tried to let me sleep. If you have ever tried to sleep on a three-inch bamboo pole lashed to other bamboo poles, you know how impossible that is. I sat up the remainder of the night. The next morning they took me in a huge canoe that was twenty-to twenty-five-feet long and was paddled by ten natives. I sat in the center section. The natives paddled for hours without missing a stroke, until we got to Kennedy's quarters near a place where the Marine Raiders had just come ashore. That portion of the island was newly secure. Kennedy gave me a big tumbler of Scotch, and again I couldn't keep it down. Then Kennedy took me to review his troops. They consisted of about a dozen natives with different caliber rifles, and they were really a sight to see.

The next morning a PBY "Black Cat" picked me up and took me back to the Russells. There I learned that my dear old squadron buddies had drunk my bottle of Old Forester, raided my Cokes, and toasted to "dear old Jim." They were also celebrating the return of Manny Segal, who had been rescued by a destroyer the evening of our battle over New Georgia, taken to Guadalcanal, and then flown home to the Russells. Manny had beat me back by a few days. I was back on flight status almost immediately. The only thing really wrong with me was that the sun had burned the living bejesus out of me.

I got credit for only a probable from the first Betty on July 11, because I had not actually seen him crash, but I did get credit for the other Betty and the Zero that had been chasing Manny. I have since learned the names of some of the Japanese Zero pilots that I shot down. Three or four of them were Zero aces. Unfortunately there were quite a few pilots killed on the days that I nailed Zeros, and it's hard to determine who gets credit for which victory.

One of the memorable things about our time in the Russells was when the SeaBees "accidentally" killed a cow. The SeaBees were extremely innovative, as everybody knows. They had a grinding machine; they had a freezer, and they had some flavoring. There was a baker who could provide some hamburger buns. The SeaBees had a "mechanical cow," a milk-shake machine. They decided to provide the fighter pilots with hamburgers and milk shakes, your choice of vanilla or chocolate. We pigged out for quite a while, and then the word got around. There were a lot of emergency landings in the Russells. Pilots claimed engine trouble when, in reality, they just wanted a hamburger and a milk shake. They would have sold their souls for them.

We went down to Sydney in early August, then returned to Espiritu Santo later in the month. Next we were moved to the Quoin Hill base at Efate in the New Hebrides. On September 9 we flew to Turtle Bay fighter strip in the New Hebrides, where I was presented with the Congressional Medal of Honor by Major General Ralph Mitchell, USMC.

We practiced gunnery and division tactics for the rest of September, then moved again, to Vella Lavella in October 1943. Our skipper at this time was Major Nate Post. Almost immediately we tangled with a Japanese fighter sweep on Kahili. I got a Zero and another probable in that fight. Unfortunately I lost my wingman, Milt Schneider. He was following me and I never saw what happened to him.

On November 2 we flew from Vella Lavella on landing force cover for the Empress Augusta Bay landing on Bougainville. That day I got two Aichi-99 Val dive-bombers and one possible Tony fighter. I also raked a Royal New Zealand Air Force P-40 with improper markings. It didn't hurt the pilot, but his aircraft was damaged. I escorted him back to base where he landed "wheels up." I had to circle while they cleared the wreckage. The New Zealand pilot was holding a recognition talk when I got to the ready area. We got him really drunk after that. I have often wondered if he survived the war.

For the rest of November we escorted dive-bombers over the Shortlands, Kahili, Buka, Buna, and other places. On the thirteenth we had a four-hour mission flying cover for a crippled cruiser, the USS *Denver*. The following day we escorted a B-25 with engine problems. There were all sorts of "great" missions that month.

On December 11 we went aboard the Dutch motor ship NMS *Sommelsdijk.* We had a great Christmas meal on board, complete with cigars on the table and the whole bit. At two o'clock in the morning on December 31 we arrived in San Francisco. I had a brief reunion at that time with my family and my fiancée. That was wonderful. We had to be at the train depot by 2400 hours the same night. "Tiny Tim" Walker and I proceeded to the St. Francis Hotel and got bombed out of our gourds. We left for the train depot with five minutes to spare. The streets were so jammed up with people celebrating New Year's Eve, we finally had to hail a navy shore patrol paddy wagon. The navy got us to the train depot just in time to shove off for San Diego. The skipper had all the troops lined up, and here were two of his pilots, arriving in a navy paddy wagon. He was embarrassed, and he let us know about it. All was forgiven when my father put a couple of cases of whiskey aboard the train, along with about twenty cases of beer for the enlisted men. We had a hell of a New Year's celebration, but what a hangover the next morning!

At San Diego we were promptly granted thirty days leave. I went home to marry my sweetheart. We had a brief honeymoon, then I returned to duty and was reassigned to Santa Barbara NAS. Just before we took off for Santa Barbara I took a friend of mine for a ride in a Navy SNJ. We flew under every bridge in the bay. I got reported, of course. When we arrived in Santa Barbara, the colonel called me in and gave me ten days restriction to the marine corps air station. It was basically another black mark on my record, because the same thing had happened at Quantico in mid-1942, when a friend and I flew under a bridge and down the Rappahannock River just as the colonel was driving over it. That same colonel later pinned a Distinguished Flying Cross on me with the words, "Well, Swett. We meet again."

After we reported into Santa Barbara, my poor wife was able to see me for only half an hour each day when we came out for meals. We had only five of our original guys, and we were training a new squadron. I had wanted to meet Joe Foss, who had been stationed there, but he had left just before we arrived. We took over the same hangar that he had used. All of the new pilots had flown torpedo planes, and when we put them in the new Corsairs, they learned to fly the hard way. We had about forty pilots in a close-knit squadron. We learned that we were going to the USS *Bunker Hill,* so we spent a lot of time in field-carrier landing practice and made some actual landings on the USS *Ranger* off San Diego.

We got on board the USS *Bunker Hill* and left for overseas to join Task Force 58. Life aboard the ship was wonderful, like the difference between the Waldorf-Astoria and the slums of the worst area of the world (which was our life in the mud and among the flies of the Solomon Islands, particularly Guadalcanal). We got along well with the crew of the *Bunker Hill* and the other squadrons on board. We had two marine fighter squadrons on board—VMF-221 (mine) and VMF-451 (our brother squadron). There was also VF-84, commanded by Commander Roger Hedrick of the "Skull and Crossbones" Squadron. There were a torpedo squadron and a bombing squadron, all commanded by air group CO G. N. "Bunky" Ottinger. Unfortunately we would lose Bunky on a raid over Okinawa.

When we got out to Ulithi, we saw a long row of fast carriers called "murderers row" and we became part of it. Task Force 58 stretched from horizon to horizon and included ten major aircraft carriers and ten light aircraft carriers. God knows how many support ships there were, but it was an absolutely incredible sight. The task force was commanded by Admiral Mitscher. Admiral Spruance was there, commanding the fifth fleet from the battleship USS *New Jersey.*

VMF-221 participated in the fleet strikes over Japan. I made two flights over that country. Then we supported the landing at Iwo Jima and operations on Okinawa, where we made a lot of interceptions of kamikazes. On May 11, 1945, we were in one of those battles. I shot down a low-flying Judy torpedo plane, probably flown by some young kamikaze pilot. He didn't have a prayer. He didn't do any evasive tactics. He just let me shoot him down. My wingman, Walter Goeggel, downed a Judy the same day. Section Leader Ralph Glendinning got a Betty bomber with a Baka bomb (piloted suicide bomb driven by a rocket motor) attached to it. By then we didn't have any ammunition left and were low on fuel, so we returned to the *Bunker Hill*.

We were assigned to the carrier's starboard quarter, where we would circle at about 1,000 feet. At that point I saw two kamikazes diving on the *Bunker Hill* and screamed that there were two planes diving on her. The word just barely got out and very few people actually shot at the Japanese planes. The first one hit the parked airplanes at the rear end of the afterdeck. It dropped a bomb that went through the flight deck, out the side of the ship, and exploded in the water. It cleaned out an awful lot of the gunners on the gallery deck. The second kamikaze did a wingover, then came back and dropped a bomb that exploded in the navy fighter pilots' ready room and our squadron office. That bomb killed a lot of pilots. The kamikaze then crashed into the flight deck at the point where it meets the island. It totally destroyed him and his airplane. The *Bunker Hill* suffered about seven hundred casualties. The destruction was unbelievable. The mess was a horrible thing to clean up.

Many crewmen had gone over the side without life jackets. I had twenty fighters and two photo planes. We dropped life vests, rubber boats, dye markers—anything that would help the destroyers pick them up. I have no idea how many survived because of us, but after we rejoined the ship, many people gave us thanks.

We were stuck in the air with no place to land. When we got low on fuel and began declaring an emergency, they told us to land on the USS *Enterprise*. This was the old *Enterprise* with narrow flight decks. They had never received Corsairs aboard, but now we had twenty of them coming in, plus two F6F Hellcat photo planes. I landed my Corsair. They got me out of the cockpit, got the plane out of the wires, and pushed it over the side. Of those twenty Corsairs, only half a dozen survived without being sent over the side. All of our other equipment was on the *Bunker Hill*.

We were taken back to Guam, and finally Ulithi, compliments of the air force. We got back to Ulithi just in time to board the *Bunker Hill* as it was pulling anchor to head for Hawaii. When we returned to the United States, I was assigned to El Toro and we began training two squadrons to go overseas a third time on Operation Olympic, the invasion of Japan. The war ended before we could go over again, and that saved many lives, including my own.

My fighter squadron, VMF-221, finished the war as number two in the Marine Corps with 185 enemy planes shot down. We had eleven air aces. I ended up with 103 combat missions, sixteen and a half official kills, and nine probable kills. I am very proud of the enlisted ground crew that worked so hard to keep our aircraft in top-notch condition. I also have great admiration for the men who flew with me—my wingman, my section leader, and "Tail-End Charlie," as well as the rest of my squadron mates.

CAMERAS AND GUNS

Lieutenant William Shomo took off on a simple mission to photograph Japanese installations on Luzon, but that changed when he and his wingman spotted twelve enemy fighters escorting a Betty bomber. Shomo shot down ten Japanese aircraft in a seven-minute battle and won the Congressional Medal of Honor for his bravery.

In October 1942 I transferred to the 82nd Tactical Reconnaissance Squadron of the 71st Tactical Reconnaissance Group to fly Bell P-39s. The unit was later assigned to the Fifth Air Force and entered combat operations over New Guinea in November 1943. The 82nd's job was to provide the Fifth Air Force with visual and photo intelligence about Japanese military activities, chart jungle escape trails, and attack targets of opportunity. When the 82nd found something, the recon pilot picked up a K-25 hand-held camera from his lap and dropped a wing while snapping pictures. By June 1944 the 82nd had only two claims for Japanese planes destroyed in aerial combat, due to the range limitations of the P-39.

By December of that year American forces had returned to the Philippine Islands, and the 82nd Tactical Reconnaissance Squadron went with them. I was the squadron commander by then. We were based at San Jose Airfield on the island of Mindoro. We received an early Christmas present when we traded in our war-weary P-39s and P-40s for a mixture of P-51D Mustangs and the camera-equipped version of the P-51D, the F-6K. It was while we were flying out of Mindoro that I shot down my first enemy aircraft, a Val dive-bomber, over Luzon Island on January 10, 1945. I will never forget the following day.

The American invasion of Luzon at Lingayen Gulf was imminent, and the high command needed some hard intelligence about what the Japanese Air Force could throw against the invasion forces. The squadron was assigned to make a reconnaissance with two F-6Ks (P-51Ds) up the center of Luzon, to photograph the airfields at Tuetuegararo and Aparri in the northern part of the island, and Laoag in western Luzon. Since the Japanese were likely to challenge the mission, six P-51Ds from the newly arrived 3rd Air Commando

Group were assigned to provide top cover. The 3rd Air Commando Group was largely made up of combat veterans from the ETO, and they craved Pacific theater combat experience. Their six Mustangs roared down the runway, took off, and circled over San Jose airfield until the tower called and canceled their mission.

My wingman, Second Lieutenant Paul M. Lipscomb, and I were taking off when we heard the tower cancel the fighter cover. I immediately called the tower and asked about our mission. They responded, "Bulldog Red Leader, we have no information about your mission." I gave Lieutenant Lipscomb the order to continue with the mission.

We headed north and found very little of interest until we approached Clark Field. On the main railroad headed south near the field, a Japanese supply train was moving. I ordered my wingman into a trail position and commenced a strafing run with a long burst of machine-gun fire. The engine's boiler blew up, and the majority of the train was set on fire.

We climbed to 200 feet and continued north over Luzon until we were over Tuetuegararo in the Cagayan Valley. We had been flying for exactly two hours and were getting ready to start an on-the-deck photo run on the Japanese airfield. We were right on schedule. Suddenly, through a break in the clouds approximately 3,500 feet above us, I spotted three bogies headed in the opposite direction. I called out the bogies to Lipscomb, and he replied that they might be U.S. Navy planes on patrol in the area from offshore carriers. I told Lipscomb to follow me and did an Immelmann off the deck and a rollout on top of the clouds, in the opposite flight direction. We were now above and behind the bogies, on the left side of an enemy formation. An electric shock ran through both of us. The sky was full of "red meatballs."

A Japanese fighter squadron of eleven Tonys and one Tojo was escorting a Betty bomber. The enemy formation was stepped down in a wide V, like geese following the leader—the Betty bomber. The Japanese fighter pilots were flying in two-ship elements rather than in their usual three-ship elements, and each element was higher than the Betty and/or the element to its front. There were three two-ship elements on each side of the V. I had initially seen only the last two fighters on the left side of the formation and the wingman of the element to their front. I immediately ordered an attack. The aerial battle that every fighter pilot dreams about was about to take place.

I called for one pass down the left side of the Japanese formation with a pull out in front of the Betty. We would return to Tuetuegararo when we completed this pass. I warned Lieutenant Lipscomb: "Don't drop your fuel tanks unless you are shot at, because we will need the fuel to finish our mission."

We dived to within forty yards of the unsuspecting Japanese fighters and I began firing short bursts that destroyed the wingman at the end of the formation and then his element leader. Both Japanese fighters exploded as they were hit. I continued down the Japanese formation and set fire to a third Tony—the second element wingman. Just before the pilot was hit, he opened his canopy, looked over his shoulder, and frantically tried to wave me off. The suddenness of the attack had obviously caught the Japanese completely by surprise.

Lipscomb overshot me and destroyed the second Japanese element leader. This was a problem because the integrity of our flight was threatened. I immediately assumed the wingman position to protect Lipscomb's tail.

The Japanese apparently panicked and now began a counterattack. The second element of fighters on the right side roared out of formation and made an attack on Lieutenant Lipscomb. They missed. I shot down the wingman as they passed directly in front of us. Lipscomb continued his straight pass down the left side of the Japanese formation, and, firing at close range, exploded one of the Tonys on the left side of the Betty bomber.

We dove below the bomber because the Japanese tail gunner was now shooting at us. Lipscomb was still leading. He pulled up in a close-in skid and tried to use his guns like a garden hose to rake the exposed belly of the Japanese bomber. He missed and skidded out in front of the Betty, which exposed him to point-blank fire from the bomber's nose gunner. Lipscomb climbed out of danger in a tight vertical spiral.

I was still underneath the bomber, so I pulled back on the stick and began firing at a slight angle, raking the belly of the Japanese bomber across the right wing root. It erupted in a large fireball of orange flame. Then I pulled out in front of the Betty and followed Lipscomb up in a tight vertical spiral. The Betty, belching smoke and fire, began to descend in an attempt to land in a grain field below.

I looked up and saw Lipscomb directly above me, turning back north across the flight path of the Japanese formation. The third element leader on the right side of the Japanese formation realized that his mission to protect the bomber was a failure and was now going to follow the samurai code. He would destroy his enemy by ramming him on a head-on pass! The two pilots closed on each other with guns blazing, and neither one deviated. I saw it all happen as I climbed from below. Lieutenant Lipscomb stopped firing at the last split second and dove his F-6K under the Japanese suicide pilot. The Tony fell spinning to earth past my plane, trailing dense, black smoke with a dead pilot at the controls.

I looked down and saw the burning Betty attempting a crash landing in a grain field. Two Japanese fighters remained in a tight formation on the right wing of the crippled bomber as it descended.

A burst of gunfire from below warned me of a new threat. The Tojo that had flown "Tail-End Charlie" on the right side had now come across the top of the formation and latched on to my tail while I was still climbing vertically. It looked like a P-47 with a large radial engine. The Tojo had begun firing as I continued climbing in my vertical spiral. I looked back over my shoulder and used the rudder to turn more tightly inside the Japanese pilot's gunfire, thereby preventing him from gaining sufficient lead to hit me. The Tojo finally stalled out, flipped over, dove with me hot on his tail, and escaped into the nearby clouds.

Now I spotted Lipscomb flying south, heading back toward me. The last two Tonys were on the deck below us, leaving the burning Betty as it crashed, and heading for the low hills close by to the south. Their prop wash was blowing through the grain fields like two giant fans. I called for one last pass on the two remaining Japanese fighters. I overtook them in a full-power diving pass and I quickly destroyed the element leader. I followed the wingman in a ninety-degree wingover to the right at grass-top level, and watched as the Tony cartwheeled into the ground from a short, point-blank burst of machine-gun fire.

Suddenly the sky was clear. On the ground were the smoking and burning wrecks of ten Japanese aircraft as testimony to the effectiveness of our seven-minute attack. With the exception of our attacks on the Betty bomber, all firing had been at ranges of forty yards or less and had consisted of very short, point-blank bursts. We flew over the wrecked Japanese aircraft and took pictures of them with the side-mounted recon cameras to verify our claims. This took another five minutes. We had now been flying for two hours and twelve minutes. Score: Lipscomb, three Tonys; Shomo, six Tonys and one Betty.

Lieutenant Lipscomb reported that his aircraft was damaged and he was returning to Mindoro, so I had to make a decision. I could let him fly alone over 500 miles of Japanese territory, or escort him home. There was really no choice but to escort him safely back to our base.

When we arrived over San Jose Airfield, I made seven victory rolls in three passes. The entire base turned into a beehive of activity. My victory rolls had delayed the takeoff of a three-squadron P-38 fighter mission of the 475th Fighter Group. After I landed, Colonel Jerry Johnson, a famous P-38 ace and the 475th Group Commander, taxied his fighter back and ran over to my plane to chew me out. When I assured him that the victory rolls were authentic, he smiled, clapped me on the shoulder, and left to catch up with his fighter group.

Two days later Tokyo Rose announced on her radio program that "a high-ranking Japanese air marshal and his staff had died two days earlier in an aircraft accident while inspecting Japanese forces on Luzon Island in the Philippines."

Lieutenant Lipscomb and I were both promoted. He received the Distinguished Service Cross, our nation's second highest award for gallantry in action. I later received the Medal of Honor. I served my country in uniform for twenty-eight and a half years, until retiring as an air force lieutenant colonel in 1968.[5]

COMPASSION

First Lieutenant Bill Cullerton passed the test to become an army fighter pilot and then was counseled that he would never make it. He went on to become the 355th Fighter Group's second-highest-scoring ace. On a second tour in the ETO he was hit by flak over a German airfield and began one of the most amazing adventures you will ever read about. After evading for about ten days, he was captured by the SS, shot, and left for dead. Nursed back to health by a Jewish doctor and other kind people at the risk of their own lives, he escaped again and was eventually rescued by an armored spearhead.

I was the ten thousandth cadet from Chicago to join the army's aviation cadet program. I was signing the papers when someone said, "You're the ten thousandth guy to sign up!" They swooped me into Mayor Kelly's office and gave me a complimentary night on the town.

I took the required written test and passed it, but when results came back, the counselor had some advice. "We have to give you a shot at being a fighter pilot, but as an experienced counselor, I'm here to tell you that you scored seventy, the minimum qualifying score. There's no way you're ever going to make it." All I needed was someone telling me that I couldn't make it. Ironically I finished the war as the second highest scoring ace in my fighter group.

My war experiences took place in what I call "my other life." We were young men at the time. I was flying combat missions at ages nineteen and twenty, and I was hot stuff. There wasn't a German pilot or any groundfire that could hit me, and I felt invincible. I'm no hero, but I did exactly what I was trained to do. Those of us who returned must have done something right, but the important thing is to tell young people what can happen to them in this world. A couple of things happened to me that will be hard to believe, but truth is always stranger than fiction.

The 355th Fighter Group was stationed near the English town of Steeple Morden at an airfield we called Station One-Two-Two. We began the war in P-47 Thunderbolts. P-47s were heavy planes with a limited range for the important bomber-escort missions. They were later replaced with long-range P-51 Mustangs. We finished the war with a score of 862 German planes destroyed and one of the best aerial kill ratios in the ETO. Fifty-six of our pilots became air aces.

The group excelled at ground-strafing attacks. The idea was to get as close to the ground as possible, because the lower you were, the less armament could be aimed at you. This was safer and made you more dangerous to the enemy. Many of our passes were so low that we literally blew out the windows of buildings as we roared past them. We suffered heavy losses from groundfire on strafing missions, but they earned us the nickname "Steeple Morden strafers."

In mid-September 1944, the B-24 bombers we were escorting were jumped by approximately forty long-nosed Focke-Wulfs, with ME-109s flying top cover. As the FW-190s headed for the deck and we gave chase, we passed over a German airdrome. We were able to destroy fourteen enemy aircraft in a strafing attack. Seven of them were mine.

My best day was in early November when fifty-six of our Mustangs rendezvoused with the bombers west of Merseburg, Germany. We were engaging targets of opportunity north of the main bomber track when a group of FW-190s and ME-109s was spotted landing at an airdrome near Wernigerode. I was engaged for some time in the air and shot down an ME-109 and an FW-190. As I was coming out of a maneuver on the deck, I spotted about fifty parked enemy aircraft and opened fire. My wingman and I strafed the field through intense groundfire, until we were out of ammunition. Gun-camera film later showed that I had destroyed six more German aircraft on the ground, in addition to two gun installations.

I completed my first tour in early December 1944. My boss, Colonel Everett Stewart, invited me back for another tour with the promise of a promotion and, eventually, a squadron of my own. I was really on a high when I returned to the States for the customary thirty-day leave. I had gotten so taken by the publicity that I must have really believed in my own invincibility, reading my own clippings, so to speak. While in the States, I broke my own rule and got engaged. That was a terrible spot to put a young girl in. I damned near got killed when I returned, and my death would have been a sad thing for her to go through. It turned out well. We've been married forty-five years as of June 1990.

I returned to England in late December, just in time to get in on the cleanup following the Battle of the Bulge. The weather during the peak of the battle had been bad, socked in right to the deck, and this allowed the Germans freedom of the roads. They moved a hell of a lot of tanks and other equipment into the fight. When the weather broke (about December 15 to 18) the Eighth Air Force got to them. By the time I returned, the 355th Fighter Group was strafing every day. There were miles of roads lined with burning German vehicles. For all practical purposes, we had broken their backs.

The next couple of months were one strafing mission after the other. We were aware of the German rocket fighters and the ME-262, a pure, twin jet. The 262s were doing a number on our bombers (B-17s and B-24s) with high-speed passes through the formations. I tried to chase a few down, but no luck. Our strafing, or target of opportunity, missions were directed at digging out hidden airfields that might be housing rocket fighters or jets. The day I got hit was such a day. We were looking for airfields, or any concentration of tanks or other vehicles.

I can't remember if I was leading the squadron or just a flight, but I was the first one to jump the field. There were some planes hidden in a treeline, so I divided the planes into two flights. My flight went in first from east to west, and the other flight hit from north to south, right after us. The flak was fairly heavy and we hugged the treetops, but the Germans had built gun platforms just below treetop level, so we were looking them right in the eye as we passed by. I could get a "sight" on the planes under the trees, and got off a couple of bursts. One or two of them began burning. I was just starting evasive action when I got hit.

I was down on the deck (which means that your prop is kicking up dust) when I took a direct hit in the fuselage tank right behind the cockpit. That tank held eighty gallons of gasoline. For a moment I thought that I had hit something on the ground. It was a hell of a jolt. I looked in the rearview mirror and saw a mass of flames and knew my plane had been hit. I started to climb as fast as I could, jettisoned the canopy, and waited until it was safe to bail, because I was very low. The plane hit the apex of its climb and I bailed, pulling the rip cord simultaneously. I am sure that whatever forward momentum I had saved my butt. No sooner had the chute popped than I landed on my ass, although I didn't know it at the time. A few days later I realized that my rear was black and blue from waist to knees.

I was so scared that I jumped up and ran for a clump of woods, dragging the collapsed chute behind me. Realizing that I was totally panicked, I stopped and took inventory. My training took over. I took a small "escape" kit out of my seat pack, unhooked my chute, and continued running across a field toward the woods. I could still hear the sirens on the airfield, and my plane was a mass of flames about 200 yards away. I knew damned well that they'd be hunting me down—soon. I decided to conceal the chute in the closest woods (where I had originally been heading), then thought of a better idea.

I got to the woods and kind of "half hid" the chute in some small trees, then took off back across the field in the other direction. As soon as I got to the other side of the field, I looked for a place to hide. I figured they would be gauging how far I could get away from the plane in any one direction, and they wouldn't spend much time in the immediate area. They would find the chute and start searching in that direction. That's just what happened, except they left some guards near the wreckage of my plane. They had decided to search all the woods around my plane, and I hadn't counted on that.

I found a thicket of small pine or fir trees and coiled myself around the trunk of one of them. Because the branches drooped almost to the ground, I was well concealed. The German guards came by, one at a time, so close that I could have reached out and touched their boots. Two of them stood at my tree, talking and smoking, for about half an hour. They would have found me if the search hadn't been so halfhearted, and I'm not sure what I would have done if they had. The .45 was in my hand the entire time the two Germans stood over me, and I probably would have tried to kill them if they spotted me. Fortunately the search party left after about an hour. I decided to wait until dark to make a run for it.

One thing I had been blessed with was an instinct for direction. I had spent many a day in the woods with my grandfather. In high school I had been a guide in northern Wisconsin. I had a compass, matches, a silk map, some benzedrine tablets, and a chocolate bar, as well as extra .45 ammo (as if I were going to shoot my way out of there). I headed west after dark. I've been in some dark places, but an overcast night in the German forest, under the strict blackout rules they lived by, was dark. I mean *dark!* Over the next several nights I walked smack into fences, stepped into a deep creek, almost stepped on a bedded-down deer, and had the living hell scared out of me by the glow of rotting, phosphorescent trees. I thought they were flashlights. The night I almost stepped on the deer, I ran into a huge tree before I knew what the hell I was doing. I wasted about three matches before I realized that my "button" compass glowed in the dark.

Most daylight hours were spent trying to get to a distant goal that might have a nighttime outline. This was wooded country with occasional small villages and some farms. On the farms were guarded field workers. It was spring, and they were planting potatoes or beets. I went into the fields at night and tried to dig up whatever it was they were planting, but it never worked. My hands were so cold and raw that they were bloody. At one point I decided to get to one of the field workers and take some food. I watched a girl for two or three hours, until she finally headed home along my treeline. I intercepted her and scared her half to death with my .45. She thought I was a German. I got her calmed down and, through sign language and pointing, identified myself as an Americanski. She was either a Polish or Czechoslovak slave laborer.

I got a piece of bread, some potatoes, and good directions, and had a hell of a time telling her that she couldn't join me.

I have no idea how many miles I covered in the next several days. I was starving and it was so cold that I'd fall asleep and wake up with my eyelids frozen shut. I was either delirious by then, or my mind had just gone blank. I shot a crow or raven and chewed on the meat and guts. Then I started hearing trucks, tanks, and big guns. I saw our bombers and fighters and watched some dogfights, and could see that the Germans were in flight, both in the air and on the ground. They did very little moving around on the roads while the Eighth Air Force was over Germany, but word always got out about the "all clear," and the roads would soon be jammed with tanks and trucks.

I worked my way across southern Germany until I came to a place where there was small-arms fire in the distance and I knew that the front was close. The Americans were advancing, pushing the Germans back, and I thought the safest thing to do was hide out in a small woods and wait for our forces to overrun me. Then the Americans started shelling the woods. The treebursts were unbelievable. Fragments smacked into trees and lodged there. Other trees were torn apart as if a tornado were roaring through. I expected to get hit, so I decided to move to another clump of woods about a quarter mile away. I hadn't gone more than thirty feet when I ran into a group of twenty to twenty-five Waffen SS men. They had been running the other way and weren't interested in taking any prisoners.

They disarmed me. One of them put my gun in my belly and said, "For you, the war is over." He shot me on the spot.

The Germans must have counterattacked and pushed back the Americans. I lay there for a day or two or three. I don't know how long. Then along came a German farmer with a two-wheeled donkey cart. I think he saw my flying suit and thought that I was one of their flyers. He loaded me on his cart, and the next thing I remember, I was in a hospital, laid out in the operating room. I am a Catholic and wore a crucifix around my neck. A German doctor was holding it and saying, "Katholik."

I replied, "Yes."

He said in broken English, "My name is Meier and I am a Jew. There aren't any priests here. I am a Jew and I am your friend." He told me that he was running a small German hospital that was crammed with 400 to 500 patients, then he said, "You have been shot through the liver and you are bleeding to death internally. If you want, you can take a piece of paper and write a message to your mother and father. I will give it to the Americans."

I told him, "Forget it."

I asked him if he knew anything about sulfa. He didn't have any. They were using newspapers for bandages. Some of the patients in the hospital had walked all the way back to the German lines after their defeat at Stalingrad and had lost hands and feet to frostbite.

The local military knew that I was an American flyer and told the doctor that they wanted me. He recognized their obsession with paperwork, so he told them, "Fine, but you'll have to sign for him. If I have to turn this pilot over to you, somebody will sign, because if you move him, it will kill him." He was putting his life on the line.

The Germans refused to sign for a couple of weeks. During that period I had found many people who were willing to gamble their lives for a perfect stranger. The small hospital was staffed by Lutheran nuns in their typical habits, and they would sneak food to me. A little eleven-year-old Dutch boy, a slave laborer who cleaned bedpans, etc., spent half of his waking hours stealing little scraps of food for me. When he walked past my bed, he would slip them under the cover, risking his life for another human being.

The doctor and I had become very close. One day he came to me and said, "They are going to move you. They know the Americans are coming and they are taking you with them. They want you." My room was on the second floor of the hospital. The doctor told me: "I had a load of manure dumped under your window this afternoon. You had better leave tonight."

I jumped into the pile of manure that same night. The fall made my wound start bleeding again. I crawled to the edge of town, found a big underground culvert, and crawled into it to hide. It was cold in there. Again, my eyelids were freezing shut at night from the moisture. After two or three days in the culvert, I heard German tanks passing overhead and knew that they were retreating. Then there was a day or so of absolute silence, except for the roar of the big guns. One morning I heard tanks that sounded different from the German ones. I thought that it was the Americans, but I was afraid to crawl out of the culvert and take a look. Finally a tank rolled over the culvert and stopped. I could hear guys calling back and forth, so I began crawling out of my hiding place.

There was a huge black soldier standing on top of a tank behind a machine gun that looked like a gatling gun. I leaned out from the culvert and said, "Hey!" He turned and pointed that big gun right at me. "I'm an American!"

"I don't know who you are, buster, but you make one little hoot and you're gone!"

When they established that I was one of them, they began shouting, "We got an American! We got an American!" They radioed back for an ambulance while saying things like, "God! He's wounded! He's sick! Give him some brandy! Give him some food!" It turned out that they were part of a 14th Armored Division spearhead that was thirty-five miles in front of our lines.

They laid out a bunch of blankets for me and gave me some liberated brandy and boiled eggs. The meal made me sick as a dog. By the time a medical lieutenant jumped out of his ambulance a couple of hours later, I was in bad shape.

He shouted at the tankers, "Who the hell got this guy and gave him the booze? He's drunk!"

Anyway, I had been liberated. What I will always remember is a Jewish doctor, a little Dutch boy, and a big black tanker (and his smile when he recognized me as an American). They all risked their lives for me.

SALVATION FOR A DOOMED ZOOMIE

Lieutenant John Galvin's F6F Hellcat was shot down on his fifth mission, at a place called Woleai Atoll. He was rescued by the submarine USS *Harder,* which was commanded by the navy's most decorated submarine commander, Samuel Dealey. Galvin's adventures aboard a combat submarine are a story in themselves. He returned to his squadron, VF-8, to participate in memorable actions over the Marianas, Formosa, and the Philippines.

Woleai Atoll should have remained a remote, obscure chain of tiny islands in the South Pacific. Instead, Japanese troops were shipped in, followed by the bulldozers that gouged a crude landing strip out of dense jungle. Corrugated huts were erected, and aviation fuel and other supplies were stockpiled. The fronds of palm trees that had once swayed in the tropical breeze became tattered and shredded from the harsh wind blast of aircraft propellers. The quiet of that isolated place was violated with the sounds made by Japanese medium bombers, fighter aircraft, and bulldozers. This was only the beginning. The installations at Woleai Atoll had been discovered by U.S. forces.

The job of locating the airstrip, monitoring its traffic, and rescuing downed airmen fell to Commander Samuel Dealey and the crew of the submarine USS *Harder*. These men had three combat patrols under their belts and had sunk seven Japanese ships. The *Harder* was already known throughout the Pacific as the "submarine of submarines." An hour after arriving off Woleai on March 29, 1944, the *Harder* spotted an enemy aircraft leaving the island. The submarine dived to eighty feet. Japanese aircraft were spotted six more times that day, and the submarine dived each time one of them came too close. In an effort to pinpoint the strip, Sam Dealey maneuvered his vessel as close to the shoreline as possible. The jungle hid everything. Then he boldly sailed submerged into the lagoon and panned the area with his periscope. No ships were at anchorage that day. A few moments later the executive officer, Lieutenant Frank Lynch, sighted the airstrip. It was about 3,000 feet long and had a Betty bomber at one end, preparing to take off.

The navy's plan was to destroy the enemy air bases at Palau, Yap, and Woleai as part of a massive operation against the western Caroline Islands and along the New Guinea coast to the south. The USS *Harder*'s intelligence information was just what the planners needed. Army B-17 bombers hit the Japanese while they slept, at 0105 hours on March 31, and took them so much by surprise that there was no antiaircraft fire. Sam Dealey watched through his periscope as bombs hit parked planes, vehicles, buildings, and supply dumps. Two more waves of B-17s hit within the hour, and this time the defenders of Woleai were awake and manning their guns. The men aboard the *Harder* wondered if anything could be left intact on the island after such devastating attacks. That question was answered when several aircraft rose into the air later that day. At 0725 hours on April 1, the sub's radar picked up a flight of planes at 36,000 yards. Dealey grinned as he watched the first wave of fighters peel off toward the airstrip. I was piloting one of those Hellcats.

April Fool's Day, 1944, was supposed to be a day of rest for us. For the past two days we had pounded the Japanese on Palau Island with bombs and machine guns. What an experience that had been. We had caught the enemy completely by surprise, and everything we shot at burned or blew up— planes, gas tanks, hangars, everything. I didn't think much about the killing, but about the incredible display of flashing explosions and the huge mushroom clouds of fire and smoke.

When the general quarters alarm sounded that morning, and the impersonal voice squawked, "All hands! General quarters! Man your battle stations!" I groaned and realized it was only three o'clock. As I waited for our briefing to begin, I wondered if this day would be like the others. Commander Collins, the squadron skipper, gave us our briefing. "You're going in to attack Woleai Atoll because we're going to be retiring by this little place." He smiled at us, but nobody smiled back. "Actually, it's a stepping-stone between Truk Island and New Guinea."

After breakfast we received information from a teletype screen that was mounted on the bulkhead about wind course and speed, target heading and distance, homing-device frequency and call letters, and the frequency of "Falstaff," the lifeguard submarine. An intelligence briefing told how many enemy planes and antiaircraft guns to expect, then we waited for the squawkbox to announce, "Pilots, man your planes!"

The flight deck was alive with activity. Our F6Fs, wings folded to conserve space, were already fueled and armed. We started our engines on command and awaited our turn on the catapult. You never got used to the catapult. When the catapult crew rushed forward and connected the hook to the underside of my Hellcat, I released the brakes, put the throttle full forward, and trusted in the hook to hold me. Full throttle and no brakes. I was launched upon command of the catapult officer, and 2.1 seconds and 110 feet later, I was airborne. The rapid acceleration pushed me back in my seat, and the plane vibrated so hard that everything became a blur, then the vibration stopped and the plane smoothed out at ninety knots. Two hours later we sighted our target.

We flew high over the atoll at 25,000 feet. Gus, my flight leader and former All American end for the University of Pennsylvania, gave us the "close-up" signal and we brought the aircraft within ten feet of each other, in a tight diving attack formation. I activated the gunsight and armed the machine guns and bomb. The airfield was below us now as we dived at 450 knots. I squinted through the gunsight and spotted Japanese planes parked in random little alcoves that were hacked out of dense jungle. I squeezed the trigger on the front of my joystick and six .50-caliber machine guns blasted away, sending a shuddering convulsion through the aircraft and filling my oxygen mask with the smell of burned gunpowder. The shells were ripping and exploding the targets to shreds. At precisely 3,500 feet over the strip, I pressed the "pickle" button on top of the stick and dropped the bomb.

Our bombs exploded behind us as we flew fifty feet off the ground. Then I saw the Betty bomber parked all alone at the end of the airstrip. I rolled the Hellcat to the right, stupidly leaving Gus alone. T.I. and Chris, the rest of our four-aircraft flight, were to my right and had no choice but to follow me. We all opened fire at the bomber at the same time. The Mitsubishi exploded in a brilliant flash in front of our eyes. Beyond the burning plane was an ack-ack emplacement, and the Japanese gunners were firing strings of 20mm tracers right at me. I saw them whizzing by my cockpit. *Clumph-clumph!* The aircraft shuddered and already I noticed that the right wing was shredded, as if someone had gone after it with a giant can opener. I could see some of its ribs. Shells were still hitting the ship, so I instinctively dived to the ground and started jinking (rapid, erratic turns in both directions).

T.I and Chris told me that both sides of the aircraft were on fire. Both wing tanks were burning furiously, and I have never felt such panic. By the time I was able to eject from the plane, at 300 feet above the water and 250 mph, the cockpit was on fire. I was slammed hard against the plane's tail, then went spinning off into oblivion. I was unconscious for only a few seconds before I tried to open my chute and realized that the 300 mph wind and my collision with the tail had already done that. One pendulum swing below the chute, and I slammed facefirst into the water with the kind of jolt you'd expect from hitting dry land. The chute dragged me through fifteen-foot waves. I gulped seawater and fought for breath until I managed to cut the risers with my survival knife. My life raft had a deep gash and was useless, so I had to swim for it after all.

I had a torn and useless Mae West and no life raft, the heavy G suit was soaked now, and weighting me down, and then I saw the shark fins. Marking dye was supposed to keep away sharks, not that I had much confidence in the survival manual right then. I ripped open six bags while turning my body to see if one of the sharks was sneaking up on me. When the bright green dye covered the surface of the ocean around me, the sharks left. I gulped more seawater, snapped out of my stupor, and tried to swim.

I had quit struggling when a strange and remarkable thing happened. There was an invasion of brilliant light, and the water around me took on the appearance of morguelike luminosity. Time stood still during this surrealistic experience, then a voice called, "John!" I didn't recognize the voice, but I was drifting beneath the surface with an oxygen-starved brain by then. I was starting to drown and didn't realize it. The voice snapped me back to reality and I thrashed upward until I broke surface, coughing and gurgling, gasping for air.

I no longer had the strength to fight the huge waves, then thump! I had cracked my head on something. I desperately kicked back toward the surface, but my feet hit something solid. I stumbled to my feet in shallow water. Another breaker slammed me against a coral head and I desperately clung to it for safety. The razor-sharp coral cut my hands painfully. After an endless struggle through 500 yards of coral and breakers, I pulled myself up on the sand and passed out. It had taken four and one half hours to reach shore. I was now the only American on a Japanese atoll. When I awoke, I saw three Hellcats circling overhead. Where was the rescue submarine?

Sam Dealey had watched our strikes on the atoll and was impressed. The bombs had blown buildings into the air, causeways had been bombed, petroleum storage tanks had exploded, and the islands were cloaked in heavy clouds of black smoke. The attack planes had reformed and hit the islands again from east to west, diving through the blanket of smoke and a hail of ack-ack fire. The *Harder* received the command to rescue a downed "Zoomie" while all these other things were happening, and he calculated that it would take three hours to reach me.

The sub was one mile off the northeast corner of Woleai when the replacement flyers that I had seen guided him toward my location "on the northwest tip of the second island west of Woleai." He surfaced and moved to a spot 1,500 yards off the beach with "white water breaking over shoals twenty yards in front of the ship." The fathometer had ceased recording. Dealey had calculated that the Japanese would be too busy with their own problems to worry about his submarine.

One of the aircraft above us had advised the *Harder* that the rescue was too difficult, but Dealey decided to back off and attempt an alternate approach. He had watched me stand up on the beach and then collapse, and assumed that I was suffering from physical exhaustion. He was right. My suit looked black because it was wet, and my face didn't look like an American's by then. I had a blistering sunburn that was coated with dried blood. The attack and cover aircraft were running low on fuel, and to complicate matters, a second man was squatting on the beach a short distance from me. They didn't know if he was native or Japanese. Dealey radioed Admiral Spruance to "prolong the attack and provide air cover and we will effect the rescue." The *Harder* made a second approach, and nearly every man on the crew volunteered to push a rubber raft to shore to rescue me.

When the three volunteers neared the beach, I pushed myself into the surf and inflated a rubber raft that had been dropped to me, then tried to paddle out to them. My hands barely reached the water. As my boat drifted parallel to the beach, two submariners waded and swam through the rough surf in an attempt to reach me. They tried for half an hour before they got there, and just as they did, snipers opened up from the shore. Hellcats dived to strafe the jungle, but the Japanese kept firing at us and the submarine. Sam Dealey got a bullet through his cap as he watched the rescue from 1,200 yards out to sea. They finally got me aboard, even after a rescue float plane had accidentally severed the tow line between the raft and the sub and set us adrift once again. The second rescue operation is a story in itself. I was saved by a crew of extremely brave men.

I gradually healed and recovered my strength over the next few days while the *Harder* remained off Woleai. As soon as I was able to work in those cramped quarters, Sam Dealey assigned me the job of encoding and decoding messages. It helped my injured pride to feel useful again. The other officers remarked to Sam what a welcome relief it was to have me take over the decoding duties, and one of them suggested that they should rescue a downed Zoomie on every trip. I learned that a submarine is both a weapon and a home. It was actually larger than I had imagined, about the length of a football field, but very narrow.

Sam Dealey had a theory. He wanted to sink Japanese destroyers because that would leave the resupply convoys vulnerable. He told me that the Japanese fleet was desperately short of destroyers, which were about the only ships, other than light cruisers or other submarines, capable of defending themselves against submarine attack. He theorized that a destroyer would steam straight toward a periscope and attack on the assumption that the submarine would submerge and run. If the unexpected happened and the submarine fired its torpedoes, the natural impulse would be to try to turn the ship away from their frothy wakes. That would be the mistake. "My plan," he said, "is to deliberately attack destroyers and sink them." That scared me, and I thought the guy was nuts.

The only activity around Woleai was the appearance of occasional Japanese patrol planes. When they came too close, we dived. It got monotonous after a while and the crew became edgy. The routine broke on the night of April 12 when I decoded a message for the *Harder*—"Target priority restriction lifted." Sam had won his point with headquarters. Now he could go after Japanese destroyers. Several days later he spotted the mast of a destroyer that was resting in Woleai's lagoon. He began cruising on the surface near the atoll, trying to get airplanes to spot us. Whenever they turned in our direction, we dived. The pilots didn't know how quickly or how deep we would dive, and they consistently set the depth charges to explode at depths above us. I only hoped a pilot wouldn't drop a bomb and sink us by accident.

We baited another plane on April 14 and waited. Every fifteen minutes Sam would rise to periscope depth and scan the horizon for more planes. In late afternoon a sonar operator reported pinging. Only destroyers pinged. The destroyer's sonar was on a swinging, circular sweep, scanning 360 degrees for a submarine. We could hear pinging come into audible range, fade out, and then come back into range. The *Harder* aimed its bow toward the destroyer, and the other ship's captain reduced the sweep to fifteen to twenty degrees. He thought he was going to sink an American submarine. A Japanese land-based medium bomber appeared and circled over us, then Sam spotted the destroyer's mast, not more than six miles away. It was steaming directly toward us.

As the destroyer got closer, Sam identified its silhouette as one of the new 1,950-ton *Fubuki* class. It was later identified as the *Ikazuchi*. The range was down to 5,000 yards by 1847 hours. From that point on, the radar man called out the range every 1,000 yards. Sam readied eight torpedo tubes, four forward and four aft. I could picture two knife-edged ships racing at each other. At 2,500 yards, the Japanese skipper put his ship on a zigzag course that would bring it to within 800 to 1,000 yards from us, but it stopped the maneuver and came straight at us when it was 1,500 yards away. At 900 yards the destroyer made an abrupt turn, probably because we were so close that the sonar began confusing pings and the operator's interpretation was that we had turned. We wouldn't have to fire the first torpedo point-blank to get the destroyer to turn. The ship's captain had done that for us.

"Right full rudder!" Sam ordered. "Match gyros!" An officer quickly keyed the command into the TDC (torpedo data computer) and it calculated a new gyro angle for the fish. "Fire one!" yelled Sam. At eight second intervals, "Fire two! . . . Fire three! . . . Fire four!" Sam got a good look at the destroyer as the torpedoes white-tailed their way to the target. "Down scope!" "Take her down! Dive! Dive!"

Someone with a stopwatch counted off the seconds. "Five seconds . . . four . . . three . . . two . . . one!" There was a long silence. Balloom! We felt the concussion and a shout went up through the ship. Balloom! The submarine went up to periscope depth and the officers took turns watching. When it was my turn, I saw the stern end of the destroyer sticking straight up out of the water. The sight of a destroyer slipping nosefirst beneath the water, carrying its crew to their deaths, was something that I could no longer watch. I had seen them hanging on the rails as she went down. We were only 400 yards away and had to clear the area as the ship settled toward the bottom and we were rocked by explosion after explosion as the preset depth charges on her deck detonated. We later surfaced, but there were no survivors. The Japanese had been victims of forty or fifty depth charges going off like a string of giant firecrackers. The *Harder* slowly cruised through a nightmare seascape of mangled bodies and pieces of bodies.

On April 16 the *Harder* struck again. Sam sank one merchantman and at least damaged a destroyer. The torpedo hit on the destroyer sent up a sheet of flame, but we lost track of her in a rain squall. A second destroyer depth-charged us for the next two hours. The next morning we spotted the burning merchant ship, but no survivors, and could find no trace of the two destroyers.

On April 20 the *Harder* was down to just enough fuel to make the 3,300-mile trip back to the American submarine base at Freemantle, Australia. The next morning we surfaced 2,000 yards off the beach and pounded Woleai with the four-incher and the smaller 20mm cannon. We dived within two minutes of opening fire, long before the Japanese had time to react. Six of us were on the bridge that night for the midnight watch when we heard a high-pitched, screaming whine that sent a chill down my spine. When it stopped, someone yelled, "Torpedo!" Heading for the submarine's midsection was the telltale streak of white bubbles. The torpedo was "porpoising," rising to the surface, then diving deep, then coming back to the surface again. There wasn't time to sound the alarm. It dived under us. We never did find what had fired it.

We arrived at Freemantle on May 3, 1944, thirty-three days after my rescue. It was there that I learned that Admiral Spruance had prolonged, by two and a half hours, an operation involving 110 warships, including sixteen carriers, just to rescue me. That's excluding one 30-million-dollar submarine and its crew of eighty-four men. The admiral had done this at the request of Sam Dealey. I will never forget the last conversation with Sam on the night of my farewell party. I still get goose bumps when I recall his words.

"Zoomie, I want you to remember all the rest of your life about the wind and the tide and the current that carried you ashore. Never in my entire naval career have I seen anything like it. You had a lot of help going for you that day. So don't you forget it." Then he told me about the request to Admiral Spruance that saved my life. Today I believe that a power far greater than a fleet admiral wanted me to be rescued.

After those memorable days at the submarine base, I was reunited with the crew of the USS *Bunker Hill*. My return sparked a great reunion aboard the carrier, but the warmest welcomes came from Gus, T.I., and Chris. They greeted me as if I were the prodigal son. Things had changed within me. My great ego had been humbled by the shootdown. It could happen again, and maybe the next time I wouldn't be coming back.

One of my first missions after returning was a sortie over Guam on June 14. We were told to expect stiff opposition from the Japanese who were concentrated on the three-mile-long half-mile-wide, Orote Peninsula. They had five hundred antiaircraft guns with three-inch and larger bores, and an unknown number of rifles and machine guns. We flew in before sunrise from 25,000 feet, and just as we pushed into our vertical dive, the ground lit up like a Christmas tree. I thought the fools had turned on all the lights for us! What I was seeing was the open ends of gun barrels. We lost some good men that day.

On September 21, 1944, our flight of four (Gus, T.I., Chris, and me) were among the first group of two hundred fighters sent on a major strike against Manila. No American planes had overflown the city since MacArthur had left it in 1942. We had been launched from sixteen carriers and all converged on Manila and Clark Field. The Japanese had barrage balloons up, and going after them was like shooting sitting ducks. We sprayed them with our .50-caliber machine guns. Just when we thought that things would be easy that day, down came the Zeros to get us. I don't know how many there were, but they easily outnumbered us. They were the older army "Oscars," but their vintage did not affect the determination of those pilots. They came at us like a swarm of angry hornets and the dogfight was on. The radio crackled with shouts and warnings of pilots reporting the locations of Oscars.

I got on the tail of an Oscar and stayed glued to him as he tried to outrun me in a steep dive. I got a lead on him and peppered him good. That's all it took. Japanese planes had little armor plating and no self-sealing gas tanks, so when you scored a good hit, you could generally count on setting the target on fire. My Oscar burst into a flaming torch, arched toward the ground, and crashed in a huge fireball.

Seconds later I spotted another Oscar that was heading for a landing at Clark Field. It was either already damaged or low on gas. I swung down and got it in my gunsights, blasted away, and splattered the plane as it flew a few feet off the ground along a hedgerow. The plane bellied into the ground, sliding and digging a long furrow. Then it exploded. I climbed back into the clouds in search of more targets, but there were none. I spotted another Hellcat and flew side by side with him back to the carrier. The pilot was George Kirk from Moline, Illinois. He had bagged three Japanese that day.

There was great elation over shooting down Japanese airplanes, almost like scoring a touchdown in football. I never felt remorseful about killing, and I don't recall any of our pilots expressing regret. We were taught that the Japanese were the enemy, and that we were to hate them and shoot them down.

On October 16 we catapulted off the *Bunker Hill* for an escort and bombing run over Formosa. I was on the first flight sweep of twenty-four fighters from several carriers. Our primary mission was to blast in there and try to shoot down all enemy planes, so that the following waves could bomb the installations and a large aircraft factory at Matsuyama Field. As we dived out of the overcast sky, we were immediately jumped by about eighty Japanese Tojos, new frontline fighters that were comparable to the F6F in firepower, armament, and armor. Tojos were everywhere, darting back and forth in pursuit, bent on bagging Hellcats. I eluded by finding sanctuary in a cloud.

Maybe a minute went by before I poked my nose out of the clouds to encounter more Japanese planes, only Japanese planes. None of ours were in sight. I started shooting by reflex, and most of the subsequent action was so harried and fast that it's a blur in my memory. I spotted a Tojo and went full throttle after it, concentrating on getting it in my gunsights. When I had it locked in, I blasted away and zapped it. Then I went looking for another one. They weren't hard to find because they were looking for us too.

I saw a distant plane coming head on for me. I slouched in my seat and peered through the gunsight. Just as I was about to squeeze the trigger, I heard Gus's voice over the radio. "Dumbo! [My nickname] Do you have a plane coming at you head on?"

"I sure do!"

We realized that we were heading for each other. Both of us had thought that the opposite plane might be an F6F, but the Tojos resembled a Hellcat when seen head on. Good old Gus! He was a welcome sight. I succeeded in knocking three Tojos out of the sky that day, which brought my total victories to five. The fight ended with fifty-two claimed Japanese planes shot down and no Americans lost.

On our next mission Gus and I were on a three-hundred-mile search for the Japanese fleet. As we neared the area where we expected to find them, I spotted the first enemy aircraft high above us, just below the cloud layer. I yelled excitedly over the radio to Gus: "Topsy! Twelve o'clock high!"

The Topsy was an old American DC-2 that had been sold to Japan before the war. I had forgotten that it carried no armament and that I could easily have closed in for the kill. I bore down on the plane, shooting like crazy, but in my excitement to beat Gus there, I pushed full throttle ahead and overran it. I looked back over my shoulder as I circled around and saw that the Topsy was in flames. Seconds later Gus closed in and finished off the plane. Chalk one up for good old Gus.

Gus ordered me to fly above the cloud layer while he stayed below it. A few moments later he called on the radio. "Hey, Dumbo! Make a diving left turn through the clouds and come in shootin'!"

I did just that and what I saw was unbelievable, like a picture from a storybook. There were three Nells flying in a close V formation. Nells were old twin-engine, eleven-passenger Japanese high-level bombers. I came through the clouds and was right on top of them. I made a "beam" run from the left side and a little above them, and set my gunsights on the lead plane, really drilling it. The rays of sunlight through the early morning clouds made the Plexiglas glitter as it shattered and popped out of the cockpit. The Nell lurched and started a nosedive, leaving a trail of black smoke in its wake. I had gotten the pilot. I switched targets to the nearer of the two remaining Nells and hit it good. The left prop stopped turning, the right landing gear dropped, and the bomber caught fire. Gus saw what was happening and came in behind me to finish it off.

I bore down and peppered the last Nell with machine-gun fire. Its gunner was throwing everything he could at me. I came in too fast and overran the plane, then pulled up at the last possible second, just missing the bomber's twin tails. The Nell started to turn away. I kept zigzagging back and forth to slow down enough to come back around for another shot. I finally reduced airspeed, made another pass, and sprayed the aircraft with my .50s. It exploded into a ball of flames and plummetted.

On October 18 we were flying an escort and bomb run over the island of Luzon when we spotted some small Japanese ships far below us. Gus and I peeled off and went down first. We missed. Then I went into a shallow dive, called a skip-bombing run on a 6,000-ton transport. I fired all six machine guns as I closed with the target. Just before I had to pull up to avoid crashing into the ship, I dropped the bomb. It sank the transport. The ship slid into the ocean, sternfirst.

Late in my series of combat missions I was coming in on a flat, 300 mph downhill dive on a Japanese ship, flying into a shower of bullets, strafing all the way, until I could release a bomb. All six machine guns jammed at once. Having one gun jam wasn't uncommon, but to have all guns jam was an incredibly rare event. In a split second I instinctively stooped forward and down to punch the gun charger buttons and clear the jam. *Crack!* The inside of the cockpit exploded in a shower of glass splinters that was accompanied by the shrill whistle of rushing air. "What the . . . ?"

I bolted upright in my seat and looked straight ahead. My gunsight was shattered and most of the windshield had been blasted away. There was a bullet hole in my headrest. A Japanese .50-caliber shell had entered the cockpit through the windshield, shattered the gunsight, and lodged in my headrest. A split second before, my eye had been in front of the gunsight. I was so shaken that I don't remember if I punched the pickle to drop the bomb. Later I was able to calculate that the shell had been in the air and on its way toward me when my wing guns jammed. I had been saved once again. Today I have to wonder if it was mere coincidence or divine intervention.

A new policy in effect when I arrived in the Pacific was that a carrier squadron should serve for twenty-five combat missions, or six months in the combat zone. While the army and marines counted every flight as a mission, the navy counted only those flights in which there was combat. That's why we had so many flights. During one period, we never dropped anchor for 138 days. We would clobber a place, pull back 300 to 800 miles, get resupplied, and do it all over again. I had 123 combat flying days and ninety-six combat missions.

This was less than or average because of the time I had spent aboard the USS *Harder*. One man was up to 120 or 125 missions. By that stage of our experience all thoughts of heroics and high medals, and all dreams of conquest, were gone from our minds.

It seemed that every time we attacked a target, somebody would get shot down. The stress was real and hard to deal with for some of our pilots. Some of the guys let the fear of dying really get to them, and it eventually shattered their nerves. The navy finally altered its policy and consented to allowing pilots to be grounded from "combat fatigue." Manliness had nothing to do with it. The stress was real, although it wasn't a problem for me. My squadron was eventually withdrawn from the combat zone with one third of its pilots lost, another third grounded, and the last third still flying.

We didn't get back to the States quite as fast as expected. Our squadron left the *Bunker Hill* and took up residence on the stinking little island of Ponam, off the coast of New Guinea. Later we were transferred to Pearl Harbor. While I was there, I learned about the fate of Sam Dealey and the USS *Harder*. After I left them, the submarine went on another combat patrol where Dealey managed to sink five Japanese destroyers in six days. The navy tried to pull him out of combat when he returned. It was the military custom to pull highly decorated officers out of combat, and Sam Dealey eventually earned the Medal of Honor, five Navy Crosses, and the army Distinguished Service Cross. Sam insisted on leading a wolf pack on a sixth combat patrol. They sank two, and possibly three, Japanese destroyers, then his sub was sunk while he conducted a bold maneuver to lure a small enemy antisubmarine vessel away from another American submarine. This was the type of bravery and self-sacrifice that Sam Dealey was famous for by then.

The other American submarine, the USS *Hake*, reported that a string of fifteen rapid depth charges were dropped. The Japanese report stated that a periscope had been sighted at 2,000 yards and a depth charge attack was immediately delivered. After this single attack, a huge fountain of oil bubbled to the surface, along with considerable quantities of wood, cork, and other debris that floated in the slick. I was able to tell Mrs. Dealey the whole story and return some of Sam's personal mementos to her while I was on a thirty-day leave back home.

The squadron finished the war at Saipan aboard the USS *Bennington*. We were part of the huge Allied invasion force that was preparing for the final assault on Japan. Atom bombs ended the war. An estimated 200,000 Japanese were killed by those bombs, which was a fraction of the one or two million Japanese and Americans who would have died in an all-out attack on the home islands. I was eligible for an immediate discharge and took a fifty-five-day trip home aboard a liberty ship from Saipan. Though the war was finally over, and I was going home, the loss of Sam Dealey and the crew of the *Harder* left me in no mood to celebrate our country's great victory.[6]

BAILOUT OVER CHINA

Lieutenant Colonel Edward Rector had spent one tour with the AVG and returned to China in 1944 to command the 23rd Fighter Group. On his second mission after returning he was hit by antiaircraft fire over Quemoy Island and forced to bail out. There followed a remarkable escape through the heart of Japanese-occupied China.

I was a navy dive-bomber pilot stationed at Norfolk NAS and serving on the old USS *Ranger,* and later the USS *Yorktown.* We participated in exercises in the Caribbean and neutrality patrols in the Atlantic, and it was during this one-year tour that I was allowed to resign from the navy and join General Claire Chennault's American Volunteer Group (AVG) for duty in Burma and China. When the AVG was disbanded by presidential decree, I was one of five pilots and twenty-eight ground personnel who signed on with the army air corps. We formed the cadre for the 23rd Fighter Group that supplanted the Flying Tigers. After Chennault requested me for a second tour, I arrived back in China in the fall of '44 and served briefly as assistant director of operations for the 68th Composite Wing. Then I assumed command of the 23rd Fighter Group.

By that time the Japanese had pushed south from Hankow along the north-south railway system to Canton and Hong Kong. They had forced abandonment of Hengyang, one of our key bases, and from there had pressed southwest along the Siang River, necessitating abandonment of more bases at Lingling, Kweilin, and Liuchow. However, east of the north-south railroad axis was an area of unoccupied Chinese territory. The 23rd Fighter Group (now a four-squadron unit) continued to operate with impunity from two air bases inside the pocket. Two squadrons, one at Kanchow and another at Suichwan (less than ninety miles away), had continued to give the Japanese holy hell by raiding seaports and airfields from Hong Kong–Canton northeast to Wenchow.

That was the situation in early December 1944 when I moved the two other squadrons to those bases to participate in a massive raid, by 14th Air Force standards: seven hundred planes, including 100 B-29s from Cheng Tu. We blasted Hankow, the very heart of the Japanese offensive. The following day Major Phil Chapman, CO of the 74th Fighter Squadron, took me on a familiarization mission to the occupied southeast China coast ports of Swatow, Amoy, and Wenchow.

We took off in our P-51Bs and headed at low altitude south-southeast toward Swatow Air Field, flying over low hills until we arrived. On the field were two revetments, each containing a single-engine scout plane that was covered with camouflage netting. Phil strafed one of them and I took the other. There was desultory groundfire, and after two more strafing passes we called that portion of the recce complete.

Phil signaled for me to join up, and we headed northeast along the coast toward Amoy. I became concerned at this point. The Japanese had a rudimentary ground warning net and some radar, and I was thinking that we should have departed north-northwest, as if returning to our base. It was 9:45 A.M. and we were flying under a dark, overcast sky when we skipped over a low ridge near the airfield on Quemoy Island. The perimeter of the field lit up with groundfire like a diamond necklace, and I thought, "Uh-oh! Someone will probably get hurt!"

There was a bomber and two smaller aircraft parked on a ramp adjacent to a small control tower. Phil headed for the bomber. I kicked out forty degrees to starboard to line up the two smaller aircraft and the tower, and to ensure that my ricochets didn't endanger him on his pullout from his target. I felt and heard the small-arms fire hitting my plane, then one hell of a thud! As I jinked, I looked down at my right wing and saw the ground through a hole in it! I headed north and inland with Phil telling me to do just that. The engine was missing a beat every ten to twelve seconds, and the windscreen was now covered with engine oil. As I crossed the coast, I climbed to 1,800 feet and informed Phil that I would have to bail out. Later I learned that he had switched on his gun camera to "camera only" and filmed my subsequent jump. I treasure that film.

By now the engine was cutting out more frequently and the red oil-pressure light was on. The canopy release mechanism on the "B" was a long, horizontal handle on the right side of the cockpit. I pulled it to the vertical release position, but the canopy stayed in place. A report I had read flashed through my mind. A 23rd pilot had been found in the wreckage of his P-51B with fingertips clawed to the bone. Something was wrong with those release handles. After several more pulls and hard hand shoves, the canopy remained in place, so I loosened my shoulder harness and half stood, giving the canopy one hell of a heave with my shoulders. It instantly released and I felt the welcome rush of cold air. By this time I was inland over some low hills and had lost altitude.

I crouched in the seat and put considerable forward trim on the tab. In level flight at low altitude I let the stick go and simultaneously kicked straight up, pulling the rip cord immediately. The chute opened, I swung twice and hit the ground with a thud! There's a reason why the ground came up like a runaway elevator and I hit it so hard. I had lost a close friend and former navy squadron mate, Burt Christman, while the AVG was fighting over Rangoon. His bullet-riddled body was returned to us after a dogfight, and the natives confirmed that he had been strafed while descending by parachute. The same thing had happened in China. On my way through Kunming for a second tour I had requested a twenty-two-foot canopy chute rather than the standard twenty-eight-foot chute. The smaller size would allow more agility in sideslipping and maneuvering if I bailed out and came under strafing attack.

The extra flow of adrenaline allows individuals to do extraordinary things under stress. The first example of that had been my physical shouldering loose of the Mustang's canopy. After hitting the ground I quickly bounded up, although dazed from the rap I had taken on the head. I heard rifle fire over the next hill and assumed it came from a Japanese force that made occasional foraging raids on the mainland from their base on Quemoy Island. I put my foot on the parachute straps and tore the survival kit from the back of the parachute. The chutes of that era were sturdy, and the survival kit was sewn in place with strong waxed twine and doubly secured. This feat would have been physically impossible under ordinary circumstances. I was never able to physically tear a kit loose after that day.

I threw the kit over my shoulder and started running along a trail around the hill where I had hit. After about a mile I heard voices ahead of me and quickly turned uphill to hide in the undergrowth. A scattered group of Chinese came hurrying along the trail toward my landing site. Now I had to make a decision. I could lie low, or I could reveal myself to them. Knowing about the remarkable record of Chinese assistance and rescue of downed pilots, it took me all of twenty seconds to decide to come out of my hiding place. It was a good judgment. I later learned that the firing I had heard was exploding ammo from my crashed fighter.

I lost more than my airplane when I bailed out. Between overseas tours I had been a test pilot at Elgin Field, and, among my other duties, assisted in operational testing of the K-14 gunsight. Its effectiveness amazed us. When I learned that I was returning to China, I wheedled a breadboard model for the P-51B, got myself designated a courier, and used the fifty-eight-pound additional weight allowance to take over a K-14, complete with engineering and installation drawings. That sight had been on my fighter for only two missions after all that effort! However, the following Ds and Ks came equipped with the K-14.

The Chinese escorted me back along the trail until we came to the semblance of a road running north and south. They turned right toward Amoy and I demurred, pointing north. We hand-argued for three or four minutes, but they appeared so smilingly confident that I finally gave in and nodded "okay." Then my right leg collapsed and I fell flat on my ass! I had banged the hell out of my right knee when I hit, and with that final decision the adrenaline was gone.

The Chinese brought up a small horse which I rode to Amoy, straight to the mayor's guest house. Word traveled quickly in China. I was the first American flyer they had seen, and a large crowd had gathered by the time I dismounted. They helped me into the house and gave me a delicious lunch before I went to bed. The mayor came calling in the afternoon, and through his hastily acquired interpreter, we had a delightful two-hour chat. As he was leaving, the mayor asked me to address the townspeople before I departed. I agreed, then had a scrumptious meal and slept the sleep of the exhausted.

About one A.M. I was aroused by a house servant, accompanied by Mr. Lo, a young, college-aged Chinese man. He apologized for waking me and said that he was from the Air Ground Aid Service (AGAS). Chennault had organized the AGAS to assist downed flyers. The service consisted of hundreds of young, mostly English-speaking men, spread all over China. Mr. Lo asked me to sign a chit, proving that he had "found" me and offered his assistance. While we were talking, the servant brought in a second AGAS man and I signed his chit as well. I noticed that the young AGAS men were having difficulty communicating (China has one written language but five major spoken languages and over four hundred dialects). One man was from Shanghai and the other was Cantonese. I asked them why the hell they didn't speak to each other in English. The problem was solved.

Two days later I was sedan-chaired two miles out of town to the northeast. From this secluded point I was able to observe the Japanese airfield one mile across a strait on Quemoy Island. There were infrequent takeoffs and landings and the usual airfield activities. That was a unique experience, and I recall it in clear detail to this day.

On my last night in Amoy I addressed a full assembly of townspeople in the town hall. They were hanging from the rafters. Through the mayor's interpreter, I brought them up-to-date on the war situation in China and around the world, and thanked them for their hospitality, kindness, and support, locally and throughout China. Warmed by their cheers and applause, I related some war stories about bombing, strafing attacks, aerial victories, etc. I went to bed that night with the full realization that I had experienced a brief four-day interlude that I would treasure and remember forever.

AGAS had made arrangements for my departure. I still hobbled, so my travel would be by sedan chair. Mr. Lo would be my escort. The next morning the town square was filled: thousands of people. After many good-byes and again expressing my thanks, I was helped into the chair. Two "toters," one fore and one aft, stood between the carrying bars and grinned, proud to be chosen to transport the "*megwa fegerin*" (American flyer). They lifted on signal and nothing happened. I weighed 170 pounds and the weight of the chair with me and the gifts I had received must have been nigh on 210 pounds. They hoisted me on the second try, and off we went with Mr. Lo trotting alongside. Once it was apparent that my two toters were laboring hard under the weight, Mr. Lo obtained an additional carrier. Off we went.

We traveled throughout the day and arrived just after dark at a hamlet situated at the confluence of two rivers and a small bay. It was there that I first met an AGAS American, the area director. He told me that I would be traveling by night to avoid the occasional Japanese patrol boats. We boarded a very large, motorized, covered sampan and left. We debarked the next morning, and I was turned over to another AGAS sedan-chair crew, this time with six carriers. The carriers would spell each other every fifteen minutes, with four toting and two walking along beside. This phase of our journey took several days.

We arrived at Changan, the capital of Fukien Province, on Christmas Eve. I was taken to a two-story guest house and bade farewell to my carriers. Further travel would be by truck. As I prepared for bed at about ten P.M., I heard the strangest thing: young voices singing Christmas carols in English below my second story balcony. I went out and saw below me some thirty youngsters, gathered in the bright moonlight and holding lighted candles. After listening to two more renditions, I thanked them and went back inside. They were a young people's choir from the local church. As I said before, news travels fast in China.

The following morning I resumed my journey by riding in the cab of a pine-oil-fueled truck whose bed was loaded to the top of the cab with assorted goods. We took a narrow road with hairpin curves and sheer dropoffs through steep hill country, often encountering unexpected oncoming traffic. I was a nervous wreck by the time we stopped for lunch. When we had finished eating, I silently vowed that after what I'd been through, I wasn't going to be killed in the cab if our truck left the roadway. I was almost one hundred percent mobile by now, so I rode atop the cargo, just behind the cab, ready to bail out left or right if the need arose. That's how I finished that phase of the trip.

On New Year's Eve we arrived at some sort of American outpost. I walked into the compound at about eleven P.M. and entered a well-lit house. What a surprise! I was greeted by eleven Americans who had gathered there from outlying posts to join the local cadre for New Year's Eve and New Year's Day. This group of fellow countrymen from OSS, OWI, AGAS, etc., had delayed their banquet, knowing that I would soon arrive. I borrowed some clothes, took a quick hot shower, and rejoined them. We sat down to a great feast at 12:30 A.M. and then wassailed until late predawn.

I immediately handled the problem with our faulty canopy-release handles. Using the secure communications facilities at the American compound, I ordered the grounding of all P-51Bs and a thorough inspection of their canopy-release systems. Two aircraft were found with inoperable systems, if normal canopy-release procedures were followed.

There was an airstrip close to the compound. Two days later I was picked up and transported to Suichwan in a De Havilland Otter. I borrowed a P-51 the next day and returned to the 23rd Fighter Group Headquarters at Luliang, fifty miles

301

east of Kunming. I later learned that Chennault had known I was okay within six hours of my bailout, but under the circumstances his headquarters could only send a "missing in action" report to my parents. Three weeks later their anxiety was alleviated by a wire stating that I was back in the saddle!

—THE—
KOREAN
WAR

The Korean War was a strange war with strange rules of engagement. It began with propeller-driven planes, but soon escalated into a jet war. The Americans fought at first with F-80 Shooting Stars, and later, F-84 Thunderjets. These were fairly evenly matched with the Communist MiG-15s. The tables turned when the United States introduced its progressively improving versions of the F-86 Sabrejets. The enemy jets were armed with both 37mm and 23mm cannon, while the F-86 carried six .50-caliber machine guns. Except for the ability to climb quicker to a higher altitude, the Communist fighters were now far outmatched. Of the 958 enemy aircraft destroyed in the air, 810 were destroyed by Sabrejets in a ratio of over twelve to one.

There were forty American aces in Korea. Thirty-nine of them flew F-86 jets and one flew a piston-driven F4U Corsair. This collection has memoirs from five F-86 aces (Fischer, Jones, Lilley, Marshall, Wescott) and the Corsair ace (Bordelon). George Jones and Bill Wescott had already flown combat missions during World War II. Harold Fischer served two tours—one flying ground-support missions in an F-80, and one in which he became a double ace in an F-86. William Marshall participated in a battle where F-86s savaged an escorted mission of TU-2 bombers, then watched the same thing happen in reverse as MiG-15s decimated a formation of B-29 bombers. Leonard Lilley flew a lot of interesting missions, including one where he shot down a pilot with blond hair. Guy Bordelon flew night-interdiction missions against the Communist supply routes before assuming a night-fighter role and shooting down five enemy propeller-driven aircraft.

AIR WAR IN KOREA—THE EARLY DAYS

Lieutenant Colonel George Jones arrived in Korea the month after the first American fighter pilot became a jet ace, and things seemed oddly familiar. He had seen a lot of it before in the Pacific in World War II. This interesting story describes some of the early combat missions to the Yalu and the planning and execution of a successful aerial ambush over North Korea.

As the Korean War progressed, tactics changed, facilities changed, and many fine combat leaders and pilots rotated through. Some became aces or double aces, and two became triple aces. But some things never changed in that war of jet aircraft against jet aircraft, pilot against pilot, where specks in the sky rushed at you or receded at 1,200 miles per hour. Jabara had become the first jet ace in May 1951. I joined the 4th Fighter Wing the following month.

After arriving at Johnson AFB in Japan and filling out the usual papers, I was on my way to the war the next morning in a C-47. We circled Kimpo Airfield to allow time for a flight of F-86s, returning to land from a fighter sweep to the Yalu. Everything I saw below us was strangely familiar—the PSP (pierced steel planking) used in runway construction, revetted antiaircraft guns staring skyward, and sandbagged revetments with aircraft. It was as though I had been there before, and I had. Just a few short years back I was flying P-47s on fighter-bomber missions against the Japanese. Only now there was no island with coral strip runways. This was a rugged peninsula with a fighter strip hacked out of raw red earth, compacted with quick-set asphalt and laced in places with PSP. F-86 Sabrejets were crouched in the sandbagged revetments, ready to go or being prepared for the next mission. I felt elated, but underneath the elation was a little warning—Take care! This is war!

I reported to Colonel Herman Schmit, the 4th Wing CO. I liked him on sight and would find him to be a dedicated officer and a fine gentleman. It really wasn't like checking into a strange group, because I knew many of the pilots from previous days. Here was a crackerjack fighter outfit, led by such renowned Top Guns and combat leaders as Colonel Glenn Eagleston, Colonel Bruce Hinton, and Colonel Francis S. Gabreski. "Gabby" had just reported in a few days earlier.

He greeted me with a big smile and a handshake and said, "Hurry up, get ready, and let's go get them!"

Lieutenant Colonel Ben Emmert was assigned to get me settled in, briefed, indoctrinated, and ready for combat. There were many procedures I needed to know before flying combat against the MiG-15 pilots. He led me to the officers quarters, the tent area where I stowed my gear and erected a mosquito bar over my bunk, then showed me where to dig my air raid foxhole. All the time we were talking about the MiG-15s.

As we were leaving the area, Ben said, "George, there is a very important thing that you need to know." I leaned forward, straining my ears to hear what I expected would be some key trick in busting MiGs. Ben continued. "George, don't urinate on the ground outside your tent at night. The Old Man will have your butt if he catches you." I assured Ben that I would heed his advice.

We went to a mess-hall tent that had bowls of yellow Atabrine pills on each table. We were supposed to take a pill each day. It was just like in the Pacific in World War II, but more fresh vegetables were served here. There was also a bathhouse with a row of hot showers, and that was great. The latrine was ingenious. The stools were holes sawed in a board that was fastened over a water trough that periodically flushed itself. The water mechanism, a seesaw with a container of rocks on one end and a watertight empty container on the other, was in almost perpetual motion. The rocks held the empty container in the air under a constantly flowing water pipe. Water flowed into the container until it weighed more than the rocks, then it seesawed down and dumped twenty gallons of water into the trough. When it was empty again, the rocks lifted it back to the water pipe. That was a gimmick worthy of the Navy SeaBees in the Pacific. Those jokers could make anything from washing machines to walk-in coolers, in addition to building airfields.

Now about the war. The rules of the game were deceptively simple. It was okay for the Communists to load the airfields north of the Yalu (in Manchuria) with as many MiGs as they wanted. Antung was probably the major air base. The others stretching across Manchuria were satellites. Since we could not strafe them, they needed no revetments, and supplies came and went at their pleasure. Intelligence told us that there were over one thousand MiGs up there and they could put a hell of a lot of them up in the air. In those days, thirty-two F-86s on a mission was a good number for us. The MiG-15s could take off, climb out to altitude (usually higher than the F-86s), circle, and then speed up and pour across the Yalu like water out of a boot. Meanwhile the F-86s swept back and forth between the MiGs and friendly fighter-bombers that were working over North Korean targets of opportunity, in addition to gun emplacements and supply dumps. When the MiGs came across the Yalu, we could jump them.

We covered for B-29 daylight raids for a while, and those raids brought the MiGs out in force. They would come in high upon instruction from their controller at Antung, then come screaming down after the bombers. It was almost impossible to prevent a determined MiG pilot from getting a shot at a B-29, usually with bad results for the bomber. We would latch on to the MiGs as they peeled off from altitude, and when they broke off from the B-29s. We put weaving close cover and top area cover over our bombers, but the MiGs still shot them down. We shot down MiGs. MiGs shot down bombers. The B-29s really took a beating, and Fifth Air Force stopped the daylight heavy bomber raids over North Korea.

When B-29s were over North Korea, "Listening Post" reported that the Antung controller kept telling the MiG flight leaders, "Get the big boys! Get the big boys! Disregard the Sabrejets! Get the big boys!"

I flew a couple of local flights and got my intelligence briefings. I also received air-sea rescue information and a cockpit flight chart showing distance and heading information, geographic code names, and IFF (information, friend or foe) procedures. I was ready to go. I was scheduled for a fighter sweep to the Yalu, flying Ben Emmert's wing. We were briefed and then picked up our personal equipment—Mae West life jackets (we already wore G suits under our flight suits), parachutes, helmets, and handguns. Some pilots carried .38 revolvers. I carried a Colt .45 auto pistol in a specially designed pocket in my flight jacket. Already aboard the aircraft, in the bucket seat where we sat, were life raft dinghies. We just got in and snap-hooked them onto the parachute D-rings. I climbed into the cockpit, strapped in, and watched the seconds count down until startup, said a little prayer, and hit the start button at Ben's "wind-'em-up" signal.

We taxied out and lined up sixteen aircraft on the runway. Red Leader gave the "run-up" signal, and holding brakes, we ran the engines to full power. Black clouds of exhaust gases rolled back as sixteen fighters strained to start rolling. Red Leader nodded, and he and his wingman released brakes and started rolling down the runway in formation. Thirty seconds later the second pair was rolling, and every thirty seconds thereafter another pair began moving. It was our turn. Ben nodded, then we released brakes and rolled. On reaching takeoff speed, the noses came up and we leapt into the air, climbing out on course. It was a straight climb out, with the lead aircraft throttled back to 300 knots, until all sixteen fighters were in formation. Then Red Leader pushed the throttle up for climb speed. Four flights of four aircraft spread out almost line abreast, with each flight of four in "Fingertip" formation (look at the back of your hand, fingers extended and thumb tucked under, to visualize the fingertip formation).

As we reached 15,000 feet, Ben gave the signal to spread out and test-fire guns. The six .50-caliber machine guns each fired at a rate of five hundred rounds a minute. The load was usually a combination of ball, API (armor-piercing incendiary), and tracer. The .50 cal is a hell of a good round, with a muzzle velocity of almost 3,000 feet per second. I switched on the gun switch, pressed the trigger on the stick, and six guns blasted out a burst. As I looked through the gunsight, the tracers appeared to float through the orange dot. We were ready!

Combat flying is a teamwork job. Ben had briefed me to cover him—he was the shooter. Unless he called me to take the lead to fire, my job was to keep him clear of attacking MiGs.

We were at 28,000 feet over Sinanjo, a few minutes south of the Yalu, when friendly radar called out, "Big train moving out at the station!" He was saying that many MiG-15s were taking off from Antung, climbing out to altitude, and massing for an attack. Soon we heard, "Big train leaving the station. Casey Jones at the throttle!" Casey Jones was the code name for a hell of a good MiG-15 combat leader, probably a Russian. He knew his aircraft and he knew the fighter game. Now we heard, "Big train headed for Racetrack!" Racetrack was a geographical location we knew well. Correcting our course to the right about ten degrees, we headed for Racetrack.

Heads swiveling, eyes searching the sky, we strained to catch sight of the MiGs. We wanted no surprises. Suddenly contrails broke out straight ahead and high above us, followed by bursts of sunlight flashing off MiG canopies and fuselages. It was like a mirror catching the sun's rays and bouncing them back at us. Judging from the glints of light, many MiGs were headed our way at 600 mph. We dropped our empty fuel tanks and headed for the contrails. The contrails quickly disappeared and we knew that the MiGs were letting down. Seconds later we met twenty to thirty of them head on. Red-nosed, stubby aircraft with big red stars flashed by on my right side. We whipped into a hard right turn, the MiGs turned hard left, and the fight was on.

A flight of F-86s came in, and another flight of MiGs dropped down from altitude. Except for an occasional burst of cannon fire from them, or a .50-cal snap-shot from us, nobody was firing. MiGs and Sabrejets were turning and twisting, trying to get into shooting position. Ben called that he was "locked on" (in shooting position) but still out of range. Cutting across, we were gaining on a MiG-15.

I was holding my position on Ben's wing when we suddenly flashed by another MiG-15 that had climbed up under us. We were so close that I could look through the canopy and see the big red stars on the pilot's helmet. I couldn't shoot. My job was to stick with Ben, and we were still closing on his MiG, but now we were across the Yalu. The MiG sped north and we broke off. Flights were calling in "bingo fuel" (only enough to get back to base). The fight was over for the day—no MiGs. But tomorrow was another day, and I would be leading my own flight.

In July 1951 I was given command of the 334th Fighter Squadron. I had been flying with that squadron, knew the officers and men, and felt that it was a great honor to be their commander. As CO, I took my place on the roster for briefing 4th Fighter Wing combat missions. About the middle of that month it was my turn to brief and lead a fighter sweep to the Yalu. It had been tough going for the past week. The MiG pilots were aggressive and came barreling across the Yalu at altitude, like yellow jackets out of a nest. As we sat in the briefing room and listened to the weather report and the intelligence briefing about the enemy air order of battle, I could see that the pilots were as tense and taut as a tuned fiddle. Twenty F-86s (Red Flight, Black Flight, White Flight, Blue Flight, and Green Flight) were going on this mission and, more than likely, sixty to eighty MiGs would be on hand to greet us.

When it was my turn on the rostrum, I took the pointer and walked over to the big briefing map. This huge chart covered Korea and north into Manchuria. On it were posted various geographical code names, such as Mizzu (a reservoir near the Yalu), Racetrack (a large, circular area below Mizzu), our home base, and other bases in the south. Raising the pointer, I began my briefing.

"I'll be leading Red Flight today. Red Flight and Blue Flight will take off and penetrate along this line." The pointer traced a route from home base, along the east side of Korea, and up into North Korea to the vicinity of Racetrack. "Red and Blue will climb to thirty thousand feet. Green Flight and Black Flight will follow Red and Blue at twenty-second intervals on takeoff and penetrate along this line," (the pointer went from home base, along the west side of Korea, up to the west side of Racetrack) "and climb to thirty-five thousand feet.

"White Flight will take off first and be at an altitude of forty thousand feet by the time you reach the Yalu. Red, Blue, Black, and Green flights will maintain *absolute* radio silence from the time you start up to the time you tangle with the MiGs. White Flight will *talk* on the radio periodically from start up to the Yalu. At the Yalu, *talk* it up and call bingo fuel.

"The MiG controller will direct his MiGs toward you. White Leader, when they start getting in your area, turn south and start a high-speed letdown, coming back between Red and Blue on the east, and Green and Black on the west. The MiGs won't be able to catch you, and when they all pour into our funnel, we will snap the lid shut on them."

There was a moment of silence and then the pilots roared with laughter. The tension was gone. "Get up and git!" I said. "Let's get 'em!"

We filed out and the mission started to roll—pilots and equipment to the hard stands, start up, taxi out, and liftoff. We rendezvoused the assigned locations and had not even made a circle when White Leader from up on the Yalu said, "Red Lead, you wanted MiGs and here the son of a bitches come with me in the lead!"

We dropped tanks, pushed throttles forward, and sped toward the incoming MiGs at 600 miles per hour. At a closing speed of 1,200 mph, it takes only thirty seconds to close ten miles. We met head on and turned, and I picked out a flight of four MiGs diving through. Racing through the melee of red-nosed MiGs and F-86s, I saw what the Communist jets were after. A flight of British Meteors was carrying out a fighter-bomber mission against a North Korean supply dump, and the MiG leader was almost on the Meteor leader's tail by the time I got to him. He broke off, pulled up sharply, then turned toward me and dived to shake me off.

My throttle was open and I didn't shake off. I was closing slightly now, but we were pulling so many Gs that I couldn't get the gunsight on him. The pipper (a small dot in the sight which told you where the bullets would hit) was clear out of sight. The gunsight computer was saying that I needed more lead. I cranked the throttle handle, putting the gunsight in manual, and the orange dot appeared back on my windscreen. Now I had a reference point.

Relying on my wingman to keep my tail clear, twisting as I turned, I continued following the MiG. The pull of gravity in the turns was seven or eight Gs, but the G suit was inflating, compressing against my body, keeping the blood from pooling in the lower extremities and pushing it back into my face. The MiG reversed, turning left, and I gained ground on him. We were covering a lot of miles in this turn. In spite of the Gs, I pulled the stick a little more and the nose of my aircraft cut off the MiG. I pulled a bit more and, at about 1,500 feet, I twisted the throttle handle and put the gunsight back into computing mode. Now it would figure the lead as long as I could get the pipper on target and track him for a second. The pipper settled on the MiG about halfway up its sleek fuselage.

I fired a short, one-second burst and watched armor-piercing incendiary lace his fuselage, sparking and arcing like a high voltage electric wire gone berserk against grounding metal. The burst cut behind his cockpit and flames shot out. The MiG immediately slowed in midair. Now the pipper was on his tailpipe. A long burst at 600 feet from all six machine guns sent a bullet stream up his tailpipe. The MiG stopped. The .50s were firing almost fifty rounds a second, and over 200 rounds crashed up the MiG's tailpipe and flashed into the fuselage in arcing sparkles. Black, oily smoke poured out. He was blacked out by smoke clouds in an instant. I whipped the stick over to avoid crashing into the burning, shattered MiG. As I cleared the smoke, I watched the MiG spinning down toward the ground.

My wingman called out, "He bailed out, Lead! He bailed!"

More MiGs came in on us. We turned, looking for a shot, and a MiG fired on us from a high side pass. When he fired, the MiG's nose lit up with orange and red flashes. The cannon shells looked like a string of red golf balls streaming by. The shells passed behind and below us. Then the MiGs were gone, back to their sanctuary across the Yalu. We were at bingo fuel by then.

My wingman had stuck with me through all this action, and now we were heading back home line abreast. I took a chance (we were still over enemy territory) and waggled my wings for a "close it up." He slid in, wingtip to wingtip, and we looked at each other across thirty feet. I nodded my head and gave him a thumbs-up. He nodded and returned the greeting. I signaled "spread out" and we continued on our way to home base. Now was the time to check your fuel gauge again, turn off the gunswitch, and relax a little. When the field was in sight, I signaled a "close it up," and called the tower for landing instructions. The mission had worked out fine. The group downed two MiGs and damaged three others. The Meteor pilots invited us across the field for drinks and dinner.

The air war in Korea was like all wars. It was a time when, on the ground or in the air, inside your macho image you ran the gamut of human emotions. Teamwork was the all-encompassing element. From the ground crews who prepared your aircraft for flight and combat, to the air crews with whom you flew, it was teamwork. Skill, confidence, and teamwork brought you through.

I was blessed with great wingmen. On the ground we shared drinks and thoughts, and ideas about busting MiG-15s, among many other things. In the air we shared the danger and the teamwork it took to make a MiG kill. Some of them shared in the kills. I felt that they deserved one half of our success. May God bless wingmen, and may God especially bless those wingmen who flew with me. Without their help I probably wouldn't be writing this today.

KISMET AND THE PAPER TIGER

Captain Harold Fischer really has four stories to tell. On his first tour in Korea he flew ground-support missions in an F-80. On the second tour as an F-86 pilot he shot down at least ten MiGs. Then he spent a couple of years as a prisoner of the Chinese Communists. Later he flew Hueys in Vietnam. This story mainly concerns his experiences in F-80s and F-86s. Taken together, they give an intense in-depth view of the air war in Korea, and a glimpse into the mind of a great fighter pilot.

I left for Korea from San Francisco, the port of embarkation for millions of personnel in World War II (and still functioning as such for the Korean War), for the Far East. My aircraft touched down on Japanese territory that still bore the scars of war. We were driven by bus to Area B at Camp Fuchu. On the way there we passed a tori, two pillars supporting an arch, which marked the park where the first American raiders on Tokyo were beheaded. When questioned, none of the local residents knew anything about it. Two of us were assigned to the 80th Fighter-Bomber Squadron of the 8th Fighter-Bomber Wing, APO 929, Fukuoka, Japan.

A line of tents greeted us, and on the first tent was a picture of a headhunter's head painted in yellow and black. My friend and I were assigned to a GP tent with six other pilots, then assigned to an RTU. Probably at no other time in our careers would we be so finely trained, so expertly honed, and here we were being retrained. Our instructor pilots had already completed their required missions, and since the mission came first, some replacement pilots had to wait days and weeks for aircraft to be made available for their checkouts. I waited through the alloted time until those who had reported earlier passed through RTU. Finally, after almost an anticlimax, they said that I was ready for my first bleeding. It was the practice at the time to send the newly graduated RTU pilot on a mission as soon as possible.

The number-two spot was always allotted to the newest pilot. It was a place I occupied literally, because two pairs of eyes were always on me from number three and number four. Each mission was preceded by a briefing two hours before takeoff, and since takeoff was not always at the same time, it might be a briefing at 3:15 or 3:30 A.M. My first strike was against the frontline, against the village of Suijui, and I don't remember much about it. It was like the three monkeys—I felt nothing, heard nothing, and saw nothing, but reacted as I should. After the first mission, just as it is after the first airplane you shoot down, there is much reliving of the actual event.

The F-80s carried a huge load of over 930 gallons of JP-4 aviation fuel, around 1,800 rounds of ammunition for the six .50-caliber machine guns, and either 500- or 1,000-pound bombs, rockets, or napalm. We would fly 200 to 250 miles, with ten to fifteen minutes to the target area, conduct the strike, and then return. The climb out to Korea would take about 125 miles and the maximum ceiling with our heavy loads would be about 23,000 to 24,000 feet. We could reach 30,000 to 34,000 feet coming back. My philosophy was that if I could not be a leader, then I would be the best damned wingman in the air force.

Actually carrying the fight to the enemy was probably never like one first supposed it to be. If he was terribly afraid, it was not so frightening after all; if he was courageous, courage being only the ability to overcome fear, he might find it fear-inspiring. When the Communist gunners began to fire the 20mm and 40mm cannon, and the projectiles started to float toward his aircraft, then suddenly converge at tremendous speed, it would increase the adrenaline flow of the most courageous man. The cannon shells were termed "golf balls," and they had somewhat of the appearance of luminescent golf balls which grew into tennis balls as they passed the aircraft. You could become fascinated, almost hypnotized, by them. It was exhilarating to be shot at and missed.

When flying as number two on a leader that I could trust, I would go in on a strafing pass and actually be hitting a target underneath the lead as he was pulling up and over it. I would commence firing as he finished firing and pulled over the target. This worked when the target was the same and both aircraft were very close together. Some leaders would complain because it was distracting to pull over a target and see it come alive with light from tracer bullets and armor-piercing ricochets, although it was safe. If flying and dropping ordnance against a living target can be termed fun, napalm drops were the most interesting, followed by skip-bombing, rocketry, and dive-bombing.

To drop napalm, the pilot would get down as low as possible, usually less than fifty feet. When the target disappeared under the nose of the aircraft, the napalm would be released—both tanks at once, or one at a time for better coverage. According to reports from prisoners of war, napalm was the most feared weapon we had, and it was impossible to miss with it. We skip-bombed with delayed-fuse bombs, using the same method we used with napalm, and it was difficult to miss. The bomb bounced once into the air and then exploded on target. We used skip-bombing against railroad tunnels. I recall one instance when a bomb went all the way through a tunnel and exploded harmlessly on the tracks on the other side.

Rocketry was more difficult. In order to be effective, it was necessary to get almost a direct hit, and since the launching technique was from 3,000 feet at an angle of thirty to forty-five degrees, many factors entered into a successful launch. Our gunsights had a setting for rocketry, but most pilots estimated the correct range and altitude and, in many cases, the attack was about as successful as throwing rocks at the enemy. Dive-bombing was similar to rocketry, but the angle of dive was steeper and the altitude higher. Accuracy and devastation could be increased by using proximity fuses which exploded the bombs one hundred feet above the ground and rained death and destruction on all those below them.

A technique used late in the war was glide-bombing, and I am sure it must have been a rewarding sight to the Communists to see an entire squadron or group of American planes fly over a railroad, straight and level, with no gunsights or bombsights to aid them, and try to cut the tracks. Twenty-four airplanes might get three or four good rail cuts, and as soon as the whine of the jets died away, thousands of laborers would be swarming over the tracks, repairing the slight damage. A few bombs would have delayed fuses of up to twelve hours, and this might deter them from too rapid a repair.

The two most effective weapons used against the Communists, as far as fighter aircraft were concerned, were napalm and the .50-caliber machine gun, just as in World War II.

One of the great tragedies of the Korean War was that there was no way to determine whether a village contained peaceful Koreans or was a billet for enemy troops. The pilots discussed the problem and unofficially decided that we would not hit villages unless we had been briefed that they contained troops. Two incidents that happened to my friend may give an indication of what some of us felt. He was on a support mission to attack a village that supposedly had enemy troops. Napalm was used in the attack and he had lined up on a home in the center of the village. Just as he dropped the napalm and the thatched house passed under the nose of his aircraft, he saw the woman of the house, surrounded by children, reaching out for her husband and trying to help him to the safety of their house. It was a direct hit, not only on the house, but on my friend's conscience. Another time a bullock was running for a safe place when its life was snuffed out by napalm. My friend was a rancher and this also affected him. The lives of animals and human beings cannot be compared, but senseless killing can be.

During the Communist spring offensive of 1951, our unit was flying continuously. As soon as our aircraft returned from a mission, they were refueled and rearmed and ready for takeoff again. While one mission was still in the air, pilots were briefing for the next one. Under these circumstances, the line crews worked night and day. They were an indispensable part of the organization, and can never be given enough credit. My crew chief was a southerner totally devoted to his job. I always made it a habit to cue in the crew chief on the mission that we were to fly, and tell him about the results after we landed. Since the crew chief was responsible for the safety of the aircraft the pilot was going to fly, without him there would be no mission.

Being one of the lowest-ranking first lieutenants, I was given the oldest plane in the squadron, number 659. Since the problem of survival seemed to be in the hands of fate, I decided to call the airplane Kismet. The name was placed on the left nose, my name on the right side of the canopy rail, and the crew chief's name on the left side of the canopy rail. Kismet was a good and reliable airplane, and no one was more proud of his airplane than me, which is akin to the feeling one has for his first car. It would sometimes throw a turbine blade in the accessory turbine, which we called a "bucket," and this could set up a dangerous vibration, but it always got me home.

Rumors began to fly that the unit was going to be stationed in Korea, and the thought of going there was not pleasant. I was determined to fly as many missions as I could, so I would stand by in a spare aircraft as missions took off, hoping that one of the pilots would abort. The idea was to get all my missions completed and get back to the States and on to other things. In one thirty-day period, I logged thirty missions. As soon as this was discovered, I was forced to slow down in order to keep pace with the rest of the pilots.

The F-84 had been introduced into the theater with the arrival of a Texas National Guard outfit. It was considered a newer plane and more advanced than an F-80, but could carry only half its load and had to use JATO (jet-assisted takeoff) to get airborne. They took more runway to get airborne than F-80s with comparable loads. Temperature conditions were critical for takeoff, and some missions had to be canceled because of the runway length available. The F-84's advantage was that it had a slightly greater range and was better suited for bomber escort work. However, they had a propensity for blowing up or burning. It was a constant wonder why a newer aircraft could be less effective than an existing one and still be put into production.

On May 1, 1951, the United Nations decided to make a show of force on the traditional Communist holiday. We would hit the officers training school at Sinanju, within sight of the Chinese mainland. All fighter aircraft in the Far East were used on this mission. All the airplanes of the 8th were flown to K-2 and then armed and fueled and the pilots briefed. The airplanes from the 8th were lined up on the west side of the runway and those from the 51st were lined up on the east. The 51st F-80s took the runway and reached 100 mph, then their JATO jets would kick in. The first few aircraft were successful, but the smoke from the JATO lay on the runway like the thickest cloud cover. One could hear the roar of jet engines, and then the airplanes would appear at the end of the runway, either a few feet above the PSP or about to become airborne.

A few pilots, thinking they would not get airborne, hit the panic button and dropped their ordnance and wingtip tanks. Bombs and rockets would fall on the end of the runway, then the F-80 would leap into the air. One pilot aborted in the smoke and slowed down. The next aircraft collided with him. Another pilot inadvertently fired his JATO as he was lining up for takeoff and was forced into the ground-controlled approach shack in spite of brakes and stop-cocked throttle. Since our armament was restricted to rockets, we had lighter loads and an easier time of it. It was a political mission, and we expected a great deal of enemy fighter activity over the target area. As it turned out, the only losses were on takeoff.

We were assigned to K-14, Kimpo, in Korea. The first American aircraft of the war had been lost there when a Yak-9 had burned a C-54 that was waiting to take a group of evacuees to Japan. The one permanent structure was gutted with bomb craters and bullet holes from strafing by both sides and was unusable by the time we arrived.

The missions continued. Once I was leading a two-ship mission when we went into the heavily defended valley of Chorwon. It fairly spouted groundfire, both small caliber and 20mm and 40mm. As I scouted the valley, I looked around for my number-two man and he informed me that he was over the broken overcast at 1,000 feet above me. He wasn't afraid of being shot at, but the Chinese and North Korean gunners invariably fired behind the jets, and he was afraid of being hit by the groundfire aimed at me. On another mission in the Iron Triangle, I made repeated passes at a 40mm emplacement and, each time, was sure I had taken out the position. Each time it would loft flaming golf balls at me as I pulled out. When I was out of ammunition and low on fuel, the gun was still firing. It was a draw.

At that time we were trying to knock out the enemy airfields in North Korea so that the Communists could not bring in airplanes from China at night or during inclement weather to launch attacks against our poorly camouflaged frontline troops. You could always tell that you were over the United Nations lines because of the many vehicles and troops in the open. On one mission to "Post Hole," the airport north of Pyongyang that was heavily fortified with antiaircraft, the airplane that preceded me in the dive was hit and crashed on the runway. The Communists were using 88mms, and you could tell when a burst was close because of the red flame in the black ball. I had been concentrating on hitting the runway with my thousand-pound bomb when I noticed the black pall of smoke at the end of the runway. Only later did I learn that it was one of our planes. A few days later Kismet was hit by a .50-caliber round while I was strafing a village. The round had evidently been fired at me from the front and I was not aware of any groundfire whatsoever. By now the truce talks were in progress and the war was supposed to be over in thirty days.

I was then selected to spend sixty days with the army as a forward air controller. My job was to fly low and slow in a spotter plane and direct air strikes against specific targets. Losses among FAC pilots were heavy, as I was able to observe first-hand. After ground school we were required to fly a mission in a two-seater T-6 spotter plane. The one I used was old and patched in many places from bullet hits. We were assigned to the east coast of Korea. As we headed inland from the sea, the pilot began to circle one small valley and I asked what he had seen. He reported one soldier sitting under a tree. I couldn't see a thing. Next, we marked a village that harbored enemy troops and watched as four P-51s set up a rectangular gunnery pattern similar to that used at Nellis AFB. They came in with rockets, then dropped their bombs, then ended up strafing. I was amazed at the amount of ordnance a P-51 could carry.

Just before I was to leave for the ROK forces, a call came for volunteers for a special mission. I attended jump school in Japan, then the mission was postponed and we were returned to our units. I was sent to complete my FAC requirement with the Commonwealth forces. The British battalion had been pulled back, and there wasn't much activity at the time.

One day while I was waiting around I drove the jeep up to see my old friend who was assigned to the Canadian unit. When I arrived, the plane was being turned around and the propeller was being pulled through to start it. My friend ran from his tent and I jumped from the jeep and ran over to him, since there was an air of excitement about the place. He jumped in his plane and asked if I wanted to go along. "Yes." The radio didn't work and there was no way to contact the strike planes that had been ordered to hit a hill that the Chinese occupied in force.

He handed me three smoke flares and a Very pistol to mark the target. As we circled the hill, we saw a group of light olive-drab figures moving on it. P-51s circled to the west as we opened the door of the airplane and dove down over the hill. The airspeed crept over the red line, and the door propped open by my friend's foot caused the aircraft to skid from the uneven air pressure. I fired the Very pistol, and a large red flare spiraled down to the ground. We emptied our .45s at them on the next dive, a senseless gesture, but it made us feel better. Then we moved aside as the Mustangs saturated the hill with napalm and machine-gun bullets.

When my time as an FAC was finished, I returned to my squadron. The unit was now at K-13 at Suwan. The Korean War was no longer a war of movement. Both sides were dug in along a narrow belt across the peninsula, and neither side dared to cross for fear of upsetting the political war. Missions were now limited to ten per pilot per month. If a person flew his ten missions in the first week, he could count on sitting out the rest of the month. I had to be checked out in the F-80 again, the same old army game of hurry up and wait. I had to wait until aircraft were available for the low-priority training flights. While I had been gone, Kismet had met a warrior's death when it was hit in the engine section while on a strafing mission. The pilot had been able to bail out. We continued ground-support missions in the popular places for attack—the Punch Bowl, Heartbreak Ridge, and other bloody places.

The targets in North Korea were well damaged by our air force, although there were a few areas that fighter planes did not attack. One was Pyongyang, the capital of North Korea. It had two excellent airfields, but they were too heavily defended. Pilots with World War II ETO experience viewed the flak over North Korea with contempt, but it was all a matter of conditioning. The North Koreans preferred to concentrate a tremendous amount of small-arms fire, in addition to 20mm and 40mm weapons, on the low-flying United Nations aircraft.

Railroads were prime targets and train engines were the most desirable. Locomotives were hidden in tunnels during the day. Ferreting them out became a game as exciting as shooting down enemy airplanes. In fact, there were locomotive aces, primarily the B-26 night units. They would fly with no running lights and engines idled back, then glide down to attack the engines. Those B-26s had all kinds of armament firing forward, in some cases as many as fourteen machine guns.

I flew on one of those B-26 missions. As we crossed the front lines, with the heavy guns flashing on both sides, I thought of the hundreds of thousands of dollars being spent down there and the men on both sides who were dying. The communiqués read that there was a little patrol activity along the front. Again it makes me wonder why men fight for ideologies when, in some cases, they might be compatible. We attacked a truck convoy. As the first bomb dropped, the headlights went out as if tripped by a single switch.

I completed my 105th mission with little fanfare. I was interested in a career and decided that the place to be was in the Far East. I'd applied for a job with FEAF (Far East Air Forces) in Tokyo, had been accepted and told that it would be waiting for me when my combat tour was completed. The job was as assistant officer in charge of combat crew assignment in the combat crew branch of personnel. Although the job was not impressive, the place where I worked was. It had the status of command, and anyone who worked for FEAF exhibited an aura of greatness, whether or not he deserved it.

On the morning I was leaving in the wing's C-47, my friend was just leaving for a mission, one of his last. I crawled up on the wing of his fighter to say good-bye to him. That was the last time I saw him. He applied for Germany and went directly there after a thirty-day leave home. While overseas, he was making a pass on two British Meteors when he hit the second one. He bailed out, but his parachute streamed. And so my very good friend, who had worried about old people and oxen during his combat tour, was lost. He was killed by an accident over which he had little control.

I was sent to Johnson AFB outside of Tokyo. My boss was a captain, and it seemed that all my life I had been working for captains. After I had been at work a few days, I began to get chronically tired. As I was being introduced to other people in the office, I passed out for the first time in my life. I was soon very sick and hooked up to an IV in a hospital. A month went by before I became well, or what I felt was well, and it became torture to remain in bed. To alleviate this, I spent some time working on a model of an old Republic P-47, the Thunderbolt. By then I would rather have been in prison than in a hospital. Later I found out that a hospital was better. I spent Christmas 1951 in the hospital and it seemed like forever before I was finally allowed to return to work.

After recovering from the illness and being on the job for a while, the lure of combat and my talks with jet aces began to excite me. One of the aces told me that experienced pilots were needed and, with diligence, I could become an ace. I requested another combat tour and was eventually allowed to stay on with the understanding that I would be there a short time and then be reassigned to a fighter unit. I spent the time honing my skills and again checking out on the F-80. Eventually the fruit of much ground work and long overwater flights to Korea, prior to my assignment at Johnson AFB, were realized. My orders to Korea came through.

I found myself again traveling the road I had first taken to the Far East—FEACOM, airlift to Korea, then to Suwon. Someone said that everything travels in circles and, if his particular theory needed support, then my return added validity to the premise. It was September 1952.

Six squadrons comprising two wings were utilizing the base. Across the base to the east was the 8th Fighter-Bomber Wing, my old outfit, still flying F-80s. The 51st Fighter-Bomber Wing on the west side of the runway was now flying F-86s. They were the only modern aircraft in Korea. All others were obsolete by the standards of enemy aircraft. It was rumored that the F-86 and the MiG came from common parentage. After the cessation of hostilities and the inevitable dismemberment of Germany, the Americans got the German designs for advanced swept-wing aircraft, and the Russians got the designers. So in the Korean War the two aircraft with a common ancestry but different tail designs met and did combat in the name of freedom for both sides, as the fate of a nation was decided in the clear, cold sky over North Korea.

After reporting to the 51st, I was required to attend a ground school on the F-86 at Tsuicki, Japan. The systems of this fighter were diverse, complicated, and, according to all reports, highly efficient. Here was an aircraft conceived and funded by free enterprise, and it was meeting the best the

Communist world had to offer. After ground school I returned to Suwon. It was still dusty, with the yellow clay and the ageless Koreans. The only change was a few new buildings that gave the airfield a more permanent look, in addition to more gun emplacements and more aircraft. Just as we landed, there was a flight of aircraft landing, and one of them, the leader's plane, had a dirty black nose from firing the .50-caliber machine guns. It signified that the leader had fired his guns in anger or fear. That night the world would read about another enemy aircraft shot down or damaged. If the pilot had a number of victories, his name might be mentioned in the dispatches, and perhaps a feature article would be written about him.

After completing an exam on the F-86 I was ready for checkout in the aircraft. After a lengthy briefing and a blind-fold cockpit check, it was time. The Sabre accelerated so fast that its landing gear had to be retracted quickly. As I reached for the gear, the airplane started porpoising up and down a few feet in the air, a sign that a novice pilot was flying. Then it climbed at an amazing rate of speed. After more familiarization, I was ready to seek the foe and slay him wherever he could be found. A long-sought goal was within my grasp, that of being in combat with other aircraft and having the opportunity to shoot or be shot. The ancient Greeks had said, "I will return with my shield, or upon it." This was it—the time of harvest.

My first combat mission was an uneventful indoctrination flight. The flight leader called out landmarks and the places we were not permitted to fly over. The frontlines were not apparent, but men were fighting and dying down there. Newspapers extolled the virtues and accomplishments of the pilots and did not pay proportionate attention to the infantry, the artillery, and the rear-echelon troops. To die in the mud was mundane, but to die in the air, thousands of feet above the ground, this was heroic, and the warriors always went to Valhalla.

Soon an exchange officer from Canada assumed command of my squadron. This squadron leader was a rare individual who was dedicated to getting the job done, and results were more important than the methods employed. The Canadian had flown Spitfires from Britain in World War II and was an ace against the Germans. He was truly my first flight commander, and it was he who taught me to fly combat.

Our first combat flight went north of the Chongchon River (which bisected the area above the frontlines) and ended up on the Yalu River. We were at 40,000 feet and I was wingman to the squadron leader. The basic strategy was for one flight to follow another in a gigantic orbit over known landmarks, making a huge racetrack pattern. Even the airspeed was prescribed, so that flights would not overrun each other and leave gaps in the pattern. Theoretically if the Communists attacked one flight, the following flight would be in a position to help it. These tactics were merely an extension of the old Lufbery circle of World War I fame and merit. This time I got separated from the others and notified them that I was proceeding to rendezvous at a predetermined altitude. As I orbited to the right as briefed, three airplanes appeared and I sheepishly joined them. Instead of the verbal dressing-down I had expected, the squadron leader stated that I had done the right thing. It was a lesson I never forgot.

I was flying number two on another mission. The U.N. radar voice controller on Cho-Do Island, north of the battle lines, had called a bandit train near Ta-Tunk Kou, an airfield about thirty miles inside the Manchurian border. Bandit trains were reported taking off from the airfield, and the dust could be seen rising even from our distance away, over the Yalu River. It was always a thrill when the high-tailed swept-winged aircraft of the enemy would appear, often with no warning at all.

Number three and number four had become separated from us, so the leader and I were on our own. The leader turned his airplane northward and headed for Ta-Tunk Kou Airfield. We crossed the Yalu and headed into the sovereign territorial air of China. This was an infraction of the written rules, but certainly not the unwritten rules of aerial combat in the theater. A few miles south of the airfield we could see the alert aircraft taking off and disappearing over the terrain at the end of the runway. We dropped in a steady descent to overtake the aircraft quickly and ensure that the rate of closure for aircraft attacking us would be minimal. Then I spotted an aircraft heading due west and climbing at about 20,000 feet, and called it out to the leader. The MiG had either been separated from the other formations or was an observer.

The enemy fighter began a gradual letdown to the left and we were soon in an ideal position for all fighter pilots— six o'clock, right on the tail of the MiG. Our speed was so great that we had to reduce throttle, a tactic not recommended in the combat area. I called clear as we closed to within the optimal firing range of 1,200 feet, but still the leader did not fire. I called clear again, in case he was looking around and not firing, but still he delayed. As he closed within 150 to 200 feet, a short trail of smoke indicated that he had squeezed off a few rounds. I had expected to see a MiG literally blasted out of the air as our pilot fired many bursts.

As it was, we zoomed for altitude and both looked back at the MiG. It began to turn to the left and gradually start to spurt puffs of smoke. Diving at about forty-five degrees, it seemed to be headed straight into the ground. Just before it hit, the entire aircraft turned into a flaming orange torch and then leveled off momentarily. It was doomed. Nine rounds of ammunition had been fired. When we landed back at home base, the crew chiefs expressed concern that I did not taxi all the way into the revetment area and follow their hand signals. They were amazed and amused when they learned that I had just run out of gas.

Soon thereafter I was able to fire back at the enemy. I was number four in a four-plane flight. We were orbiting in an oval pattern over the Chongchon River, midway between the frontlines and the Yalu, when bandits were reported crossing the Yalu and heading south. Suddenly the voice from the GCI (ground control intercept) station called, "Heads up in the Chong-Jo River area," and almost immediately MiG fighters appeared at three o'clock and began an attack on a flight in front of us. As they broke, the number-four man in the MiG formation passed in front of us. He was behind the rest of his planes and I saw that he would pass at a position ninety degrees to me and 2,000 feet in front. Pulling the nose of the aircraft up, I estimated range and lead and fired about one hundred rounds. Gun-camera film later showed that my tracers had reached out for the high-tailed MiG and passed twenty-five feet under it. The lead was correct, but the range was wrong.

As the missions progressed, so did my desire for a kill. A wingman needed permission from the flight commander to fire, and given the speed of the jets, if permission was given, it came too late. I was flying on the wing of a blond Swede from Minnesota who was on his hundredth (last) mission and had yet to get even a damage claim. He had flown well, but always on the wing, and the general mood was that this was the day the Swede would get his MiG. Now he was flying lead and had been given a mission in the afternoon period on a clear day when the possibility of enemy contact was greatest. A victory for the Swede would be a victory for all of us. As we climbed into the bright sunlight, bandit tracks already being reported from Cho-Do Island.

Soon we were in the area heading northeast. A flight of MiGs was above us and crossed our flight path heading southeast. We turned to follow them, knowing that they would have to head back north toward the Yalu, but we lost distance and fell about a mile behind them. I cleared the Swede and he began firing short bursts. Then I looked right and saw four more MiGs. I was between them and the Swede. Calling the lead, I informed him of the MiGs and said that I thought we might have to turn left, and I would tell him when. All the time he continued squeezing off those short bursts. Alternately looking at the lead and the MiGs, I saw them move into position at about six o'clock high, then called a turn. When they opened fire, I thought that they were not pulling lead when suddenly a sound like a hot knife slicing through butter told me my airplane had been hit.

Calling a break (a break from formation—evasive maneuvers), I proceeded to make the most unorthodox maneuver in the history of aerial combat—a combination turn, roll, split-S, and control reversal. The moment after the break is hazy. I recall going straight down toward a deck of clouds and seeing a spinning aircraft. When I came out of the clouds at about 3,000 feet, I saw a swept-wing aircraft. Thinking it was the MiG I had seen before, I banked around to fire, but it was an F-86. On the ground below was a spiral of smoke, all that was left of the MiG and its pilot. The plane had spun out and never recovered.

I made it home on the hydraulic emergency system. There was a jagged 20mm hole in my right wing. The Swede had gotten his MiG, but I was disappointed. The flight commander understood and told me at the briefing: "You will get your airplane." Even now I remember every detail of my first kill. The Canadian had told me that he could not sleep the night after his first kill. Neither would I. Instead, the aerial battle was refought in my mind a hundred times. That is an indication of the thrill an individual experiences after a victory.

My position was number two. Our flight was over Kang-Ye, almost at the source of the Yalu and the farthest distance away from home base, almost to the outer fringes of "MiG Alley." The Communists used the familiar tactic of sending their fighters into the area when we were low on fuel. The air quickly filled with MiGs. They were all around us in the blue sky, and we were like goldfish in a bowl, in the center of them. We had been given freedom of action, so I called that I was going to make a pass on one of the enemy. As soon as I called the bounce, I turned to the left and surveyed the scene. Then I saw two MiGs heading north about 1,500 feet below me. They disappeared under my aircraft and then reappeared over the nose, traveling at high speed toward the Yalu. I began my attack.

I eased down from higher altitude and fell about a mile

behind from the loss of thrust I had experienced when I allowed my aircraft to slow down so the MiGs could overtake me. Even though I was out of range, I had to fire to justify my initial bounce. The enemy aircraft were at least 4,000 feet away. My radar gunsight would not work at that distance, so I moved the selector to fixed position, raised the nose of the aircraft, and fired. Tracers reached out in a long arc and seemed to fall around the two airplanes. There didn't seem to be much chance of hitting them, and they appeared to be pulling away. I fired two long bursts as they approached the Yalu, then prepared to stop the attack. An amazing thing happened. The enemy wingman on the left began to turn left and slant downward. I told the flight leader that I would continue the attack. He said that he could no longer clear me. I was on my own. Later he told me that he had turned into two MiGs while clearing the deck for my action.

There was nothing behind me. The attack continued. Squeezing off bursts, I slowly gained on the MiG. He seemed to slow down and leveled off deep inside China. My airplane was bucking and rolling from the high-speed dive at full power, but whenever I could control it, I fired again. As the MiG slowed down and began a gradual climb about 2,000 feet above the ground, I was able to close rapidly. The wing roll began to diminish, indicating that I was out of the critical mach area. This gave me a stable gun platform at an optimum range of about 1,000 feet. Two bursts went right up the tailpipe and lit it up. The MiG seemed to stop in midair as I closed and gave it a final burst. As I rolled to the right around the MiG, I was surprised to see that the canopy was missing. The pilot had already bailed out. I had been closing on a derelict aircraft. I dropped my speed brakes and watched the MiG crash into a rocky mountainside.

I returned to fire a burst into the side of the mountain to allow the gun camera to record the smoke and wreckage, then headed toward home across a barren, brown mountainous countryside that seemed devoid of life. A lonely feeling overtook me. Applying full power and looking forward, I saw a white object in the sky. The MiG pilot was sitting back in the risers of his parachute at 20,000 feet above the ground. I aimed to the side of the pilot and squeezed off a short burst to register the chute on film. I had no intention of strafing him, but am sure that the pilot thought otherwise. As I flashed by a hundred feet away, I saw that he was dressed in a wool flying suit with a great deal of fur on it. He wore winter trousers and fur-lined boots. His parachute was a ribbon chute, similar to what the Germans used in World War II. I dipped my wing as I passed.

Landing with the nose of the aircraft black was a sign that I had arrived, that I was one of the fighters that had fired back in anger. The flight leader was there to greet me. He was as happy about the kill as I was. He had also claimed a victory over one of the pilots he had taken off my tail. Of course, that night I couldn't sleep.

One of the most interesting speculations during the war was whether we were fighting Oriental or Caucasian pilots. One of the pilots had damaged an aircraft on a mission, and seeing that it was helpless, decided to move in for a closer look. The enemy pilot had jettisoned his canopy. He was large, had red hair, and was definitely not Oriental. He shook his fist at the victor. Some of our pilots had been flying in the Far East at the end of World War II and were offered money to fly for the Communists. Speculation was that they were still flying, still being paid, and believed in what they were fighting for.

Victories were important to fighter pilots. Roy Brown from World War I was credited with only one victory, but it was he who killed Baron von Richtofen. Now I had one victory, and having been involved in innumerable skirmishes with the enemy and having listened to many descriptions of other encounters, my chances for another kill were greater. My position moved from wingman to assistant flight leader, and the squadron leader recommended that I take over the flight when he left. Our Canadian was nearing the fifty-mission normal tour for his countrymen. He left with his two kills and the desire to be the first Canadian ace of the jet age, and turned the flight over to me. I was a first lieutenant. When I had initially arrived, there were majors leading flights.

One day the call came for a flight to hurry over to the group briefing room for a hurry-up mission. The object was to search for a pilot who had crashed near the Yalu. Four of us were soon airborne. As soon as we passed the Chongchon River, contrails could be seen approaching us from the south at well above the 40,000 feet that we had just attained. I called for the fuel tanks to be dropped. Seven of the eight tanks fell away, glittering in the sun. The man with the hung tank was sent home with my wingman as escort. The element leader and I remained to face the MiGs. Twenty miles north of the Chongchon we suddenly found ourselves in another goldfish bowl with MiGs all around us. None seemed to be in a good firing position, so we immediately started turning to keep our tails clear. The Communists would fire if the noses of their aircraft were pointed in the general direction of ours. Since there was little likelihood of a hit, it was no more than a bit disconcerting. We squeezed off a few bursts ourselves to upset them.

Each time an opportunity came to attack a MiG and I commenced firing, my wingman would call a break to fend off other MiGs attacking us. This happened many times in a matter of minutes. The enemy evidently had less fuel than us and now began to gradually withdraw. This was our chance. Turning to the left, we dropped down on a flight of two heading north toward sanctuary. We were at 40,000 feet and I was able to position myself behind a MiG at 600 feet, an ideal range. Before I could get settled down to fire, the MiG pulled up into an almost perfect loop. My F-86 floundered around the top of the loop and made it only because of the excessive speed of the initial attack. Then I squeezed off a short burst to prevent my airspeed from diminishing from the recoil of the guns. My wingman called minimum fuel. I told him to leave when he had to but to call me before he did so.

The MiG executed consecutive loops, and my advantage

became greater as we lost altitude. Just over the Yalu River the MiG straightened out momentarily. I was preparing to fire a long burst when my attention was diverted by an object going by my aircraft. It was the canopy, followed immediately by the pilot in his ejection seat. He had apparently given up on shaking a pilot determined enough to follow a MiG in a loop at altitude. All the time that I had been firing, I had not seen a hit, and the only reason I had fired was to shake him up as much as possible. Gun-camera film later showed the pilot ejecting. As had happened so many times during the war, the Communists seemed to abandon their fellow pilots when they were in trouble.

Later, while I served as flight leader to the wing commander, a flight of MiGs passed over us, heading south. Assuming that they would have to head back north, I turned my element around and headed south. We were lucky. The MiGs appeared in the distance after completing their race-track pattern. Setting up an interception course, our element joined up with them and opened fire. One enemy element broke away and this left us behind the other element. It was an ideal situation, until they realized what was happening. They began to zoom up, taking advantage of their lighter construction, and we tried to follow. As their altitude increased, our aircraft began to mush under full power, and it was impossible to raise the noses without stalling out. When the MiGs approached the Yalu, I raised the nose of my fighter and squeezed off a burst. There was a light twinkle on the other aircraft's wing and tail, but he continued on. I claimed a damage that one time. Many other aircraft were damaged by me, but never again did I claim them.

Under similar circumstances my third aircraft was claimed and verified. Only this time the MiG was heavier with fuel, or the pilot was not so adept. He elected to go down after he had tried to zoom away. Evidently he was psychologically defeated. As soon as he started down, my .50 calibers chewed him up. He was not observed bailing out, and the

MiG disintegrated on contact with the ground. Now I had flown thirty-three F-86 missions.

One of the members in the flight was made assistant flight leader, having been chosen because of his high number of missions and his eagerness to seek out the enemy. He had some unusual ideas, but it was a pleasure working with him. On one mission near the mouth of the Yalu, we staggered up to our highest altitude of around 43,000 feet and let our airspeed diminish until we were virtually standing still in the thin air. Our intention was to invite attack. Two aircraft appeared to our left and immediately made their attack. At that altitude a turn would suffice to remove the threat from our tails. I called a turn to the right. He reversed under my directions, and I told him to pull up his nose and fire. He got many good hits on a MiG. It was damaged but not downed. With our low airspeed and poor acceleration capability, the enemy fighter could easily outrun us. It disappeared into the high, clear blue sky.

On another mission we were given freedom of action. As soon as bandit tracks were called on the other side of the Yalu, we turned off our IFF equipment and crossed into China behind a flight of four MiGs. We knew that they would soon be letting down and landing at an airfield close to the river. The enemy pilots were unaware of us as we dropped at great speed behind them. They were making their approach from a long distance out from the field, to preclude attacks on them as had happened in the past. I chose number four. Letting down at a tremendous rate of speed from almost on top of him, I squeezed off a burst at about 400 feet. The tail cone lit up with a bright flash. As I settled down for another shot, I hit his jet wash and was jolted so hard that the binoculars around my neck were shattered. The gunsight went off and my guns stopped firing. I thought of ramming the tail of the MiG and disabling it that way, but I swerved at the last second and missed by about six inches. Then I realized that the jolt had caused the cover to turn off the gun switch.

I turned on the switch, completed my roll, dropped speed

brakes, reduced power, and literally blasted the MiG out of the sky. The aircraft immediately caught fire. The altitude was about 2,000 feet and I waited for the pilot to bail out. Now the MiG's airspeed made it a gliding derelict that was impossible to stay behind. With a completely closed throttle, my aircraft slid alongside the MiG, and then in front of it for a moment. The pilot could have hit me, because the range was only about one hundred feet. I looked back and saw the burning fighter and a surprised pilot looking down and to the side of me. I noted the huge number 341 on the airplane's right side and later reported it to the intelligence officer with much pleasure. The MiG crashed into a hillside close to the field. Evidently the pilot had been so panicked that his reaction was no reaction at all. I mentally painted a red star on the side of 958, my excellent steed and valiant old war horse. But the battle wasn't over.

Turning the element over to my wingman, I joined up on his wing so that he could lead us into battle. MiGs were all around us, but not in positions to invite attack. Climbing over Antung, the element leader saw a group of MiGs going into a landing pattern. He called a bounce and headed down into the traffic pattern of the airfield. I cleared him. He entered the pattern behind a MiG that was flying in trail formation, and fired as soon as his terrific closing speed brought him into range. He was going too fast to slow down and track the MiG for very long, but he hit the aircraft and it headed for the ground. I am sure that it crashed. We were low on fuel by then and had to return to base. The day's tally was one MiG destroyed (my fourth) and one probably destroyed. I now had forty-five missions in an F-86.

The fifth kill came sooner than expected, and brought with it a great deal of trepidation and mental anguish. I never hated the individual enemy, although I could hate the ideology that controlled him.

Our flight had been scrambled for a search mission. Since the only way to have fuel remaining for the search area was to climb to altitude and then let down, we were at 40,000 feet. We checked in with the ground controller when we reached the Chongchon area, and he told us to head due west. He stated that the enemy would be at our altitude fifteen miles ahead, and he was setting us up for an interception. The controller must have been one of the very best. Having little faith in the usual instructions, his very words inspired confidence. To my amazement, four dots rapidly became larger and merged into a flight of four MiGs on a southerly heading. That was the only perfect vector I ever received in the Korean War.

We set up an interception turn and fell in behind them. Just as we were ready to fire, the MiGs utilized their favorite tactic and zoomed for altitude. The number-two man evidently panicked and his wings rocked back and forth. He either could not continue the zoom, or chose what seemed to be a more logical action. The other three aircraft continued up while he went down. I fell in behind him and ended up at a distance of 4,000 feet. He seemed to be too far away for the radar gunsight, so I switched to fixed and began squeezing off short bursts, hoping to slow him down. This went on for a long time, with no indications of a hit. Once, a spark went off and I called to the wingman that I had finally hit him. We had been slanting in a dive for a while, and after what seemed like an agonizingly long time my wingman and I drew nearer. We were well into northern China by now. It was an eerie situation.

Gradually a light began to grow in the tail of the MiG: first a small pinpoint of light, then a candle lit on a dark night. It grew to envelop the entire tail section. By the time I drew within ideal firing range, there was no need to expend ammunition. The MiG was dying. The entire aircraft was engulfed in flames by now, so I pulled alongside it. I wish that I hadn't. The pilot was beating on the canopy and trying to escape. The heat must have been insufferable, because the smoke was intense and the canopy was changing color. Until then the enemy had been impersonal, but now he was another man who was trapped in the cockpit of a burning aircraft, with no power and no place to land. That sight is impossible to forget.

The MiG pilot saw me and attempted to turn his aircraft to ram me. It was easy to evade the ramming maneuver. Sliding behind the MiG, the molten metal of his airplane came over my airplane like a light rain and partially obscured my windshield. I pulled up the nose and fired a few short bursts before three of my guns quit, my left rudder pedal went to the fire wall, and my heart went into my mouth. The engine sounded different, but it responded. The change in sound was due to the loss of pressurization, and it was affecting me as well. My stomach began to expand from its gases and the life raft under me became hard as a brick. As I headed for home, my left shoulder began to hurt from the bends and I had to loosen my belt. Everything possible was done to relieve the pressure, including belching, and breaking wind, but my stomach remained rock hard. I somehow landed at the field by controlling direction with aileron, stop-cocking the engine and using right rudder on the runway. It was very close.

The day before, one of the pilots had made ace on forty-eight F-86 missions. I did it with forty-seven missions. Both of us had previous combat experience—he in F-84s and I in F-80s. I received a telegram wishing me success from the general in command of the Fifth Air Forces, got some publicity, and learned that I was the twenty-fifth ace of the Korean conflict. I had achieved everything for which I had originally striven. Now it was time to assess just what I wanted to do. My basic decision was to continue flying missions and do no more than any other pilot to seek out the enemy. No one could say that I had gotten my kills and then gotten out. There was also the first opportunity to have an actual flight command and the control of eight to ten other pilots on a day-to-day basis.

One day I was on an afternoon alert when the buzzer went off and energized everybody into action. We were taking off within minutes with no checks and no stops for wingmen to get into position. As I climbed for altitude, my wingman, a young pilot on his second mission, fell in beside me. Our job was to patrol the Chongchon River from its mouth to a point about one hundred miles inland. We set up a sausage-shaped patrol and edged the aircraft higher. As we made turns, our flight path moved increasingly closer to the Yalu River and "MiG Alley." The controller kept calling us back to our intended patrol area. My position was at the mouth of the Chongchon when the flight at the other end of the orbit began calling out bogies. Suddenly they were calling breaks. We had freedom of action, so the element leader and his wingman departed. My wingman and I climbed as high as we could. I turned the flight to the east, hoping that MiGs would come underneath me, to the right, ninety degrees to my course. For once this "by-the-book" planning paid off.

Two flights of MiGs appeared to the right. The second flight came right underneath me. I chose the number-four man, turned left, and dropped line abreast to him at a distance of a few hundred feet. It was an excellent position for a World War I dogfight. No matter who won this encounter, it would be a fight to remember.

Both of us started to scissor, each trying to get on the other's tail by turning into him, then away. Our flight paths resembled an interlacing pattern. The situation was static until I took a calculated risk and dropped speed brakes. My fighter fell behind the MiG. Seeing that the advantage was with me, he headed for the border with heavy contrails forming behind him. I was 600 feet behind, and the contrails were so heavy that when I pulled up to shoot, my canopy would enter them. The radar gunsight was working perfectly. The first burst lit up his aircraft, almost from wingtip to wingtip. Every round seemed to find its mark. Before I could fire again, the canopy went by, and then the pilot. My wingman verified the bailout.

My wingman was off to the left and slightly higher than me. As I looked at him and the MiGs to our front, he fired and the wing root of a MiG sparkled from an excellent hit. Before he could press his advantage, we turned and he called a break. I had a MiG on my tail. A shiver of fear coursed through me when I looked over my shoulder. There was a single MiG at seven o'clock, about 1,500 feet behind me. Rolling over and over, I pulled as many Gs inverted as possible without stalling the aircraft and losing airspeed, then split-Sed. That shook the MiG, but my wingman had lost sight of me. I took up a course for the front lines.

Looking above, I saw a lone MiG heading south. Behind him was another MiG about 3,000 feet directly astern of me. The lone MiG was apparently out to avenge my victory. Now it became the hunted stalking the hunted as I took up position behind the lone MiG that was now about 3,000 feet away. Calling my wingman, I told him about the second MiG that was headed in his direction, and instructed him to level off, build up his Mach number and run for it. I saw him ease his aircraft down. The second MiG followed. I told my wingman that I would tell him when to turn. There was little danger, because the range between him and the second MiG was too great. When the MiG turned, I would be in an excellent attack position. The MiG would not turn without firing, so I warned my wingman about that as well.

Nearing the Chongchon, my range had decreased. Looking back, I saw that I was being followed at long distance. It was easy to tell the attackers from the attacked, because our airplanes were not in the heavy contrail area like theirs. I finally squeezed off a few bursts at the lone MiG. When he turned, I was able to decrease our distance. When he tried to zoom, I ended up about 300 feet behind him in almost a full stall. His plane was a beautiful silver color and looked like it was just off the assembly line from a Russian factory.

I couldn't miss at that range. The burst hit directly behind the cockpit and lit it up in an encircling glare of light. He snapped into a spin at 38,000 feet, and I followed him in a spin of my own. Squeezing off another burst in the spin, I was able to register a hit on the wingtip of that beautiful plane. His spin continued all the way to the ground. My wingman couldn't verify this kill, but a member of the other flight did. The second MiG was now heading back to the north. I fired the rest of my ammunition at him, but the range was too great.

During this time I became interested in learning as much about the Korean and Chinese people as possible, and trying to find out why the Chinese Revolution was so successful. I checked out books about Korea and China from the base library and read them during alerts. I read about the Powells and their decision to stay behind in China under the Communists and support their cause. After reading a book about the new regime in China that referred to Americans as paper tigers, I chose Paper Tiger as the name for my aircraft. The idea was to show the enemy that not all Americans were paper tigers.

The eighth victory held the most danger and was fraught with the most mistakes. It began with a new pilot, a former professional musician with an uncanny ability to play the clarinet. I would take new men out on my wing for a few flights to judge them and get them combat seasoned, so he was my wingman. We were about fifty miles northeast of the Yalu, at about 40,000 feet and climbing, when we saw a great panorama of contrails and visible aircraft in the swirling blue sky. Through this melee, two MiGs flew on a course northward. Like a pack of dogs after two rabbits, the full complement of flights in sight turned and gave chase. One F-86 pilot must have used up every bit of power to attain a tremendous altitude and, in making his attack, came straight down through the MiG formation. He had evidently underestimated the recovery time from that high altitude and pulled out when he was probably 10,000 feet below the target.

After those two MiGs stole the show, from behind came four more in the standard fingertip formation. Six of us (two in my group and four in the other) followed them into China. The MiGs let down into a thick overcast and began disappearing and reappearing in a moderate cloud layer. It was easier to follow contrails through overcast. I had guessed where the MiGs were headed and continued after them with my wingman. Suddenly we broke out of the clouds and saw the four MiGs to our left in a turn. It would be easy to join up with them.

My joinup with the number-two man on the inside of the turn was too good—I was too close to fire effectively. My wingman called me clear, but before I could fire, a great number of cannon tracers went by my right wing and within a few feet of the canopy. It gave me a tremendous fright. The wingman again called me clear. Just as I was able to get settled down, another burst of fireworks passed over the right wing and past my canopy. Again my wingman called me clear. By now I was probably the most nervous pilot one could imagine. Finally the barrage of fire from behind me ceased, and I quickly dispatched the MiG ahead of me. A few good bursts and the battle was over. The aircraft was on fire and the pilot bailed out. The only reason I had escaped was that I had been so close to the MiG I shot down that the one behind me couldn't get a good shot for fear of hitting the friendly aircraft.

As I pulled up and looked around, I saw two other F-86s that had evidently been observing my kill, but my wingman was gone. When the other fighters departed, I was very much alone. I searched the sky and called, for he said that I was in sight. The sky was empty. I headed for home. As I crossed the Yalu, the wingman called and said that he was low on fuel and would have to go into a friendly island off the coast. I returned to home base and received a call at squadron operations after landing. A lieutenant colonel from K-55 had witnessed my kill and wanted to emphasize that he couldn't understand how my aircraft had not been hit by such a quantity of ammunition at such close range. I agreed with him. The more I thought about it, the madder I got at the pilot who was supposed to be flying my wing. It was bad enough to lose your leader, but calling him clear when he was under attack was almost murderous. The entire situation appeared to be more ludicrous than tragic.

The next day the courier from Cho-Do Island brought back the wayward wingman. I was waiting for him in personal equipment, where he would turn in his parachute, survival gear, helmet, etc. I had alternately stewed and fretted over what I was going to say, and finally settled on the approach of calm outrage. This fitted my personality. I explained just what had happened—that I was being called clear when I was actually in the process of being fired upon—and impressed upon him the fact that except for a great deal of luck, I would have been left up there on the cold Chinese countryside. I was just getting wound up, really raking him up one side and down the other with calm, cold contempt, when an unusual event occurred. Tears came to his eyes. There was nothing else to do but dismiss him and assure him that greater mistakes had been made. All my rehearsals evaporated, and that was where the one-sided interview ended. I later recommended the musician pilot for first lieutenant. That surprised him.

On another day in the battle area we immediately encountered a flight of MiGs heading south and turning. Just as I reached an excellent position on one of them, there was radio chatter from number two, saying to break, then very rapidly calling that he had been hit. I debated for a split second whether to fire or check on my element, then broke off the attack. Below me was a lone F-86 heading for the deck and the friendly offshore islands. It was being shepherded by the squadron commander and his wingman. The MiGs we had run into were reported to be from Czechoslovakia. They were dull green with red noses, and supposedly were one of the crack units of the satellite nations. They were certainly either very good or very lucky to hit my wingman's aircraft. This was the first time that it was confirmed that the satellites were participating in the Korean conflict.

The issue of flying across the border varied from time to time. For a while we were ordered not to fly closer than twenty miles to the border. Then it was permissible if you were in hot pursuit. On one mission we were briefed to patrol thirty miles inside China to protect F-84 and F-80 aircraft that were attacking the Suiho Reservoir on the Yalu River.

Once, my flight took off and headed north into the combat area. There was no activity on the legal side of the border, but there was a great deal of activity on the other side. One could hear pilots reporting breaks and being cleared, presumably for firing. We could see aircraft contrailing down below us. Our flight had used up a great deal of fuel pursuing a fictitious enemy, but we had enough left for one more attack. Seeing the activity below us and to the north, I decided to attack one aircraft and hope that it was the enemy.

Picking out a speck in the sky, I began a full-power dive. The speck, which happened to be at a right angle to our course, grew larger and began to fire short bursts at another aircraft. Puffs of smoke issued from its cannon, and that was a sure indicator that it was a MiG. Although out of range, I began to fire, hoping to frighten him away from his quarry. The MiG had been zooming up behind a lone F-86 at about a 1,000 feet range. When the enemy pilot saw or felt my attack, he headed north. I fell in easily behind him. It was a simple task to get the MiG burning. The pilot bailed out. Turning away from the doomed aircraft, I saw that I now had two wingmen. This concerned me, but only for a moment. The extra F-86 belonged to the commander from another fighter squadron. It was my ninth kill.

Shortly thereafter I was credited with my tenth kill. By now there was little thrill in a kill other than painting another red star on the side of old 958. The Paper Tiger still wore the tiger's teeth we had painted on it, but they required frequent retouching as the ravages of weather and high speed took their toll. Both the crew chief and I loved that airplane and felt that it was the fastest fighter in the unit. Other pilots agreed.

I was leading a four-plane mission on the afternoon of April 7, 1953. I wasn't flying my Paper Tiger that day. Numbers three and four left to investigate two enemy aircraft heading north, but the MiGs climbed and disappeared from the contrail level. Continuing northward with my wingman, I saw a flight of four aircraft come across the border, pulling contrails. I positioned my element above me, and we attacked as they passed 2,000 feet below us. As we gained position, they zoomed. I fired my guns at a range of 1,000 feet and the bullets went 200 feet to the right. The guns had not been boresighted after the previous mission. It was organizational policy to boresight the guns after each mission where the guns were fired, just because of results like these. Before I could correct for the error, we were attacked by four MiGs that came from above the contrail level. We tried to break off our attack by turning, then reversing the turn, so we would again be the attackers, but it was no use. The enemy aircraft were traveling too fast. We set course for the Yalu and home.

My wingman evidently had a tip tank that had not fed, because he called that he was getting low on fuel. At the same time, two more aircraft came across our noses, heading north. It was an ideal situation. I called a bounce and my wingman called that his fuel was getting lower. I made the wrong decision, telling him to head out and I would follow him later. I continued the attack. But now there were three aircraft— the first two and a straggler. I went after the straggler, dropping and closing at a tremendous speed. Getting off a shot, I made a gigantic roll around him and then fell in behind him. I was now heading south with minimum fuel. My wingman was somewhere in front of me, and I was responsible for getting him home safely.

The straggler accelerated and pulled even with the other two MiGs. I rolled over on the number-two aircraft, and this time the guns were calibrated. A long burst stopped his engine and he dropped back. This gave me the opportunity to hit the lead aircraft. From 1,200 feet, all six .50s literally tore the MiG apart. Debris came by my F-86 in large pieces, and I unconsciously ducked. I could either go under the aircraft, as I had done the time I had looked back at the burning MiG's guns, or I could go up over the debris. I chose the latter course.

Directly over the enemy fighter, my engine stopped. The throttle came back in my hands. The engine instruments read that the engine was dying. My speed began to decelerate rapidly, and I was pushed forward against the shoulder straps.

I thought of calling, but didn't. It might be interpreted that I was crying for help. I could reach the mouth of Yalu, but would be at zero altitude by then, and the ditching characteristics of the F-86 were not predictable. The aircraft would probably blow up in a short time. If I wanted to live, I had to bail out. Reaching down for the left handle, I jettisoned the canopy, then pulled up the right handle, leaned back in the seat, put my feet in the stirrups, and squeezed the trigger. Altitude was 2,000 feet, airspeed 450 knots.

The 37mm shell that activated the seat gave me a tremendous upward impetus. I blacked out momentarily and came to with the wind rushing around me as I rotated rapidly in space. I unstrapped my safety belt, stepped away from the seat, and pulled the rip cord. The chute deployed with no opening shock, and this surprised me. I looked around for other aircraft and saw a MiG that was a derelict in the sky, trailing a stream of flame as long as the fuselage. It turned lazily toward me, and I thought for sure that it would fire. My only defense was a chrome-plated .45 pistol. It had to be one of those aircraft that I had hit, and the pilot must certainly have had a desire for revenge, but fortunately he did not pursue it. The MiG turned away just as lazily.

My landing in a rocky, hilly country of scrub brush and trees was the start of a long period as a Chinese Communist prisoner of war. It involved several prison camps, numerous and endless interrogations, constant manipulation, and an almost successful escape. During the more than two years I spent in various Chinese prisons, I learned many things, including the meaning of comradeship.

They held five of us in a cell block at Murkden. One of them was Andrew Mackenzie, the Canadian squadron leader who had flown Spitfires from England during the Big Hassle. Andy had made an attack on some aircraft and was hit as he pulled away. His aircraft began an uncontrollable roll and he had to bail out. An F-86 went by him as he pulled the rip cord. He was sure it had shot him down, and he was bitter about it, as he had every right to be. Another pilot was Ronald

Parks. He had gotten hit, then flown into China by following what he thought was the coast of Korea. He had put out a great deal of radio chatter until one of his fellow pilots told him to shut up and die like a man. Ron had bailed out over Port Arthur and was held by the Russians for a while. Lyle Cameron was the fourth pilot. The four of us communicated with one another, but could not contact the man in the fifth cell.

Much later our group was joined by Ed Heller, another ace. Andy, Ed, and I had shot down at least twenty enemy aircraft in two wars. Two of us were there because we had made our own rules. Andy had just been unlucky. The three of us were different from the population in general because we had been better than average in our profession. Andy went home to Canada first. Four more of us were released after a show trial in Peking and a warning that ". . . if you are ever to enter China again, you will be duly punished." We ate our last meal in captivity in a room whose walls were festooned with "hate America" posters, then a train took us to Hong Kong. The first man who greeted us was a Jesuit priest. He said, "Welcome to a free land again."

In another war, in another place, I flew Huey helicopters and served as an advisor to the South Vietnamese.

CORSAIR ACE

Lieutenant Guy Pierre Bordelon, Jr., has the distinction of being the only navy ace and the only propeller ace in the Korean War. This memoir covers the hazardous navy night resupply interdiction missions behind Communist lines, and the special mission that resulted in Bordelon's five victories over Yakovlev and Lavochkin aircraft.

In August 1942 I left Louisiana State University and answered my country's call by enlisting in the U.S. Naval Air Corps. Fortunately I was immediately called as a naval aviation cadet and reported for the very strenuous preflight training program at the University of Georgia at Athens on September 3, 1942. Shortly afterward I attended what was billed as a "motivational lecture" by two young veteran pilots of the Battle of Pearl Harbor. Their message (most earnestly proposed) was "Be prepared to die for your country! Those Nip pilots are the best! You can't beat them!"

This angered me and a lot of other cadets. Never having been a quitter or a loser, I resolved that I was going to live, not die for my country, by being better than the best the enemy had to offer. I didn't get the chance to test my resolve on the actual enemy, as they had been battered back to their islands, and two large *bangs* ended the fray before I saw an airborne Japanese for real. However, I had found my occupation, naval aviation, and when the chance arose applied for the Regular Navy. The following years flew by and saw me circumnavigating the globe as part of Air Group 11 on the carrier USS *Valley Forge,* then serving in various fighter squadron, command, and staff billets until the outbreak of the Korean War.

During the KOWAR, as we called it, I first served as operations, logistics, and intelligence officer on the staff of commander, Cruiser Division Three, on board the heavy cruiser USS *Helena.* Serving in this billet was hectic, because I was exposed for the first time to the other navy, the "Black Shoes." I had never understood the competition between brown and black footwear, but soon became disenchanted with my "we're all on the same team" attitude. Our admiral hated aviators of any type, and did all he could to convince me that the naval air warfare doctrines were not the way to achieve victory in any conflict, past or present. Fortunately my tour in purgatory soon ended. I was ordered by a prescient BUPERS to Composite Squadron Three (VC-3) at Moffett Field, California.

Composite Squadron Three was the only all-weather combat fighter squadron in the Pacific Naval Air Forces, and I was tremendously excited by the opportunity to fly actual combat missions against an enemy in the Communist, or Red, camp. My only concern was that we would be flying what many considered to be an obsolete, propeller-driven, World War II aircraft against modern high-performance jets. This meant that we were relegated to a night-attack role against enemy resupply efforts over and through tortuous mountain terrain. It rankled when we saw the air force daily engaging the hottest Communist jets with great success over North Korea. We avidly followed their actions in the daily news and wished (oh, how we wished!) for a miracle—air-to-air combat, a dream!

Now, don't get me wrong. The Corsair was a great old plane. Known as the "Hose-Nose" or the "Ensign Eliminator," it was a proven success against the Japanese during World War II. But now we were not even in the ball game, and I mean high ball, not low ball. As officer in charge, team dog, VC-3 aboard the USS *Princeton,* I had five combat aircraft, five pilots with a unique combat capability and, of course, a mission that was dirty, dangerous, and essential. All the airborne victories the air force scored didn't stop the North Koreans or ChiCom forces from killing American and U.N. troops on the ground. We *had to stop* the continual resupply of frontline Communist forces. So we did the job. During the day, and night after night, naval aviation pounded the supply routes. Communist trains and trucks were destroyed by the hundreds as they rolled down heavily defended railroads and twisting, dirt mountain roads with the persistence of ants.

As a fellow pilot put it, almost in wonder, "They want to win the war! You can almost walk on the antiaircraft!"

That concentrated antiaircraft fire almost ended my "Ko-

rean experience," even as it started. My first night launch
called for recon of enemy resupply railroads and trucking
routes in the central mountains and rugged northern mountains. My plane, Nan Papa 21, was loaded for bear with eight
250-pound "frag" bombs, equipped with daisy-cutter fuses set
to explode just above the ground to take out any rolling stock
in the vicinity. The most important item in Nan Papa 21's
load was 200 rounds of 20mm high-explosive-incendiary ammunition per cannon. At 1,200 rounds per minute from each
of four cannon, we could literally burn the air around any
surface or air target. It was deadly against both trucks and
aircraft. Finally NP-21 carried a 500-pound bomb on a centerline rack, but these World War II–era heavyweights were
all but useless, as they invariably failed to explode. During
nine months of deployment, only two of mine went off, and
I brought all my "wires" back. We checked everything from
fuses to explosive compound, but never found a satisfactory
solution to the problem.

Launching from the *Princeton* just at twilight, I led a
flight of four Corsair 5Ns toward a point off Wonsan Harbor,
North Korea, with each fighter maintaining a two-mile interval. Enroute to IP (initial point), we checked our communications and guns. All worked well, so we continued to IP,
then broke up for our own target areas of responsibility. My
target routes were west and northwest of Wonsan, formerly
a major North Korean port, but now patrolled within the
harbor by U.N. naval forces under a U.S. commodore in a
destroyer or frigate. I called this commander, known as the
"Duke of Wonsan," before entering airspace over him. He
gave permission to proceed. After crossing the northern perimeter of Wonsan Harbor and reporting "feet dry" to Task
Force 77, I entered my first recon route and began visual
search for truck headlights on the mountainous inner portion
of the route. Sighting moving lights on a roadway north and
west of Wonsan, I immediately turned hard starboard to close
the target area.

As I turned, I observed a cluster of three sharp hills

passing directly underneath me. Just as quickly, I was surrounded by fluorescent pink balls of fire. I jinked hard port,
finding more pink balls that seemed even closer. Rolling hard
aport and diving sharply, I pulled back over Wonsan Harbor
and set up for a dive-bombing run. Going in strafing, I pickled
the five-hundred-pounder. It failed to explode. I jinked violently away toward my other truck routes to the northwest
and saw no more antiaircraft fire from the three hills. At about
this time the Duke of Wonsan called to apologize for failing
to warn me about the apparent AA buildup in the area! Lesson: Call for the word; don't expect it to be automatic.

On the next night that we flew, there was high humidity
with scattered light stratus clouds, and I learned another lesson. After sighting apparent truck headlights on the ground,
I turned toward them only to observe all lights go out as I
closed. "My flares will handle that," I thought, and released
one over the suspect area. Zap! I was suddenly in the middle
of the worst "milk bowl" conditions I had ever seen! It took
all of my instrument training to get out of that one. Lesson
two: Never drop a flare for target illumination when conditions are soupy.

In spite of these learning experiences, we were still burning trucks. "Strafe and bomb the front of the convoy, then
strafe and bomb the rear, and follow on with coordinated
multiplane attacks if others can be called in." Our favorite
circumstance was to be up on a clear night and catch a convoy
of trucks winding down a "switchback" mountain road. This
happened to me one night when I had expended all but cannon
ordnance. No other aircraft were near, so I pulled up to 7,000
feet, reduced power for a quiet run-in, and pushed over in a
shallow dive. At estimated effective range I opened fire with
short bursts. Suddenly I could observe tracers bouncing
straight up in front of me and, just as rapidly, understood
that I was firing into a ridge directly between me and the
trucks. I was low and slow, and sinking right into the ridge.
This was before afterburners, but my Corsair took me out of
there like JATO. I pulled out directly over the trucks and

must have barely missed them. The next day's photo recon of the area showed three trucks off-road.

Meantime, back around Seoul, the air force was beginning to ask for the type of aerial assistance that we navy types had dreamed of providing since KOWAR started. The seventh fleet commander, that famous old Cherokee Indian Admiral "Jocko" Clark, learned that the air force had received disastrous setbacks while attempting to stop night intrusions of enemy aircraft of late–World War II vintage. Several Fifth Air Force "all-weather" jets had been lost trying to intercept Communist propeller types, collectively known as "Bed-Check Charlies." The enemy aircraft ranged in variety from observation planes to multiengine bombers of the TU-2 class. Using such aircraft and the cover of night, the enemy had successfully destroyed fifteen million gallons of aviation gasoline and other supplies in a well-planned attack at Inchon Harbor shortly before Admiral Clark visited the joint operations center in Seoul.

When what had occurred was explained to Admiral Clark, and he learned that the air force problem was the inability of high-performance jets to maneuver at the low altitudes and low airspeeds of enemy aircraft, he immediately volunteered the services of "our navy planes which fly low and slow on every night mission." JOC Korea accepted the offer, and within two days a contingent of ecstatic navy night-fighter pilots flew in to the Kilo 14 Airfield being used at Seoul by the air force. No bands and no parades, but we were resolved to solve the critical problem of cashing Charlie's bed-checks.

As Admiral Clark had declared, almost all of our Korean night combat experience involved flying low and slow, around and through the most hazardous mountain terrain. These nightly interdiction missions, attacking trucks and trains on the twisting, precipitous resupply routes in North Korea, were an invaluable experience in coping with an airborne enemy who was also flying low and slow. There were problems, of course, and these involved the nature of combat in Korea.

There was a long front crossing the peninsula with many commands engaged, and a general lack of control over local flight operations.

JOC Korea briefed us on the necessity of intercepting any "bogie" from the rear, and closing to the point of letting us identify it as friend or foe. Further, we were required to obtain permission to open fire from our joint ops center (JOC) controller. This turned out to be an absolute necessity. On any given night there were always various types of friendly aircraft flying through our area on unknown missions, without the least benefit of the *mandatory* flight plan. This did make it difficult. On several occasions, in fact, I was vectored onto a transport aircraft flying blissfully through our combat patrol zone. On reporting "friendly" contact, I would be informed by the omnipotent JOC controller that no friendlies were in the area, and that I should open fire at once. It was necessary to identify some friendlies as such several times before the order to fire was rescinded.

Our identification procedure, which we practiced religiously, was by eyeballing aircraft silhouettes and engine exhaust patterns. Fortunately the aircraft utilized by Charlie had very distinctive engine exhaust flame patterns and/or silhouettes, like nothing being flown by U.N. pilots. I particularly espoused the exhaust stack pattern technique and found it to be infallible. However, it was not an easy task.

One evening when I was fortunately not airborne, a U.S. Marine sergeant pilot, flying a specially configured night AD-1 Skyraider, put multiple 20mm cannon holes through a fabric-covered Piper Cub being utilized as an artillery spotter aircraft. As usual, the Piper was on an "unfiled" mission. Shortly thereafter, a large and very unhappy infantry officer showed up at our field at Pyongtaek (K-6), waving a big .45 pistol. He complained loudly about his "20mm haircut" and was actually frothing at the mouth. *He was fortunate.* The 20mm cannon load we utilized for this mission was all high-explosive incendiary. Had they struck something solid—no more Piper!

On another evening, while flying CAP north of Seoul, I

was vectored on a target that barely appeared to be moving and soon acquired it by radar. It was easy to pick up, but on closure for identification zipped off the radar screen. I tried everything but sticking my feet out to slow and set a flight path to pass directly under the bogie for possible visual. Finally (after the third pass) I detected the brief but characteristic flicker of rotor blades. I requested JOC to confirm the presence of rescue choppers operating from the U.S. Navy hospital ships USS *Haven* or USS *Hope,* but was immediately ordered to "Shoot! Shoot! Shoot!" After again asking for verification of any helo rescue in the area, I was suddenly and frantically told, "Hold fire! Repeat, don't fire!" The chopper was from a hospital ship. That was a close one.

Now to our mission to get Charlie. First we were transferred from K-14 (where we had been briefed) to K-6 at Pyongtaek, about thirty miles south of Seoul. K-6 was the major operating base for the Marine Corps in Korea. Better yet, it was loaded with Corsairs, AU-2s, and other Marine Corps aircraft. A HAMS (headquarters aircraft maintenance squadron), magnificently equipped to support and maintain Corsair operations, accepted our "odd" birds with great enthusiasm and efficiency, which was a definite relief.

After numerous briefings we flew some very thorough orientation hops and used our radar on "search" to map the area. At least that's what I did. K-6 had two runways, but the principal one was on a 130- to 310-degree heading. Built recently by the SeaBees, the field topography included a declining gradient that transversed the main runway. On landing or takeoff you were going first uphill, then sharply downhill. Visiting aircraft, despite warnings, were prone to self-induced ground loops or swerves off the runway when they thought they had run out of strip prematurely. In actuality, they still had 3,000 feet remaining.

Initially we stood by for operations in a ready hut just west of the northern and western side of runway 31. On our first night we launched under field GCA control when area radars picked up "unknowns headed our way from the northwest." We orbited for a while on a bright moonlit night, then GCA vectored two of us to the west of the field. I finally picked up a target on the search feature of my radar, and using that for headings and the GCA for altitudes, was able to obtain a visual on what was immediately identifiable as a YAK-18.

I had closed to point-blank range before being cleared to fire and almost immediately saw a stream of tracers from the YAK, all passing below my left wing and to the left. Realizing that the enemy rear-seat gunner would soon have my range, I opened fire with all four 20mm cannon directly into the enemy's fuselage. The tracer fire stopped. He turned left and I gave him another burst of cannon fire. With that, the YAK literally blew to bits. I was temporarily blinded but, pulling up, was soon able to see again.

Almost immediately I was vectored on a second target approaching from the north. Closing to visual range, I was able to again identify the target as "foe," another YAK, and was given clearance to fire. It took a good long burst from my cannons before the bogie disappeared in a flash of fire. The K-6 GCA sergeant operator had accurately vectored me into visual range of both targets in a concise, professional manner. He was a major factor in the mission's success.

The next night's mission, a four-hour CAP, (combat air patrol) found me patrolling from seaward of Inchon, north up the west coast to the mouth of the Imjin River, thence eastward and along the river to "Marilyn's left and right ones" (distinctive northerly bends in the river). On my first sweep north I was vectored by JOC radar onto two aircraft operating to the seaward of Inchon. I was able to acquire and close to visual range on two high-performance aircraft of the La-vochkin LA-9 or LA-11 type.

Reporting "foe," I was cleared to fire and closed the trailing wingman. One short burst blew him away. His wing appeared to crumble and he went down burning. The lead aircraft turned to follow his wingman down, then seemed to realize that I was there and led me into a hairy tail chase over the AA batteries around Kaesong. Playing it safe, I pulled in tight, then stuck right on his tail until we cleared the antiaircraft fire. Then I gave him a series of short bursts of cannon fire until he broke up. I watched the aircraft explode on the ground. A strange feeling, just like observing night bombing practice!

After this there was a period of several days during which the enemy disappointed us by not venturing south. However, it gave us a chance to further equip our aircraft for night ops, and after six days we were pleased to learn of the arrival of radio ADF equipment for our birds. My plane and Ralph Hopson's NP-24 were equipped at once and we were ready for bad weather navigation. That evening when I assumed CAP station off Inchon, I was vectored well out to sea to eventually acquire a formation of two TU-2 bombers that were flying southeast toward Inchon. Cleared to fire, I closed in behind the wingman and—my guns would not fire! I tried to notify JOC, but they could not understand. The only thing to do appeared to be to scare off the bogies. The TU-2s could do a whale of a lot of damage in the Inchon area.

Remembering a sly practice a VCN-1 instructor had tried on me during night training, I pulled off to the side and went full throttle ahead of the slow TU-2s. Arriving two miles ahead at a forty-five-degree angle, I turned head on into the bombers, dropped my landing gear, and turned on my landing light. I was almost on them when one aircraft dove vertically left as I just missed the other one. It pulled straight up.

Later I learned that a single vital wire to the ordnance system had been left unfastened during the ADF installation in Nan Papa 21. My crewmen, Ballard and Gabbard, were highly embarrassed. As far as I can remember, it was their only mistake while based at K-6. They kept NP-21, or "Annie-Mo," as I called her, in like-new condition, if not better. They were the best.

A few nights after the incident with the TU-2s, my wingman, Lieutenant "Hoppy" Hopson, was flying CAP when he was vectored by JOC Korea on a fast-moving target up by

"Marilyn's left and right ones." He acquired the target by aircraft radar and started to close, but his radar suddenly malfunctioned. JOC vectored me on the target, which I was able to acquire with some difficulty because the bogie was changing course and altitude. He soon stabilized, and I was able to close to visual range by picking up his dim silhouette and stack pattern. It was another LA-9 or LA-11 fighter, and I reported "foe" to JOC. Clearance to fire was quickly given.

As I closed to a "sure kill" firing position, he began to turn away and was apparently under ground radar direction. I pulled in close as he turned hard left and right, leading me through the Kaesong AA field of fire. Things got hectic. Finally he straightened out long enough for me to fire a long burst directly into him from below and dead astern. He turned hard right and his aircraft exploded with a tremendous flash. My aircraft was bounced severely and I was nearly blinded. Flicking on the auto pilot (previously set for level flight), I let Annie-Mo fly herself until my vision cleared. She performed like a Thoroughbred, and I could have kissed her.

The Korean War was the last true "fighter" war and has been neglected as such by military historians. During that conflict we learned many lessons in tactics that are still of great value today. However, the most important lesson is that of teaching and nurturing the "winner's concept" in combat flying. During World War II, some armchair hero came up with the catch phrase "There are old pilots and there are bold pilots, but there are no old, bold pilots." I believe that he was of the same school of loser philosophy which thought that "tigers are stupid—they accomplish nothing but getting themselves and others killed." Anyone who has experienced actual combat on a day-to-day basis knows that these two aphorisms are, if not the words of congenital cowards, at least words that characterize the proverbial loser.

You can't learn the razor's edge of skill, or the informed level of confidence required to succeed in combat, by flying only a Link trainer or other cockpit simulator. To put it more succinctly: Until you become an integral part of your aircraft, the thinking-acting part, you can never succeed as a combat pilot. The requirement is twofold—experience and realistic training, training, training! Training should be administered by the finest, most able pilots in the service, certainly not by losers. This is my story and my philosophy.

MIG ALLEY

Major W. W. "Bones" Marshall, in this powerful story, shares some of the action-packed experiences of his Korean tour. He was in the unique position of participating in the attack on the only North Korean TU-2 bombing raid of the war, and flying escort for a disastrous B-29 daylight bombing mission.

The words in the U.S. Air Force song, "Off we go into the Wild Blue Yonder," perfectly describe the skies over North Korea, particularly "MiG Alley" (the valley of the Yalu River). When I first flew over the two Koreas, I was struck by the endless hues of blue. Most of the roofs of their homes are blue. The hills take on various shades of purples and blues and browns as the day wears on. The skies over MiG Alley were absolutely spectacular in their blueness, which reaches from the blue-black of the ocean to the brilliant white-blues of the high sky, where the MiGs patrol.

The white contrails of the MiGs could be seen for miles against that blue background. If the MiGs were not conning, we were blind until they were next seen, in a firing position on our tails. The best flying and fighting altitude for the F-86s was 28,000 feet. We seldom if ever conned at that altitude. That doesn't mean that we were invisible, for the enemy ground radar system kept us under constant surveillance. There was no escape from them.

All my fighter pilot dreams came true in those action-laden blue skies over North Korea. There was the thrill of being there, of being able to twist your airplane and body through the most impossible flight configurations and maneuvers, ending sweetly in position on the MiG's tail. Then came the thrill of pulling the trigger and blasting him out of the sky. If you don't like these words, you had best not read any further, because that's all I am going to talk about—flying and fighting, like a good fighter pilot should.

The Korean War added a long string of aces to the history of all air wars, and I was fortunate to become the fifth jet ace of the war. My score was six and a half destroyed (kills), seven probables, and six more enemy aircraft damaged. I get many questions like, "How in the hell did you get a score like that?"

It all depends on when you were there. A destroyed enemy aircraft was often downgraded to a probable or damaged if you didn't have gun-camera film of your kill or another witness who saw the aircraft crashing into the ground, or burning, or exploding, or the crew bailing out. Sounds reasonable, except that not many months later, after I had departed Korea, the rules were changed and some, or all, of my probables could have been upgraded to destroyed. It's just another roll of the dice.

Usually your wingman was your witness. However, unless you had a super wingman like mine, John Honoker, he couldn't stay with you in the wild gyrations to get on the MiG's tail, or shake him off yours. Some of my kills were witnessed by other flights that happened to be in the area, like the time I snap-rolled and spun down in formation with a MiG, and was finally able to blast him before we both hit the ground. That time I was lucky that Hoot Gibson (in another flight) witnessed the kill, for my wingman was long gone from the scene. A tremendous amount of luck was involved in the game of "was he killed or not?" Hoot's flight just happened to be in the area. It's a classic example.

During the early days, the 4th Fighter Wing Awards Board was overly conservative in awarding the "enemy aircraft destroyed" category. If there was any doubt in their minds, they downgraded it to a probable. It was done in my case too many times. It was a sore point with me to be credited with only a damaged MiG after a hell of an air fight that ended when the MiG fled home with my gun-camera film showing smoke pouring from his engine.

The event that tilted the awards process in favor of the pilot's destroyed claims was the establishment of an Allied listening post located on an island, almost in the mouth of the Yalu River and practically in the traffic pattern of the MiG base at Sinuiju. It was staffed by language experts, and they listened and reported all MiG transmissions during combat operations. The information they were able to provide the F-86s during air battles was instrumental in turning the tide of warfare over Korea in favor of the F-86s. In addition, we finally had another witness to our MiG claims after a big air battle.

The F-86 pilots might report only three MIGs destroyed and four damaged, and a lot of MiGs shot at with unknown results. The listening-post report on that battle would state that forty MiGs took off but only thirty returned, and two of them crashed on landing due to battle damage. They would further report hearing four MiG pilots bailing out of their burning airplanes during the fight, and intercepting a Communist headquarter's report that six additional MiGs were missing in action. So, in accordance with intercepted information, twelve MiGs had been lost. The F-86 pilots, following the restrictive 4th Fighter Wing criteria, had only reported three enemy fighters destroyed. Now the rules were changed to more accurately report air battle results, but it was too late for me.

In one of my probable claims I had moved into close range on the tail of a MiG and looked to my wingman to make sure that it was safe to fire. There was no MiG on my tail, but my wingman wasn't there. The rules were to get out of there if you didn't have the eyes of your wingman. I fired a long burst into the MiG and prepared to run for it. The MiG blew up in my face. I couldn't see ahead because of his fuel or oil all over my windshield. My engine seemed to be running rough from ingesting fuel and possible parts of his exploding aircraft into the intake. On landing, the intelligence people swarmed all over my F-86, taking samples of the oil from my wing and windshield. My gun camera did not work, and not having a witness, I could claim only a probable.

Same story again. A MiG blew up in my face, except this time I had a wingman for my witness. On landing, my crew chief climbed into the engine intake to check for damage. He came out quickly, white in the face. He had found the MiG pilot's helmet on the engine intake screen. One MiG destroyed.

And finally the question: "How do you get a half a kill,

and why wasn't it called a probable or damaged?" One of our squadron's greatest pilots was a guy called Sam. He was a huge guy and barely fit into the small cockpit of an F-86. Generally, big pilots are assigned to bombers and transport aircraft, and skinny little guys go to fighters and recce. But Sam loved fighters so much that he had fought to stay in them, and now here he was, flying and fighting to his heart's content, every day in MiG Alley. But Sam was miserable. He was approaching the end of his combat tour and hadn't had the opportunity to shoot at a MiG. Many pilots complete their combat tours without firing their guns, but Sam was different. He was smarting from the criticism of some "big mouth" types, who said that he was too big to be a fighter pilot and couldn't hit the side of a barn even if given the opportunity.

Sam was a hell of a good fighter pilot and a great wingman, and I loved to have him with me in a tough fight. One day, with Sam as my wingman, I fired into a MiG, followed him down, and ended up on his tail as he flew ten feet off the ground while violently turning left and right to shake us. Although I was at point-blank range, I was holding my fire, waiting for him to fly straight and level long enough to pour gunfire into him. The best way to avoid being shot down is to make maximum G turns so the pursuing fighter can't get his gunsight on you long enough for effective fire. This MiG pilot was very good at it. Then I noticed that he was taking us down a valley that was ringed by antiaircraft guns, all tracking us, but holding their fire for fear of hitting their own plane.

When he finally slacked off on his turning, I fired a long burst up his tail. He caught on fire but continued to fly. I told Sam to take over the attack and finish him off, which he did immediately. In a matter of seconds the MiG had exploded and the antiaircraft guns opened up on us. We hugged the earth to avoid their fire and headed for home—full speed. After examining our gun-camera film, the 4th Wing Awards Board gave Sam and me each credit for one half kill. Our squadron had a super celebration for him that same night. Sam returned to the U.S. with a feeling of great pride.

Twenty-two F-86s of the 4th Fighter Group, spread out in wide combat formation, had been on combat patrol in MiG Alley for an extended period of time. There had been numerous MiG contrails overhead throughout the mission, but none had come down to fight. Several pilots had already reported bingo fuel. Of course, any radio calls that we were low on fuel, or that an F-86 was experiencing engine problems, was like offering raw meat to a starving lion. The North Korean radar controllers continuously monitored any radio transmissions by American pilots and, should any of us report problems, down came the MiGs to attack the lame duck fighter. We had often played their game by faking radio calls about aircraft problems or low fuel to lure MiGs down from their lofty perches and surprise them. We were just hungry for MiG kills.

Today we were patrolling deep inside North Korea and had a long way to go home, so there was a bothersome fuel situation. The combination of low fuel and numerous MiGs overhead put us in a critical posture from a fighting standpoint. As a result, we were tensed up and expecting an attack at any time. In a low fuel situation, you couldn't do much to fight the MiGs, because it took full engine power throughout, which means maximum fuel consumption.

Our fighting plan was to stay on station long enough to be able to intercept and fight the MiGs until the fighter-bombers had completed their mission and departed for home. We were supposed to have enough fuel remaining to return to our home base and be able to go on to a second base in the event that a battle-damaged aircraft had crashed on our primary runway and closed it. That was the plan, but after a fight we never had enough fuel to do more than make it back to our home base, period. During a big air battle it was not uncommon to run out of fuel and glide the last few miles to our airfield on a dead engine. With only a few gallons of fuel remaining, I have shut down my engine, glided, then restarted the engine for the landing.

On this mission we received a call that the fighter-bombers were clear of the area. It was time for us to get the hell out of there. Our fighter group commander called the turn for home and cautioned us to keep alert for MiGs. The Communist pilots were clever in attacking formations in their turns, when the American pilots were paying more attention to where the other F-86s were than looking for MiGs.

While in the turn, and in the midst of all that tension, an unidentified F-86 pilot suddenly shouted, "Break! Break! Break!" over the radio.

I say "unidentified" because we didn't know which one of us had reported it, so for a split second we didn't know who was being attacked by MiGs. A call like that scares the hell out of you and, if you are an experienced combat pilot, you don't ask questions. Instead, you immediately break as hard as you can to prevent the MiG from having a clear shot at your tail. This time every fighter in the formation did a hard break for insurance. As you can imagine, we had F-86s all over the sky. As it turned out, the MiGs were attacking me.

At the exact moment of the break call my fighter was surrounded by bright orange tracers, which I swear were as big as tennis balls. I was already in a hard turn, but I took the control stick in both hands and pulled it as hard as I could, exceeding the maximum G force on the airplane and on my back. I had been looking back over the tail when the MiG call came, trying to watch my wingman's rear and my own, so my spine was twisted into a full corkscrew to the right. When I applied maximum downward pressure in the break, it all centered on my back.

I shook the MiG off my tail but experienced excruciating back pain as we proceeded home. I could not move after landing, so the canopy was removed and I was lifted out of the cockpit by a crane. I was flown to a hospital in Japan for a week of recuperation (where little Japanese nurses walked on my back with their bare feet), delaying my return to MiG alley.

The unidentified pilot who had given the MiG warning had saved my life, as would happen on many missions during my combat tour with the 4th Fighter Group. After such a mission the pilots might fuss and grumble about some idiot pilot making a life-or-death call and not identifying himself. That's all well and good under normal circumstances, but if you're a wingman and you suddenly see a MiG at the firing position on your leader's tail, all standard procedures go out the window and you scream, "Break! Break! Break!" And we all break so that we can live and fly another day.

You can bet your sweet ass that as soon as I was able, I proudly shook the hand of the unidentified pilot (who happened to be my own wingman). Grateful for his alertness in immediately sounding the alarm, I gladly bought him all the cool ones he could hold. We lost too many pilots who were not as lucky as I was in having such a great wingman. He died in combat after I left Korea for home.

I was involved in four incidents where I almost got my ass shot down. In every case I exceeded the max Gs on the airplane and my body through violent evasive action, which usually resulted in shaking the MiG off my tail and, often, my own wingman as well. A wingman with "good eyeballs" was our most valuable asset in MiG Alley.

The closest I came to being shot down was by a MiG in my "six o'clock" position while flying with a "new guy" as a wingman. I still break out in a sweat when I recall the MiG opening fire at me, unseen by him. Hoot Gibson, flying in another squadron formation, saw the MiG attacking and shouted, "Break!"

I saw the tracers coming by my right wing, so I broke to the left as hard as I could. Too hard, because my F-86 did a snap-roll and fell off into a violent spin. That didn't shake the MiG. In his attempt to stay with me, he had also exceeded his flight envelope and was spinning down in formation with me. We both recovered simultaneously, except that I ended up directly in front of his guns with no airspeed and little maneuverability. Before he could fire, I again jerked back on the stick and snapped off into another spin. The MiG reacted the same way and was again spinning down in formation with me, canopy to canopy. This type of acrobatics is best left for air shows.

I was getting very concerned. This MiG pilot was good. He was determined to shoot me down and was willing to take the risk of a midair collision to stay with me in a spin. We were fast running out of altitude, so I had to attempt another spin recovery. Lady Luck was with me this time. He was dead ahead in my gunsight when we had both recovered. I poured fire into him until, with smoke and fire coming from his aircraft, he dove straight into the ground. It was with tremendous relief (and thanks to Hoot) that I headed home to fight again another day.

The following may sound like a training mission, but to those new pilots flying their first combat mission in a sky full of MiGs, just being there was a terrifying experience. One day I had another new guy on my wing. He was flying his first mission in MiG Alley. He was well trained, with many stateside hours in fighters, and had even completed a combat training course at Nellis Air Force Base that was especially tailored for Korean air combat. And finally he had completed the 4th Fighter Wing's combat indoctrination course, required in order to be qualified to fly and fight in MiG Alley.

There were numerous MiG contrails overhead when we arrived in MiG Alley. Because we had several new guys in our 335th Fighter Squadron formation that day, we had been assigned to fly in the relative safety of the southern patrol corridor, well away from the MiG threat, or so we thought. I was surprised, then, when I spotted two MiGs diving in on my new guy's tail. I quickly ordered him to follow me in a hard break, but his break was only mediocre. As a matter of fact, it was terrible. The MiGs were easily turning inside of him and rapidly closing into a firing position. I quickly yo-

yoed up and back down onto the tail of the two MiGs, firing as I did so. They immediately broke off their attack.

My new guy was in a gentle turn on my right. I was shocked to see two more MiGs on his tail, and they were much closer this time. So I shouted for him to break. Again he did a half-ass hard turn. As I rushed in with guns blazing to scare the MiGs off his tail, I begged him to pull his turn tighter. The two new MiGs broke off. Now we had four MiGs on our tails. I was in no position to shoot at anyone, and had I been by myself, I would have split-Sed and gotten the hell out of there. But there was my new-guy wingman, sashaying around the sky, about to get his ass shot off. He was doing nothing but gentle turns, while I frantically did acrobatics to keep myself between the MiGs and this poor fellow. Now we were getting low on fuel due to our continuous full-throttle operation.

The four MiGs and I continued our rat race and lost sight of the new guy. The MiGs probably got tired of playing with me, or were low on fuel, because they finally broke off the fight and headed north for home. I called the new guy on the radio, and there he was, wisely circling out over the water, our 4th Fighter Group procedure in the event that you became separated from your formation. MiGs never flew over the water for fear of being captured if shot down. He quickly joined me for the flight home.

The group formation had listened silently to my frantic directions to "Break! Break! Harder! Harder!" They told me later that they had damned near wet their pants every time I screamed "Break!"

Surprise attacks on our F-86s were repeated a hundred times during my combat operations in MiG alley. The MiGs had a tremendous tactical advantage over the F-86 forces. They had the element of surprise and always outnumbered us in every air battle. They also had the reassurance of flying and fighting over their own territory. We were faced with the specter of a terrible prison camp if we were shot down. Their greatest assistance came from the North Korean and Chinese radar control and surveillance system. In those early days we had nothing but our eyeballs.

The Communist radar controllers would direct the MiGs in an attack at our low tail position (six o'clock), where it was most difficult for the F-86 pilots to see. As a result, it was mandatory to fly in two-ship elements, in spread-combat formation, so that we could watch one another's tails. In spite of our best efforts, the MiGs continuously slipped in on us, right up our tails. Most of our F-86 combat losses were from MiG attacks in the tail quadrant. Of course, most of our MiG kills were made from the six o'clock position as well. There was very little deflection shooting in Korea, except by George Davis, commander of the 334th Fighter Squadron and the best deflection shooter in the air force (as attested by his outstanding MiG kill record).

Eventually the United Nations Command installed that listening station to monitor the departures and recoveries of the MiGs at Sinuiju Field in China. These brave people—I heard they were Australians—would listen to the MiG commanders directing their pilots in on the attack. The information was passed on to us, materially changing the outcome of the air battle in the F-86 pilot's favor.

It was a bright, clear, cold winter morning. I was leading one of the three F-86 squadrons of the 4th Fighter Group, and we were en route to MiG Alley. We were not flying in our normal, fuel-conserving manner—a slow climb in loose formation on a straight line from Kimpo Air Base to the Yalu combat patrol area. Instead, we were in a relatively close formation, remaining low to avoid detection by North Korean and Chinese radar, and flying on the east side of the north-south mountain range that cuts through the Korean peninsula. Everyone was maintaining absolute radio silence in accordance with the plan. Surprise would be the key to our success. We were en route to attack the first (and only) North Korean bomber operation of the war.

You can well imagine the surprise and excitement we

pilots had experienced during the morning's briefing when we had been told that our mission was to attack a formation of thirty Russian-built TU-2 medium bombers escorted by LA-9 propeller-driven fighters with a top cover of MiG-15s. Never had the Communists massed such an armada of combat aircraft. The TU-2s' mission was to bomb and destroy the United Nations listening post at the mouth of the Yalu. It was vital to the survival of the MiGs' combat machine that this station be knocked out.

The three fighter squadrons of the 4th Fighter Group (the 334th, 335th, and 336th) were fully manned with every available F-86 aircraft for that top-priority mission. The fighters were to be flown by only the best and most experienced pilots. The formation was led by the group commander, Colonel Ben Preston. All of our top combat pilots in the wing and the group were flying in key, lead positions. With so many VIPs aboard, I was lucky to be leading my own 335th Fighter Squadron.

The time had arrived. We turned west and crossed the ridgeline, and were immediately exposed to their radar as we started our climb to altitude and moved into our spread-combat fighting formation. There, directly in front of us, was the biggest Communist air show that we could ever have hoped to see, let alone participate in. It was a huge and strangely beautiful panorama of enemy aircraft, seemingly flying at every altitude. The TU-2s, growing nearer by the second, were in a large, loose formation with ten flights of three bombers each. The LA-9 fighters were flying close escort and were weaving back and forth over the bomber formation. Overhead, the sky was filled with more MiG contrails than I had ever seen. They knew that the F-86s were airborne, but hadn't picked them up on radar. As a result, the MiGs were swarming about like mad wasps, looking for us.

It must have come as a deep shock when the MiG, LA-9, and bomber crews were told that the F-86 Sabrejets were already among them. The bomber formation was headed directly for the island and was about fifty miles from target, so our timing was perfect. The plan was for the 334th and 336th Fighter Squadrons to immediately attack. My 335th Squadron was to pull up into a covering position to meet the expected MiG attack. From that point on it was the greatest show on earth. The air exploded. The bombers tightened their formation as the F-86s started their attacks. The LA-9s turned head on into the F-86s, while overhead the MiGs dove straight down on our formations. What a show!

I was terribly disappointed that my squadron had to remain on high perch as the air below us filled with burning bombers. An LA-9 fighter was on fire and diving into the ground. Parachutes everywhere, and MiGs and F-86s mixing it up all over the place. It seemed to go on for a lifetime, but the initial attack had taken only seconds. At last the group commander called me to bring down the 335th into the fight. It was as bad a traffic jam as I have ever experienced in Bangkok, Thailand, as we dove in on the target.

We had to weave our way through LA-9s going in all directions, with MiGs and F-86s in combat at every level. In front of us were the bombers, a beautiful sight as they lumbered in close formation on their last few miles to the target, apparently bombing on the leader. I fired and my bomber immediately started smoking, but it continued on without breaking formation. We pulled straight up off the attack and spotted several LA-9s in front of us. My great wingman, John Honoker, immediately told me I was clear to fire (before I could ask him), meaning that there were no MiGs on my ass. My bullets hit an LA-9. It exploded in a ball of fire. We saw no chute.

We were no longer in squadron formation, but in individual elements of two—our best fighting posture. John and I dove back in on the bombers, or what was left of them. Of the original thirty TU-2s, only six or seven remained. As I dove down firing, my bomber immediately caught on fire, resulting in a mass bailout of the crew. Now I was out of ammunition, so John Honoker would take over the lead on the next attack.

I will never forget my fantastic panoramic view of that enormous air battle as we pulled up from the second attack. The enemy bombers were burning as they fell from the sky. Several LA-9s exploded as I watched, and MiGs were using violent evasive tactics, trying to shake the Sabrejets. Overhead, a MiG fell in a lazy, flat spin. There were parachutes absolutely everywhere, like a mass airdrop of the 82nd Airborne. And the best sight of all. Almost at their "bombs away" point, the last of the remaining bombers were turning back while still under attack. John would have to hurry if he was going to get a kill.

I was still watching the show when John suddenly called me to "break hard!" Then I lost consciousness. I was later told that an LA-9 fighter had made a head-on attack on my F-86, scoring hits on the left wing, penetrating and destroying the canopy, and scoring hits on my headrest. John Honoker immediately attacked and destroyed the LA-9, then followed as my fighter spun earthward in a slow, inverted spin. I was in a hell of a situation.

When I regained consciousness, the earth was spinning and I was being blasted by the freezing air of a cold winter day over North Korea. As I recovered from the spin, I could hear John saying that I had spun in and he had seen no chute. However, he spotted me again as I began a climb back to altitude, and immediately joined on my wing. My helmet had been split open from the cannon shell blast, so I could not transmit on my radio. I could hear John, but no one else. I had to hold one hand over my face to keep the oxygen mask in place. My face and hands were already numb. I was bleeding enough to scare the hell out of me, and was having a hard time concentrating on flying my battle-damaged aircraft home to our base at Kimpo.

If you ever needed a wingman it was then, and John Honoker was the greatest in the world, both in combat and most certainly in the severe emergency that I was now experiencing. We were worried that the MiGs might decide to go after the wounded duck. I was 150 miles into enemy territory and low on fuel (made more serious by the extra drag from the hole in my left wing and the missing canopy). I had one hell of a morale problem. I was freezing and hurting. There was blood on my hands, face, and neck, caused by slivers of Plexiglas from the canopy and fragments from the shell that exploded against my headrest. At that moment everything looked like hell.

John reported that he saw cannon shell damage on top of my fuselage, directly behind the canopy. This immediately got our attention, because the F-86's hydraulic flight control lines are located there. If they were damaged and I lost hydraulic fluid, the flight control system would become inoperative and I would have to bail out. Upon looking back, I was startled to see white cloth streaming out of my parachute pack. The parachute had probably saved my life by shielding me from some of the shrapnel from the cannon shell explosion on my headrest, but now I couldn't bail out. After I made John aware of the problem by looking and pointing, he quickly told me to belly in on the North Korean beach below us, while I still had flight control. He also informed me that air rescue helicopters were on the way.

Unless it's on fire, a pilot does not readily bail out of an aircraft that is still flying under its own power. Moreover, I will admit that I was chicken, as well as being cold and sick at heart. I was afraid that I would do a bad job of landing on a narrow beach under those conditions. So, whether with good sense or not, I proceeded to fly to home base.

After what seemed a lifetime, we were within gliding distance of Kimpo. All aircraft were cleared from the traffic pattern, and crash equipment stood by the runway. I felt like a kid who falls and scuffs his knee, but holds his tears while he runs home to Mommy. Then he lets it all hang out. With the runway straight ahead of me and John on my wing in case of further emergency, I was so relieved that I suddenly wanted to cry.

Then the impossible happened. An unannounced F-86 pulled in only a few feet in front of me with his landing gear down. We were now occupying the same airspace and one of us had to go! Not me. I was the emergency. Both John and the control tower called for the unidentified aircraft to go around immediately, to leave traffic for an emergency aircraft on final approach. The runway jeep fired a red flare at the unknown F-86, but the pilot ignored it. We would soon be landing at the same spot at the same time. In spite of my pains and the doubtful status of my aircraft, I had to pour on full power and go around for another landing. There was a lot of celebrating when I finally touched down, mostly by John Honoker and me.

The unknown F-86 had been flown by one of the great aces of the Korean War and a close friend. He had been returning from the attack on the bombers with his radio out, so he could neither receive nor transmit. Being out of fuel, his engine had flamed out and he was "dead sticking" it in. He could do nothing when the jeep fired that red flare. My friend was following rules of the air that were similar to those at sea. A nonpowered craft has priority over powered craft, and the latter must give way when both are on a converging course. He had no way of knowing the desperate state of my aircraft and no way of announcing his own situation.

Oh, well. We all survived, but it sure was exciting for a while. That was about as much action as you can cram into an hour-and-forty-five-minute flight. How bad off was I? Not bad at all, once I was on the ground. The hydraulic flight control system lines were not cut. My parachute would have supported me in a bailout. My head, neck, and hand wounds were minor. I still had enough fuel for one more go-round, and that was all I needed.

The North Korean Air Force's bomber formations had been devastated when they attempted their only daylight bombing raid of the war, although the thirty TU-2 medium bombers had been escorted by many MiGs and LA-9 fighters. Our F-86s so decimated the Communist bomber formation that they aborted their bomb run just prior to reaching their target. To add insult to injury, more of the bombers had been destroyed before they could reach the safety of China. In addition, a large number of LA-9s and MiGs had been lost.

So here we were, thirty or more big B-29 bombers headed north, just across the line into North Korea, escorted by well over one hundred American and Allied fighters above and on both sides of the formation. Previously the B-29s had been making night attacks on targets in North Korea. Like the fighter-bombers, they had to fly through the most effective antiaircraft gun systems in Asia. However, they had been free from MiG attacks. MiGs didn't operate at night.

Why, then, were the B-29s on a daylight bombing raid? The answer is that they needed the additional accuracy that comes from inserting visual identification points into their bombing computers. Precise accuracy was required, for they were bombing military targets within the Pyongyang city limits, and they wanted to avoid needless civilian casualties. Fighter escort tactics had been worked out jointly with the bomber command. My 335th Squadron was flying to one side, about 5,000 feet above the bomber formation, to block any MiG attacks out of the sun. Just prior to the bomb run, fighter-bombers were scheduled to attack the North Korean AA gun emplacements and their radars in an attempt to knock them out. The plan looked good on paper.

On our northerly heading we had flown outside the range of our own radar, so we could not expect any help from anything but our eyeballs and some intelligence reports as they became available. Many doubted that MiGs would come that far south. These so-called experts would be proved sadly wrong. At last the waiting was over; the MiGs were airborne and proceeding south on a direct line to intercept our bombers. Both B-29 and F-86 pilots spotted the contrails at the same time. At that word our fighter group commander ordered us to drop external fuel tanks and advance our engines to full combat power. We had our best combat pilots and our best aircraft, and we were ready for the MiGs.

The bad news was that there was no air fighting as far

as the F-86s were concerned. Instead, we were helpless observers to a complete disaster as the MiGs attacked the B-29 formation with little interference from us. The MiGs and North Korean antiaircraft guns combined to decimate the bomber formation. After thirty-eight years my memory is very vague on figures, but I believe that twelve of the B-29s were shot down or crash-landed on South Korean airfields, and many more recovered with severe battle damage.

The harrowing story of the American bomber losses was spread all across the U.S. media. It reflected adversely on the survivability of our bomber forces on daylight operations and the credibility of the fighter forces that had been glorified daily for their ever-increasing victories over the MiGs (resulting in new jet fighter aces every other week). It was a period of gloom for us as various U.S. agencies sent specialists to Korea to determine what had happened. General Curtis LeMay, Commander-in-Chief, Strategic Air Command, immediately flew to Korea with a SAC investigative team. Every other "wheel" from U.S. Air Force headquarters, the Tactical Air Command, and the U.S. Navy arrived on the scene to participate in the "wake."

From a SAC perspective, the bombing plan seemed solid. On the surface nothing was wrong with the fighter escort plan. It was obvious that in the minds of the SAC, lack of initiative by the F-86 pilots in a critical combat situation was the most probable cause factor. General LeMay met with us in the briefing room for a round-table discussion of the mission. Round table, hell! We were chewed out for a lousy job. We were crushed. It was a bad day at Black Rock and remained so for many days to come.

However, I have another view of that mission. I am an 8,000-hour fighter pilot with extensive experience in both tactical and air defense operations. I have made hundreds of practice attacks against SAC bombers to train both SAC defensive weapons operators and our fighter pilots in bomber attack techniques. I participated in both the attack against the TU-2 bombers and the escort for the B-29 Pyongyang raid. Without the support of radar surveillance and control, without ECM and communications jamming, without fighters with a decided speed and power advantage over the attackers, the bombers of that day had no option but to stay on the deck and fly only at night.

After completion of my Korean tour I participated in tests in the United States to develop procedures for escorting SAC bombers in combat. Two F-86 squadrons participated, with one squadron acting as escort and the other being the attacker. On each subsequent mission their roles were reversed. Throughout these tests the attacking aircraft could not be stopped by the escorting F-86s. Even today, if you don't have AMMRAM or Phoenix air-to-air missiles, forget it.

The MiGs and F-86s did a great job in air-to-air combat during the Korean War, shooting each other's asses out of the sky. But both types of aircraft were ineffective in a bomber escort role. It's too damned late to fight the air battle in and around the bombers. That's a losing situation. The enemy has to be engaged and fought to a standstill a minimum of a hundred miles in advance of the bombers' target. You need radar surveillance and control for that type of operation, either from shipboard radar or AWACS. They were not available in the Korean War.

The escorting fighters, and the gunners aboard the bombers, could not stop our devastating attack against the North Korean TU-2 bombers. All of them were shot down. Over one hundred Allied fighters could not stop the MiG attack against the B-29s. They were never again used on deep, daylight bombing missions.

The burning and exploding of so many TU-2s, and the picture of the big B-29s falling out of the sky, has left such a deep impression on my mind that I can't put those scenes away once and for all. I will say it again. Surely we know today that bombers can't survive in daylight operations in an environment where the fighter interceptors have superior speed and weapons system advantage over the bombers. The bomber crews have enough to do just trying to survive the enemy's ground defenses.

I flew escort for North American RB-45 and Lockheed RF-80 recce aircraft on deep reconnaissance missions to the Yalu River. Again we were helpless to stop determined MiG attacks against them. When threatened by MiGs, the RB-45 would go to maximum power and run off, leaving both the MiGs and the F-86 escort behind. MiGs had an overtake speed advantage when they dove to attack from altitude. Under our weight conditions we were underpowered and not capable of catching anyone. It was both humorous and embarrassing when the RB-45 pilot asked us what we were going to do about the MiG coming in on his tail. If we didn't have a good answer, he would take off and leave us all behind. Like the F-86s, the RF-80s could jettison fuel tanks, split-S, and run for it if attacked.

Contrary to the tactics manuals, I found the best escort position to be squarely behind your bomber or recce aircraft, so that the attacking MiG had to fly by you. He usually was so intent on shooting at the bigger target that he never bothered with you. From that position you could slide in behind him as he went by, then shoot his ass out of the sky or run him off by threatening a midair collision. Oh, well. I was only one of thousands of combat air tactics experts who all seemed to be in Korea at the same time.

The story of one of the saddest events in my entire fighter pilot life requires some introduction. Early in my Korean tour I had completed my 4th Fighter Group indoctrination training and had flown several combat missions, all milk runs with no MiGs seen. I was scheduled to fly my first combat element lead on an early morning mission in a formation being led by Colonel J. C. Meyers, 4th Fighter Group Commander (later Commander-in-Chief, Strategic Air Command). Our group formation consisted of six F-86 aircraft. In those early days the group was critically short of fighter assets, so those six F-

86s represented the total combat resources available for a mission to provide cover for a fighter-bomber strike.

We had crossed the bomb line into North Korea when one of our pilots reported that he had a rough engine. Meyers ordered him to return to home base and, in accordance with our long-standing rule of not flying alone in combat, his wingman went with him. Now we had four aircraft. As we approached MiG Alley, we saw numerous MiG contrails, so Colonel Meyers gave the order to jettison external fuel tanks. But one of the colonel's tanks wouldn't jettison. The F-86 cannot engage in combat maneuvers with the MiG, with one tank still attached. Colonel Meyers told me to continue on to MiG Alley; he was returning to home base. The colonel's wingman escorted him out of the area, leaving two of us as the total group escort effort.

There were twelve to fourteen MiGs overhead and, with superiority in numbers, they lost no time in diving to attack. For the next thirty minutes we fought them as best we could with our two fighters. We shot at the MiGs and they shot at us with no one hitting anyone. However, we kept them fully occupied that morning, and none were able to attack the fighter-bomber formations. Mission accomplished.

That was to be the modus operandi throughout my combat tour. Regardless of how outnumbered we were, our primary job was to prevent the MiGs from attacking the fighter-bombers and other American and Allied air operations. We could not do that by maintaining a safe, defensive posture while on combat patrol. The MiGs could have easily flown around our formation to the Allied mission aircraft. We attacked the MiGs, broke up their formations, shot them down, ran them out of fuel—anything to keep them occupied so that they couldn't attack anyone.

Later, when we were able to read some of the Allied listening station reports, we laughed to see the MiGs reporting flights of ten F-86s as a hundred F-86s, attacking them from all directions. With some exceptions this was to be their pattern—break and run when attacked by F-86s and report that they had been outnumbered ten or twenty to one. Great! Mission accomplished.

Ten months after that first encounter I was leading six F-86s of my 335th Fighter Squadron on a combat mission. One of my element leaders was a very senior and experienced fighter pilot who was flying his initial combat missions with each of the 4th Group's three squadrons, to gain MiG-fighting experience prior to taking command of a combat wing. He hadn't seen MiGs on any previous missions, and I had guaranteed him that I would find MiGs today.

We entered MiG Alley and, as advertised, dead ahead of us was a formation of forty enemy fighters. We dropped our fuel tanks and charged full throttle into the middle of the MiGs, scattering them all over the sky as they broke formation in panic. One of our pilots was able to destroy or damage a MiG, but the majority of them fled back across the Yalu River to China. Intelligence later reported that the MiG pilots told their ground commander that they were under attack by a large force of F-86s and had been forced to withdraw from the area.

During our attack I had suddenly become aware that our senior pilot wasn't with us. I had called him at once and he replied that he was okay, so we continued to pursue the enemy fighters. I was feeling fine about the results of the mission when I returned to base. However, once on the ground I was called to wing headquarters, and instead of being congratulated was told that I was relieved from command of my beloved 335th Fighter Squadron for displaying reckless leadership in attacking a force of forty MiGs with only six Sabrejets, thereby endangering the safety of our pilots and aircraft. I was shattered.

I spent three miserable days sitting around, wondering what was coming next. Fortunately the matter was quickly resolved when it was determined that I had been following correct 4th Fighter Wing combat directives to always attack. It was with great relief that I again assumed command of the 335th Fighter Squadron. The senior pilot became one of our most aggressive senior commanders and we became the best of friends.

On a more happy note, during one of my final combat missions I reported to our group leader that I was directly below a formation of thirty MiGs heading north, returning to their home base at Sinuiju. He told me to look them over for markings or insignia that would help identify any of the East European combat units rumored to be flying with the North Koreans and Chinese. We had already been in a big fight, so everyone but my wingman and I were headed home. We were out of ammunition but had plenty of fuel. Our plan was to get as close as possible for a look, but be ready to run for it if they turned to attack us.

The next events were amazing. The MiGs were flying in a V of elements on both sides of their leader. It reminded me of a great formation of geese heading north. We pulled into the center of the formation behind the leader. We looked at them and they looked at us, and nothing happened. They held formation as good Communist pilots do. We were so close that I could see that the pilots were not wearing helmets or oxygen masks like American or Allied fighter pilots. We were so excited that we almost forgot to look at the markings on the MiGs which identified them as a North Korean squadron just entering their combat phase. We finally broke off and headed for home.

The F-86s won air superiority over MiG Alley and maintained it for the rest of the Korean War. Our American pilots will always feel that we own that piece of real estate. For me, it represented everything a fighter pilot dreams of. My Korean tour was a steady stream of exciting and amazing events—the unmatched thrill of shooting down an enemy aircraft, and the excitement of being shot at and taking your F-86 through impossible maneuvers to escape. I attribute my success to my pilots, and especially my wingmen (the finest in the business), like John Honoker and Sam. We had the greatest ground crews. Rick Johnson, my operations officer, was the best.

Yes, contrary to the Pan American captain's description of his job as being thousands of hours of utter boredom broken by occasional panic, I would say that my Korean War tour involved hours and hours of flying and fighting broken by occasional milk runs. It was a great life.

GUNNERY

Major William Wescott had flown close-support bombing missions in the Aleutians and the Pacific in World War II, then served as a gunnery instructor at Nellis Air Force Base prior to requesting assignment to Korea. In one month there he destroyed five MiGs and damaged two others. This is a story about combat flying, but also about the performance of men and machines under stress.

I had served during the occupation of Japan in 1946 and 1947, and my arrival at K-13 was accompanied by odors reminiscent of my earlier arrival in Japan. It gave me a sort of "homey" feeling. I was assigned to Group Operations and attached for flying with the 25th Fighter Interceptor Squadron (FIS). The squadron was commanded by Major Bill Whisner, who had scored sixteen kills with the Eighth Air Force during World War II. "Whiz" directed Captain Kurt Utterback, squadron executive officer, to show me around the outfit and give me a command briefing. Kurt was outstanding. His personal attention was a great help in understanding the nature of the beast we were up against.

Captain John Heard, squadron operations officer, was given the job of "wet-nursing" me through a local checkout and ten combat missions. My first encounter with the enemy was observing two or three cannon balls going by my canopy while I was flying wing on John. Two MiGs were sitting on our tail at a range of about 600 feet. We shook the MiGs with a hard downward break—about ten Gs—followed by a rolling pull-up. They had missed a great opportunity. It was obvious that they didn't know gunnery.

After a series of combat air patrols (CAPS, but not to be confused with the CAP set up for downed pilots) I was elevated to the status of flight commander.

April 1952 was a month of significant activity. I shot down five MiGs, including two double victories. Much credit for those victories, and my successes during a twenty-six-and-a-half-year career as an engineering test pilot has to go to the crew chiefs, armorers, electronic technicians, and specialists who maintained my aircraft. In combat I never experienced a problem that led to an abort. My guns never failed to fire, except for a few jams in the A-20 (six nose-mounted M-1 .50s).

In Korea my F-86's guns were accurately harmonized with the gunsight. They never jammed or failed to fire. However, after several long bursts, a "cook-off" might occur about five minutes after firing. Cook-offs were caused by temperature buildup in the gun bay. This caused the powder in a shell to explode/fire. Most likely the cook-off occurred in one of the top two guns, the ones closest to the pilot's head, and the unexpected sound could cause a physical reflex action on the part of the pilot.

A different sort of unexpected event happened during a cover mission for the 8th Fighter Group. Just north of Pyongyang at about 40,000-foot altitude, my canopy released from the closed position. This caused "explosive decompression." My oxygen mask actually moved away from my face for an instant, but I immediately felt the effect, secured it, and selected pressure breathing. The event lasted only about four seconds, and I was alert and completely conscious throughout. Aside from a day-long headache, the only anomaly was that my entire visual world contained polka dots. I found myself trying to look around them for MiGs.

Credit for one of my first two MiGs destroyed must go to Captain Bill Craig, who was one of the most dedicated and loyal air force officers/pilots I knew. We had already served together at Nellis for several years. His flying skill and air discipline allowed me to gain advantage on the MiG and shoot it down. It happened this way. We had just broken off a successful attack when I observed a MiG closing on Bill's tail. I told him to break right. This caused both of them to turn away from me. I followed them in the turn for a few seconds, then told Bill to break left. This gave me the position to close on the MiG and shoot it down.

During the same engagement I had the opportunity to fly alongside a MiG and observe the pilot. The pilot was either dead, or seriously injured and unconscious, slumped forward in the seat. I thought that I could see long hair, like a woman's. The pilot wore a tan jacket similar to a parka without a hood.

The second time I got twin kills was almost a disaster

from the onset because of a complete breakdown in air discipline. Our flight consisted of four F-86s in a "fluid four" formation. We were still climbing to our patrol altitude when a flight of four or more MiGs hit us on our tail. Each pilot covers the other's tail, visually scanning the hemisphere. The element covering the tail of the two of us in the lead (my wingman and I) obviously didn't see the MiGs. After looking over my shoulder and seeing them, I called a break. We still had fuel in our external wing tanks. My accelerometer showed that I had exceeded the limit load factor during the break maneuver, and the force ripped the tanks off the wings.

Later my wingman overshot his position and came into my line of fire. He was relatively new, and definitely inexperienced, and moved in front of me as I was firing. He was looking at the target rather than trying to maintain his assigned position. After the first burst the MiG slowed considerably and I had to throttle back and extend the speed brakes to maintain a good firing position. That was when my wingman screwed up. Fortunately he wasn't hit and was able to resume his proper position.

The F-86's ability to take high-G loads is important. It was designed for 7.0 G, maximum in a clean configuration. Also, it was built to withstand 1.5 times the maximum G as a safety factor. So it was basically a 10.5 G aircraft. Although it might be overstressed, it wouldn't come apart. With tanks on and containing fuel, the aircraft was slightly tail heavy. Applying full elevator along with about one-half aileron caused what is called "dynamic overshoot." If nose-up trim was applied along with hard back-stick movement, extreme pitch-up rates would occur, resulting in dynamic overshoot. This quickly changed the direction of the fighter away from the MiG's potential line of fire.

Being able to get maximum performance from an aircraft in combat required using maximum energy climb and cruise. This means flying at a speed high enough to be able to pull maximum G without getting into a stall buffet. At 25,000 feet and higher, the aircraft's ability to turn and maneuver was limited by Mach effect. The air over the wings and control surfaces reached supersonic speed, accompanied by an increase in dynamic pressure (compressibility). This caused the effective power of the controls to be reduced and wing buffet to occur at lower pitch angles. This decreased performance increased the possibility of being shot down if an enemy happened to get on your tail.

The F-86 had an advantage over the different brands of MiGs I encountered in Korea. It could outdive them. Being lighter, the MiG could outclimb the F-86. It could also turn tighter at high altitude. The maneuvering and control characteristics of the F-86Es and F-86Fs were possible through the irreversible hydraulic flight control system that controlled the combination horizontal stabilizer and elevator, and the ailerons. The dive characteristics of the F-86 were used to great advantage against the MiG. The F-86 was able to attain a higher Mach number in a dive. In addition, the MiG could not pull as much G as the F-86. At the higher Mach number, while pulling more G, the F-86 could convert airspeed to altitude (pull up into a climb) and regain maneuvering superiority over the MiG. This was possible from about 25,000 feet and below. Most MiG pilots wouldn't even try to follow the F-86 in a dive from high altitude.

The dive characteristics of the F-86E provided the pilot with the confidence that he could dive away from a fight and the MiG would be unable to get him. This played a major role in the action that resulted in my fifth victory.

Midmorning on April 26, 1952, I was on duty in Group Operations when Captain Al Moorman, 36th FIS, walked up to my desk. "Let's get a mission from JOC. I know the MiGs are up over the Yalu," he said.

I replied, "Okay, Al," and called JOC for a two-flight sweep south of the river.

We received a frag order for the mission and Al departed for the sweep with a four-ship flight from the 36th FIS. I called the 25th Squadron and set up a four-ship flight for me. We took off about ten minutes behind Al's flight and headed for a point about sixty miles east of Antung. This would give us a slight advantage, with the sun behind us, as we turned west and paralleled the Yalu at a 38,000-foot altitude. We neared the west coast, performed a left 180-degree turn, and headed east about thirty miles south of the river.

The exercise had so far cost Al about twenty minutes of patrol time, dragging wing tanks at high Mach number. As we reached our turn point, about sixty miles east of Antung, he called out "bingo" (minimum fuel remaining). No sooner had he said these words when "many cons" (contrails) appeared over Antung. At least eighty MiGs had climbed into the tropopause (the origination of a layer in the atmosphere where the heated exhaust from a jet engine leaves a visible contrail). A few seconds after that my element leader called bingo and headed for K-13. I asked my wingman, Captain John Mackey, if he could stay with me. "Affirmative." We proceeded to engage the wily MiG.

Based on their formation, the group of MiGs were probably undergoing crew training. We jettisoned external fuel tanks. I positioned myself below "tail end Charlie" and started a slow climb, trying to hold the highest possible speed. I finally got in firing position at a range in excess of 3,000 feet, at close to a 43,000-foot altitude. At no time did John concentrate on the target. He was busy clearing our tail. I, too, had my head "on a swivel," clearing John.

Immediately after the second firing burst John called out MiGs coming in at eight o'clock. "Okay, let's call it a day and head home." I rolled nose down, increasing speed to .95 Mach number while descending to about 25,000 feet. When we were convinced that there were no MiGs on our tail, we climbed to 38,000 feet and continued to K-13. We started our letdown for a landing a few miles north of K-14.

At the debriefing I asked John if he had observed my hits on the MiG. He said that he hadn't. He was totally occupied clearing our tail. Exactly right; he did his job perfectly. Without his verification I submitted a damage claim, pending gun-camera film assessment. The next morning, while shuffling papers in Group Operations, I received a phone call from our group gunnery officer. He said, "Congratulations, ace." I thought he was kidding and didn't appreciate the joke. He insisted, however, and told me that Colonel Gabreski and Colonel Shinz had viewed my gun-camera film. It showed the MiG pilot bailing out. I hadn't seen that during the engagement.

I previously mentioned "brands of MiGs." Of course, some of their aircraft were painted blue, and others were unpainted, but here "brand" means variation in performance—higher speed and increased climb capability.

Once I encountered a flight of four taking off at Field X. My wingman and I were descending through 15,000 feet, closing on the flight at an airspeed of 500 knots. As we were closing into firing range dead on their tail, the two elements split. The lead element pulled up and to the left, and the second element pulled up and to the right. We were closer to the second element and pursued it. The element lead broke down, continuing the hard turn to the right. I followed, but could not get close enough. Then I saw a MiG getting into position on my wingman and broke off, telling him to break left. As I pulled around to engage the second MiG, he pulled up sharply and headed north. I told my wingman to break right and call when he had me in sight. We joined up and headed for K-13.

Several other encounters with the MiG convinced me that they not only had models with better performance ("super MiGs"), but that experienced pilots were flying them. In some cases their tactics (as a flight of four) were equal to or better than our own.

Before I assumed command of the 39th FIS, while I was still assigned to Group Operations, I became friends with a young first lieutenant. He was a religious man who neither drank liquor nor smoked. We talked about many things, including combat tactics and rules of combat. One afternoon, while I was standing outside Group Operations and talking with some fighter pilots, the young lieutenant came up to me with tears in his eyes. His closest friend had been assigned to fly a wing position, and had left the flight of his own volition to attack a MiG. Apparently he didn't see the other MiGs, because he was shot down before his flight commander could help him. I hated to do it, but I told the lieutenant that his friend had asked for it by leaving the formation. His friend had violated a cardinal rule of combat flying. The young lieutenant found this hard to swallow, but he became an outstanding fighter pilot. I ran into him a few years later. He was the commander of a special operations squadron and held the rank of bird colonel.

Another pilot, who was shipped to Korea and assigned to the 51st, lacked adequate training for air combat. A flight commander in my squadron reported that Lieutenant "A" had spun out of a turn at high altitude. He was also very poor at maintaining his position in the fluid-four formation while the formation was maneuvering. Further, it was reported that he would lose the formation, thus becoming single, and then proceed back to base, a very dangerous thing to do. I flew with "A" several times and had some discussions with him. The result was that I recommended him for combat-crew training at Luke or Nellis, which he received. He apparently did quite well, because he later became a fighter squadron commander.

All air action in Korea was not dogfights against MiGs. Lieutenant Ivan Kinchloe downed several Yak-9s and shot up a locomotive after a patrol on the Yalu. Another type of mission was reconnaissance of airfields to count the MiGs parked on them. I was assigned a recce mission on Antung one evening. Lieutenant Kinchloe was my wingman.

Arriving over Antung, we found the airfield overcast by coastal fog. The fog layer ended about ten miles inland, so we proceeded visually to line up with the airfield and let down from the top of the fog layer, about twelve miles north of the field. The fog layer was about 500-feet thick, with a base about

200 feet above the ground. We were holding 400 KIAS (knots indicated air speed), heading toward the Yellow Sea. I was level, about 100 feet above the runway, when I noted a pile of blue and silver-tone metal on my left. On my right were several revetments, each holding a parked MiG. At the far end of the runway were several batteries of guns, probably .50s and 40mms. You could see the orange color of the muzzle blasts clearly, since the light was quite low. More gun batteries opened up on the right. This was expected, because they would have received plenty of advance notice of our arrival from their radar sites.

The sightseeing tour ended abruptly when a 40mm shell hit my aircraft. It exploded at the base of the armor plate glass windshield at the left support structure. I was stunned, but instinctively pulled up. Not realizing that I had put some +G on the aircraft, I felt light-headed and thought I was "transitioning" from life to death. Suddenly I was aware of a receding overcast and a dark blue sky. The aircraft was in a normal high-speed climb, only a few degrees right of course for K-13. I couldn't see forward through the windshield, but I could see that the combining glass for my gunsight was missing. I found it on the seat, between my legs. It had been restrained by the heavy webbing of my parachute's leg straps. There was a hole in the lower left side of the canopy which allowed ice cold air into the cockpit. Maximum heat and pressure helped reduce the effect since there was no outflow exit hole, and the cockpit's airflow valve remained closed. I had a small cut on the little finger of my left hand, probably from the glass.

Shortly after arriving on top of the fog layer, "Kinch" asked if I was okay. I said, "Affirmative," but added that he should lead and I would fly his wing. He rogered the lead and said in typical Kinchloe verbology, "Jeez, Major I thought you had it." Well, at the time so did I.

Our flight back was uneventful. We had sufficient fuel to return at low altitude (25,000 feet), and I had enough oxygen left to stay one hundred percent. Pure oxygen lessens the effect of low atmospheric pressure. On entering final approach for landing we switched lead and Kinch gave me a poor man's version of a ground-controlled approach (GCA).

A final vignette about oxygen. During a sweep near Antung my wingman got lost and returned to K-13. I became engaged in a fight that resulted in neither the MiG (another super MiG) nor my gaining a significant advantage before he left. Starting at 40,000 feet and using one hundred percent oxygen in preference to Normal, our dogfight terminated at about 500 feet above the ground. I headed for K-13, cleared my tail, and abruptly stopped breathing. This happens when you select the one hundred percent position on your oxygen regulator and use up all the oxygen. The reason is that the regulator is designed to stop the inflow of cockpit air while it provides the pilot with pure oxygen, a desirable function when the cockpit air is contaminated.

An additional problem became apparent. Having 600 pounds of fuel remaining for a flight of 200 miles meant that I would have to head for maximum attainable altitude, cut the engine and glide, and restart the engine if needed. I knew that the quickest way to pass out when oxygen was reduced was to perform physical acts such as looking around to check the six o'clock position. Therefore, I decided to loosen the straps, lean back, and relax, and exert as little physical effort as possible. If I was jumped by a MiG, I could tell by the hits on my aircraft. I would then pull power off, pop the speed brake, put the aircraft into a wind-up diving spiral, eject at the right altitude, and delay opening the chute until about 1,000 feet above the ground.

An F-86F with no external stores, no ammunition, and only 600 pounds of fuel remaining is very lightweight, and will double or triple its normal-weight rate of climb. At 39,000 feet I cut the engine and held best glide speed (about 185 KIAS). Cabin pressure decreased with the engine off and steadily climbed to about 29,000 feet cabin altitude. Continuing to glide, I arrived over K-13 at about 7,000 feet and air-started the engine. After landing and taxiing to the revetment, there were about 100 to 200 pounds of fuel remaining.

It is difficult to end a document such as this. There are so many events that will remain untold. There were many contributors to the success enjoyed by the 51st. So many of their names and contributions will forever remain unknown.

KIMPO (K-14)

Captain Bill Lilley had seen Kimpo Air Base in 1947, but the field had changed when he returned in 1952. This story covers the types of missions Lilley's unit flew from that bustling field and two of his victories, one against a pilot with blond hair, the other against a "lone eagle" attacker.

I arrived in Korea on June 5, 1952, seven years to the day that I graduated from West Point. I had 1,800 hours flying time, most of it in fighters, including one hundred hours in jets and forty in F-86s. I was assigned to the 334th Fighter Squadron of the 4th Fighter Interceptor Wing at Kimpo Air Base, not far from Seoul.

Kimpo and Korea were familiar sights because I had flown border patrol along the 38th parallel with the 8th Fighter Group back in 1947. The Far East Air Forces rotated this duty among the fighter groups stationed in Japan on occupation duty, and four P-51s were the only USAF combat aircraft allowed in country at any one time. Our job was to fly along the parallel and count the aircraft on North Korean airfields. The count was unbelievably high—very sobering indeed. A single airfield at Haeju had over two hundred conventional fighters parked so that they covered the place, leaving hardly any room for takeoffs and landings. These aircraft were, of course, among those that made the first strikes in 1950 at the start of the "police action."

Kimpo (now K-14) was a startling contrast to what I had known in 1947. Formerly very quiet, very peaceful, the increase in the level of activity was at once noticeable. Aircraft filled the skies, taxiways, revetments, and parking areas, coming and going. Aircraft everywhere—a wing of F-86s, a squadron of Royal Australian Air Force Meteors, a photo reconnaissance squadron. Being the closest airfield to the front lines meant that a variety of aircraft returning from combat missions was always landing, either for fuel or from battle damage. The operations terminal remained, proudly bearing scars from that initial attack back in 1950. The dust was the same, gray and choking, only now there was more of it. And it was hot—the sticky, humid kind of hot that was only temporarily cooled by a refreshing shower. But all these matters were quickly overlooked for the prospect of once again flying F-86s and actually having the opportunity to fly them against the MiG-15.

One week later, after five training flights in the local area, I flew my first combat mission in number-four position in a flight of four F-86s escorting a marine Banshee on a photo-reconnaissance mission along the Yalu. The mission lasted one hour and thirty minutes and, though we saw nary a MiG, it was an enormously eventful moment in my life up to that point.

In the summer of 1952 the war had stabilized with the frontlines roughly along the 38th parallel. Our area of operations was from the base at K-14, two hundred nautical miles north to the Yalu River (the boundary between North Korea and China). We operated mostly along the western coast of Korea, sometimes in the middle and extreme northern part of the peninsula, but rarely on the eastern coast. The most active MiG bases were in Manchuria, near the mouth of the Yalu, where it emptied into the Yellow Sea.

Our basic fighting unit was a flight of four aircraft in fingertip formation. We might send several flights of four on a mission, but they rarely flew together. Large gaggles had been tried in the first engagements between MiGs and Sabres and had been found to be unnecessary. They were too cumbersome and reduced flexibility. Under attack the four-ship flight would often break down into two elements of two aircraft each, the lead aircraft firing, the wingman clearing. The wingman was our unsung hero. This was tough duty that required the utmost in flying skill and discipline.

We had learned early in jet aerial warfare that when a target was sighted, one simply could not lose that target from sight, or the chances were excellent that it would disappear from view. In other words, you could not check the target, concentrate on the gunnery problem at hand, and clear yourself at the same time. Things moved too quickly. A system evolved as follows. When the leader sighted a target, he called out, "I'm padlocked!" This told the wingman that no one was clearing the element's tail but him.

The wingman immediately replied, "You're clear."

The leader would repeat, "I'm padlocked!"

With his head on a swivel, straining to be sure that no one was closing on them, the wingman would repeat "You're clear" every few seconds. Through the most violent maneuvers—tight spirals, high-G turns, half loops—the wingman had to follow, not losing his leader, doing all this and looking to his rear. I lost a MiG once when my wingman didn't reply to my call of "padlocked." He was there, but was so excited that he didn't hear the call. When a wingman doesn't answer, a quick chill settles in, and you're certain that he's been zapped by the bad guys. A quick look—he's there. A return to target—it's gone. It's hard to believe that a target could disappear that quickly, but it's true. Milliseconds counted.

The absolute minimum number of aircraft that were allowed to remain in the sensitive area was two, an element. Should a leader and his wingman become separated for any reason, both were to head for the coast and effect a rendezvous. If they rejoined, fuel permitting, they could reenter the area. If they were unable to find each other, they both returned to base. This was the absolute rule, at least in our squadron, and it was responsible for our low loss record while still scoring as highly as the other squadrons. We lost one pilot to MiGs, one who swooped down from a daisy chain and was gone before anyone saw him. Our pilot was recovered from a prison camp after the war. I think it is safe to say that the majority of those shot down were alone in the area, concentrating on firing at a target and unable to clear themselves properly, the wingman or leader having been lost. Had all Sabre pilots adhered to our rule, the ratio of Sabre versus MiG kills would have been even higher than it was.

We flew fighter sweeps, photo-reconnaissance cover, fighter-bomber cover, and alert scrambles, all with the four-ship flight as a basic formation. On fighter sweeps a flight of four would be assigned to a certain sector, usually along the

Yalu, to patrol and prevent the MiGs from penetrating into North Korea to interrupt our air operations. This was a popular mission, much coveted by our pilots. Great flexibility was allowed in this task and most MiG kills were on this type of mission.

Photo recce escorts were another matter. They were not as popular. In fact, they were very hard work if you were escorting a slower RF-80 (we also escorted the equally slow marine Banshee and the faster RF-86). Photo recce escorts required the close cover to scissor over the RF for the entire flight. One flight of four was assigned close cover, and could leave the RF under no circumstances. Additional flights were assigned medium cover (generally 5,000 feet above the RF) and occasionally there was a high flight 5,000 feet above the medium cover.

At the first sign of MiGs, the two higher flights departed to engage them prior to their contact with the RF. This left the close cover with their hands full—responsible for the safe return of the photo recce plane and its pilot. We didn't particularly like the close-cover role, especially with a swirling dogfight raging all around. But discipline was good. We stayed with the RFs and never lost a single one. I shudder to think what would have happened if we had. In fact, we never even let one get damaged.

The fighter-bomber cover missions were not as restrictive as photo recce escorts. We usually stayed high while the fighter-bombers were hitting their targets. We kept them in sight and were prepared to attack any MiGs attempting to attack them. We had learned not to get too close to fighter-bombers unless they were under attack. The reason was simple. Fighter-bombers fired at anything with a swept wing that came close to them. They were not long on aircraft recognition, and "better safe than sorry" was their byword. I really can't blame them, although MiGs seldom got to the fighter-bombers unless they were working close to the Yalu. Again, a relatively popular mission.

Alert scrambles were another matter. Generally we stationed four aircraft at the end of the runway, fully armed and ready to go at a moment's notice. We usually were not scrambled unless MiGs were already interfering with certain of our mission objectives. Many days we waited in vain and were never scrambled. Other days we barely had the aircraft in place before we received word to go. Once airborne, the mission complexion was much more like a fighter sweep, but directly under the control of our ground-based radar operators.

A word about the F-86, truly the Cadillac of fighters in its day. That was a first-rate aircraft. I never met a fighter pilot who didn't want to fly an F-86. It was fast, had an excellent flight-control system, and efficient, accurate armament. Maintenance was superb. We were most fortunate to have support facilities and dedicated personnel that allowed us to do our job so well over North Korean skies. The MiG was a worthy adversary, but was flown by pilots who lacked our training and discipline. Some of them were exceptional pilots. Most were not.

September 14, 1952. Another hot day. Our squadron was scheduled to escort an RF-80 on a photo reconnassiance mission to the Sui Ho Dam on the Yalu River. The briefing in Group Operations was routine. We might expect to see MiGs. Be alert. Be sure and bring the photo recce bird back safely. Fortunately my flight was assigned to one of the medium cover positions. My wingman was to be Squadron Leader Eric Smith, a Canadian exchange officer who had flown night Intruder missions against the Germans in World War II. Absolutely fearless, and with superb flying skills, he was a joy to be with both on the ground and in the air.

We were the third flight to take off, and our climb to altitude and flight to the Sui Ho were uneventful. Upon reaching the dam, with cameras whirling the RF pilot turned left and started down the south shore of the Yalu River, photographing the airfields at Uiju and Sinuiju. Four flights of four (sixteen F-86s) were providing an aluminum umbrella for the subsonic RF-80—one flight high and weaving, two flights medium (also weaving), and one flight close, scissoring.

Suddenly a rash of MiGs struck from across the river. The top flight became engaged immediately and a high-pitched babble of voices on the radio attracted other F-86s in the area. Now a full-fledged battle evolved. Aircraft heading in every direction—down, up, left, right—filled the sky. It was difficult to tell MiG from Sabre. It seemed that everyone was shooting at somebody. Watching all this and still trying to keep the RF-80 in view, I sighted a lone MiG behind an F-86 firing his cannon and getting hits. I yelled for the 86 to break, but my call was probably blocked by the high saturation on that particular channel.

A short dive to the right and Eric and I closed directly behind the MiG as it continued to fire. I fired at 1,000 feet, putting a strong burst up the MiG's tailpipe. This caused an explosion in his engine compartment. Fire streaked along the outside of his fuselage. The MiG was breaking up. Debris from his aircraft began to hurtle past us, but we were lucky enough not to suck any of this junk into our airscoops. Despite all of this, the MiG continued straight and level, still firing at the F-86 ahead of him.

I gave the MiG another burst just as the turbulence from his jet wash raised my aircraft ever so slightly so that my tracers traveled along the top of the MiG's fuselage. Simultaneously the MiG pilot ejected and I observed strikes on his seat. The seat must have malfunctioned in some way, because it barely cleared his aircraft, rocked forward momentarily, and then flipped over backward so that it passed immediately over my canopy, inches from my head, with the pilot still in the seat, upside down. Only a flash, but a shock of blond hair and a wildly contorted face were instantly burned into my memory. I can still see that face today. No parachute was sighted, and I was queried many times about the pilot's shock of blond hair—very unusual but true. Mission number 45; victory number 3.

MiG pilots were totally unpredictable tactically. We saw

every imaginable maneuver, from four ships diving line abreast, all firing cannon simultaneously, to the daisy chain of several MiGs circling high above us with an occasional Lone Eagle swooping down on our flights for a quick firing pass then pulling back up into the daisy chain. We met and terminated such a Lone Eagle on November 18, 1952.

The mission of our squadron that day was to be part of a fighter sweep along the Chongchon River which was fifty miles south of the Yalu. Fighter-bombers were working the bridges just south of the Chongchon, and our job was to keep the MiGs from interfering with their work. Our flight of four F-86s was slightly delayed in making our takeoff time, and consequently was the last to leave K-14. At that time I was operations officer of the 334th Fighter Interceptor Group and was leading the flight. Lieutenant Danzer was my wingman; Captain Pete Fernandez was leading the element with Captain Merlin Mitchell on his wing.

Shortly after takeoff we switched to our combat radio channel and heard excited chatter from flights ahead of us that had been attacked by MiGs as soon as they had reached the Chongchon. We continued to climb to our assigned altitude of 38,000 feet, punched off our external wing tanks, checked guns by firing a short burst, and began a shallow dive toward the river, building our speed to the Mach. We strained for signs of the fight but saw nothing.

Suddenly, and now I am speaking of microseconds, a MiG—apparently a Lone Eagle who had recently vacated our altitude—dived on a flight below us, firing his cannon all the way. He pulled up from his pass and arrived back at our altitude almost at a stall, certainly at a very low airspeed. We were closing at an enormous rate of speed, and popping up directly ahead was this target practically at a standstill. The distance between us flashed to no distance. I squeezed the trigger, almost no burst at all, a snap-shot at best, but it probably saved my life. That brief burst hit him in his fuel tank, causing an internal explosion that rocked the MiG violently to the right just as I rocketed over his wing. All this in a second or two from first sighting him. My heart had never hammered harder.

I looked back and saw him commence a long spiral earthward, belching a trail of white smoke that hung in the sky until he hit the ground. The trail of white smoke, like a white, milky corkscrew, stayed in the sky for some time, a rare sight indeed.

Finishing a fight with an abundance of fuel and a practically full load of ammunition was a new experience for me. Normally our flights back to K-14 after a fight involved critically low fuel levels and zero ammunition. But on this day things had happened so quickly we were more than prepared for additional encounters. None came. The MiGs had had their fill and retired north of the Yalu. After patrolling down to "bingo," our call sign for a safe withdrawal fuel level, we commenced an uneventful trip back to K-14. Later the armorers informed me that 180 of the 1,800 rounds aboard had been expended in that short burst. The gun-camera film, as might be expected, was very short in length but exceptional in its clarity. One could see the rivets in the MiG as I flew by. All in all, a most eventful day—one less Lone Eagle and a moment in time never to be forgotten.

—THE—
VIETNAM
WAR

The United States used many different types of aircraft during the Vietnam War, but the majority of victories were claimed by variations of the F-4 Phantom. Because the cold war philosophy of the 1950s had stressed technology over conventional hardware, the Phantoms went into combat without machine guns or cannon, relying instead on radar-guided and heat-seeking missiles. Dogfighting techniques had also been neglected as outmoded. The Americans faced MiG-17s, MiG-19s, and MiG-21s armed with 23mm and 37mm cannon and piloted by men schooled in dogfighting. The results were a forgone conclusion. The sophisticated electronics systems on board the fighters failed too often, as did the missiles themselves. If something went wrong with the electronics or missiles, a pilot had no backup gunnery system.

The air-to-air tactics deficiency was addressed when the navy founded its famous "Top Gun" school. The "no guns" problem wasn't corrected until very late in the conflict, but the lessons weren't forgotten. All American fighter planes are now equipped with both missiles and guns.

Our pilots over Vietnam overcame these handicaps, in addition to the hazards of dense, multilayered antiaircraft defenses and ground-controlled enemy fighters, to achieve a more than two-to-one superiority over the Communists. Two U.S. pilots, one navy and one air force, became aces. Randy Cunningham's story follows.

FOX TWO!

Lieutenant Randall "Duke" Cunningham is one of only two American aces from the Vietnam War, and the only navy ace of that conflict. He flew jets without guns, while his North Vietnamese opponents had cannon and plenty of opportunities to use them. This is a gut-wrenching story about flying against the most sophisticated antiaircraft defenses in the history of warfare—against SAMs, radar-guided cannon, and a variety of MiGs.

During the 1965–68 period of air combat over North Vietnam, the navy's kill-to-loss ratio was 2.42 to 1, while the air force came out slightly behind with 2.25 to 1. This simply means that we barely managed to down two MiGs for every fighter we lost. During the second major air combat period, in 1972, the navy's kill ratio soared to 12 to 1, and the air force ratio actually dropped to 1.88 to 1. There are clear reasons for this disparity.

Through the end of the Korean War and a bit beyond, air combat maneuvering (formerly dogfighting, hasseling, red-dogging) was as much a part of fighter-pilot training as were guns mounted in the aircraft. In the late 1950s, however, the concept evolved in western air forces that missiles would replace guns in aerial combat. The next war was supposed to be fought with ICBMs and long-range bombers, and the projected need in fighter aircraft would be for fast, high-flying interceptors armed with missiles and sophisticated radar. The enemy would be hunted on the scope, and the pilot would never see the target aircraft. Thus were born the ideas which produced the F-4 Phantom II, the F-106 Delta Dart, and other fighter-interceptors of the era.

Because of these concepts, the first American air offensive over North Vietnam, Operation Rolling Thunder, was a painful slap in the face to both the U.S. Navy and Air Force. From 1965 through 1968 we shot down 110 MiGs in aerial combat, but lost forty-eight of our own fighters. The 2.29 to 1 ratio was a disaster compared to the 10 to 1 kill ratio achieved in the Korean War. The navy ordered a report that uncovered the basic fact that pilots were not trained for the combat maneuvering battle. By September 1968 the fledgling Navy Fighter Weapons School was established at NAS Miramar near San Diego. Thus was born "Top Gun." The navy's foresight paid off during the Linebacker operations over the north in 1972, where the average kills per engagement soared from 0.20 to 1.04. When I went into combat I had over two hundred simulated dogfights behind me.

My first cruise, aboard the aircraft carrier USS *America,* had been relatively quiet since President Johnson had restricted all bombing in North Vietnam. During that nine-month period in 1969–70, the entire squadron had been fired upon only twelve times, and very few of us had ever seen a SAM. We left San Diego harbor for my second cruise on the morning of October 1, 1971, aboard the USS *Constellation* ("Connie"). Entering Strike Operations just before our first mission gave me a joltingly unpleasant surprise. The chart marking the known AAA (antiaircraft artillery) and SAM locations with color-coded pins looked like a Christmas tree. A year before, the chart had been virtually absent of pins.

The gomers, as someone had nicknamed the North Vietnamese early in the war, had moved SAM sites south of the DMZ and into Laos. Many of the guns that had once fortified the North were moved south with the apparent notion that the United States would never resume the bombing there. The supply route, the Ho Chi Minh Trail, that had once consisted of gomers walking and carrying equipment, piece by piece, had changed into a highly complex logistical network. Trucks had replaced bicycles. Bulldozers had etched out hundreds of roads beneath the jungle canopy. Tanks and troops readily moved south, and their gunners had more shells than they needed. I was prepared for the MiG threat, but wasn't counting on being shot at by more than small-arms fire. Now we faced 23mm, 37mm, 57mm, 85mm, 100mm, 120mm, and SAMs on every mission. We would drop more bombs during my first two weeks of combat than we had on the previous nine-month cruise.

Our first mission was near the valley of Tchepone in Laos. The gomers were infiltrating heavily there, supply trucks lined the roads, and enemy defenses had been increased to protect supplies streaming in from Russia and China by way of transport ships in the gulf ports. Four F-4 Phantoms, four A-6

Intruders, and four A-7 Corsairs would rendezvous with an OV-10 forward air controller, call sign "Covey 632." The small four-ship formations would afford better maneuverability if we were fired upon. Since we could not overfly North Vietnam, we would proceed through the corridor just north of Da Nang Air Base and on into Laos.

Lieutenant Brian Grant, my assigned wingman, was on his first combat mission. He was teamed with Lieutenant Jerry "Sea Cow" Sullivan, a combat-experienced RIO (radar intercept operator) in the backseat. This would also be the first combat mission for my RIO, Lieutenant (jg) Bill "Irish" Driscoll. The navy normally placed a combat-experienced pilot with a "nugget" backseater, or vice versa.

Our F-4 was ready. The ground crews had done a good job, and now it was our turn. I remember the look on Driscoll's face as he climbed the ladder and said, "Go get 'em, Duke. I'll be right behind you." A voice blared over the loudspeaker: "Start your engines!" Connie turned her skirts into the wind, giving us about thirty knots across the deck to get airborne during the cat shot. Canopies closed as the furnacelike heat blast burst from the jet engines. Sweat poured down my face.

The catapult officer lifted his right hand in the air, pointed his index finger, and motioned for one hundred percent power. Then the signal was given to select full afterburner. The F-4 strained forward on the hold-back bridle. The air-conditioning system blasted into our sweaty faces. A quick final check by the cat officer, then he saluted and we returned the traditional affectionate finger. Leaning down to touch the deck with two fingers, the signal was given by the cat officer for the catapult operator to fire us off. The G force was so great that my vision blurred, but it was a good shot and we were free as eagles. I never ceased to wonder at the catapult's ability to get a 56,000-pound fighter airborne in a matter of seconds, particularly on a hot, sticky November day like this one. Gear and flaps up . . . the F-4 was accelerating smoothly.

As we approached the assigned rendezvous point, all of

us scanned the jungle floor. FACs normally flew above 3,000 feet to keep themselves out of small-arms range. Their OV-10 Broncos plodded along at just over one hundred knots, and even though enemy gunners saved their fire for the jets most of the time, an FAC that ventured too close was in for a barrage. Those FAC crews really had our admiration. With his upper wing painted white, Covey was easy to spot. "Show-time, I've got three trucks for you parked alongside the road." Circling at 15,000 feet, we watched Covey go into action. The light propeller-driven aircraft nosed over into a steep dive, heading for trucks we couldn't ever hope to spot from this altitude. He fired a smoke rocket that hit ten meters south of the trucks, but by the time Brian and I flew around a large cloud, the smoke had dissipated due to high surface winds.

We asked for a second rocket, and a sharp, crackling air force voice burst from the UHF: "Come on, you navy pukes, I don't have all day!" Once again he arched over toward the target. This time little white puffs of 37mm AAA appeared all around the OV-10. I called out, "Covey, they are shooting all around you! Look out!"

He kept pressing into the target and placed a rocket smack in the middle of the trucks. With relief I watched his nose pulling skyward. "Okay, Navy," Covey radioed, "the score is six to nothing. Air force six, navy . . ." The Bronco erupted into flame as a 37mm made a direct hit! I sat there in utter horror. I had never seen a plane shot down. Help-lessness washed over me in sickening waves. As he hit the jungle floor, rage poured into me. "That damned gun is open-ing up on us!"

Two A-7s had joined our orbiting flight, and the lead Corsair called out, "I see gun flashes!" In seconds he was down and in the slot for a run. The bombs pickled off with uncanny accuracy, and they must have hit the gun and its ammunition dump. Secondary explosions rocked the jungle floor. For the first time in my life I really wanted to kill someone. Brian and I rolled in, putting our bombs square on the trucks, but nothing could be done for the air force FAC.

My guts ached as I flew over the burning aircraft, looking for signs of life. Our fuel was low and air force F-4s were now overhead directing SAR (search and rescue) efforts, so we headed back to Connie. We never found out if the FAC made it. I was sickened knowing someone back home would soon receive a letter from the Defense Department.

The first days of combat rolled on and settled into a routine. The two F-4 squadrons, my own VF-96 and VF-92, were assigned four basic missions: bombing, photo escort, fleet combat air patrol, and flak suppression. The majority of Phantom sorties fell into the latter two. My first photo run was for an RA-5 Vigilante driven over Vinh Airfield by Commander Murph Wright. He never got slower than 500 knots, and I fully expected to get fired upon, but it was quiet and almost peaceful below. With a false sense of security I was assigned to make the same run the next day. No sooner had we hit the coast than the sky filled with black puffs from tracking AAA sites. Near Vinh, the electronic countermeasures (ECM) gear lit up in the cockpit. The enemy was getting ready for something.

"SAMs!"

My stomach contracted in honest to goodness fear, a reaction I would never lose at a SAM call. Sweat was pouring out of Willie (a nickname I often traded with Irish) and me. The Vigie driver broke toward one SAM and defeated it with a high G maneuver. The second one was after us. "Duke, SAM at three o'clock!" Willie called out.

I could see the RA-5 heading on its way, but I would have to leave him to deal with the missile. I turned starboard, and the approaching white pencil corrected toward us. I broke port and so did the missile. It was locked onto us and tracking. I was in full afterburner—36,000 pounds of thrust was accelerating the F-4 to 600 knots. My hand was almost numb from gripping the control stick. Willie and I both kept our eyes on the SAM as it came closer and closer. My mouth was drying up. Holding the fighter at zero G, or unloaded, as we called it, I was counting on breaking at the last moment. We broke hard into the SAM and I couldn't turn the corner. We could see the fins moving as it passed by like a snake strike. The gomers failed to get us that day, but no matter how many SAMs a pilot might defeat, he respected them. Each SAM call brought doubts of survival and numbing fear.

The tension aboard ship was mounting. Each mission was more dangerous than the last as the enemy brought in larger AAA and moved more SAM sites into Laos and South Vietnam. By December the war had taken on an even grimmer outlook. More and more supplies were making it down the trail. We were hurting the VC with our strikes, but they were getting through enough men, weapons, and supplies to give our ground forces a rough time. Air Force B-52s began to bring their awesome weight against the flow of traffic. The destruction wrought by a section of stratofortresses was the most feared weapon we had according to captured VC. Ultimately the 52s earned the lion's share in bringing North Vietnam to the negotiating tables.

I remember finding the passageways alive with activity one night when everyone should have been trying to relax. Attack pilots were cutting up maps of North Vietnam. For the first time in three years we were going to strike North Vietnam. There were mixed emotions on the faces of my buddies. Most of us felt that it was about time to stop pussyfooting around and stop the enemy cold, but this meant higher risks. Many of us would not come back. After intense study and preparation on our part, orders for the first strikes north were canceled by Washington.

When preparations began again it was obvious that the United States was intending to make full use of its airpower. The navy was slated to strike coastal interdiction points, MiG fields, and supply storage areas. The air force would concentrate on inland targets, while the South Vietnamese Air Force would provide ground support for their troops. Recce photos uncovered large supply stockpiles in each target area—millions of gallons of fuel oil, tanks, SAMs, launchers, and military equipment lay out in the open awaiting shipment south.

It seemed that the enemy was confident that we would never reenter the North.

From 1965 through 1967 the planners had learned never to attack above an overcast, let alone fly a predictable path at subsonic speeds and allow the AAA and SAM radars to pinpoint formations for a final firing solution. Instrument tactics were unthinkable in a low-threat area and a double hazard over the North. All this didn't make much difference. Operation Deep Proud came off under all the above conditions, and we lost twenty-six aircraft in five days. A tactical risk had been chosen with an increased loss rate to divert a possible Viet Cong offensive.

We went in with A-6 Intruders, with a small group of A-7s and F-4s flying wing on each. The idea was for the A-6 computer and radar systems to locate targets from above the 12,000-foot overcast. When the A-6 dropped his bombs, we would drop ours simultaneously from straight and level a few thousand feet above the clouds. We flew into SAM salvos and intense AAA fire. While I maneuvered to defeat successive SAM launches, other aircraft were hit and downed around us. Preplanned missions often were aborted in favor of groundfire suppression missions in our efforts to rescue downed crews. It's difficult not to look back on the whole thing and feel frustration. We flew under hazardous conditions, got poor bombing results, and lost too many aircrews killed or taken prisoner.

MiGs had not been much of a problem during Deep Proud because they had an aversion to jumping any strike force where the odds did not favor them, but MiG activity increased during the first months of 1972. Each night MiG-21s would stage out of Kep, Yen Bai, Phuc Yen, and Quang Lang airfields. Very little individual initiative was given to the MiG drivers. They were closely controlled by GCI (ground-controlled intercept) radars. If an intercept was attempted by our fighters, the MiGs would land at the nearest field or run into China, where we could not follow. The enemy cleverly attempted to entice our fighters to give chase on several occasions. As the MiGs flew south at supersonic speed, their GCI controllers would compute exactly when the intercept would be made by American aircraft. As we neared, the enemy would turn and head north just out of missile range. Enemy GCI had direct liaison with SAM and AAA under the MiGs' flight path, and pursuing fighters would be lured over lethal antiaircraft fire.

North Vietnamese planes out of Quang Lang Airfield had made several attempts to shoot down B-52s over Laos, so far without success. It was only a matter of time until they scored, so a photo-reconnaissance mission was ordered to overfly Quang Lang and establish enemy MiG strength. An RA-5 photo bird was escorted by a large strike force of A-7s, A-6s, and F-4s, and when the Vigie was fired upon by AAA, the strike force conducted an effective "protective reaction strike." Postmission photos revealed MiG-21s being rolled into caves. Numerous SAM sites and gun emplacements ringed the field. The field was repaired within a few days, and MiGs continued to harass our air operations. A second recce was required, but two attempts by other carriers to photograph Quang Lang failed due to low visibility and cloud coverage.

On January 18, 1972, I was told to prepare to escort a strike group over Quang Lang. The news excited me. MiGs had been airborne on the previous strike, which left the slim possibility that we might engage one. I took out my lucky rabbit's foot, rubbed it, then set out for the mission briefing. I had carried that crazy piece of fur and nails for two years, ever since a friend from the University of Missouri had given it to me. I rubbed it on every mission, saying, "This is the one I get a MiG." The guys in the squadron used to ask if the foot twitched when things looked promising. The briefing was lengthy. Instead of attacking from the gulf side, we were going to attempt surprise by flying south of the DMZ, then turning northward through Laos. We were trying to appear as a large force targeted on Laos.

Our formation of thirty-five aircraft got off without a

hitch, and no one broke radio silence as we went "feet dry" over South Vietnam and Laos. The countryside below passed in lush green. This was the first time any of us had flown that far north, and we felt as if no other human had set sight on the jungle below. We continued north past the familiar mountain passes of Ben Nape, Mugia, and Ban Kari, easily identified by the barren bombed-out sandpits created by the thousands of bombs delivered in attempts to slow supplies moving south. The farther north we flew, the less the destruction was visible. Radio silence was finally broken as Commander Eggert called out Point Alpha, our first checkpoint. All ordnance switches were armed.

Point Bravo was three minutes north. One third of our force detached, and thirty seconds later a second element split off toward the target. The tactic was to establish positions southwest and north of the field. If fired upon, we could attack simultaneously from three directions. As "Point Bravo" sounded over the radio, my pulse rate jumped, almost like being awakened from a long sleep with a bucket of cold water. A-7 bombers and F-4 flak suppressors pulled off to starboard, my cue to accelerate our section ahead of the second element. As I called for Brian, my wingman, to jam throttles to one hundred percent, I could see Quang Lang twenty miles away, nestled in a small valley in the middle of a large river bend. The mountains separating Laos and North Vietnam passed under my nose as the third element was called to turn inbound.

The ECM gear lit up. The gomers knew we were in town. Fifteen miles out, Brian and I began to take 57mm fire. To avoid flying a predictable path, we jinked, turning and varying altitude. Then the wonderful little black box that detects SAM radars operating flashed its warning. "Showtime, SAM low!" Showtime was VF-96's radio call sign. We were smack in the middle of two active SAM sites. We roared over an empty field and headed north to place our section between Quang Lang and the enemy fields farther north, to cut off any attempt by MiGs to reach the strike force. It was a fighter pilot's dream job.

The field was behind us in seconds. The northern SAM site had us locked up on radar, and I was looking at the missile pad as two SAMs lifted. Dust and dirt flew up as a missile's booster propelled the telephone-pole-like ordnance into the air. There is nothing, absolutely nothing, to describe what goes on inside a pilot's gut when he sees a SAM get airborne. The booster dropped off, replaced by a white glow of flame accelerating the missile to Mach three plus. I called Brian to turn hard port. As he did, the missile followed him, indicating that it was tracking his aircraft, but he and Jerry hadn't seen it yet. As it closed rapidly, I called for a break turn of maximum G. The SAM passed close to Brian and failed to detonate, possibly because we were inside minimum arming range. If it had gone off, Brian and Jerry would not be around, or they would be eating pumpkin soup in the Heartbreak Hotel.

Our A-7 Corsairs were doing some good work on the field and the AAA sites. I heard Norm McCoy call out, "Let's hit the SAM site to the north." He and his wingman did just that with finesse. The attack birds were drawing most of the heavy flak as they rolled in on their targets. The southern SAM site locked up on us and fired two missiles. Breaking the other way, we came back over the field as two more SAMs were launched simultaneously from both sites. Brian and I quickly were separated as the MIGCAP became a secondary mission to simple survival. They fired eighteen SAMS, often in pairs from both sites. We had made a terrible misjudgment by getting penned in between the two sites. As we desperately maneuvered to avoid tracking missiles, one went off very close but caused no damage.

Quick glances around revealed the attack birds pounding everything. The A-7s found the MiG storage areas hidden deep in the mountains south of the field, and Norm and his wingman demolished the hated northern SAM site with Rockeye bombs. A-6s were on the mark, cratering the airfield with thousand-pounders. One A-7 made three passes through a maze of AAA, attempting to drop ordnance that was hung up on his aircraft due to an electrical malfunction.

"Duke, look at that A-7, three o'clock," Willie called out. A SAM was chasing him downhill. At the last second he pulled up and the missile whistled by to plummet into the field's runway. Normally a SAM was set to explode anytime it came within a few feet of a solid object. Thankfully most of them were not performing very well. I noticed what I thought were two more A-7s exiting the target area to the north about four miles ahead. There was something unusual about them. They were too far away to identify, but they had white glows near their tailpipes, indicating afterburning engines. Corsairs don't have afterburners.

"Irish, we have two bogies [unidentified aircraft] heading north, but I can't tell what they are." I thought they were MiG-21s, but I hadn't seen a MiG for two years and my rabbit's foot wasn't twitching. Two days before, a pilot in VF-92 had called out "MiGs, MiGs, MiGs!" when it was our own RA-5. The pilot had a hard time living it down, and I wasn't about to make the same mistake.

Still nosedown, I accelerated to 650 knots and reversed, placing me in a perfect position behind the unknown aircraft. As we closed, I saw two of the prettiest delta-winged MiG-21s. The leader was about 500 feet off the ground in a canyon, with his wingman stepped up to his right at about 700 to 1,000 feet in fighting wing. "Showtime," I cried, "bandits, blue bandits [code for MiG-21] north of the field!" Brian heard the call and headed north after us. Then something strange happened. I leaned back against my rabbit's foot. It dug into my flesh and I carry the mark from it today.

Willie and I were 200 feet above the ground, doing 650 knots, looking up at the lead fighter. I went boresight on the radar and called for Willie to do the same. "Duke, he's locked on the radar, in range! Shoot! Shoot! Shoot!" This was just the situation to fire a radar-guided Sparrow, but my prior experience with this missile in training had not been good. In several of our practice engagements with drones, I had fired Sparrows and missed, while scoring consistent hits with the Sidewinder. I reached over, selected "Heat," got a good aural tone (indicating the missile was sensing the heat of the MiG engine), squeezed off a Sidewinder at dead six, and called, "Fox Two!" The Sidewinder was not selective of friendly or hostile, so when a pilot called "Fox Two!" it warned other aircraft of the impending launch.

Just as the missile left the rail, the MiG did what all MiGs do well—he executed a maximum G, tight-turning, starboard-break turn. Either his wingman called a break or his tail warning radar was working. I had an instantaneous plan view of him, and he was really hauling, still in afterburner, at treetop level. His only defensive move would be either a nose-level or a nose-high turn. I pulled up and rolled the F-4 toward the MiG's belly side in a lag pursuit roll, placing us on the outside of the MiG's turn rate. In the middle of the turn I looked back over my starboard wing to find the enemy wingman running away to leave his leader to fight me alone.

I could see my adversary's head thrashing around in the cockpit. He was not well trained, making the fatal mistake of dissipating his energy in the break turn. He apparently could not see me. His wings nearly clipped the rocks of the valley floor as the first 'Winder attempted to match his high G turn. The missile couldn't handle it, and exploded out of lethal range.

Our Phantom was upside down 200 feet off the deck, doing 500 knots. "Blue Angels can fly inverted at these altitudes, but I'm no Blue Angel!" Panic rose in my throat again as I thought we were going to crash. I jammed the left aileron and full rudder while pushing forward on the stick. Instant negative G forced us into our straps, and I ended up doing a fast aileron roll (which I hadn't planned), but we were right side up, pointing straight at the MiG with forty degrees to go to his heading. His left wing started to drop as he reversed his turn. Irish was telling me to watch our altitude,

421

no MiGs behind us. His voice quivered with excitement. "Get 'em, Duke." I knew that if I waited to fire another Sidewinder after the MiG's turn was completed, the missile could be defeated just like the first one, so I squeezed the trigger and called "Fox Two!" at the moment he started his reversal.

The MiG was no more than 3,700 feet out in front of me, and I was zero degrees angle off, a perfect envelope for the missile. Just as the enemy fighter's wings leveled, the Sidewinder hit him. The effect was spectacular. The whole tail came off, and the remainder of the airplane went into a violent pitching, tumbling crash into the ground, creating a huge fireball. We passed through some of the debris as it scattered into a nearby village. It was like a dream, like none of this was really happening. I experienced a momentary relief that the enemy was finally beaten, then excitement beyond description. For the first time in eighteen months a MiG had been sighted and destroyed by a fighter pilot of the United States. Irish was screaming in the backseat with exhilaration.

I picked up a silver glint at two o'clock. Brian saw him at the same time and called, "Duke, MiG-21 at two o'clock, three miles. I can barely see him." The MiG was out of missile range, so I lit the afterburners and accelerated to 650 knots, but he was opening the gap by 50 knots. No MiG-21A, C, or D model could do that. This had to be one of the newer MiG-21Js with hydraulically boosted controls. The enemy fighter was so small that each time it ran straight away from us, we lost sight of it. Russian training was the only aid I had. Communist pilots were taught to turn from side to side in an attempt to clear their six o'clock. Each time he turned, we regained sight of his plan form. The supersonic chase a hundred feet off the deck, weaving over trees, rocks, and canyons was no picnic.

I would have chased him into China. Willie snapped me out of it by forcing me to check our fuel state. We had only 7,500 pounds left and were taking small-arms fire by now with tracers coming up from directly ahead. A slingshot could have brought us down from that altitude. As a last resort before breaking off, I decided to fire a Sparrow. "I might get lucky, or it might make him turn into me" were the only rationalizations I had. There was a short in the ejector cartridge and the missile failed to come off the trail. The E-2 radar and radio relay vectored two fighters from the gulf north of us toward the escaping MiG, but he got away into China. I wonder what he told his comrades when he got back.

I pulled on the stick and looped back toward Laos. Quang Lang came into view with its familiar SAM sites. Three SAM sites had been destroyed, two AAA emplacements damaged, the runway bombed, the MiG storage caves demolished, and a MiG-21 destroyed. Radio Hanoi said that we violated northern airspace and attacked many hospitals and schools, losing two aircraft "blown to pieces" and many others damaged. We had only one A-7 damaged, and I didn't see hospital patients manning the weapons. The enemy radar locked on again on our journey south, but we were well out of range.

Back at the Connie, I requested permission for the traditional victory roll and was tersely refused. I could see thousands of her men watching from below, so I made a six-G break turn, ninety-degree angle of break. We landed after one of my best passes of the cruise. The flight deck was alive with men full of excitement and joy, arms waving, victory fingers held high. A hastily scratched-out flag read "Congratulations Lieutenant Driscoll, Lieutenant Cunningham."

The deck flooded with men as we raised canopies. Willie White, one of my favorite ordnancemen, nearly knocked over the captain, leapt up on the F-4, and shook my hand. "Mr. Cunningham, we got our MiG today, didn't we?" He and thousands of others had spent two years toiling in the heat, lifting Sparrows and Sidewinders and bombs aboard. Today his Sidewinder, his effort in making sure it was connected properly, his inspection of all the systems, allowed that missile to perform effectively, just as all the men working elsewhere on the ship made it possible for us to carry out the mission.

Five thousand men had just shot down a MiG-21 and they were proud of it.

The USS *Constellation* was scheduled to sail for home in the latter part of March 1972. After our last scheduled day in the Gulf of Tonkin, some of us headed home on space-available air force flights. I had two combat tours under my belt and thought that I would never see Vietnam again, but the Communist spring offensive changed everything. I drove back to San Diego, caught a 747 for Manila, and arrived shortly thereafter back aboard the Connie. She was already conducting operations against the besieged town of An Loc, seventy miles northwest of Saigon.

Pressure increased along the DMZ, and the Connie moved north. Then the dike really broke. Twelve thousand rounds of rocket, mortar, and artillery fire slashed across the DMZ, followed by 25,000 fresh North Vietnamese regulars equipped with Russian-built tanks and artillery. The objective was Quang Tri, the South's northernmost provincial capital. Next, Kontum came under siege and An Loc was pressured by a fresh supply of troops and tanks, but the South Vietnamese defenders held their battered positions. The Viet Cong were waging an effective multifront campaign alongside the regulars. Loc Ninh, a rural capital north of Saigon, was captured. General Giap had committed fourteen of his fifteen divisions across Indochina, and they demanded maximum logistical support. This is precisely when President Nixon decided to act.

The invasion had shattered President Johnson's 1968 agreement to stop bombing the North, and a resumption of unconditional bombing was ordered. Four aircraft carriers were in the gulf, and the USS *Midway* was en route. Our B-52 strength had doubled since 1971, and air force F-111 and navy A-6 aircraft could interdict supplies in the worst weather. Two more Phantom squadrons flew to Da Nang from Okinawa and Korea. American air power was effectively increased from 450 to 800 planes.

On March 30 at two A.M., hundreds of blips came to life on the Russian surveillance radars near Haiphong and Hanoi. Our A-6 drivers were the first aircraft over the North, flying at fifty feet to knock out SAM sites that might affect the B-52s. Air Force F-105 Wild Weasels joined them with radar homing missiles. The intense action was incredible. Over two hundred SAMs were fired into the pitch-black night, and pilots said North Vietnam looked like it was on fire. Even though the Electric Whales (EA-3s) and EA-6s jammed the enemy radar effectively, the attack pilots had a rough go of it down on the deck in the middle of it all. I know of one pilot who turned in his wings.

The linemen created a hole for our fullback. Seventeen B-52s dropped thirty tons into the darkness over Haiphong. I could imagine that the only thing visible on the Russian, Chinese, and foreign ships in the harbor would be rear ends. Fuel farms and petroleum storage areas exploded, sending fireballs skyward that were visible to the carrier crews 110 miles away. By 0930 Hanoi was in panic. Loudspeakers blared warnings as thirty-two air force F-4s attacked warehouses and any petroleum storage areas that remained on the city's out-skirts. To a small group within Hanoi, the holocaust was music. The POWs were overjoyed at the American show of strength. Their supposedly fearless guards quivered and dived under anything available. One guard curled up in a tight ball in a corner, crying, "Don't kill me!"

At 1430 Sunday, forty navy jets launched against heavily defended Haiphong to hit truck parks, SAM sites, AAA em-placements, storage areas, and other military targets. Lieu-tenant Dave Lichterman rolled in on Kien An Airfield, dropped Rockeye bombs, and watched the MiGs parked in revetments go up in flames. As the day neared its end, 250 SAMs had been launched but only two aircraft had been hit, not the fifteen claimed destroyed by Radio Hanoi. Only four MiGs had gotten airborne, and three of them were shot down.

I was part of a forty-plane strike into Happy Valley south of Haiphong, the entry point to the mountain passes leading into Laos. The A-6s and A-7s hit the rail yard and storage areas, and my F-4 section went after flak emplacements with Rockeyes. Whenever the enemy's guns opened up on the rest of the force, Brian and I would destroy them. Flak suppression was normally a rough mission, but the AAA was surpisingly light. Irish noted all the empty gun emplacements left over from the 1965–67 period, when Happy Valley was one of the hottest areas in Vietnam. Evidently the North had not expected us to return. There were a few SAMs and some AAA fire. One village housing two 23mm and four 57mm gun emplacements was destroyed.

We returned to the Connie after a second strike group had been launched. We trapped, went off to Flight Operations for the debrief, then prepared for the next launch, only two hours away. Each of us had to memorize the target location hidden among the thousands of tributaries and fingerlike coves that make up Haiphong harbor. This time I got into the center of the action. We hit a supply storage area where Russian ships had unloaded war materials. AAA was thick in the area, making identification that much more difficult if one was not thoroughly familiar with the target area. We were within range of six MiG bases, and gomer radar had us from the time we rendezvoused over the ship, but the North Vietnamese were leaving the gray navy jets alone.

As our force moved up the coast just out of SAM range, the ECM strobes started ticking off enemy radar tracking. Six SAMs were fired out of range, exploding several miles away. The Red River Valley lay south, glimmering in the sun's reflection. We covered the strike birds with air-to-air missiles and Rockeye bombs. Amazing weapon, the Rockeye; it broke in half at altitude to disperse hundreds of tiny dartlike bombs capable of penetrating tank armor or fragmenting against soft targets. The Rockeye could cover an entire gun emplacement, preventing it from firing on strike aircraft. Our air-to-air mission entailed watching a sky full of twisting aircraft, and identifying each one as it raced by at supersonic speed, lest it prove to be a MiG.

"Mayday! Mayday!" An A-7 not far off the beach was hit and going down, a parachute popped open, and enemy gunners kept shooting at the pilot as he floated down. As happened on so many occasions, the entire mission was diverted to rescue the downed pilot. I had a chance to look around. Roaring oil fires could be seen for fifty miles, and the harbor itself seemed to be on fire. The downed pilot's buddies were circling him, but most of them had dropped their ordnance. Two Russian freighters were headed straight for our man, and I told Brian to arm his bombs and take a one-mile trail position. Irish was busy checking our six o'clock for MiGs. They loved to sneak in on slow-flying SAR birds. If the Russians fired on us, which we deeply hoped for, Brian would blow them out of the water.

Before leaving the area, one of our A-7s flashed in front of us and placed a few 20mm rounds in front of the first freighter. It kept coming, and so did I. I let down to 200 feet, jinking back and forth just in case the ship opened fire. I could see the Russians on the deck as we neared. There would be no "accidental" running down of one of our pilots today. The Russkies got the message and turned away from the raft. One of our helos was hovering over the raft now, totally vulnerable to the guns firing from the beach. I lined up the tracers and pressed in for the kill, and the gomers switched their fire to us. Tracers flew past my canopy as Brian attacked another gun about a mile ahead of us. A SAM was launched, failed to track, and exploded high above me, but the bombs from both of our Phantoms were dead on target. Another gun opened up as I pulled off my target, but we had bought enough time. The helo had made it out with the injured pilot.

On May 6, things really busted loose. The navy scheduled major strikes on Haiphong, Vinh, and Bai Thoung, and intelligence reported as many as fourteen MiGs at the latter field. Fighters from the USS *Coral Sea* downed three of them that day. We learned on May 7 that we would be in the middle of the action the following day, and we partied in anticipation. A couple of friends launched a top secret mission on the captain's ice locker to get ice for a popcorn party. Of course, we were avoiding deep thought about the next day's mission. Things like stealing ice helped us all keep our sanity.

By the time we arrived over the target area on May 8, we had already been fired at by two SAMs and 85mm AAA. We were ten miles north of the strike force. For all I knew, they might be flying into a nest of MiGs, so I ordered a 180-degree turn to cover them. Just as we got turned around came the call, "Bandits closing at your six o'clock and twenty miles." We turned again and headed west. From 10,000 feet the haze obscured the ground below and concealed any MiGs that might be lurking there. Red Crown called again, but my radio garbled it. I started to call Brian to get the dope when he called out, "Duke, in place, port! Go!"

As I called Brian's six clear, I selected full afterburner, then pulled hard up and to the inside of the turn to place myself abeam of Brian at one mile. Now we could clear each other's tails. No sooner had I taken a look behind him than a MiG-17 came screaming up through the haze layer in afterburner, shooting at Brian! The MiG's 23mm BBs were falling short. "Brian, MiG-17 at your seven o'clock!"

"*What?*"

"You've got a seventeen on your tail and he's shooting! Get rid of your centerline [belly fuel tank], unload, and outrun him!"

Brian punched off the big tank and started to extend away from the MiG. The MiG driver must have come from the last gunnery class, because he wasn't pulling enough lead. "Brian, I'm high at your nine o'clock. Don't push negative Gs or you'll fly through his BBs."

Our intelligence boys had told us that the 17 didn't carry Atoll missiles, so all we had to do was get out of gun range. When Brian had opened the gap to around 3,500 feet, I saw a missile blast out from under the enemy fighter! "Brian, Atoll! Break port!" The F-4 hauled around in a tight six-G turn and the missile, though it tried, just couldn't make the corner. But the break enabled the nimble MiG-17 to cut across the circle and get back in gun range. "Brian, he's closing again! Unload and go again!" The MiG still couldn't get the proper lead, but I was about sixty degrees off its tail and couldn't get a Sidewinder shot.

As Brian pulled away, Willie called, "Duke, look up! Two MiG-17s meeting us head on." They passed 200 feet over my canopy. "Irish, watch 'em. By the time they get turned around, they'll be out of the fight." I was about to get my first lesson in the turning ability of the MiG-17.

My concentration was boresighted on the fighter chasing Brian and Sea Cow. Their F-4 had reached the same position ahead of the MiG as before, and I was afraid the gomer was going to shoot another Atoll. I still had sixty degrees off the MiG's tail, and no 'Winder could hack a shot now, but I fired anyway. The missile tracked and strained for its quarry, finally giving up to fall below, but it sure scared the MiG driver, who made a hard break and got off Brian's tail. He reversed right in front of me and started to run. This was too good to be true. Surely I could catch him. Yeah.

"Duke, MiGs at five and seven shooting!" came Willie's strained voice.

"Impossible," I thought. "No plane can turn around that fast." Irish later told me that the 17s were 4,000 feet apart when they passed over. They turned in toward each other and completed 180-degree turns without crossing each other's flight path! Yep, impossible, but they were firing away at us.

I had a tone on the fleeing MiG, so I squeezed the trigger. It was a classic shot. The missile came off the rail, did a little wiggle, and flew right into him. The fighter crashed into the mountain it had been heading for, but it could still be an effective sacrifice play for the enemy. With Brian sitting high over me, I called "All right, Brian, I'm going to pull hard down into your port turn and drag the MiGs out in front of you! Shoot them off my tail!"

It was my turn in the barrel and I was anything but calm, cool, and collected. The cannon shells flashing past my canopy unnerved me. The 23mm twinkles out of the wing roots, but the 37mm puts out a BB the size of a grapefruit. Its muzzle flash looked a good five feet long. As I went to port, the MiG at seven o'clock closed in, sending grapefruits over my head in large numbers. "Well, that's not going to work!" bounced through my mind as I turned to look the enemy in the face. I could see his eyes, his hat, his goggles, and his scarf.

I reversed and tracers began zooming by the right side of my canopy! "Brian, get in here! I'm in deep trouble!" I tried one more reversal, but Hanoi Charlie was still there, blasting away. Training adages were bouncing through my mind, "Never turn into a MiG-17." Yeah, definitely good advice, but I couldn't go up and deplete any more airspeed and give the slower MiGs more of an advantage. I rolled my beautifully constructed McDonnell product into a 120-degree nose-slicing turn, burying the stick in my lap. I put a good twelve Gs on the aircraft, tearing wing panels, popping rivets, and breaking a flap hinge. The MiG turned inside of me and I looked out of my canopy to see him a scant ten feet away! I could read his side number and count rivets, and he still had two missiles slung under his wings.

I called for Brian to pitch up into the vertical. He was at my one o'clock, and I wanted to pull to the inside of his port turn. If the MiG followed me, Brian could roll over the top and get a shot. Hanoi Charlie and his gomer buddy weren't buying the goods. They started pressing me again. "Brian, I'm diving for the clouds." Full stick forward and I was in the milky deck with the MiGs right behind me. Up to this point I hadn't used afterburner because I was afraid of the remaining Atolls. Two J-79s at full cooker would have presented a great heat source. Now I went into full burner and accelerated out to 550 knots real quick.

Brian radioed that he couldn't see all of us. "That's good. They can't see me either," I thought. "Brian, I've got 550 knots coming out toward the sun." If the MiGs did fire a heat-seeker, it would most likely select the sun's heat and not my tailpipes. Hopefully they would be blinded by the sun, if nothing else. As I popped up, Brian let out a "tallyho!" and there he was, high at my five o'clock, in perfect position to jump the MiGs if they followed me. Sure enough, they popped out right behind me. They wanted no part of Brian, and dived back into the sanctuary of the overcast. We went hunting for them, but they escaped.

Another patrol over Gia Lam, Hanoi's main field, produced no results, although we were following up on a report of MiGs staging out of there. All attack aircraft had exited safely and other Phantoms had launched to cover our withdrawal. I spotted a five-mile-long line of trucks on the way out. The air-to-air fighting was over, so I rolled in on them. I figured that a truck might provide enough of a heat source for a Sidewinder, so I was trying to get a tone. I had tried it once before with no success, but one of the trucks must have needed a valve job. I got a good tone and squeezed off the missile. It slammed into the truck, dead center, sending a fireball into the sky. Back at the Connie, our fuel was too low for a victory roll, so permission was again denied. Instead, we were greeted with five thousand handshakes.

Throughout the war in Southeast Asia, foreign ships crowded the harbors of the North, delivering military supplies through Haiphong and other major ports. We had flown over Chinese and Russian ships loaded with surface-to-air missiles, fuel oil, tanks, MiG crates, and who knows what else. Brian and I flew over these ships, taking pictures of their lethal cargo, while the crews waved at us. The rules of engagement were really something. We could bomb the supplies once they reached Laos and South Vietnam, but trucks are hard to find in the jungle. Inside the passes just over the North Vietnamese border, trucks were backed up for miles, waiting to run past our air attacks.

All of that changed on May 8, 1972, when President Nixon announced the mining of North Vietnamese harbors. Operation Linebacker missions would be increased, and more B-52 strikes laid on for military-industrial targets. The mines were deployed on May 9 with activation commencing in three days to allow all foreign ships to leave. Again Brian and I were flying over enemy ships, this time twenty or thirty of them parked outside the harbors with decks full, fearful of entering and failing to get back out before the three-day deadline. They waved again, but this time we were the ones laughing.

The sophisticated AWT-1 shipping mines were incredibly efficient. Some went off when metal neared. Others would allow a ship to pass, giving the impression the area was clear, only to explode on a subsequent detection. Others detonated by sound or pressure or who knows what gizmo. There were immediate results for us. Before the mining, strikes into the Haiphong area would bring numerous SAM launches (over two hundred) and heavy flak. After the mining, strikes drew a maximum of four or five SAMs and less AAA. The only disadvantage to us was the MiGs' lack of fuel, which meant they couldn't get airborne so we could hassle. Eighty-five percent of foreign supplies, nearly 250,000 tons per month, were prevented from reaching the enemy.

On May 10 I was assigned to fly flak suppression for a strike on the Haiphong rail yard that served as a funneling point for the Ban Kori, Mugia, and Napi mountain passes. It was smack in the middle of several MiG fields and was supposed to be heavily fortified with AAA ranging from 23mm to 120mm, not to mention the SAMs along the flight path. Brian and I stepped up above the main strike force of A-6s and A-7s, and Irish commented on what a shame it was that such a beautiful country had to be bombed. Winding waterways glistened through emerald green valleys as the sun reflected off the roofs of the populated wetlands.

The attack craft sailed over the target, then rolled back over from west to east, looking for all the world like a column of ants as they went down the chute. The rest of us orbited overhead while AAA bursts dotted the sky. Commander Henry Blackburn, who was right across the circle from me, took an 85mm hit. His RIO, Steve Rudluff, survived to spend the remainder of the war as a POW. His wingman was hit by the same barrage, and he went out single engine. MiG-21s made one pass at him, then let him go.

The first attack aircraft demolished the primary target, so the rest of us were directed to secondary targets. Brian and I were sent to the large supply area adjacent to the rail yard. We decided to close in tight to a fighting wing formation and release simultaneously. We rolled over just as two SAMs were launched. They failed to track and whizzed up past us. I looked back down at the target to see it disappear in a cloud of smoke and debris from thousand-pounders. We dropped our bombs and pulled off, and I made the mistake of looking over my right shoulder to see what we had done to the target. My head was down and locked when Brian called, "Duke, you have MiG-17s at your seven o'clock, shooting!"

Two 17s flew right by Brian's F-4, about 500 feet away, and I was about 1,000 feet in front! I popped my wing back down and reversed hard port in time to see a 17 pull in behind and start firing. That damned 37mm put out a BB the size of a pumpkin (they had grown from grapefruit size in two days), and a muzzle flash that seemed to jet out the length of a football field. My instinct was to break into him. Then I thought, "I did that two days ago and the guy rendezvoused on me." A quick glance at the MiG told me that it was closing at high speed, meaning that his controls would be hard to move. I broke into him anyway.

The MiG driver just didn't have the muscle to move that stick. He overshot over the top to my two o'clock, but his wingman was back 1,500 feet. He pitched up and did a vertical displacement roll out to my belly side. "Duke," Brian called, "I'll take care of the guy at your six." With utter confidence in Brian I turned my attention to the other MiG. When I squeezed off a Sidewinder, the enemy fighter was well within minimum range, but by the time the missile got to him, he was about 2,500 feet in front of me. That's how fast he was going. The 'Winder blew him to pieces. That engagement had lasted about fifteen seconds.

On two previous occasions Brian had dragged MiGs out

for me on his tail, and now it was my turn to reciprocate. "Brian, here's your chance. I'm gonna drag this guy out for you." I accelerated down in a turn with the MiG hot after me. "Brian, get that SOB! Brian?"

"I can't help you, Duke! I've got two on my tail!" I lost my pursuer with a quick disengagement maneuver, accelerating out to 600 knots. I looked to my right and saw Brian. He had seen me take off, had shook off his two MiGs in the same fashion, and then pulled back into combat spread position. There simply could not have been a better wingman on all the earth. We had all kinds of fuel left, so we pitched into the vertical, came over the top at 15,000 feet, and rolled out of the Immelmann and back into the fight. Below us a MiG-17 burst into flames. The pilot ejected before the stricken fighter smashed into the ground. The scene below was straight out of *The Dawn Patrol*. There were eight MiG-17s in a defensive wheel with three F-4s mixed in! Our guys should never have been there. They were down to 350 knots, which is a good place to die. I called for Brian to cover and rolled in.

I no sooner got nose down when a Phantom came out of the circle, missing us by a hair. "Willie, who's in 112?" It was Dwight Timm, the XO, with Jim Fox in the backseat. "Jeez, look at that!" Timm was in a port turn with a MiG-17 about 2,000 feet behind him, a MiG-21 about 1,000 feet behind the 17, and what he couldn't see, a 17 on his belly side, flying wing! We were back at seven o'clock, behind the trailing MiGs, but the real threat was the 17 flying wing, about to pull up and start shooting. I called for Timm to maneuver his fighter and get a tone, but he was in burner. If I squeezed off a Fox Two, it would most likely go for the Phantom. I called for him to reverse starboard to kick the MiG across his tail, underneath, allowing my Sidewinder to home on the MiG's tailpipe. He thought that I was talking about the trailing MiGs (he still hadn't spotted the real threat), so he kept going on. I called again. "Showtime, reverse starboard! If you don't, you're going to die!"

"Duke," strained Willie, "we have four MiG-17s at our

seven o'clock." They were out of range, but Timm's arching turn was allowing them to slowly gain on us. Willie was on the ball. "Duke, look at two o'clock high!" I looked up and saw two flashes, not airplanes, just flashes, since they were too high. "There can't be any more 17s in the world!" my mind retorted. I was right. They were MiG-19s. As they rolled in on us with guns firing, I reversed and they went out to our six o'clock. This put the fight over to our ten o'clock with a deep lag position to the MiG behind Timm, but out of range of the MiGs which were trailing us, except for one just about in the firing position.

One of the only things I did right that day was to have about 550 knots just then. The MiG behind me couldn't close as long as I didn't turn too tight. At 500 knots I was opening up on him. The problem was, I had to turn to stay behind Timm and his MiG. I told Willie to keep an eye on my MiG and tell me when it started to pull lead. When it did so, shooting those blasted BBs, I'd straighten out and open up the gap a bit. This all happened in a few seconds.

Finally Timm broke. I had a tone, no tone, then a tone again. I squeezed the trigger. "Fox Two!" Jim Fox looked out of the backseat of Timm's Phantom and saw the MiG for the first time, just as my missile hit. The lethal heat-seeker traveled the entire length of the 17, blowing it to bits. Commander Timm's wife later rewarded me with a super-sized kiss.

The MiG pilot ejected behind the F-4, and I had to break hard port and drop the wing to miss him. Then four MiG-21s rolled in on us. They must have been pretty upset when I popped their comrade, who would probably end up driving water buffalo down the Ho Chi Minh Trail. As they rolled in, I pulled hard into them, putting them 180 degrees off me. Timm was already on the deck and heading for the coast. Everywhere I looked there were MiGs and no F-4s, so I headed east myself. At about the same time, an A-7 driver had pulled off target and heard a MiG call. He decided he wanted to see a MiG just once, so he turned around. He came through the fight with two 17s on his tail. Matt Connelly shot one off and told the Corsair pilot to get the hell out, that the A-7 was no match for MiGs. The A-7 headed out, but was soon back with two more MiGs on its tail. Matt knocked a second MiG off the A-7 pilot's tail, and this time he got the hint and hauled his aircraft toward the gulf.

The aerial maneuvering was going on all around us and we were badly outnumbered. It was time to get out. As we headed for the coast at 10,000 feet, I spotted another airplane on the nose, slightly low, heading straight at us. It was a MiG-17. I told Irish to watch how close we could pass the MiG to take out as much lateral separation as possible so he could not convert as easily to our six o'clock. We had done the same thing against A-4s back at Miramar, since the two aircraft were virtually identical in performance. This proved to be my first near-fatal mistake. A-4s don't have guns in their noses. The MiG's entire nose lit up like a Christmas tree, and pumpkin-size BBs sailed past our F-4. I pulled sharply into a vertical to destroy the gomer's tracking solution. As I came out of the six-G pullup, I strained to see the MiG below as my F-4 went straight up. I was sure that it would go into a horizontal turn, or just run as most had done in the past.

I looked back over my ejection seat and got the surprise of my life. There was the MiG, canopy to canopy with me, barely 300 feet away! I could see a gomer leather helmet, gomer goggles, gomer scarf, and the intent gomer expression. I began to feel numb. My stomach grabbed at me in knots. There was no fear in this guy's eyes as we zoomed some 8,000 feet straight up. I lit the afterburners and started to outclimb my adversary, but this excess performance placed me above him. He began shooting as I started to pull over the top, which was my second near-fatal mistake. I had given him a predictable flight path, and he had taken advantage of it. I was forced to roll and pull to the other side, and he pulled right in behind me.

Not wanting to admit that this guy was beating me, I blurted out to Willie, "That SOB is really lucky! All right, we'll get this guy now!" I pulled down to accelerate with the MiG at four o'clock. I watched and waited until he committed nosedown, then pulled up into him and rolled over the top, placing me at his five o'clock. Even though the close range and the angle didn't allow me to fire a missile, the maneuver placed me in an advantageous position. I thought that I had overflown him, and overconfidence replaced fear. I pulled down to press for a shot, and he pulled up into me—shooting. I thought, "Oh, no! Maybe this guy isn't just lucky after all!" He used the same maneuver I had attempted, pulling up into me and forcing an overshoot. We were in the classic rolling scissors. As his nose committed, I pulled up into him.

I had fought the same situation in training. I learned that if my opponent had his nose too high, I could snap down, using the one G to advantage, then run out to his six o'clock before he could get turned around and get into range. As we slowed to 200 knots, I knew it was time to bug out. I had been taught to disengage in these situations. The MiGs superior turn radius, coupled with higher available G at that speed, started giving him a constant advantage. But when he raised his nose a bit too high, I pulled into him, placing my aircraft nearly 180 degrees to follow. Willie and I were two miles ahead of him, out of missile range and at 600 knots airspeed.

With our energy back, I made a 60-degree nose-up vertical turn back into the MiG. He climbed right after us, and again I outzoomed him as he squirted BBs in our direction. It was a carbon copy of the first engagement as we went into another rolling scissors. Again we were forced to disengage as advantage and disadvantage traded sides. As we blasted away to regain energy for the second time, Irish came up on the intercom. "Hey, Duke, how ya doin' up there? This guy really knows what he's doing. Maybe we ought to call it a day."

This almost put me in a blind rage. To think that some gomer had not only stood off my attacks but had gained an advantage over me twice! "Hang on, Willie. We're gonna get this guy!"

"Go get him, Duke. I'm right behind you!" Irish was all over the cockpit, straining to keep sight of the MiG as I pitched back toward him for the third time. Man, it felt good to have that second pair of eyes back there, especially with an adversary who knew what air fighting was all about. Very seldom did U.S. fighter pilots find a MiG that fought in the vertical. The enemy liked to fight in the horizontal for the most part, or just run if he didn't have the advantage.

I met the MiG head on, this time with an offset so he couldn't use his guns. As I pulled into the pure vertical, I could see the determined pilot a few feet away. Winston Churchill once wrote, "In war, if you are not able to beat your enemy at his own game, it is nearly always better to adopt some striking variant." I came up with a last-ditch idea. I pulled hard toward his aircraft and yanked the throttles back to idle, popping the speed brakes at the same time.

The MiG shot in front of me for the first time! The Phantom's nose was 60 degrees above the horizon with airspeed down to 150 knots in no time. I had to go full burner to hold my position. The surprised enemy pilot attempted to roll on his back above me. I used the rudder to avoid stalling the F-4 with the spoilers on the wings, and rolled to the MiG's blind side. The other pilot attempted to reverse his roll, but as his wings banked sharply, he must have momentarily stalled the aircraft. His nose fell through, placing me at his six, but still too close for a shot. "This is no place to be with a MiG-17," I thought. "At 150 knots, this slow, he can take it right away from you."

But he stayed too long. He pitched over the top and started straight down. I pulled hard and followed. Though I didn't think a Sidewinder would guide straight down, with the heat from the ground to look at, I called, "Fox Two!" and squeezed one off. The missile came off the rail and went straight into the MiG. There was a little flash and I thought it had missed him. As I started to fire my last 'Winder, there was an abrupt burst of flame and black smoke erupted from the 17. He didn't seem to go out of control. The fighter simply kept descending until it crashed into the ground at a 45-degree angle. We later found out that this superb fighter pilot was "Colonel Tomb" of the North Vietnamese Air Force. A man who reputedly had thirteen American aircraft to his credit. He had refused to disengage when his GCI controller ordered him to return to base.

"Duke, check ten o'clock! MiG-17 rolling in on you!" Irish had his eyes open. We had 550 knots, so I pulled nose high into the attacking craft and told Willie, "Here comes number six." Just then Matt Connelly, who had been watching the fight, yelled out, "Duke, get the hell out of there! There are four 17s at your seven o'clock!" I saw Matt with his nose down on us just as he fired a Sparrow. It went over our tail and sailed into the center of the MiG formation, and they looked like fleas evacuating a dog, splitting off in every direction to get out of the way.

Five MiGs were enough. We rolled and headed for the coast with Matt on our wing. To our left, a heavy barrage of 85mm blackened the sky. ECM gear said SAMs were on the way as well. Two of them raced for us head on, but we were able to defeat them. Then came a sudden lull. Something was wrong when enemy gunners just plain quit firing, and Willie found the reason. "Duke, MiGs chasing us!" As I pitched up, there was a 21 smack in front of my windscreen. I was going to shoot, but he was well within minimum range. I flew right by him. Before I could comprehend what was happening, a MiG-17 flashed by within close range and then yet another 17. If I'd had a gun instead of just missiles, I might have made three more kills.

I pitched off, broke, and headed out again in burner. There was another SAM call as we neared Nam Dinh. Glancing over to starboard, I watched an SA-2 heading straight for us, and before I could maneuver, it detonated. The concussion was not too violent, but my head felt like it went down to my stomach. We'd had closer SAM explosions than that, and there appeared to be no damage. I immediately went to the gauges to check for systems malfunctions, but everything looked normal, so I continued to climb and watch for more SAMs. Irish couldn't understand how the thing got so close without our ECM gear warning us. Neither could I.

About forty-five seconds later the aircraft yawed violently to the left. "What's the matter, Duke! You flying instruments again?" asked Irish. I steadied up and looked into the cockpit to see the PC-1 hydraulic system indicating zero, the PC-2 and the utility systems fluctuating. Fear, that ever-present companion, wanted to run the ship. "What now, Cunningham?" raced through my mind.

I remembered that "Duke" Hernandez, another navy pilot, had rolled his aircraft to safety after losing his hydraulics. When an F-4 loses hydraulics, the stabilizer locks, forcing the aircraft's nose to pitch straight up. The stick has no effect on the controls, and only the rudder and power are available to maneuver the aircraft. Sure enough, when PC-2 went to zero, the nose went straight up. I pushed full right rudder, yawing the nose to the right and forcing the nose down. As it passed through the horizon, I selected idle on the throttle and put out the speed brakes to prevent a power dive. I quickly transferred to left rudder, yawing the nose through the downswing to force it above the horizon. Full afterburner, retract speed brakes, and the F-4 was in a climbing half roll. Just before the Phantom stalled, the process was repeated.

I rolled the aircraft twenty miles in this manner, I don't know how many times, since all I cared about was reaching the water. We began at 27,000 feet and worked down to 17,000 by the time we were over the Red River valley with its wall-to-wall villages. The greatest fear I had ever known was thinking that we were going to become POWs, especially if the gomers knew that we were the first American aces of the Vietnam War. I told Irish to set the ejection sequence handle so that if he decided to go, I wouldn't go with him. I wasn't going to spend nine or ten years in the Hanoi Hilton. He told me that he was staying with me, and set the handle so that we would both eject when I gave the word.

The next few seconds were full of fear. I even prayed, asking God to get me out of this. The aircraft rolled out, and I thought that He didn't have anything to do with it. Then the F-4 rolled uncontrollably again, and I thought to myself, "God, I didn't mean it!" An explosion ripped through the Phantom, and I almost ejected, but we were still over land. The radio was full of screams from our buddies to punch out. They knew the burning F-4 could explode at any second. A-7s and F-4s were all around us. I could see them as we rolled up and down. Any MiG wandering within ten miles of the area would have been sorry—a situation like that gets pilots hopping mad.

Just as we crossed the coast, we lost our last utility system and another violent explosion shook the fighter. If it had happened a few seconds earlier, we would have been forced down over enemy territory. At that moment I prayed the classic foxhole prayer and pledged myself to seek and accept Jesus Christ if I made it out of there. With the hydraulics gone and the rudder useless, I was unable to force the nose back down on the upswing. The F-4 stalled and went into a spin. On each revolution I could see land, then ocean, then land again. Fear kept me in the aircraft. We were close to the beach, and the winds normally blew landward. I told Irish to stay with me for two more turns as I attempted to break the spin and get more water behind us. I deployed the drag chute with no effect. The controls were limp.

Willie and I had often discussed what to do should the need arise to leave the aircraft. I would say, "Irish, eject, eject, eject!" and he would pull the cord on the third "eject." I got out "Irish e—" and I heard his seat fire. I heard his canopy go and thought my seat had malfunctioned. As I reached for the ejection cord, my seat fired, driving me up the rail and away from Showtime 100. There was no pain from the G-loading, and everything was quiet as I tumbled through space. I saw Willie's chute opening, and again felt fear that something would go wrong and I would not separate from my seat. Then it detached, the cord lines rushed past me, and the chute opened with a crack-the-whip jolt into a beautiful full canopy. Sharp pain ran through my back. Below us was a large freighter and several junks coming out of the Red River toward us. I just knew that I had no taste for pumpkin soup. Corsairs and Phantoms dived through the AAA and SAMs to turn back the boats.

Then it dawned on me that I had a survival radio. I could talk! "Mayday! Mayday! This is Showtime. One Hundred Alpha is okay." (Willie was One Hundred Bravo.)

"Hang on, sailor, we're on our way," replied the SAR team. Wow! In my joy I looked around for the first time. The biggest boost of the day was to see Irish a few hundred feet away, waving like crazy to let me know he was okay. He flipped me the bird. No doubt about it, he was fine. I cordially returned the "salute."

Thinking about my wife, I cried like a baby for a minute or so. My life was falling apart in a great emotional upheaval. Again I vowed to change it if I ever got out of this. My mind jolted back to present difficulties when the wind caught my survival raft hanging several feet below me on a tether. I started to swing back and forth like a pendulum. At the top of each swing, the side of my chute would tuck under and, having never parachuted before, I thought that it would fold and let me fall. About twenty feet above the water I jettisoned the chute while looking down at the raft. I went belly first into the warm, muddy water. Muddy? I was in the mouth of the Red River! In scrambling for the tether attached to the raft, I noticed something floating in the water next to me. A closer look revealed a rotting Vietnamese corpse, apparently washed down the river. For a second I thought it was Willie, but the body was too good-looking. I swam for my raft with Olympic speed.

Willie was later asked by the Boston press: "When you were hanging in your parachute after killing three North Vietnamese pilots and bombing their country, and after being shot down and nearly killed, what was going through your mind?" Sensing the leftist leanings of the interviewer, Willie replied, "My thoughts were that perhaps I had made an incorrect decision in leaving the Army Reserve in Boston." Needless to say, the laughter overwhelmed the interviewer, who retired discreetly.

We were in the water fifteen minutes pending fifteen years when three marine helos from the USS *Okinawa* rescued us. Fighter pilots make jokes about funny little machines with rotors that chug along just over one hundred knots, but my views changed radically at that moment. We were first taken to a hospital ship. My back was stiff and out of place but pronounced okay, so we boarded the helo again to get back to Connie. The decks were lined with waving, cheering men. As we gently set down, the cheers were audible above the chopper's roar. My back was throbbing, but damned if I was going to be carried aboard on a stretcher. Irish helped me out of the chopper. By the time my feet were on Connie's deck, the tears were flowing—Irish too. It was impossible to express our joy at being home and not under a VC gun.

I think all five thousand guys on the ship were waiting for us. Captain Ward, Al Newman, and Dwight Timm ran over to help us off that sweet marine helo. A few of the men looking on made no effort to hide their tears. A black enlisted trooper made his way over and said, "Mr. Cunningham, it's nice that you shot down three MiGs today, and it's nice that you became the first ace, but from the men of Connie, we're just glad to have you back, sir." This gesture overwhelmed me. Later at the evening meal some of the attack pilots walked over. "Hey, Duke, remember when we said that all you F-4 drivers were good for was taking our gas and flying our wing? Well, we take it back." It had been more than nice when those attack guys risked their lives to keep the enemy away when Irish and I were in so much trouble.

We had beat the air force to produce the first ace of the war. Up until that time, the leading MiG killer in Southeast Asia since 1967 had been General Robin Olds with four victories. May 10, 1972, had been quite a day for both the navy and the air force. "Turkey shoot" was certainly a proper term. Eight MiGs had fallen to navy pilots, including six kills belonging to my squadron, VF-96. The 555th Tactical Fighter Squadron, the famous "Triple Nickle" of the USAF, downed three MiGs. One of those was the first kill made by the team of Captains Steve Ritchie and Chuck DeBellevue. Steve went on to get five kills as a pilot, while Chuck ended the war with six as a weapons system officer, the equivalent of the navy RIO.[7]

Notes

[1] Special thanks to Mr. Bill Ryan for his editorial help and his kind assistance with this story.

[2] Story based on personal communication and the book *Happy Jack's Go-Buggy*, by Jack Ilfrey with Max Reynolds. Exposition Press: Hicksville, New York, 1979.

[3] Based on a speech by Robert Scott. Versions of this story have previously appeared in print. This particular one was prepared by General Scott exclusively for *Top Guns*.

[4] Story based on personal communication and the document, *Interview of Lt. Cdr. Sam L. Silber, USNR*, Air Intelligence Group, Division of Naval Intelligence, Office of the Chief of Naval Operations, Navy Department: Washington, DC. 24 May, 1944.

[5] Story based on an interview with Colonel William Shomo, taped and initially composed for publication by Colonel Travis Cutright, PIO, Keystone Wing/CAF, Pittsburgh, Pennsylvania. This historical interview was recorded on August 25, 1988, when an honorary CAF membership was conferred on Colonel Shomo by Colonel Ralph Royce, Executive Director of the CAF, in West Mifflin, Pennsylvania. With permission.

[6] Story condensed from *Salvation for a Doomed Zoomie: A True Story*, John Galvin with Frank Allnutt, Allnutt Publishing: Indian Hills, Colorado, 1983.

[7] Story condensed from *Fox Two*, Randy Cunningham with Jeff Ethell, Champlin Fighter Museum Press, 1984. With permission. The book itself is highly recommended.

Dedications

Tom Blackburn. To the superb Marine and Navy enlisted men who kept VF-17 flying.

Guy Pierre Bordelon, Jr. To Anne Taylor Bordelon (a great Navy wife).

Arthur Raymond Brooks. To my valiant comrades who fought for supremacy in the sky with selfless dedication to duty and preservation of the American way of life, and by their courageous efforts paved the way for the eventual development of the magnificent U.S. Air Force as we know it today.

William Cullerton. To my wife, "Miss Steve," whose love pulled me through.

I also want to acknowledge the incredible devotion that Bob Kuhnert of Dayton, Ohio, has displayed in holding our group (355th Fighter Group) together.

Kenneth Dahlberg. To my wife, Betty Jayne.

Jeff De Blanc. To my wife, Louise Berard De Blanc, our children, and grandchildren.

Harold Fischer. To Harold E. Fischer and Pearl M. Fischer of Swea City, Iowa, for all the support and love they have given me.

John Galvin. To the memory of Samuel David Dealey.

Roger Haberman. To "Joe" Foss, my inspirational leader, then and now.

Jack Ilfrey.   In Memory
Of our fallen comrades who gave their lives
in the cause of freedom
1941–45   Lest we forget

To you from failing hands we throw the torch—
Be yours to hold it high

George Jones. To Margaret, my wife, whose support was unwavering through thick and thin.

Leonard Lilley. To my lovely and very understanding wife, Bonnie.

John Lowell. To my patient, loving, faithful wife, Penny.

James Morehead. To my mother, Ophelia James Morehead, who, with her heart in her throat, awaited so many months and years that awful notice by telegram of the fate of her three sons. The lady taught school for thirty years and made more men out of boys than the average barnyard full of teachers is doing today. She taught her first school in a dirt and log dugout in the Oklahoma Indian Territory. She proudly offered her sons in the defense of her country, one of which she gave. Her service was that of the silent service, of those who toiled by day and trembled by night in serving their homeland. She made me the man I was and if it had been any less, I would not have made it through the awful times.

Edward F. Rector: To the ground personnel of the American Volunteer Group "Flying Tigers." Without their dedication, expertise, long hours and devotion the Group would have been grounded within three months.

Robert Scott. To General Claire Lee Chennault. Whose fighter commander I had the honor of being in China and who never asked me to do anything I didn't think he could have done better.

Working under his command and living in the same house with him was like living with your dad, only The General was a genius . . . in air war tactics.

Sam Silber. To the men of Fighting Squadron Eighteen.

Leslie Smith. To my wife, Marion, who missed all the excitement, but endured a full measure of fear, uncertainty and loneliness.

James Swett. To the pilots and ground crew of VMF-221.

Stanley Vejtasa. To the officers and men of the Grim Reapers (VF-10) and the Fighting Flattops—USS *Yorktown* (CV-5) and USS *Enterprise* (CV-6).

Alexander Vraciu. To my skipper, Butch O'Hare, who taught me my lessons well.

William H. Wescott. To my wife, Frances, who has "sweated me out" for forty-one years.

Ace Biographies

WORLD WAR ONE

Arthur Raymond Brooks graduated from MIT prior to entering the service. He was discharged from the Army Air Service with the permanent rank of army captain. Commander of 1st Pursuit Group, Ellington Field, Texas (1920–21); flew mail and passengers for Florida Airways Corporation with Eddie Rickenbacker and Reed Chambers (1925–26); Aeronautics Branch, US Department of Commerce (1926–28); AT&T, Bell Telephone Laboratories, organizing, supervising and operating Aviation Section in development and testing of air navigation and communication equipment (1928–60). Member Air Force Association, Air Force Museum Foundation, American Institute of Aeronautics and Astronautics, Military Order of World Wars, New Jersey Hall of Fame, Order of Daedalians, Quiet Birdmen, Smithsonian Air and Space Museum (where his original Spad XIII is preserved), Wings Club, NYC and others.

Hometown: Framingham, Massachusetts
Current Home: Summit, New Jersey
Victories: six.
Decorations: Distinguished Service Cross, World War One Victory Medal w/five battle clasps.

WORLD WAR TWO

Tom Blackburn graduated from the United States Naval Academy in 1933. He is a retired navy captain. He came from an established navy family. His father was a graduate of the USNA Class of 1904 and retired as a captain after serving on submarines and battleships. His brother, Paul P. Blackburn, graduated from the USNA in 1930. He was a naval aviator who retired as a vice admiral. Tom commanded VGF-27, VF-17, Air Group 74 (USS *Midway*), VC-5 (Heavy Attack), and Heavy Attack Wing One (USS *Midway*).
  Hometown: Annapolis, Maryland
  Current Home: Jacksonville, Florida
  Victories: eleven.
  Decorations: Navy Cross, Distinguished Flying Cross.

William J. Cullerton attended Wright Junior College prior to entering the service. He was discharged as an army captain after the war. He married "Stevie," his high school sweetheart, raised a family and continues to work with the Cullerton Company, a specialty tackle and fishing firm. He has served on the board of directors of the American Fishing Tackle Manufacturers, Sport Fishing Research Foundation, and Sport Fishing Institute, and was president of the Tackle and Shooting Sports Representatives Association. Member International Sport Fishing Hall of Fame; listed in the book *America's 100 Sportfishing Legends*. Bill has received numerous trade and public awards for his work with youngsters and disabled veterans. Recognized in Illinois Military Hall of Fame. On the board of trustees of Chicago's Shedd Aquarium. Currently outdoor editor of WGN Radio in Chicago, where he produces the "Great Outdoors" show. He is a contributing columnist to *The Sporting Goods Dealer,* a monthly trade magazine. Bill and his wife had seventeen grandchildren at last count.
  Hometown: Chicago, Illinois
  Current Home: Oak Brook, Illinois
  Victories: six in the air; twenty-one on the ground.

Decorations: Distinguished Service Cross, Silver Star, Distinguished Flying Cross, Purple Heart, Presidential Unit Citation.

Kenneth H. Dahlberg was discharged after World War II with the rank of major. He later founded Dahlberg Electronics and became its CEO. Member Chief Executives Forum, Young Presidents' Organization, Past President of the Minnesota Executives Organization, Air Force Association. Director, National City Bank (Minneapolis), National City Bancorporation (Minneapolis), Trustee, Hamline University, Board of Directors, U.S. Air Force Academy 1969–73 (Presidential Appointment). Awarded Outstanding Leadership Citation as Chapter Chairman of the Young Presidents' of the Year in 1969. Kenneth married the former Elizabeth Segerstrom. They have three children: Nancy L., Dianne K., and Kenneth J. Dahlberg.

   Hometown: Wilson, Wisconsin
   Current Home: Minneapolis, Minnesota
   Victories: fifteen and a half.
   Decorations: Distinguished Service Cross, Silver Star, two Distinguished Flying Crosses, Bronze Star, Purple Heart, Presidential Unit Citation.

Jeff De Blanc attended Southwestern Louisiana Institute prior to entering the service. He retired as a marine corps colonel in 1972. Jeff holds a doctorate in education and taught mathematics, physics, computer science and other subjects from 1950 to the present.

   Hometown: St. Martinville, Louisiana
   Current Home: St. Martinville, Louisiana
   Victories: nine confirmed; three probable.
   Decorations: Congressional Medal of Honor, Distinguished Flying Cross, Purple Heart, Presidential Unit Citation.

John R. Galvin attended Northwestern University prior to entering the service. He was discharged with the rank of navy lieutenant commander. His unique war experiences are fully told in a book entitled *Salvation for a Doomed Zoomie* (please see Notes). John left the service after World War Two and entered into a successful career as a businessman. After thirty years in the plastic injection molding business, he has retired to a life of playing golf and becoming a proficient "flower gardener." John is married to the former Susie Matthes.

Hometown: Burlington, Iowa
Current Home: Scottsdale, Arizona
Victories: seven and two assists.
Decorations: four Distinguished Flying Crosses, Purple Heart, Submarine Combat Award, two Presidential Unit Citations (one for the submarine USS *Harder*; one for the carrier USS *Bunker Hill*).

Roger A. Haberman attended The Stout Institute (now the University of Wisconsin–Stout) prior to entering the service. He is a retired marine corps colonel. Roger was a member of the Cactus Air Force's famous Foss Flight at Guadalcanal.

Hometown: East Ellsworth, Wisconsin
Current Home: Long Beach, California
Victories: seven and a half.
Decorations: Navy Cross, Purple Heart.

Jack Ilfrey attended Texas A&M and the University of Houston prior to entering the service. He was discharged after World War Two as an army major. Jack's full story is told in the book, *Happy Jack's Go-Buggy* (please see Notes). He describes his life as progressing from that of a hell-raising P-38 pilot with 142 missions and 528 combat hours to retirement as a conservative banker in only forty-five years. Jack has edited the 20th Fighter Group Association Newsletter, *King's Cliffe Remembered*, for the past eight years.

Hometown: Houston, Texas
Current Home: New Braunfels, Texas
Victories: eight.
Decorations: Silver Star, six Distinguished Flying Crosses.

John H. Lowell attended the Colorado School of Mines prior to entering the service. He became an ace after only three combat missions. John was discharged at the end of the Korean War as an air force colonel and entered the business world where he is still active. Included in the Colorado Hall of Fame (1978).

Hometown: Denver, Colorado
Current Home: Golden, Colorado
Victories: sixteen and a half confirmed; nine probable; eleven damaged.
Decorations: four Silver Stars, seven Distinguished Flying Crosses, Distinguished Unit Citation (December 27, 1944 with John as Group CO).

James Bruce Morehead attended Oklahoma University and UCLA prior to entering the service. He retired as an air force colonel. James was reared on a farm during the Great Depression and learned the realities of life and the value of self-sufficiency while working there, and later, as a fifteen-cents-an-hour oil field roughneck. He attributes his victories over superior Japanese equipment and experienced pilots to the skills he gained as a hunter early in life.

Hometown: Washington, Oklahoma
Current Home: Petaluma, California
Victories: eight.
Decorations: two Distinguished Service Crosses, two Distinguished Flying Crosses, Croix de Guerre, three Unit Citations.

James G. Percy attended New Mexico Military Institute prior to entering the service. He is a retired marine corps lieutenant colonel. Jim married Beryl M. McKinnis on February 26, 1944. They have four children (Susan, Lynne, James and Richard), ten grandchildren and one great grandchild.

Hometown: Ojai, California
Current Home: Garden Valley, California
Victories: six.
Decorations: Navy Cross, five Distinguished Flying Crosses, Bronze Star w/"V," Purple Heart.

Edward F. Rector attended Catawba College prior to entering the service. He is a retired air force colonel. He is featured in the second chapter of *High Honor* published by Smithsonian Institution Press. Edward served in China as a Flying

Tiger and a group commander, remaining there until 1947 to assist the Nationalist Chinese Air Force. He later held a variety of training and command slots, culminating in assignment to the Pentagon and attendance at the National War College. Retiring from the Air Force in 1962, he entered a successful business career.

Hometown: Marshall, North Carolina
Current Home: Arlington, Virginia
Victories: ten and a half.
Decorations: Silver Star, Legion of Merit, Distinguished Flying Cross, Distinguished Flying Cross (Great Britain), Purple Heart.

Robert Lee Scott attended the U.S. Military Academy prior to entering the service. He is a retired air force brigadier general. Robert has authored fifteen books, including *God Is My Co-Pilot*, *Boring a Hole in the Sky*, *The Day I Owned the Sky*, and *Flying Tiger—Chennault of China*. Among many other accomplishments he walked the entire length of the Great Wall of China (over 2,000 miles) in 1972, and piloted an F-16 at age seventy-six, and an F-15 at age eighty (in 1988). He is currently chairman of the Heritage of Eagles Campaign to help build the Museum of Aviation at Robins AFB, Georgia.

Hometown: Macon, Georgia
Current Home: Warner Robins, Georgia
Victories: twenty-two.
Decorations: Silver Star, three Distinguished Flying Crosses, Distinguished Flying Cross (Great Britain), Hum Whei (China).

William Shomo grew up in Jeannette, Pennsylvania. He retired as an air force colonel after twenty-eight and a half years of service. He tied for the honor of achieving the highest number of victories ever by an American fighter pilot on a single mission. Colonel Shomo passed away while this book was in the final stages of preparation and is survived by his wife, Helen.

Victories: eight in the air; twenty-nine on the ground.

Decorations: Congressional Medal of Honor, Legion of Merit, Distinguished Flying Cross.

Sam L. Silber attended the University of Maryland prior to entering the service. He is a retired navy commander. During World War Two, Sam commanded VF-18 (Fighting 18) in air battles across the Pacific.
   Hometown: Baltimore, Maryland
   Current Home: Baltimore, Maryland
   Victories: seven.
   Decorations: Legion of Merit, four Distinguished Flying Crosses.

Leslie C. Smith attended Fresno State College prior to entering the service. He volunteered to serve in World War II, leaving his job with a predecessor company of the Wells Fargo Bank to do so. After the war, he returned to his job with the Wells Fargo Bank where he held positions as branch manager, loan center manager, loan supervisor, district manager, area manager and senior loan officer. He remained active in the California Air National guard and retired as a brigadier general with federal recognition.
   Hometown: Caruthers, California
   Current Home: Pebble Beach, California
   Victories: seven in the air; four and a half on the ground.
   Decorations: five Distinguished Flying Crosses.

James E. Swett attended San Mateo College prior to entering the service. He is a retired marine corps colonel. He states that he is retired to God's Country with nothing to do but boating, swimming, hunting and fishing, and enjoying life with his marvelous wife and visits with his sons, daughters and six grandchildren.
   Hometown: San Mateo, California
   Current Home: Trinity Center, California
   Victories: sixteen and a half.
   Decorations: Congressional Medal of Honor, six Distinguished Flying Crosses, two Purple Hearts, two Presidential Unit Citations, one Navy Unit Citation.

S. W. "Swede" Vejtasa attended the University of Montana prior to entering the service. He retired as a navy captain after a distinguished military career and service in World War Two, the Korean War and the Vietnam War. He served sixteen and a half years aboard aircraft carriers as pilot, ship's officer, and later, commanding officer of the USS *Constellation*. He was commander, Fleet Air, Miramar during the Vietnam War, in charge of all West Coast Training during that period. He served as the 11th Naval District Chief of Staff from 1969–70. Swede and his wife, the former Irene Funk of Circle, Montana, have three children: Gene, Dan and Susan.
   Hometown: Circle, Montana
   Current Home: Escondido, California
   Victories: eleven.
   Decorations: three Navy Crosses, two Bronze Stars, Legion of Merit, Meritorious Service Medal, various Navy Unit Citations.

Alexander Vraciu attended DePauw University prior to entering the service. He is a retired navy commander. Top ranking navy ace in the Pacific for four months during World War Two.
   Hometown: East Chicago, Indiana
   Current Home: Danville, California
   Victories: nineteen in the air; twenty-one on the ground.
   Decorations: Navy Cross, three Distinguished Flying Crosses, three Presidential Unit Citations, Navy Unit Citation, Asiatic-Pacific Medal w/sixteen stars.

Hub Zemke attended the University of Montana prior to entering the service. He is a retired air force colonel. Hub was a career-military aviator who served with fighter units throughout his service, although he was tempted at times to transfer into other endeavors or take a position in civilian aviation. He states that the call of the "pea shooter" always drew him back. He commanded six different fighter wings or fighter groups during the course of his military career. Author of *Zemke's Wolf Pack*, *Zemke's Stalag*, and numerous military articles.
   Hometown: Missoula, Montana

Current Home: Oroville, California
Victories: seventeen and three-quarters in the air; eleven on the ground.
Decorations: Distinguished Service Cross, Silver Star, Distinguished Flying Cross, Distinguished Flying Cross (Great Britain).

THE KOREAN WAR

Guy Pierre Bordelon, Jr., attended Louisiana Tech and Louisiana State University prior to entering the service. Guy is a retired navy commander. He was the "Voice of the Navy" for U.S. Manned Spacecraft Recovery Force for Apollo Mission, up to first moon landing, and served as lieutenant governor for Kiwanis Division Six. Member Retired Officers Association, AARP, American Legion, and POETS. He is publishing a book of children's stories written during wartime for his children and is in the final stages of *A Fighter Pilot's Cookbook*.
Hometown: Ruston, Louisiana
Current Home: Ruston, Louisiana
Victories: five (all at night).
Decorations: Navy Cross, two Silver Stars, two Presidential Unit Citations, Korean Order of Military Merit—ULCHI w/silver star.

Harold Edward Fischer attended Iowa Junior College prior to entering the service. He is a retired air force colonel. Double jet ace with service in both Korea and Vietnam. Spent over two years as a prisoner of the Chinese communists.
Hometown: Swea City, Iowa
Current Home: Las Vegas, Nevada
Victories: ten.
Decorations: Distinguished Service Cross, Silver Star, multiple Distinguished Flying Crosses, Legion of Merit.

George L. Jones attended the University of Florida prior to entering the service. He retired as an air force colonel after more than a quarter-century in fighter aviation, beginning in piston-driven fighters and ending in Vietnam-era jets. He amassed 394 hours of combat flying time during his career. Upon returning from Korea in 1952, he was assigned to the Combat Crew Gunnery Training Group and led the Fighter Aircraft Gunnery Team to victory in the first USAF Worldwide Jet Gunnery Competition. Later assigned to Elgin AFB as Group Commander, Fighter Weapon System Development, he became the first pilot to shoot down a drone with a GAR-8 missile, the first pilot to break the sound barrier with a GAM-83 Bullpup Missile attached to the air frame, and the first pilot to fire this missile from the F-105. George and his wife, Margaret, have four children: George and David (both combat veterans of Vietnam); Dorothy (whose husband is an Air Force pilot); and John (who served with the airborne ranger battalion).

Hometown: Vero Beach, Florida
Current Home: Vero Beach, Florida
Victories: six and a half.
Decorations: Silver Star, Legion of Merit, three Distinguished Flying Crosses, Bronze Star, Presidential Unit Citation (navy), Presidential Unit Citation (air force).

Leonard W. Lilley attended the U.S. Military Academy prior to going on active duty. He was born in the Panama Canal Zone, the son of a U.S. Army officer who had flown in the Army Air Service in World War I. He retired as an air force colonel in 1967 after twenty-two years of service, and has been engaged in banking and investments in Washington, D.C., to the present time.

Hometown: Ancon, Panama Canal Zone
Current Home: Alexandria, Virginia
Victories: seven.
Decorations: Silver Star, two Distinguished Flying Crosses.

W. W. "Bones" Marshall is a retired air force lieutenant general. He has always had a love for flying and fighters, and was on continuous flying status throughout thirty-five years with the air force. His qualifications include tactical and air-defense weapons systems, command and control, communications and computers. He married Milfred E. Taylor, who was a WASP (Women's Army Service Pilot) during World War II. In civilian life he was vice-president for Southeast Asia, with an office in Bangkok, Thailand, for Hughes Aircraft Company, holding the position for more than ten years. Bones Marshall is a veteran of World War II, Korea, and Vietnam. He authored a story about the air battle against the North Korean bombers in the January 12, 1952, issue of *Air Force Times*.

Hometown: Beverly Hills, California
Current Home: Honolulu, Hawaii
Victories: six and a half; seven probable; six damaged.
Decorations: Distinguished Service Medal, Silver Star, Legion of Merit, Distinguished Flying Cross, Bronze Star, Purple Heart.

William H. Wescott attended Ripon College prior to entering the service. He is a retired air force lieutenant colonel. After release from active duty in 1955, he served twenty-six and a half years as an engineer/test pilot for Autometrics Division, North American Aviation, Inc./Rockwell International Corporation. From 1977 to 1982 he was with Jabveliner Division, Rockwell International. He married the former Frances LeMaire of Terre Haute, Indiana, in Las Vegas in 1949. They had four children: Diane, William Henry, JoAnne and Cynthia.

Hometown: New Lisbon, Wisconsin
Current Home: Mesa, Arizona
Victories: five destroyed; two damaged.
Decorations: Silver Star, Distinguished Flying Cross.

THE VIETNAM WAR

Randall "Duke" Cunningham, Jr., attended the University of Missouri prior to entering the service. "Duke" Cunningham is one of two American aces from the Vietnam War and the only navy ace of the conflict. He flew 300 combat missions on two tours of the war zone. The full story of his combat experiences is told in the book *Fox Two* (please see

Notes). In 1990 Randall Cunningham was elected to serve in the U.S. House of Representatives.

Hometown: Los Angeles, California
Current Home: San Diego, California
Victories: five.
Decorations: Navy Cross, two Silver Stars, Purple Heart, South Vietnamese Medal of Honor, Vietnamese Cross of Gallantry.

NOTE: All contributors are members of the American Fighter Aces Association. All (with the exception of Ray Brooks, who served before the decoration was established) are recipients of multiple Air Medals.

MATTHEW BRENNAN

BRENNAN'S WAR
VIETNAM 1965-1969

HEADHUNTERS
**Stories from the 1st Squadron, 9th Cavalry,
in Vietnam 1965-1971**

And coming in March 1992

HUNTER-KILLER SQUADRON
**Aero-Weapons, Aero-Scouts, Aero-Rifles
VIETNAM 1965-1972**

**POCKET
BOOKS**

All Available from Pocket Books

514

STEPHEN COONTS

AN AERIAL ODYSSEY ACROSS AMERICA

THE CANNIBAL QUEEN

New York Times bestselling novelist Stephen Coonts
has been hailed as the best contemporary author
writing about flying. Now Coonts takes us on an
extraordinary adventure, following highways,
railroad lines, and rivers, and touching down in all
forty-eight of the continental United States,
from sea to shining sea.

POCKET BOOKS

**Available in hardcover
from Pocket Books
June 1992**

"This is the best first novel I have ever read."
—Tom Clancy

NORTH
SAR

GERRY CARROLL

A Novel of Navy
Combat in Vietnam

In this searingly realistic novel, one of the most decorated
naval aviators since Vietnam brings us the dramatic story
of attack bomber pilots and helicopter pilots flying
combat *Search and Rescue* (SAR) — in the Navy's air war
against North Vietnam.

**Available in Hardcover
from Pocket Books**

POCKET
B O O K S

449-1